THE YOGI WITCH: BLOODLINES AND LEGACIES

Celebrating
30 Years of Publishing
in India

THE YOGI WITCH: BLOODLINES AND LEGACIES

A Jai Gill Novel

ZORIAN CROSS

HarperCollins *Publishers* India

First published in India by HarperCollins *Publishers* 2023
4th Floor, Tower A, Building No. 10, DLF Cyber City,
DLF Phase II, Gurugram, Haryana – 122002
www.harpercollins.co.in

2 4 6 8 10 9 7 5 3 1

P-ISBN: 978-93-5489-808-2
E-ISBN: 978-93-5489-841-9

Typeset in 11/15.2 Adobe Garamond at
Manipal Technologies Limited, Manipal

Printed and bound at
Replika Press Pvt. Ltd.

This book is produced from independently certified FSC® paper to ensure responsible forest management.

My incredible parents – who loved me even in times when I found it difficult to love myself.

To Madonna – for being a constant source of strength, courage, and inspiration. Your indomitable spirit and extraordinary art has saved so many lives – especially mine!

Author's Note

I channelled Jai's story one fateful August night – during the witching hour, of course! Blessed by the muses, I donned my face-shield and sat night after night at a café and wrote my heart out till the wee hours of the morning. It was in the midst of the pandemic, and I still wasn't eligible for the vaccine, but the fires of inspiration burned so fiercely that I was willing to risk it. Before I knew it, I had completed a manuscript of over ninety-thousand words in the span of less than twenty-seven nights. I wish I could explain how I did it, but clearly there was a divine force that took over my body, mind, and soul. I feel blessed that it chose me to be its earthly vessel.

Yes, this is a work of fiction. However, fiction is a beautiful way of revealing the greater mysteries of The Universe, as well as, truths about life that most of us are unable to process in their most factual state.

There are numerous occult mysteries that are hidden in the text – especially between the lines. However, there's a reason why these have been kept secret from the world. Thus, though I did my best to reveal all that I could, there is a greater responsibility on my shoulders to ensure that some still remained veiled for the safety of those who may be inspired to experiment.

Thus, I encourage all my readers – whether they're passionate believers in all things magical and esoteric, casual dabblers who enjoy reading traits about their zodiac signs online, or even staunch sceptics who roll their eyes at anything even remotely 'woo-woo' – do your research! There's so much to be discovered in the magical, as well as, in the yogic universe. I can only hope my work inspires you to take your journey to a whole different level.

This is a work of love, and is meant to be taken in the best of spirits. I thank you all for opening your hearts, minds, and souls – and making room for Jai and his journey in a warm cozy place.

Prologue

The material world is the playground of the spirit world—and Lord knows Delhi is 'materialistic'. However, Delhi is a city that's more spiritual than people give it credit for. Then again, most people wouldn't know what 'spiritual' is—even if it hits them in the face. Yes, it does hit us in the face—metaphorically, of course, though sometimes even literally. Multiple times a day. Every day. Sometimes, it'll even follow us after we die and chase us throughout lifetimes.

So yeah, most people have no idea what 'spiritual' is. That's why they're blind to the spiritual magnificence of Delhi. The smoggy sky is perfect for demons to hide while they search for vessels to possess. The constant noise is perfect to hide the wails of banshees uttering curses. The ever-increasing crime rate and corruption are perfect for lesser entities to feed off our auric shields. Not to mention the excessive materialism brought about by the ever-expanding 'mall culture', and, of course, the hellish vanity being promoted as #goals by influencers that go to excessive lengths to live up to the motto that 'image is everything'. Maya, the demon queen of illusion, has a field day with them.

Oh, don't get me wrong, there's a lot of good in Delhi too. Well, 'good' is such a judgemental word. So is 'bad', but 'good' tends to come with way more baggage. That's why it seems so much easier to be bad in this world. I know, I'm confusing a lot of you, but trust me, you'll all understand … eventually.

But for now, let's just say that there is plenty of 'good' in Delhi as well. Remember, spiritual energy is positive and negative. Just like in an atom, there are protons and electrons. You can't really say a proton is 'good', nor can you say that an electron is 'bad'. Both are needed to create the atom. Thus, if Delhi is like an atom, then there's plenty of 'good' along with the 'bad'. Sorry, I used to flunk in science when I was in school. Math too.

I tried to give the example of an atom because most people like to divide spiritual energy into 'black' and 'white'. Personally, I find that borders on being racist. I'm 'Gen Z', being socially conscious is my thing.

Oh damn! Sorry, I've been going on and on and forgot to introduce myself, I'm—

'Order for Jai! Venti green tea in a ceramic cup for Jai!'

Yes, I'm the weirdo who orders a green tea at Starbucks. At least I insist that they give it to me in a ceramic cup instead of a throwaway one. It's better for the environment. Anyway, my name is Jai. Jai Gill. Pretty cool, right? Well, it's actually Jaiveer Singh Gill, but I like to keep it short and sweet. Makes it easier to roll off the tongue. Plus, I don't like it when people automatically make assumptions about me by my name. After all, we live in a country where a person's name tells you not only where in the heavens the moon was at the time of their birth, but also one's caste, class and socioeconomic heritage. Not that

I have a problem with mine. I am Sikh on my dad's side. My mother's side, however— oh crap, he's here.

I put on a pair of Tom Ford aviators so that he can't see me looking at him as he heads over to the counter to place his order. Look at him. No, really look at him. What is it that you see? No, look beyond the shit-eating grin and the sagging skin on what used to be a chiselled jawline. Like so many men who stop exercising regularly after marriage, he has not aged well. Look beyond the prominent LV belt buckle that in a few months will be hidden by the ever-growing belly. Seriously, 'see' him. Concentrate. Breathe. Are you seeing it? You are? That silvery outline all around him? That's the etheric shield. It's kind of like the connecting force that connects your aura with your physical body. I'll explain all that eventually in detail, I promise, but try looking beyond the etheric shield. Do you see that glowing light shaped like an egg around him? That's the aura. Again, I'll explain that later. Can you see how it's not a perfect egg shape? Yeah, it's all lopsided and cracked. Also, notice how it feels like light is leaking out of it. Oh, you see the giant dark grey mass all around him? Yup, that's the demon. I guess his wife was right, he is possessed.

Okay, time to put my good looks to the test. As I mentioned earlier, I am Sikh on my dad's side. However, I am also Irish on my mother's side. Though my face resembles my father's—with his chiselled square jaw and sharp nose and defined cheekbones—I have my mother's sparkling green eyes. I believe there's even some Egyptian and Israeli ancestry somewhere in there. Yeah, that genetic cocktail makes me kinda 'hot'. Colonialism really did a number on the Indian beauty standard.

I take off my aviators and gaze straight into his eyes from across the room. There he is, grinning at someone I'm assuming is his mistress. Probably the same woman who managed to get the demon to possess him. You'd be surprised at how easy it is. Whispering under my breath, I chant a sacred mantra that can make anyone instantly attracted to me. Right after I've finished the third round of chanting, his eyes are locked with mine. Poor jerk doesn't even know what's hit him.

I sip my tea slowly, my eyes still locked with his. I smirk as his mistress tries desperately to catch his attention—clearly, it's not working. Granted, he's very obviously straight, but this isn't just about seduction. It's fun to watch even the most sexually rigid individual become fluid when the promise of exquisite pleasure is dangled before him. Especially if it's in a good-looking package.

I stand up slowly while still gazing into his eyes. I nod towards the bathroom before I start walking. I don't need to turn around to know he's excused himself and is following me—keeping a safe distance, of course. Wouldn't want to make anyone suspicious. The minute we enter, I lock the door behind us. It's a good thing that the Starbucks in Connaught Place has a huge bathroom. It's perfect for what's about to happen.

Just as he leans in to kiss me, I press the space between his brows tightly with my right thumb and begin chanting a purification mantra. He tries to fight back, but before he can hit me, I grab his arm with my left hand and press the spot between his thumb and index finger, rendering him physically helpless.

I can see his aura glow in a shade of sickly lemon green, the colour of bile. He begins to scream loudly. From what I am led to believe, he probably feels like his body is on fire. Hopefully it's muffled by Maroon 5 blaring through the speakers. As the auric field grows brighter, colouring the entire room in that bilious shade, out comes a demon from his shoulders. He hollers, 'How dare you disrupt my possession!'

The demon moves away from the man's body, causing him to collapse on the floor with a thud. 'You know you don't belong here,' I say, taking out a small velvet pouch from my pocket. 'You have two choices. Either you go into the light and find peace, or you remain trapped for all eternity within this.' I reveal an egg-shaped obsidian crystal that was in the pouch. Velvet is an ideal material for trapping spirits. So is silk, but you know, silk isn't the best for the environment.

The demon lets out a sinister but clichéd laugh—why do they always do that?

'And what if I choose to do neither?' he asks when he finally finishes laughing.

'Well,' I say, popping the obsidian egg back into the pouch and putting it in my pocket. 'I guess we'll have to fight it out then.'

I chant my mantra, and through my mind's eye, I build a sky-blue shield around my body for protection. Rubbing my hands vigorously, I activate the mini chakras within my fingertips and mounds. The demon dives towards me, but I beam out a bolt of brilliant white light at him, causing him to fall back against the wall behind him. Though it knocks the wind out of him, he gets back up within seconds and charges towards me. This time, using my index and middle finger, I create a lasso of white light and catch him around the neck with it–like a bull in a rodeo.

He tries to pull it off, but I continue to wrap his body in the lasso of white light, binding him till he can barely move.

'Do you bow to the light?'

'Never!' They always say that.

'Very well.'

I take out the obsidian egg and place it on the floor in front of the demon. I rub my hands till golden sparks begin to fly. Before the demon can even finish a taking a breath, my hands are surrounded by a golden halo. My fingers blast him with a stream of electric violet and white light. With every blast, the demon shrinks an inch further. Screaming and bellowing, the demon keeps shrinking until he is small enough to fit into my obsidian egg.

Usually, fighting a demon is almost like an ultimate fighter death match, but this isn't a high-level demon. He's just a garden variety nympho-demon used for dark-magic-based 'love spells'. Then again, all 'love spells' are essentially dark magic because no love is pure when it's based on spiritual manipulation of the soul. Forcing love is an act with many karmic repercussions. Sometimes it can even banish one's soul into places where even light is too scared to pass through.

With just a few more blasts of electric-violet beams of light, the demon surrenders. They all do, eventually. They know that 'the light' is truly where they belong.

'You sure about that?'

'Yes! Yes! Please!' the demon begs. 'That's where I know I truly belong!'

And with that, I chant another mantra, causing a column of white light to form before the demon. Removing the lasso of white light, I watch as the demon moves slowly into the light. Once in the light, he disintegrates within seconds. No, he is not destroyed. Energy can never be destroyed. He just transmutes into a light-filled etheric being. Low-level demons can do that easily. High-level ones are another story.

The guy who was possessed will wake up by the time I reach the parking lot. He won't have any recollection of what happened. He'll be too embarrassed to say he was there to hook up with another man. However, he'll almost immediately break up with his mistress and return to his wife. To make sure the mistress, or anyone else, doesn't send another demon to possess him, I cast a protective shield around him. Usually, these last around twenty-four to forty-eight hours, but mine will protect him for at least three months. That's too much usage of usually enough time for them to heal completely.

My name is Jai Gill, and I'm a yogi. Welcome to my world.

Chapter One

I was born during a solar eclipse. Not a partial one. I was told that it was a special one because it was the last eclipse of the millennium. As I tell you this tale, I'm barely a few months shy of turning twenty-one. I don't really reveal my age to others—mainly because people tend to use it to define and judge. Just like they do with our names. If only they knew that judgement is the first step towards blocking your third eye. Then again, no wonder they're blind to the spiritual reality of a city like Delhi.

My mother passed away within moments of my birth. I know this because my grandmother and aunts were there, helping deliver me in an inflatable tub at home. Yes, there was a doctor there too, but the complications of my birth were so extreme that even if they were in a hospital, they wouldn't have been able to save her. At least my mother got to hold me before she passed.

'Just before her spirit left her body,' Gran would often tell me, 'she whispered your name so sweetly, almost like angels were echoing it: "Jai". Bless her!'

That was my favourite bedtime story till my father died a few years later. The official story was a car crash on the newly constructed DND flyover. Gran didn't believe that for a second, but there wasn't anything she could do about it. Authorities don't really take nicely to interfering foreigners, especially ageing ones that march to the beat of their own drum. And there was also the whole 'witch' thing.

I first discovered my family's secret when kids at school bullied me about it. Despite being one of the biggest cities in the world, both in size and population, mortal and immortal—Delhi can be like a really small town. When people here see three strong-willed women living together without a man to protect them, tongues wag. Of course, it didn't help that they would often light bonfires on our rooftop during full moons. However, when I returned home with a bloodied nose, they realized that it was high time they became more discrete.

'Are you really a witch, Gran?' I asked her that day. I was barely in the first grade. Though I had heard this said about them before, this was the first time I was attacked for it.

'Of course I am!' Gran claimed with pride. 'So are your aunts and the other women in our family.'

'Not to mention Jemima,' Aunt Meg chimed as she drained the antiseptic water from the bowl she used to clean my wound.

'Oh hush, Meg!' Gran tut-tutted, as she placed her hand on the crown of my head, whispering an incantation to heal any internal injuries.

'He might as well know it!' Meg wiped the dish clean.

'Really? Mom was a witch too?'

'Oh, don't be bothered by that,' said Aunt Claudine, who had just entered the room.

'How was class?' Gran asked her after she had finished her healing spell.

'Pretty good,' Claudine replied. 'Had a few newcomers. Seems like the word is spreading well.'

Officially, we were a family of yoga teachers. Gran was born in India around the time of Independence. Most of her family returned to England, but her parents stayed. Her father was a scholar who had spent his life studying Sanskrit and ancient civilizations, while her mother was a disciple of a great yogi saint who was just known as 'Babaji'.

Unlike the yogis of Mysore, who were building their legacies and spreading them far and wide, Babaji chose to be more low-key. Gran and my aunts learned yoga from him too, before he suddenly disappeared. No one knows where he went, as he had no family to speak of. Some say he took up refuge in a cave in the Himalayas. Others say he attained liberation and left his body. Gran didn't bother questioning it. He had taught them all he knew, and entrusted them to spread his teaching.

We lived in a grand old house in Golf Links, with three storeys covered in ivy. The ground floor was mainly used as a yoga studio. Gran's father had built it before Independence and then struck deals with the government of the time to stay there. As it was now used as a yoga studio, Gran would get grants to maintain it. However, the current government once tried to usurp it from us. They had backed off at the last minute. Many thought it was because Gran and my aunts cast spells on the officials. They neither agreed nor disagreed with those allegations.

'Am I a witch too?'

'Yes, you are, wee one!' Aunt Meg kissed me on my forehead.

'Just don't tell people about it,' said Gran, smiling.

Before I could bombard them with questions that were fluttering about in my mind, the doorbell rang.

'Who could it be at this hour?' said Gran, wrapping a shawl around her shoulders.

'Maybe one of Claudine's gentlemen callers,' Aunt Meg teased.

'Jealous?' Aunt Claudine picked up an apple slice and took a bite teasingly.

'As if!'

The doorbell rang again. Gran went to the front door to answer.

'Come on, Jai, let's set the table for supper,' said Aunt Meg. She patted my shoulder, giving me a gentle nudge over to the china cabinet to fetch the plates while she went into the kitchen.

Unlike our neighbours, we did not have any domestic help. We picked up after ourselves. We also grew most of our vegetables at home, as well as herbs used for teas and for what I would learn later: spells.

'Girls!' Gran entered the kitchen. 'The library at once!'

I was never allowed in the library when we had company, but I would peek through a crack in the door as Gran and my aunts spoke to the guests—who were always served lavender tea. Usually it was a woman crying. Sometimes there were students who had come for a yoga class after hearing about us through the grapevine.

The ladies of the house would sit on a grand sofa with a floral print, while the guest sat on a matching upholstered chair.

The tea would calm their nerves before they spilled their life stories.

'He's cheating on me again!' cried the woman visiting us then. She wiped her tears with a tissue after a few sips of tea. 'I kept chanting the mantra for an entire lunar cycle as you had recommended. He stopped for a while and everything was back to normal, but he has begun again! Oh God! The wedding is in a few weeks! Everything has been taken care of! Invitations have been sent, caterers and florists have been paid, and we've even booked hotel suites for his family flying in from Indore!'

'That's what happens when we fall for royals!' declared Aunt Meg. 'They can't seem to keep it in their pants.'

'Meg! Don't be insensitive!' Gran shushed her and turned back to the woman. 'The incantation can only work if the other person is willing to mend their ways.'

'All healing is dependent on whether the individual wants to be healed,' said Aunt Claudine, refilling the woman's cup. 'Clearly, he doesn't want it.'

'Oh, but he must!' The woman's eyes grew wide in terror. 'I can't give up on him!'

'How far along are you?' Gran asked matter-of-factly.

The woman froze. 'H-h-how?'

'Answer me, dearie.' Gran sipped her tea.

The woman sighed. 'I took a test this morning. My doctor says about five weeks. I suspected it, but I was so caught up with the wedding preparations that I didn't even notice I was late. I figured I was just stressed.'

'Do you plan on keeping it?' Gran signalled to Aunt Meg to fetch a book from the teak bookshelf that covered an entire wall. I could see raindrops falling on the giant bay windows that looked out to our kitchen garden.

The woman covered her face with her quivering palms, sobbing into them. Gran shook her head and then gestured to Aunt Claudine to draw the curtains. I could see lightning flash before the windows were covered.

Aunt Meg placed a giant leatherbound book on the mahogany apothecary table that doubled as a coffee table. Claudine began opening the drawers on its side, taking out various tools. I saw a bronze blade and a yew wand with a quartz tied to the top. Meg took out a silver dish and a few vials of dried herbs.

'What do you want us to do about it?' Gran knelt on the Persian carpet as my aunts began lighting giant white candles.

The woman knelt beside Gran. 'I want to make him fall madly in love with me.'

'You can't force love, my dear. That's too dark for us to even get into.'

'Then I want him to be devoted to me!' The woman took out three stacks of thousand rupee notes and placed them on the table. 'I don't care what it costs—he has to be mine!'

Gran would later tell me that money was a great magical force by itself, and that it could absolve spell-casters and energy workers of karmic repercussions for rituals done on the behalf of someone else. That's why old Romani fortune-tellers would insist on having their palms crossed with silver before they read fortunes.

Meg and Claudine exchanged knowing looks as if to say the poor thing didn't know what she was asking for.

'You do realize that there's no going back after this?' Gran said, taking the woman's hand in hers. 'Once the spell is cast, there's no guarantee that he'll be the same man you fell in love with.'

'It's not about love!' the woman bellowed. 'It's about marriage!'

Gran sighed. She looked up and saw me peeping through the door, but just smiled. Perhaps she thought that it was time I learned what it was that they did. Aunt Meg turned off the lights, while Aunt Claudine placed a few crystal geodes around in a circle.

The four of them sat around the apothecary table. Gran lit a piece of camphor on fire, which was placed on a small metal cube in the centre of a silver dish filled with water.

'Do you have the things I asked for?' asked Gran.

The woman fished out of her purse a photograph of her fiancé, along with a few strands of hair and toenail clippings. Aunt Claudine put them in a small pewter cauldron, placing it in the middle of the table.

There was something so beautiful about the way Gran looked in the candlelight. Her white hair tied in a loose braid sharply contrasted with Aunt Meg's blunt raven bob and Aunt Claudine's auburn locks—which I would often call 'faerie hair'. All three of them shared my green eyes.

They sat in perfect padmasana—the most magical of all seated poses—and held hands with the woman, who was seated in a simple cross-legged pose on a small cushion. Gran sat in the centre, the woman opposite her and my two aunts on either side.

I could feel a chill run down my spine as they began chanting. I couldn't tell whether it was my imagination or if the flames were growing stronger by the second, dancing wildly as if a stormy wind was blowing through the room—which was impossible because all the windows were shut. I would later learn that sudden chills were a sign of spirits being present.

When the flames became stable again, they released hands, and Gran picked up the dagger and took the woman's hand in hers. 'Last chance. Are you absolutely sure?'

'I have no choice!' The woman answered with sheer determination.

'Very well!' Gran sighed and lightly cut the woman's palm with the dagger, causing her to yelp in pain. Aunt Meg grabbed on to the bleeding palm, while Aunt Claudine gently poured the blood into the pewter cauldron, covering the photograph, the nail clippings and the strands of hair with the blood.

'That's enough!' Gran commanded. Aunt Meg tightly wrapped the wound with a bandage, telling the woman to keep it elevated throughout the ritual. Afterwards, they would take her to the bathroom to clean the wound properly. Aunt Claudine began pouring the dried herbs into the cauldron, while Gran chanted away.

I remember letting out a gasp when flames emerged from within the cauldron. All of their faces glowed in shades of amber as the flames grew. I stood there frozen as an entity emerged from the smoke and prostrated itself before them. Gran picked up the yew wand and waved it in the air, pointing the quartz tip at the smoky entity. Aunt Meg and Claudine began chanting with Gran as the entity stood and towered above them.

'What's his name again?' Gran asked the woman.

'A-A-Anurag,' the woman stammered, bewildered by what was happening.

'His full name, love!' Aunt Meg rolled her eyes.

The woman shouted, 'Anurag Rao Holkar!'

The curtains moved apart by themselves and the windows burst open, revealing a thunderstorm outside. Lightning flashed and the entity flew out into the wind. The windows slammed shut after it was gone. The curtains pulled themselves close.

'So mote it be!' The three of them chanted in unison.

A regular kid would be shitting bricks out of fear. I was excited. I knew from that day that my life would never be the same. But I was only five. What did I know of what lay ahead?

Chapter Two

The first time I took part in a ritual was on my thirteenth birthday. Thirteen is a powerful age. In Judaism, they celebrate it with a bar mitzvah when a boy turns thirteen. It symbolizes his transition to manhood.

We weren't Jewish, nor did we follow any particular religion. I was Sikh on my father's side, and I was drawn to the teachings of Guru Nanak in particular. But I never kept my hair in a turban, nor did I wear a kara. At home, we did have statues of the Virgin Mary holding the baby Jesus in her arms, but there were also idols of Shiva, Kali, Vishnu, Lakshmi, Ganesha, Radha and Krishna, along with some lesser-known deities. You could find a copy of the Holy Quran by the Bhagavad Gita and the Guru Granth Sahib. There were many other sacred texts from around the world, including five versions of the Bible. I was made to read them all.

The morning after the night I witnessed my first ritual, Gran woke me at the crack of dawn. As always, I was to get ready to attend the morning yoga class before school began. Nothing was spoken of the night before. I had been taught that a physical asana practice was also a spiritual practice, and thus it was important to take a shower before starting, to make the body more receptive to receiving divine energies. After my shower, I was handed a mat and told to set it up in the studio.

I was usually the only child there. It was mostly women, but sometimes I noticed a couple of men. Most were in their thirties, but a few were as old as Gran. All of them, however, flowed smoothly through their poses as Gran led them through the first round of Surya Namaskaras. They were amazed at how perfect Gran's Sanskrit was as she would chant the Gayatri mantra and the names of the poses. It was one of the advantages of being the daughter of a Sanskrit scholar.

After school, I would finish my homework and then wait for Aunt Meg to teach me about the various properties of herbs. She would tell me how each was linked to a deity and a planet in the solar system. Turmeric was connected to Jupiter, cinnamon to the sun, jasmine to the moon—and all things poisonous were connected to Saturn.

Aunt Claudine would teach me how to shuffle and read tarot cards. She ensured that I learned their association with the Kabbalistic Tree of Life, but also insisted that I let the images speak to me. Theory was good to build a strong foundation, but a reading without intuition is just cold and clinical.

Gran focussed more on my yogic studies. By the time I was nine, I was able to hold an almost perfect Vrschikasana—the Scorpion pose. Often, she'd have me demonstrate the poses for the class whenever she had to explain the intricacies of technique. When newcomers or elderly students balked at how complicated a pose looked, Gran would tie her silver hair in a tight knot and demonstrate it herself. After she'd come out of the pose, she would be met with applause. But she would hush them all and say, 'I'm in my sixties. If I can do this, so can you!' Not all of them could, but Gran told me that people can master a pose only when the body is ready for it. With regular practice, the body allows all the poses. 'If not in this life, then definitely in the next one.'

After the asana practice, Gran would teach me all about the philosophy of yoga. She taught me about the five elements of creation—*prithvi* (earth), *apas* (water), *tejas* (fire), *vayu* (air) and *akasha* (space or spirit)—and about the seven chakras of the human body and how they matched the seven colours of the rainbow. She often spoke on the importance of breath. 'Our breath is the source of life as well as our magic,' she would say. 'Bheema was the strongest of the Pandavas because he was the son of the wind god, Vayu. As was Hanuman.'

'But isn't the heart chakra—'

Gran tutted, 'Say it in Sanskrit!'

'Okay, sorry, but isn't the anahata chakra ruled by the element of Vayu?'

'Yes, and?'

'Isn't that chakra all about love? What does it have to do with strength?'

'My dear, true strength comes from the love in our hearts. Falling in love is the bravest thing we can do. Hanuman was truly devoted to Lord Rama, and of all the Pandavas, Bheema truly loved Draupadi the most. Their love and loyalty knew no bounds, and thus, neither did their strength. Fear cripples us, but love empowers us.'

'But look at the many women who come to you with broken hearts. What about them?'

Gran smiled. 'Most people confuse insecurity with love. They fall in love and get married for all the wrong reasons. They're either pressured by society to do so when they reach a certain age or feel left out when all their friends start getting married. Some marry because they fear loneliness, while others do so because they want someone to take care of them. How can any love that's motivated by fear or anxiety be pure and empowering?'

'Did Mom really love Dad?' I remember asking Aunt Claudine one evening when she was teaching me about the 'The Lovers' card in tarot.

'Why do you ask?' Aunt Claudine arched a quizzical brow.

'I just wanna know!' It was strange that my father's family never kept in touch with me. Gran mentioned that he had relatives all over Delhi, some in Chandigarh as well as a few in London and in Canada.

Aunt Claudine smiled. 'They truly did love each other. That's why your father left his family for her.'

'He did?'

'Oh yes! You remember how they met when they were studying at St. Stephen's, right?'

I nodded. Gran had told me about how they had met during their freshers' orientation party, and fell in love at first sight. She was studying philosophy, and he, economics. Gran always got teary-eyed when she talked about how close they were—like lovebirds, she'd say.

'Unfortunately, your father's family didn't approve,' Aunt Claudine sighed. 'They wanted him to marry a girl in Chandigarh who was from a wealthy family.'

'Why would they do that?'

Aunt Claudine shrugged. 'Families are complicated, especially in matters of marriage. It didn't really help that we belong to a different race. And there's that witch thing too.'

'But they loved each other, shouldn't that be enough?'

'Unfortunately, it never is.'

'So, what happened then?'

'He cut ties with them!' Gran entered the room and sat beside us on the giant floral sofa. 'He renounced them all for her. That's how much he loved your mother.'

'Do they know about me?' I asked, hopeful to discover a whole family that I hadn't yet met. Maybe I'd have a few cousins my age to play with. I barely had any friends in school—where I had been branded 'the weird kid'—so the only companions I had were Gran and my aunts.

Gran grimaced. 'We did tell them, but they never replied.'

I refused to shed a tear, even though I could feel my heart shatter into a million pieces. Gran grave me a big hug and kissed my forehead, melting my resolve. I cried with my face buried deep in her bosom.

I guess all I have of my father is his last name. It's okay, it's a pretty cool last name. I did toy with the idea of using Gran's last name. Jai Byrne would have been cool too. However, Gran insisted I keep my father's family name as that's what my mother would have wanted.

I cringed whenever they'd announce my full name in school: 'Jaiveer Singh Gill!' My mother named me Jai, but my dad added the 'veer' and the 'Singh'. Well, if he could leave his family for my mother, I could keep his additions to my name. At least on paper.

'Ready?'

I nodded and Aunt Meg placed a crown of white flowers around my head. It was the night of my thirteenth birthday. Gran said it was more special because it was also a full moon.

All four of us had floral crowns that matched our flowing robes. Gran's was the grandest, with giant lilies to represent her wisdom. Aunt Claudine's had white roses while Aunt Meg's had jasmine—both representing their fertility and abundance. Mine was a mix of daisies and baby's breath to represent my innocence and purity of spirit. Good thing they didn't check my internet search history.

'Perfect for your first official ritual,' Aunt Meg smiled as she and Aunt Claudine saged my body. The sacred smoke would cleanse all negativity and strengthen my auric shield.

We were enclosed in a circle marked with candles and crystals, with rock salt tracing the perimeter. White flower petals were scattered inside the circle. The four of us sat in perfect padmasana with our spines taut. The savoury aroma of the sage was replaced by the sweet fragrance of sandalwood coming from the incense, which seemed to enhance the scent of all the flowers. In the middle was a white velvet cloth, on which was a giant quartz crystal ball, surrounded by assorted tumble stones. A silver bowl was placed in the middle to capture the reflection of the full moon. It's through that reflection that the water is energized with the moon's magic.

'Let's hold hands,' Gran smiled she extended her palms. I sat opposite her, with my aunts on each side. The minute our hands met, I felt a chill run down my spine. I hadn't felt that since that time I watched my first ritual through the crack in the library's door. I had witnessed other rituals since, but that chill had never returned until now. It was exhilarating, yes, but something seemed off.

The clouds cleared and the moon shone brightly in all her glory. Rarely could one see stars in the polluted Delhi sky. However, tonight, the sky seemed unusually clear. We closed our eyes and began focussing on our breath. Synchronizing and slowly increasing our breathing rate, we had soon reached ten inhalations and twenty exhalations.

I thought I could feel every cell in my body vibrate and my head felt as though it had detached from my body and was levitating above my neck. My spine tingled as a beam of brilliant white light shot down from above, entering my body through the crown of my head. It was as though I was bathing in a waterfall of light. Every inch of my body was absorbing the light. Had I not been holding my aunts' hands I would have probably floated into the heavens above. I could spend an eternity with this feeling.

It was a cruel shock when it all came crashing down.

'Adele Byrne!' thundered a strange voice.

I opened my eyes with a jolt. The shiver in my spine returned. Standing before us was a sinister being in a dark hooded robe. I couldn't see its face.

Gran stood up and said furiously, 'You do not belong here! This home is protected from—'

'*Was*! Was protected!' The creature laughed loudly as my aunts hid me behind them. 'But not anymore!'

It raised its hands and shot out a beam of black light towards us. Gran waved her fingers, casting a silvery shield that made the black light disintegrate.

The being laughed and shot more beams of black light towards us. This time, Aunt Meg and Aunt Claudine built a force field of silver to protect us. The black beams disintegrated immediately upon contact. Gran lifted her hands and shot two beams of white light at the thing. It deflected them as though it was swatting mosquitoes. Gran seemed surprised by that.

'You've grown soft with age, you crone!' The creature laughed as it shot more beams of black light. The shield blocked them, but I could see that Aunt Meg and Aunt Claudine were getting tired.

Gran shot a few more beams that the being dodged easily, while continuing to bellow laughter. 'Come on! Come out of that circle and fight me! After all, you are the great Adele Byrne! Surely you can take me on as you did all those years ago.'

I just remember being frozen in fear, hiding behind them. My aunts tried to talk her out of it, but Gran was having none of it. Tying her robe tighter, she jumped out of the circle with a somersault. Landing on her feet, she shot a powerful beam of light at the thing. This time, it fell to the ground.

'I banished you before, and I'll banish you again!' She spun and kicked the being even as she fired another jolt of white light. The creature seemed stunned. At that, she turned to my aunts and commanded, 'Now!'

They surrounded the being and began shooting a steady ray of white light at it. It screamed and I saw smoke coming out of it. Its terrified wail echoed throughout the house. Gran and my aunts were too powerful for it, and it was on the verge of being vanquished.

However, at that moment, it locked eyes with me. I was transfixed in its gaze. Unable to move, I could feel something pulling me towards it, like metal to a magnet.

'No!' Gran screamed and tried to cast a shield around me. But it was too late. The being shot a beam of dark light straight into my heart. I collapsed. In a fit of rage, Gran summoned all her might and vanquished the creature.

When I woke up, I found myself in the library with my head resting on Gran's lap. When she saw that I was conscious, she and my aunts cried with joy and showered me with kisses.

'W-W-What happened? What was all that about?'

Gran grabbed me and kissed me on both my cheeks. 'Welcome to our world!'

Chapter Three

'So, what exactly is it that you do?'

This is usually when the lying has to begin. 'I'm a yogi,' I reply. Well, it's not entirely a lie.

'A yogi?' His eyes lit up. 'Really?'

'You sound surprised?' I sip my gin and tonic, playing my sparkling greens to my advantage. I'm not twenty-one yet, but in Delhi, as long as you have the money to spend, no one really asks for your ID when you need to order a drink. I also play the mixed-race card to my advantage. Hey, it's just alcohol—it's not like I'm harming anyone. Besides, the legal age for drinking in this city is twenty-five, while the age to vote and for men, it's 21. That's all kinds of messed up, isn't it?

'Well, it's not exactly every day that I meet a yogi for a drink. Especially not one I met on Tinder!'

'So yogis can't drink, nor go on Tinder?' Most people who try to be sassy tend to come across as either aggressive or idiotic. Luckily, I come across as charming.

'No, um, er ...'

It's fun to see them squirm and be at a loss for words. Especially when they're cute like this one. What was his name again? Oh, who cares, it's not like I'm gonna remember him after tonight.

I needed the gin. Juniper berries are excellent for the third-eye chakra. At least, that's what I tell myself. Besides, it's great to down a G&T after a day of demon vanquishing. Company helps.

'Relax, big boy!' I teasingly cock a grin. 'You're not on the hot seat—yet!'

'Yet?' His eyes pop with excitement along with something else that his tight jeans make pretty obvious.

'Fuck! That was so amazing!' My Tinder fuck gasped as he collapsed in the backseat of my car. We were parked in an alleyway behind Lodi Gardens.

I smiled as I wiped my mouth with a tissue I pulled from a box in my glove compartment.

'Dude, I was so shit scared that someone would catch us!'

I smiled as I buttoned up my shirt and proceeded to put the car seats upright. 'You got Uber on your phone?' I asked as I straightened my hair.

'Yeah,' he said, putting on his shirt. 'Why?'

Before he knew it, he was on the side of the road, watching me speed off into the night. I'm sure he was screaming away at how I was an asshole for just leaving him there. Luckily, Lana Del Rey was loud enough to drown it.

I'm forever amazed at how thirsty Delhi men can be, something I discovered a few weeks after my thirteenth birthday.

His name was Nikhil. Nikhil Sahni. At first glance, he was your typical alpha-jock that all the boys wanted to be. All the teachers would fawn over him, especially the horny old priests. At fifteen, he was nearly six feet tall and had started shaving.

I was in an all-boys catholic school called St. Sebastian's, an institution that boasted of alumni who had gone on to be Nobel laureates, Padma Shri awardees and Bollywood stars. Now it had become a place where the elite of Delhi sent their spoiled spawn with big donation cheques. Technically, I came with one too, but I was nothing like the rest of the bullying tormentors that would use any excuse to pick on me.

I made the mistake of naming the boys who sent me home with a bleeding nose. The principal, Brother Patrick O'Sullivan, made them apologize to me in front of the entire school assembly, while making an impassioned speech about how St. Sebastian's inculcated a spirit of brotherhood and tolerance. After that, the bullying just became verbal.

It's funny how I was called a fag before I even knew I was gay. Then again, them calling me that had more to do with the toxic masculinity their narrow patriarchal lineage instilled upon them than my actual sexuality. I was also called sissy, pansy and *chhakka*. Sticks and stones may break one's bones, but words tend to scar even deeper. After all, words are spells. When uttered repeatedly they manifest into reality. Not that I'm saying their name-calling made me gay. It was just an interesting coincidence.

It didn't help that my grades were terrible. At home, I was learning about the mysteries of the universe and all the magic hidden within—which meant that I couldn't really make myself care about schoolwork. Teachers thought I was dyslexic, but that was proven wrong.

'He has so much potential,' my class teachers would say at every PTA meeting. 'However, he wastes so much time daydreaming in class or gazing out of the window.'

Once Gran was summoned to school because a teacher got scared seeing the doodles in my notebook. 'What on earth could possess him to draw this stuff?' the teacher asked her once she arrived. Gran tried her best to conceal her laughter when she saw my doodles. She obviously didn't have the heart to tell them that I was just drawing images of the faeries—spirits of nature that live within flowers and trees.

Gran had taught me all about them, and even taught me how to communicate with them. However, she forgot to mention that they could often be impish pranksters and distract impressionable children, luring them into their world. But I discovered they were harmless if you respected their space.

'It's okay,' Gran would say after each PTA meeting. 'Just lay low and pass your exams. I don't care as long as you get passing grades. Don't stir the pot too much and everything should be fine.'

It did hurt sometimes to see that I was the only kid without parents at the PTA. Though Gran and my aunts did their best to create a loving home for me, I often wondered what it would be like to feel a mother's embrace. Whenever I'd hear kids moan about how their parents were so strict and didn't let them have fun, I wanted to snap at them, 'At least you have parents, you fucking ingrates!' But I didn't. 'Orphan boy' was another name that was callously thrown at me, after all.

One day, I was carrying some books to the staff room. A bully by the name of Sahil Hada shoved me, causing me to fall flat on my face. The books scattered all over. When the teacher demanded to know who did it, I just bit my lip and shrugged, 'I tripped.' She rolled her eyes, told me to be careful and trotted over to the staff room. Sahil and his cackle of hyenas were guffawing away as I picked up the books. When I reached for the last one, he came over and swatted them out of my hands with his pudgy paws, causing them to fall again.

'Yeah, that's it, faggy boy! Bend over like the pansy you are!' Sahil snorted as two of his hyenas pushed me onto the floor.

'Please stop!' I tried so hard to fight back my tears.

'Aw, you gonna cry now?' Sahil sneered. 'Look guys, the sissy is gonna cry!'

I could feel my stomach turn as they laughed. Each cruel chuckle cut me like a blade.

'Knock it off!' A voice of mercy showered a ray of hope.

Sahil and his hyenas ran off. I was too busy picking up the books to notice half of them were already picked up.

'Here you go!' The voice appeared again.

I looked up and gazed straight into Nikhil's beautiful chocolate pools of compassion. Too shy to say a word, I grabbed the books and scurried over to the staff room.

The next week during recess, I was having my tiffin at my usual spot under the giant banyan tree in the corner of the school playground. As always, I kept an apple at the base of the main trunk as an offering to the fae and tree spirits. Gran encouraged me to do this as the fae would work their magic and prevent bullies from approaching within five feet of me. It worked like a charm. That day, however, it didn't stop a football from hitting me straight in the face.

'Oh shit! Bro, you okay?'

I blinked woozily to see Nikhil standing over me. I gulped and nodded sheepishly.

'You sure about that?' Nikhil held the offending ball in his hands. I could hear his friends calling him to return to the game, so I just smiled and quietly replied, 'I'm good, don't worry about it.'

The next day, he came over to the tree, holding that same damn football. 'Do you wanna play with us?'

It was so hard not to blush. 'No, thanks,' I replied.

'You sure?'

'Positive!' Clearly, I had no idea what it was like to be treated nicely. I could hear the faeries giggling mischievously. He shrugged and went off to play with his friends.

Throughout the rest of the week, I couldn't help but stare at him as he played football with his friends during recess. It was almost like he was kissed by sunshine, the way he exuberantly glowed as he ran about the field. He looked so freaking adorable whenever he scored a goal. That look of joy whenever he succeeded was too cute for words. Our eyes would meet a few times, and I would avert my gaze immediately. However, I could tell he noticed every single time.

Once, Nikhil came and sat next to me during our swimming period. The annual swim-meet was a few weeks away, and the swim team was practicing their diving drills. We eighth-graders were made to splash about in the shallow end.

'Wow,' said Nikhil. 'You're really fit for an eighth-grader!'

'Really? You think I'm fit?' I couldn't believe how stupid I was to say that.

'Yeah, I mean, dude, you're like ripped!'

I blushed. 'Um, thanks. I guess it's all the yoga I do.'

'Really? Yoga gives you that four pack?'

I didn't know what to say, so I shrugged sheepishly. Nikhil looked ever so sexy in his speedos. He had joined a gym a year ago, and that had made his muscles all the more sinewy. All the sports he played at school definitely helped.

'How come you're not swimming?'

I didn't want to tell him that whenever I stepped into the pool, Sahil and his hyenas would dunk my head in and try to drown me. So I just said, 'Um … It's kinda crowded.' It's the best I could come up with.

'What period do you have next?'

'Um … maths, I think?'

'Who's your teacher there?'

'Um … Sally George.'

'Oh damn, I can't stand that bitch! She's such a fucking tyrant.'

I chuckled. 'Understatement of the century!'

'You know, she's off sick today!'

'Really?'

'Yeah. You wanna bunk?'

I was caught off guard. 'Huh?'

Before I knew it, the two of us were in the one place no one would find us—the school chapel. At that time of day, the priests were either in the administration office or teaching their classes. I was nervous, as it was the first time I had ever skipped class, but Nikhil just had a way of making me feel so safe around him. It was a feeling that was alien to me.

It was strange how even our hushed tones seemed to mildly echo in the empty chapel.

'So, what's your name again?'

Oh crap! All this time, I had never really told him who I was.

'Um … Jai.'

'Hi, Um … Jai!' Nikhil smirked.

I playfully shoved him on the shoulder. 'OMG, cut it out!'

'I'm only teasing!'

I forget what we talked about that day. All I remember was that I was beaming away as Nikhil made me laugh. They were probably lame jokes, but I didn't care, I was feeling ever so happy. It was a feeling that I hoped would last forever. However, the damn bell brought an end to it.

'Damn!' Nikhil sighed. 'Time sure does fly.'

I shrugged, 'I guess!'

As I was about to get up, he grabbed me and planted a kiss on my mouth. I was caught off guard, again. A part of me wanted to push him off and run back to my classroom, but another part of me just wanted to stay and give in. I listened to the latter part of me.

His mouth felt so warm. Though I could still smell traces of the swimming pool chlorine, his manly scent filled me with such a thrill. My mouth hungered for more as he devoured me with sheer force.

Soon, we were in the toilet, sitting in one of the cubicles and making out in full glory. Our ties were undone and our shirts were unbuttoned. I was sitting astride him, pressing my bare chest against his. We were running our fingers through each other's hair as our tongues danced away with a devilish fervour.

I couldn't believe this was my first kiss. I didn't dare let him know. Wouldn't want him to think I wasn't cool.

Nikhil looked oh so hot as he towered over me. Our eyes locked as we breathlessly gazed into each other's eyes. He reached over to trace my face with his fingertips. Every single stroke sent flames down my spine.

'What's that mark on your chest?'

He had noticed the dark bruise shaped like an eye right on my chest that had been there since the attack by the hooded being during my birthday ritual.

'Um … nothing, just a birth mark!' I replied hurriedly, not wanting to draw too much attention to it.

Suddenly, there was a knock on the door of the cubicle. I froze in fear as Nikhil's mouth turned into a fiendish grin. He unlocked the door. It was a couple of his friends, guffawing at the sight of us.

All I remember was that they all unzipped their trousers. Everything that followed was a blur.

Chapter Four

Trauma has a strange and unique effect on its victims. It can happen swiftly, but can also be felt over days, months or even years. Even if it happens once, one can feel it for an eternity. It changes the victim forever. I wish I could live in denial of what happened to me. Unfortunately, it was a luxury that wasn't granted to me.

I remember Gran once told me that our soul chooses its life before we're born. The soul chooses the womb we are birthed from as well as the seed that gave us that spark of life. The soul also chooses the people we love and who love us. And it chooses those who hurt us and whom we have to hurt.

Many a times, our soul makes karmic contracts with other souls to come into our lives to teach us lessons. The lessons are sometimes traumatic, because the soul needs to go through those experiences in order to evolve to higher realms of consciousness. The way we heal from trauma is a major part of a soul's evolutionary journey.

My soul must have been masochistic when it chose this life for me. I lost my mother at birth and my father died before I could even remember his face clearly. Sure, I got to experience magic, something most souls never get to experience in countless lifetimes—but was it worth it? Was it worth going through all that happened to me that afternoon in the school toilet?

I remember just being in this strange state of shock for the rest of that day. I just kept silent and went about the day as though nothing had happened. I did my homework before Aunt Meg took me to the garden to prune the rose bushes. The thorns weren't as sharp as the pain I was feeling within. Then Aunt Claudine made me pull cards for some of the people who emailed her for readings. Every time, I pulled the ten of swords followed by the Death card. Those cards signify major changes and transformations are on the horizon. However, when it happened for the fifth time, she sent me to the kitchen to help Gran with supper.

On any other day, I would have relished Gran's roast turkey, especially when she stuffed it with apples to make it all the more juicy. I could tell that they were all concerned, but they didn't probe. Instead, they reassured me that I could talk to them about whatever was going on, once I was ready. But how could I ever be ready to talk about something so horrific?

It was only when I went to bed that I finally allowed myself to cry. I remember stuffing my face into my pillows so that my howls would be muffled. I could feel my body convulsing and throbbing with each howl. Every time I'd close my eyes, I'd see their laughing faces. I could still feel the slaps they landed on my face as they chuckled at my helpless self. Part of me wished I could have fought back. Unfortunately, I never learned how to fight. Yoga is, after all, a practice of peace. Fuck that shit!

For the next few days, I kept feigning a headache and begging Gran to let me stay at home. Usually, Gran would have just used an incantation to heal me as she cleansed my energy field. Not this time. Maybe she knew it wasn't a regular illness that plagued me. However, by the fourth day, she had no choice but to send me back to school because of a shitty rule where one needed to give a medical certificate if a student was absent for more than three days in a row.

The faeries stopped appearing. It was like they were never there to begin with. The magnificent banyan tree just seemed like a hollow vessel. I couldn't spend my recesses there anymore as I didn't want to see Nikhil Saini play football with his friends. So I just sat in my empty classroom with my head on the desk, crying. When prefects came to ask why I wasn't outside, I feigned a stomach ache. Even when Sahil Hada and his hyenas called me the most horrific names, I just remained numb. At first, they took it as a signal to up the ante. However, by the end of the week, they just stopped. I don't know if it was my lack of reaction that made them stop doing so, or if maybe Gandhi was right about the powers of non-violent protests. I didn't care, I just wanted to be left alone.

I didn't sleep for an entire month. How could I? Their disgusting faces would keep appearing like ghosts in my mind. I would just be in this weird autopilot mode during the morning yoga class. Gran wouldn't let me demonstrate advanced poses anymore. Though she had told me to talk to her only when I was ready, I could see that worry was slowly eating away at her patience. Yet, she stayed mum. However, she didn't let me take part in any ritual, even refusing to let me salt the crystals for the next full moon ritual. *Good!* I thought, *It's not like magic would make the pain go away.*

One day, the prefects, determined to get me out of the classroom during recess, cited some archaic rule that I for the life of me couldn't understand the relevance of. So, I just hid in the school chapel. Recess was when the priests would offer prayers, but I would just stare at the stained-glass windows that depicted different biblical scenes. Some were classics, such as the Nativity scene, Lazarus being raised from the dead and, of course, the Crucifixion. However, the one that stood out the most for me was the one of Saint Sebastian, the saint our school was named after. There he was, tied to a tree but standing beautiful and tall with arrows piercing his naked body from head to toe.

I wondered if it would be blasphemous of me to compare the scene with the ten of swords from the tarot and also if those who shot him with the arrows laughed cruelly as they took aim. Then again, it wasn't as though Saint Irene of Rome would come to my rescue and heal my wounds. I didn't think anyone could.

With each passing recess, it occurred to me how similar Catholic rituals were to Hindu rituals and even our witchy rituals, with the lighting of candles, burning of incense and chanting of hymns in ancient languages using words not in common parlance. True, one wouldn't dare say that to a priest of either faith. Wars have been fought over more futile reasons. But I'm sure Gran and my aunts would agree with my observation.

It was strangely peaceful to gaze up at Saint Sebastian, almost comforting to see his face be so peacefully angelic despite his predicament. I wonder if he felt the pain. I knew that pain was considered a virtue essential to one's absolution. I wonder when mine would come.

One weekend, Gran and my aunts decided to take me to the cinema to help clear my head. *The Avengers* had been out for almost two months, and Gran had quite liked *Iron Man*. She'd often tell me to imagine that the Palladium Arc Reactor on Iron Man's chest was kind of like his heart, or anahata, chakra, that keeps him alive. She truly believed comic book artists had some strange connection to the divine world, which is why almost all superheroes had their emblems on their chests. After all, the heart is the source of all strength. Mine, however, seemed to be blocked. She still hadn't told me why I had that eye-shaped scar on my chest after the attack on my birthday. I had pretty much stopped caring about it.

We were lining up at the ticket booth when an eerily familiar voice said from behind me: 'Hey, Jai.'

I didn't want to turn around. I just couldn't. I told myself that I was just imagining it.

'Aren't you going to introduce us to your friend?' Gran asked as we waited in the gilded lobby of PVR Director's Cut in the Ambience Mall at Vasant Kunj.

It took all my strength to turn around and face Nikhil Sahni, looking all cool and cute, as though nothing had happened. Look at him in his stupid washed out jeans and basic white T-shirt under his plaid shirt on top.

'Hello, Aunty,' he smiled at Gran and my aunts as though nothing had happened. 'I'm Nikhil. I go to school with Jai.'

'Oh really?'

'Yeah, but I'm in the tenth grade.'

'Oh, board exam year?'

'Yeah, but you know, can't keep studying all the time!'

To my horror, his friends were behind him grinning away. Fuck, this just couldn't be happening! How could they just talk to us as though everything was fucking peachy? Did they not know what they had done to me? Was this some sort of sick joke on their part? Were they fucking stalking me?

I was grateful that Nikhil Sahni and his friends were sitting a couple of rows ahead of us. I couldn't focus on the movie as I would often catch glimpses of their heads silhouetted by the screen. Oh, how I wanted to bash their heads with Thor's mighty hammer!

When the movie ended, I begged Gran and my aunts to take me home. When asked why, I just made up some lame excuse that I don't even remember now. I just didn't want to run into Nikhil Sahni and his skulk. However, Gran needed to use the ladies', while Aunt Claudine needed to re-do her make-up for her date later at night. Obviously, Aunt Meg joined them because for some reason, women have to go together to the bathroom every freaking time! Not being sexist or anything, but it was so fucking annoying at the most inconvenient times. Then again, I had to pee too. I opened the door to the men's bathroom and checked to see if Nikhil and the others were there. Just a bunch of random uncles and their brats. Thank God for that! Finding an empty urinal, I quickly unzipped and let out a huge sigh of relief as I unburdened myself.

'Bro! I told you there was an end credit scene!'

Oh fuck! It was Nikhil's voice.

'Yeah, like watching them eat shawarmas was so integral to the plot!'

Oh God, no, this can't be happening again, I thought. *No, no, it's all right*, another voice in my head said. There are other people here, it's not like they could do anything to me. Still, I was not willing to take chances.

I quickly zipped up and headed over to the sink with my head lowered and washed my hands. Never was I so thankful that there was a bathroom attendant present. I finished washing my hands and turned to run out as fast as I could without drawing attention.

'Don't forget to dry your hands!' called one of Nikhil's jackals. They had seen me after all. My heart sank as their chuckles followed.

Without turning around, I just opened the door and ran out. The drive back home with Gran and Aunt Meg was suffocatingly silent. Aunt Claudine was meeting her date at the mall, so she had stayed behind.

My heart was waging battle against my ribs throughout the night. I couldn't live like this anymore. Fuck my soul's contract and its evolution. For all I know, my soul was high on something weird when it made those fucking contracts. I mean, I don't remember signing on some dotted line! And hell, was my soul stupid enough not to read the fucking fine print! Fuck no! This is no way to live! This must end! This has to fucking end!

'You know you're doing it wrong, right?'

I hadn't noticed that Aunt Claudine had returned home. Nor did I know when I had entered the kitchen and taken out the knife that I was holding to my wrist. All I remember was looking up at her like a deer caught in headlights.

Chapter Five

'Was it the same boy we met at the cinema?'

I just stared down at my cup of lavender tea as I sat beside Aunt Claudine on the giant floral couch in the library, grateful that she hadn't woken up Gran and Aunt Meg.

'We knew this was going to happen. We just didn't know it would happen so soon.'

'What do you mean?'

'Oh, it speaks!' Aunt Claudine poured more tea in her cup.

Before I could think of anything to say, Aunt Claudine continued, 'The magical path isn't all cutesy and hunky-dory. The dangers are more real than most could imagine. Both on the mystical plane, as well as the physical realm. If it wasn't, everyone would be able to wield magic. Even rebellious teens that buy Wicca books to piss of their parents and decide to go all Goth chic in black. Or those bored housewives that do a weekend reiki workshop or become tarot readers in malls to make up for the fact that their husbands are too busy jerking off to some young thing instead of them. As fulfilling and enriching as our lives become when magic enters, the pain also follows.'

'B-B-But why?'

'I wish I knew!' Aunt Claudine took out a rolled joint from her purse, placing a finger on her lips to remind me not to tell Gran. Not like I hadn't seen Gran puff a doob now and then, but they usually made sure not to do it in front of me. She lit it with her onyx lighter with brass lining and continued, 'Then again, history has always enjoyed burning the witches. Not that any real witches were burned. But that's beside the point.'

'Did it happen to you too?'

'Yeah, when I was sixteen. It happened to Aunt Meg too around that time ...'

'Even Gran?'

'Honey, surely you have noticed that apart from our eyes, there's nothing really common between me and your Aunt Meg, or Jemima for that matter.'

Though I was shocked by what she said, I could see it clearly. Aunt Meg had more prominent features, with sharp cheekbones and a prominent jaw, while Aunt Claudine had a more dainty face with softer features. My mother, from the photographs I've seen of her, had a heart-shaped face with a slightly upturned nose. Gran's nose was like an eagle. Plus, even their hair was so different. Aunt Meg had a short black bob, while Aunt Claudine had long auburn faerie curls. Gran's silver locks were long and straight while my mom had had honey-blonde waves.

'Yup, we all had different daddies. None of them bothered to put a ring on Gran's finger,' Aunt Claudine took a long drag before letting out a satisfied sigh. 'Can't really blame your dad's family from objecting to the marriage. We were surprised she even got married. Then again, look how that turned out.'

My heart sank a little.

'Love isn't a luxury that we witches can take for granted. Magic and love never go hand-in-hand. There are exceptions to the rule—there always are—but I haven't really come across enough to believe in them.'

'Why?'

'Beats me! What, however, is true is that almost always, it takes some sort of sexual trauma to awaken magic within us. Not that I'm saying one should seek it out to awaken their magic. No one really seeks to be traumatized. However, when it does happen, it's a sign that the awakening has begun. Gran shouldn't have begun your training so early. However, her greater wisdom felt you were ready. Plus, you're the first boy born to us. That threw us off. We figured you'd be gay.'

I looked up in horror.

'Oh please, we knew even before you did. Besides, straight men have no true access to magic. Sure, they may study texts and find a guru to teach them various practices. However, it's women who have magic flowing through their veins. It's not like you read many tales about men being burned at the stake—except the gay ones. When they come across magic, especially in a woman, most men get very scared and do everything in their power to subjugate them. Gotta love that patriarchy!'

'But what does me being gay have to do with it?' It was the first time I had ever acknowledged my sexuality out loud.

'Well, let me put it in a way that you'd understand best. You know how we all have the magical polarities of masculine and feminine within us? You know, yin and yang, alpha and omega, light and dark, positive and negative, sun and moon, etcetera … right?'

I nodded.

'Well, straight men, because of centuries of patriarchy, suppress the goddess energy within them. They see it as a sign of weakness and value things like brute strength instead. It worked at first. They spent their days hunting, while we women observed the cycles of nature and learned how to harness the magic within the universe. Gay men were tossed aside as the weaklings of the tribes, and often hung out with the womenfolk.'

'Is that historically accurate?'

'Hey, I'm on a roll here!' Aunt Claudine took another satisfying drag. 'Anyway, haven't you wondered why the pride flag is a rainbow?'

I shook my head.

'Well, when does a rainbow occur?'

'When rain stops and the sun begins to shine again.'

'Exactly, and what energy is the sun?'

'Masculine.'

'And what energy is the rain?'

'Feminine—oh.' I had never thought of it like that.

'Bingo. Never take symbols lightly. There's a divine force attached to them, which empowers all that they represent.'

'Is that why the symbol for men is the alchemical glyph of the planet Mars, while the symbol for women is the glyph of the planet Venus?'

'Yup. And the queer symbol is both joined together, fused with the glyph of Mercury, which is the queer planet. It amazes me how people are so blind to the magic that surrounds them.'

'Okay, but coming back to sexual trauma. So many people go through it. But it doesn't really awaken magic within them, does it?'

Aunt Claudine stubbed her joint into a bronze ashtray. 'More tea?'

I hadn't noticed I had finished my cup. She refilled it.

'Look at it this way. There are tons of people who read tarot cards. Does that mean they're gifted psychics?'

I shook my head.

'And so many learn reiki or a form of energy healing. Does that make them masters or mistresses of the elements?'

I shook my head again.

'And all the people who practice yoga daily—how many of them go on to become Paramahansas or even yoga teachers? Just a fraction. And how many of them attain siddhis and can communicate with deities?'

She had a valid point.

'What age were you when we began your training?' she asked.

'Five.'

'Hmmm, figures.'

'What?'

'Well, you're thirteen now, right?'

I nodded.

'Yeah, it usually takes seven years for the body to be ready for magic. It's the eighth year when the first trauma occurs.'

'The *first*?'

'Oh, don't worry—only the first one is sexual. Afterwards, we get other tests of the soul.'

'Crap!'

'Relax, we're never tested with things that we don't have the ability to heal from.'

'So … I will heal from this?'

'We all have. Granted, it comes with its side effects. Your Aunt Meg swore off men.'

'What?'

'Oh sweetie, you really need to be more observant.'

'Aunt Meg is a lesbian?'

Aunt Claudine guffawed. 'Darling, you're not the only gay in the village. Not saying that it was because she was raped that she became one. If that had been the case, the world would be full of lesbians. Although, we're all on different sides of the Kinsey scale. Sexuality, is after all, incredibly fluid.'

'But why seven years?'

'Seven is the most magical of all numbers. Seven colours of the rainbow. Seven heavenly realms. Seven circles of hell. Seven notes of a musical scale. Seven wonders of the ancient world. Hell, seven is the number that can easily divide infinity.'

'It can?'

'Yeah, but don't ask me to elaborate on that. It's too late in the night for me to explain that.'

'What about the faeries?'

'What about them?'

'Before it happened, I could see and speak to them. Afterwards, they've disappeared.'

'Fae only speak to virgins. Innocent eyes, ears and souls unlock the veil between us and the Fae. They've not gone anywhere. They still exist and their magic is very real. However, when too much time is spent with them, they bring on such trauma even quicker. Rascals!'

That explained why they allowed Nikhil's football to hit me.

'However, now you'll be able to see and communicate with entities on different planes. Higher and lower.'

'How do I heal from what happened to me? Does that mean I have to forgive Nikhil?'

'Eventually, whenever you're ready.'

'Do I have to go through therapy?'

Aunt Claudine guffawed. 'Oh please! That's for mortals. You have something more powerful at your disposal.'

'I do?'

Aunt Claudine's lips curled into an impish grin. 'Magic!'

Chapter Six

They say that the eyes are the windows to the soul, but it's not true about the two you're reading these words with. Those eyes are pretty useless magically. The world we witness through them is merely an illusion created by Maya, the demoness of 'reality'. That's right, 'reality' is a demonic entity. And sometimes, we need to embrace demons to not just survive reality, but to thrive in it.

It is our 'third eye' that is the window to our soul. The ancients called it the 'ajna chakra', while in modern science the closest organ is the pineal gland. In old mythological sculptures and paintings, it's depicted in the centre of the forehead above the eyebrows. I suppose that's the best way artists could depict it symbolically.

However, there's no way our 'illusion eyes' can see it. Yet, those who practice magic or any authentic spiritual practice can not only feel it but also open it. The ways to do it are many, but I can only share the way Gran and my aunts helped me open mine on a fateful Saturday night at 'the witching hour'.

'Why Saturday, Gran?'

'It's Saturn's day. Saturn rules witches and magic,' Gran said, as she brewed a tea filled with brahmi, lavender, ginkgo leaves, jasmine, star anis and spearmint leaves. Gran also added a few drops of something that she promised to share with me when I was ready to initiate my magical heirs. I doubt that would ever happen.

'Doesn't Saturn rule karma, obligations, responsibility, discipline and burdens as well?' I asked as I sat in padmasana on the Persian rug in front of the apothecary table in the library.

'All things that are essential for magic. All magic comes with karma—that which we're born with, and that which we alter and play around with. Without using it responsibly, we build more karma that binds our soul to the eternal wheel of samsara. Discipline is what separates a dabbler from a true witch. And I think you already have an idea of the burdens that come with being a witch.' She shot a lovingly stern look at Aunt Claudine. I figured she would have rather I came to her that night when Aunt Claudine caught me trying to slit my wrist.

'Here.' Gran handed me a cup of the special brewed tea. 'Sip it slowly while it's still hot.'

As I sipped it, Aunt Meg and Aunt Claudine drew all the curtains, while Gran lit a lone white taper candle on an ornate black stand in the shape of an antelope's head. Aunt Meg's freshly rolled sandalwood incense burned away, filling the room with its sweet hypnotic fragrance. Aunt Claudine anointed my temples with patchouli oil so that I remained grounded. It's so easy for one to fly away into madness when opening the third eye.

'Now, my little one,' Gran smiled as she took the cup from me. 'Remember, that no matter what you see, never take your eye off the flame. Like Indra would send apsaras to distract meditating rishis from achieving their quests, there are many in the spirit world that would want nothing better than to lead you astray. Our sanity is of little to no consequence to entities and spirits. And most importantly, don't be scared—demons thrive on fear. Feed them enough, and they'll block your third eye forever.'

'It's time!' Aunt Meg alerted Gran to the giant grandfather clock that was a few seconds away from striking three.

'Good luck!' Gran kissed me on the forehead before she and my aunts exited the library, turning off all the lights, leaving just a lone candle flickering away.

Ten minutes passed, and I was just staring at the yellow flame. I wished they had at least kept the air conditioner on, but Gran said that it would interfere with the process. Irritating drops of sweat were falling down the back of my neck. I was so tempted to wipe it dry, but I had to keep my hands on my knees with the tip of my index finger gently touching my thumb. My knees were aching, and I wanted to stretch my legs. However, I could almost hear Gran going on about how physical distractions were the first hurdle to overcome.

'When it gets painful, just focus on your breath with your eyes on the candle.'

Easier said than done! Tears were welling up in my eyes, causing them to burn. The incense smoke was making even focussing on my breath difficult. At one point, it was hard to keep track of an inhale to the count of ten followed by an exhale to the count of twenty. Burdens of walking the magical path.

'Come play with me!'

Who said that?

'I did, silly!'

My eyes remained on the candle, but peripherally, I could see that it was the black antelope candle stand that was giggling away. What was in that tea?

'Don't you want to play?' The antelope began prancing about the apothecary table as the candle floated mid-air. 'It'll be really fun, come on!'

Focus, stay focused!

'Close your eyes, give me your hand, darling … ' The antelope was now behind me, whispering into my ears the lyrics of 'Eternal Flame' by The Bangles. 'Do you feel my heart beating? Do you understand?'

The lone antelope manifested into a trio, harmonizing away: 'Do you feel the same? Or am I only dreaming? Is this burning, an eternal flame … '

I wanted to tell them to shut the fuck up, but I couldn't break my focus. Was it just my imagination or was the flame dancing away to the song? The lone flickering flame had now grown three times larger. I wondered if it was just me turning cross-eyed or were there now two flames? Now three? What the—

'Say my name, sun shines through the rain' sang the antelopes. 'A whole life so lonely and then you come and ease the pain. I don't wanna lose this feeling …' Damn antelope chorus!

The three flames reunited and grew bigger in size. I gazed at the centre, but I couldn't help but notice sparks of violet, red, green and blue dancing around the flame like a mandala of light encircling it.

'Okay, your loss!' The antelopes giggled before galloping away into the void. *What the hell was in that tea? Okay, focus … breathe … watch the candle.*

'Don't forget to wipe your hands dry!' Nikhil Sahni and his jackals began guffawing. Though my eyes remained on the flame, I felt as though I was transported back to the boys' toilet at school.

'Don't worry, they can't hurt you.' I could hear Gran's voice in my head, calming me even as I felt fearful tingles run down my spine. Their laughter grew as their faces circled the flame. I couldn't tell what was more distracting—Nikhil Sahni and his jackals or the salty drops of sweat pouring down the back of my neck. I wished I had a spell to make me less ticklish. *Steady now … focus on the light …*

'Jai!'

A voice I had never heard before called out. I was no longer in the library. I was in a lush forest, sitting still in padmasana with the flame in front of me, but it was now the middle of the day.

'Jai!' the voice called out again.

Suddenly, the candle was in someone's hands.

'Do you not remember me?'

Mom?

What the fuck? It took so much strength not to look my mother straight in the eye. I could see she was gently smiling at me as she sat in front of me, holding the candle. Her long honey-blonde hair fell on each side of her shoulders, covering her bare breasts.

'I love you, Jai,' her voice echoed with angelic sweetness. 'I will always love you.'

I wanted to cry. I wanted to run into her arms and finally know what a motherly embrace felt like. My body was craving her gentle caress. I nearly gave up there and then. *Who cares about magic!* I thought desperately. *Who cares about my third eye being blocked!* I just wanted my mother! I wanted her love.

'Come with me!' She extended her hand out towards me. I could smell the fragrance of gardenias coming from her. Aunt Meg did tell me that my mother loved gardenias.

As much as I wanted to place my hand in hers and let her lead me down whatever path lay ahead, a part of me hesitated.

'Don't you love me?' Her green eyes sparkled like emeralds as she extended her hand further.

'It's okay,' said a different voice.

'I didn't die in an accident.' It was my father. As he sat beside my mother, I noticed his thick, dark, curly hair. His beard was longer than in the pictures I had seen of him. I don't know how I had the strength to resist leaping across to sit between them—but I heard Gran's voice again, gently reminding me to stay focussed on the candle.

'Don't you love us, Jai?' Their voices spoke in a sweet unison.

I could feel the earth tremble beneath me. The trees behind me were swaying as a cold breeze blew past us. My spine ached more with each passing second, making it hard for me to stay alert.

'Don't you love us, Jai?' Was it just my imagination, or did their voices turn eerily sinister?

'Don't you love us, Jai?'

I gulped as their skin began to crumble before my very eyes as their voices turned malignantly bombastic. It was hard to remain focussed on the candle as they began laughing maniacally. Their beautiful glowing skin turned into a deviant ash colour, and eventually began cracking and oozing black tar. Their eyes burned like demonic coal embers.

'They can't hurt you unless you allow them to!' Gran's voice echoed, but it was hard not to crap my pants as their laughter grew louder and louder. Their bodies had transformed into fiery figures.

'You killed us, Jai!' They taunted in demonic cackles. 'You're the reason we died! That's something you'll have to live with throughout your life! Murderer! You're a murderer! You killed us! You killed us! You killed us!'

Their bodies fused and formed a gigantic burning figure that grew so tall that it almost parted the clouds above. Its sinister laugh made the earth shake, and the lush green forest was now a burning pit.

'Remember me, Jai?' The figure before me had transformed into the hooded figure that had attacked us during the full moon ritual on my birthday!

'You're mine!' It pointed towards my chest. The eye-shaped scar on my chest began burning brightly.

'I marked you that day! And I will have you! Don't think you can escape me! Eventually, you will be mine! And not even your Gran and your aunties will be able to save you! They can't protect you forever. Soon, you'll kill them too, just like you killed your parents, you stupid miserable little twit! I've marked you and I will follow you forever!'

With a giant leap, it brought its face close to mine. Thank God that the candle flame was between us. However, I couldn't see its face. It was just a blank dark obsidian orb that reflected the flame of the candle.

'I will hunt you! I will find you! And I will have you!' It laughed maniacally and the world around me began to spin like a chaotic vortex.

I could feel the bile rise from my stomach and up my throat. I don't know how I still managed to stay focussed on the flame that danced wildly within the spinning vortex. My mind was racing at a hundred miles an hour, yet my eyes remained glued to the candle as the dark entity's laughter grew louder and wilder with each passing moment.

Then, all of a sudden, everything became calm. All my visions disappeared. I was back in the library, sitting in front of the apothecary table. Even though I knew I actually hadn't moved an inch, it felt as though I had fallen off the top of a skyscraper. The candle had melted all over the black antelope stand, with barely half an inch remaining. The flame remained stable as though nothing had happened.

'Blink gently before closing your eyes,' I heard Gran's voice say as she entered the room with my aunts and turned on the lights.

I felt salty rivers of tears flow down as I collapsed on the floor and trembled feverishly. *What was that? What the fuck had I just witnessed?* I had focussed all my attention on the candle flame, but how could I have possibly ignored everything else that I saw?

'Open your eyes slowly,' Gran whispered. I could feel a sudden wave of cold air flow over my body, taking away all the pain and fear.

'D-d-did it work?'

'See for yourself.' Gran handled me an ornate gilded hand mirror. I just saw my own reflection, flushed and red.

'Don't just look,' Gran whispered again. '*See!*'

I didn't know if it was my own imagination, but I could see a small indigo pearl glimmer between my brows. The pearl slowly blossomed into a golden lotus, and from its centre, a silver cobra arose with its hood marked with what seemed like glimmering sapphires.

'So mote it be!' Gran and my aunts whispered in unison.

Chapter Seven

Now this usually is the part in those bad teen-witch movies when the newly initiated witch hatches petty revenge schemes against all those who torment her, only for karma to bitch-slap her in the face and cause her life to fall apart. As much as I wanted to avoid that cliché, it couldn't hurt to have a little fun, right?

The Monday after the ritual that opened my third eye, I was kinda excited to go back to school. I don't know if it was the fact that I had grown a few inches taller, or that my muscles were more prominent. I enjoyed taking a shirtless selfie in the morning and making it the first-ever post on my new Instagram account.

I couldn't help but notice everyone's jaw dropping the minute I entered the school gates. My white uniform was tighter than usual, so it fitted in a sexy manner. Unlike earlier—when I would walk straight to my classroom with my head lowered, avoiding all eye contact—I now strutted with my head held high with a new-found swagger. It was sort of like John Travolta in the iconic opening of *Saturday Night Fever*. It was a little overwhelming to be assaulted by all the stares, but I loved it!

I faced my first obstacle right as I entered my classroom. Sahil Hada and his cackling hyenas were blocking the way to my seat. Backs towards me, they were hunched over a mobile phone, giggling away at a porn clip on one of their phones where a girl moaned out loud as she seemingly enjoyed being gangbanged. Who said porn stars couldn't act?

'Everything is energy.' Gran had taught me. 'We're all made up of the same things that make the trees, the stones, the air we breathe, the waters in the rivers, lakes and oceans, and even the stars in the sky. Science says we're all just a bunch of atoms, fused together by a magnetic pull. Thus, telekinesis really is about focussing on that very magnetic energy. Once you master it, you'll be able to move objects with the power of your mind.'

I couldn't help but smirk as I focussed on the legs of Sahil's chair as he made to sit down. It took all my willpower not to laugh out loud as he landed hard on his pudgy ass when the chair moved from where he thought it was. I stepped over him and strutted to my desk. I didn't need to turn around to know that they were looking at me with an alien sense of amazement. It was fun watching him freak out that his brand new phone now had a virus courtesy the porn video. Well, not just the porno.

Later, we had a free period as one of the teachers was absent. I was doodling away in my notebook when Sahil Hada and his hyenas started picking on a nerdy kid with glasses. They snatched the kid's geometry box and stood on their desks, tossing it amongst themselves and laughing cruelly as the kid tried to catch it. Assholes!

'The etheric body,' Aunt Meg had told me the other afternoon in Lodi Gardens, 'is like the creamy centre of an Oreo that connects our physical body with our aura. Usually, it's easy to see when we're in a quiet room against a white wall. Life, however, doesn't allow for such perfect conditions to be met all the time. That's why you're here when it's at its most crowded. Pick a person of your choosing.'

I pointed at a girl who was sitting with her boyfriend under a large tree. It was obvious from their body language that he wanted to get down to action with her, but she wasn't in the mood.

'Perfect, now concentrate on her. Don't strain your physical eyes—use your third eye.'

It took me a couple of moments before I could see a silvery shield of about an inch or two outlining her body.

'Good, now try to see beyond it. No stress, just breathe.'

It was tough, as her boyfriend was sitting really close to her and his energy field was interfering with hers. However, with Aunt Meg's gentle encouragement, I was able to see a yellowish field of energy outside her etheric body.

'That's the aura. Describe it.'

'It's kinda yellow, but it's cracked. I can see light leaking from those cracks.'

'She's clearly stressed.'

'Must be because of the boyfriend.'

'Now, imagine a silvery cord emerging from your navel.'

To my amazement, I immediately felt a beam of silver light emerge from my navel.

'Extend it all the way to her. Don't worry about people crossing its path, they won't be able to affect its direction. Allow it to attach to her navel. Done?'

I nodded.

'Good, you're now energetically connected. She's under your control.'

The minute my silver cord fused with her, I could feel her energy. I knew all about her life. She was the eldest of her generation in a rather conservative joint family and had been repressed all her life, so she cherished the moments she could escape to spend time with her boyfriend. However, he was pressuring her to make out with him under the tree. I could feel her disgust and discomfort.

'Don't get too attached. You'll begin to take on her karmas. Keep yourself grounded and centred.'

It took a little getting used to as I could literally feel her essence flowing to me. However, I visualized a dam in the cord blocking the karmic transference.

Just as the boyfriend was getting handsy and was trying to cop a feel, Aunt Meg ordered, 'Now!'

We chuckled as she slapped him when I waved my hand. The look on his face was priceless.

'One more time, for all the other girls he's probably pressured before they were ready.'

We giggled more as she slapped him again.

'And one more time for good luck!'

We laughed out loud as she kicked him on his shin before storming off.

In the classroom, I attached my silvery cord to Sahil's navel. I saw a glimpse of his life. He was the fat kid of his family and was constantly scolded by his parents for his slovenly appearance. I could see how his parents kept sending him to various dieticians—and even got a trainer to help him lose weight—but he would sneakily gobble chocolates in the middle of the night, or whenever no one was watching. A part of me—a tiny part—kinda felt sorry for him.

Sahil's face became pale as the geometry box fell out of his hands. Before he realized what was happening, he slapped himself. He had barely had any time to recover when he slapped himself again. And again. And again. And one more time for good luck!

'What the fuck?' he cried out loud as the entire class burst into laughter. Poor bastard had no idea why he was hitting himself.

'Always remember,' Aunt Meg had told me, 'visualize white light emerging from your dominant hand, and make a slicing motion to cut that silvery cord when you wish to end the spell. If you don't, you'll be attached permanently.'

No way did I want to be attached to Sahil Hada in any manner.

Later, during recess, Nikhil Sahni and his friends were playing football as usual. When the ball headed my way, I stood and stepped on it.

'Dude, you wanna give us the ball?' yelled Nikhil.

'Oh, you mean this one?' I picked up the ball and held it in my hands.

'No, dinkus, the two between your legs!' he snapped back.

'If they've even dropped!' snorted one of his jackals. They high-fived each other.

Focussing on the magnetic field of the football, I threw the ball high in the air. Then I jumped and bicycle-kicked it like Cristiano Ronaldo. None of them noticed that I landed perfectly with the grace of a ballerina, because the ball had zoomed towards the guy who made that comment about my balls and smashed right into his groin. He cried out in agony as he fell to his knees. The look on their faces was priceless.

'Glamour is the art of mesmerization,' Aunt Claudine once said as we were sharing a Mississippi Mud Pie at the Big Chill Café in Khan Market. 'See that guy over there?'

I turned to see a cute guy sitting with his girlfriend a few tables away, under a vintage poster of Rita Hayworth in *Gilda*.

'Watch and learn!' Aunt Claudine sipped some water before she stretched her arms above her head and exhaled to relax her body. She turned to look at him and just gazed towards his third eye. The minute he made eye contact with her, he was—well—mesmerized.

She grinned as she bit her lower lip, and I couldn't help be amazed at how his mouth dropped open. He looked as though he was in a trance. She took a spoonful of the delicious dessert and naughtily let it linger by her lips that promised sinful pleasure. He licked his lips idiotically, unable to take his eyes off her.

His girlfriend got annoyed and began snapping her fingers in front of his face. He momentarily snapped out of it, and went back to talking to her. Yet, his eyes remained fixated on

Aunt Claudine, and he ended up knocking a glass of water all over his girlfriend.

'What the fuck is wrong with you?' the woman exclaimed, livid. She got up and threw her napkin in his face before storming to the bathroom.

Immediately after she left, Aunt Claudine winked at the man ever so subtly. He got up and rushed over to our table.

'Hi!' He sounded almost as though he was out of his body. 'I'm Raghav!' He extended his hand towards Aunt Claudine. I couldn't help but judge his tacky gold bracelet.

Aunt Claudine extended her hand as if she was a princess. 'Charmed, I'm sure!'

Just as he took her hand in his to kiss, the girlfriend emerged out of the ladies' room.

'What the fuck is wrong with you?' she yelled, punching him on his shoulder.

Aunt Claudine discreetly broke the glamour spell. In less than a second, he had snapped out of his trance and was horrified to be holding Aunt Claudine's hand in his. Dropping it in a heartbeat, he turned to his angry girlfriend, who had by then turned a bright shade of red that contrasted his fear-ridden pale face.

'Baby, I'm sorry, it's not what you—'

'Oh fuck off!' She kicked him in the shin, causing him to cry out. 'I knew you were fucking cheating on me! It's one thing to do it behind my back, but in front of me?'

'Baby, no!' Cold sweat covered his face now. 'I swear I'm not cheating. I just—'

'Liar! Ugh!' She picked up a pitcher of peach iced tea from a neighbouring table and unceremoniously emptied it on his head before storming off.

'Baby, no! Please …'

He chased after her as the entire café burst into laughter.

As if reading my mind, Aunt Claudine shrugged. 'Hey, better she knows about him now than later. Saved her months of heartache!'

She triumphantly enjoyed the last bite of the Mississippi Mud Pie.

I was at the swimming pool in school when the swim team began practicing their diving drills. Nikhil Sahni was standing by the steps of the large diving pool, laughing away at some corny joke with his jackals. A part of me still burned because he still seemed oblivious to the pain he had caused me.

'Sahni!' The coach blew his whistle. 'You're up!'

'Come on, Nikhil!' the team cheered as he began climbing up the steps to the highest of the three diving boards. As he neared the edge of the board, I caught his gaze before he could put his swimming goggles on. Though he was far from me, I could see his chocolate pools soften as the glamour spell began to work.

'Move it, Sahni!' the coach yelled and blew his whistle again. Nikhil momentarily snapped out of his trance and put his goggles on, but I could still feel him looking at me. He looked so silly standing there, just gazing at me with his mouth hanging hungrily.

'Hurry up!' The coach's voice was now angry, as was the way he blew his whistle. But Nikhil didn't move. I bit my lower lip, almost mimicking Aunt Claudine's sensuality. I didn't know that it would make Nikhil step off the diving board and fall flat on his face into the water. The collective silence was deafening for a moment as we saw him lying face down in the pool.

I blinked and broke the glamour spell. *Fuck, what have I done?* The coach dove straight in and pulled him out of the pool. They gathered in a circle around him, watching on in horror as the coach began checking his air passages.

'I don't feel a pulse!' cried one of Nikhil's jackals.

'Shit!' yelled the coach as he placed his fingers under Nikhil's nose.

'Is he breathing?' someone asked. He was visibly shaking.

The coach placed both palms on Nikhil's chest and began pushing fast and hard, before blowing into his mouth. Nikhil remained limp. 'Quick, get the school nurse!' yelled the coach before he continued to perform CPR.

'Osculum Vitae,' said Gran, holding in her hands a dead parrot that had been hit by a truck moments earlier. 'Also known as the kiss of life. Only to be used when death occurs before its time. Usually, reversing death is incredibly dangerous, because when it's time for the soul to leave the body, it means the soul has completed its purpose in this life. However, sometimes death comes about before its time due to extreme circumstances.'

'How will we know if death is timely or not?'

'Oh, you'll know! Death, when final, is absolute.' Gran slowly parted the beak of the parrot. 'However, when you can see flickers of life within the eyes, you know there it is clinging on.' Gran opened the eyes of the parrot, and I could see faint golden sparks within its eyes. Gran then brought the parrot towards her lips, kissing it tenderly as she blew air into its beak. Within moments, the parrot's wings began flapping tenderly. I could see green light flow from Gran's heart through her and out of her mouth. The parrot had come back to life. It bowed gently before Gran as if to thank her, before flying off into the night sky.

'Let me through!' I cried as I pushed my way through the crowd around Nikhil's prone body. Before the coach could protest, I was kneeling beside Nikhil, feigning the CPR chest presses as I performed the Osculum Vitae spell.

It didn't work. *Fuck!*

'No magic can be done when you are stressed out,' I could hear Gran's voice. 'Remember, when a spell doesn't work, first calm your mind and focus on your breath. Then try again.'

I closed my eyes and focussed on my breath even as I continued feigning the chest pumps. When I opened them again, the school nurse was running over with a couple of the swim team boys who had gone to fetch her, barefoot and still in their speedos.

Here goes nothing, I thought as I leaned in and gently kissed Nikhil. In a moment or two, I could feel a splash of water. I backed off as Nikhil began coughing up the water. The victorious cheer was almost deafening.

'Someone exhausted themselves today!' Gran chuckled as she placed a cold compress laced with peppermint and tea tree oil on my forehead as I laid in bed trembling with a fever of a hundred and four degrees.

'It's okay,' she said and smiled, waving her hands above my crown chakra and clearing all the blockages caused by the fever. 'We all get excited when the magic courses through our veins so potently. That's why Saturn rules witches and magic. The burdens of our powers come with great responsibility. Don't worry! With time, you'll get a better hang of it.'

She bent over and kissed me on my forehead. 'By sunrise, you'll be fine.'

She turned off the lights after wishing me a good night. As I lay there, I couldn't help but smile when I thought about what Nikhil had said to me at the end of the school day.

'Hey, I heard about what had happened,' he had said sheepishly, almost as though he was filled with shame. It was perhaps a feeling alien to him.

'It's okay, I just did what anyone would.' It was the best thing I could come up with.

I could see his body squirm, but after what seemed like an eternity of hemming-and-hawing and with great effort, he finally uttered, 'I'm really sorry about what happened that day in the toilet. It was really shitty of me to do that.'

Understatement of the century much? I thought as I rolled my eyes. Words could never compensate for what he did. But before he could say anything else, his jackals called out to him. He clearly wanted to say so much more, but he just couldn't muster up the words to say it. Instead, he just turned and run over to his skulk.

Oh well, I thought, *I suppose I will forgive him. Eventually.*

Chapter Eight

'Beta, how old are you?'

'Aunty, I'm twenty-one!' I said, smiling as I sipped my cup of lavender tea.

'Twenty-one!' The lady's eyes popped out in disbelief. 'You're younger than both my daughters!'

'Is that bad?'

'No, no,' she said, taking a quick sip from her cup to calm her nerves. 'Not anything bad. Just so surprising how someone so young can be so skilled at such deep mystical arts.'

I've heard similar comments ever since Gran got me to do my very first reading at the ripe old age of sixteen.

'Once upon a time, there was a great sage called Mrikandu,' Gran told me on my sixteenth birthday as I was rolling the incense to be burned during my birthday celebration. 'Mrikandu and his wife were great devotees of the Lord Shiva, and Lord Shiva took great care of them, granting them many boons—except that of a child.'

'Why not a child?'

'Well, the scriptures aren't very clear about that ...'

'Since when do we go by the scriptures?' Aunt Meg interrupted as she handed me some dried frankincense to mix with dried sandalwood powder. 'After all, we all know they're always peppered with the beliefs of those who've written them and were changed as needed to suit the agendas of men in power.'

'Is that true, Gran?'

Gran sighed. 'An unfortunate reality of the world we live in. However, one story I was told by Babaji when I was little was that Sage Mrikandu had been cursed by the great Shukracharya …'

'Patriarchy's way of masculinizing the planet Venus,' Aunt Meg chimed in.

'Really?'

'So they say,' Gran continued as she washed her crystals in a rosewater solution. 'Though there is no clear reason as to why Shukracharya cursed Sage Mrikandu, one of the effects of the curse was that Sage Mrikandu was left impotent. For though Venus represents women and fertility, Venus also rules one's semen and our paternal legacy.'

'Shukra literally means *cum*,' Aunt Meg rolled her eyes.

'Wow!' I was taken aback.

'Anyway,' Gran continued, 'the desire for a child was so great that one day, Sage Mrikandu and his wife did an intense penance to Lord Shiva, who is known to be benevolent. He would grant the wishes of all those who worship him, whether human, divine or demonic. For Shiva never cared about things like caste, creed or even soul heritage. All he needed was one's complete love and devotion.'

Gran rubbed the crystals with a white cotton cloth before continuing, 'Lord Shiva, though happy with the penance, regretfully informed Sage Mrikandu that while he could grant them a child, there would be a catch.'

'Isn't there always?' Aunt Meg winked as she rubbed the dried herbal mixture to form incense cones.

'The story wouldn't be interesting otherwise,' Gran giggled. 'Anyway, the catch was that Sage Mrikandu and his wife would have to make a choice: either they would be blessed with a child who would only live for sixteen years but who would possess the wisdom of the universe, or they would be blessed with a child who lived to a ripe old age, but would have the intelligence of a bag of manure.'

'That's messed up!'

'However, after consulting with his wife, Sage Mrikandu said he would choose a wise child that would live for a mere sixteen years. After all, a short flickering candle could inspire the world for centuries. And so, Lord Shiva granted their wish and nine months later, Sage Mrikandu's wife gave birth to a beautiful baby boy. They named him Markandeya. True to Lord Shiva's word, Markandeya was the wisest soul anyone had ever known. The first words he uttered were hymns praising Lord Shiva. While other children would play about all day, Markandeya devoured the ancient scriptures and mastered all divine rituals. Pretty soon, people came from villages near and far to seek Markandeya's counsel on all matters. They would always leave with their spirits elevated. Eventually, on the night before his sixteenth birthday, Yama—the god of death and the underworld—appeared before them, riding on his buffalo. He gave them till sunrise to prepare for the last rites for Markandeya.'

'I wonder why Death rides a buffalo?'

It was Aunt Claudine, who had just sauntered in.

'Back so soon?' Aunt Meg raised a quizzical brow. 'Was your date that boring?'

'Nah, he was cute and all, but no way was I gonna miss Jai's birthday ritual!' Aunt Claudine kissed me on my forehead. 'Besides, there are plenty of fish in the polluted sea, but I only have one nephew.'

'I can smell the Paco Rabanne all the way from here,' said Aunt Meg, sniffing.

'Jealous?' Aunt Claudine playfully teased.

'As if!'

'Well, go get changed, we only have an hour,' said Gran impatiently.

Aunt Claudine headed to her room, giggling.

'So, what did Sage Mrikandu and Markandeya do?' I asked, curious to hear the rest of the story.

'Well, like any father would in such a situation, Sage Mrikandu panicked. His wife was distraught. Though they always knew their son's fate, no parent can accept having their child taken away while they still live within this mortal realm. However, Markandeya told them not to worry. He sat before the Shiva lingam in their hut's courtyard and began reciting the Maha Mrityunjaya mantra—an incantation to Lord Shiva that's known to be so powerful that it can even raise the dead.

'Markandeya kept reciting the mantra in perfect rhythm and tempo repeatedly without a break. Minutes turned into hours, but Markandeya kept sitting before the Shiva lingam and continued the chanting without a care in the world as his parents watched with bated breath. Soon, the moon gave a final goodbye kiss to the morning star before the sun made its grand entrance. Just as the sky began to turn a bright shade of pink, Lord Yama appeared again on his buffalo. The minute the sun could be seen clearly in the eastern horizon, Lord Yama took out his lasso of death and tossed it towards Markandeya. He was going to grab him by his neck and drag his soul to the land of Death.

'However, to his shock, the noose landed on top of the Shiva lingam. The stone lingam immediately transformed into a fierce avatar of Lord Shiva called Kalankata—the Ender of Death. Frightened, Lord Yama cowered before this form of Lord Shiva and then quickly left the scene. Markendeya went on to live a long and happy life.'

'Alrighty then, I'm ready!' Aunt Claudine called, having changed into a white flowing robe like the rest of us. Smelling now of roses instead of Paco Rabanne.

'Okay,' Gran said, standing. 'Let's get ready for Jai's birthday ritual.'

'Wait!' Aunt Claudine said suddenly. She took out her phone. 'We gotta take a selfie first!'

'Seriously?' sighed Aunt Meg.

'Hey, if it's not on Instagram, did it even happen?' Aunt Claudine said, turning to me. 'At least you'll have something to post besides those photos of you doing yoga without a shirt on.'

'I still say he's way too young to be posting thirst- traps on Instagram,' Aunt Meg complained, but reluctantly looked towards the camera as Aunt Claudine extended her arm and raised her phone.

'Oh hush! Don't be such a party- pooper!' said Aunt Claudine, running her hands through her hair and turning her head to a flattering angle, 'Everyone say "Om shanti"!'

'Om shanti!' The four of us cheered in unison as Aunt Claudine pressed the button on her phone.

'Are they your family?' The woman asked as she gazed at the framed photograph as she set her cup down.

'Yes, my grandmother and my aunts.' I stood at the far end of my studio in Defence Colony, holding two copper dowsing rods. 'Shall we begin?'

'Sure!' The woman stood up, adjusting her elegant dark trousers. 'Where should I stand?'

'Just over by the opposite wall. We're going to begin by scanning your chakras.'

'But, Gran,' I nervously whispered before I began my first-ever professional reading. 'Why do I need these dowsing rods to measure chakras? I can just use my third eye to see them, along with her etheric body and aura.'

'The rods are not for you, they're for them. I know you will accurately tell them everything you see, but they won't be able to comprehend them until they see the rods move. Seeing is believing, after all. Remember to hold the rods up, one in each hand. Speak to the rods, asking them what is the state of the chakra in question. If the rods open to a perfect hundred and eighty degrees, that means the chakra is open. If they open partially, then the chakra in question is damaged. If they remain still, the chakra is blocked, but if they criss-cross shut, then the chakra is not only blocked but also severely depleted of all energy.'

'Did your mother have a difficult time during childbirth?' I asked when the copper dowsing rods criss-crossed shut.

'Yes!' the woman exclaimed, astonished. 'As she was giving birth, they told her that the umbilical cord was choking my neck. They had to, therefore, go for an emergency C-section. How did you know that?'

'Your root chakra is severely blocked.'

I smiled in an effort to comfort her. A gentle smile always helps while talking grave matters. However, it has to be a genuine one.

'Oh. What does that mean?'

She looked surprised seeing the rods move on their own without me doing anything.

'Well, it explains why you live with a fear of abandonment and constantly worry about your finances.'

'How did you—? I didn't even ...'

'You didn't have to tell me anything—your chakra told me.'

'Amazing!'

'Always make sure that the seeker shuffles and pulls the tarot card themselves,' Aunt Claudine told me. 'It makes them feel like they're involved in the reading.'

'But if they touch the cards, won't their energies imprint on them?'

'That's the point!'

'Huh?'

'Remember, the reading is about them, not you. Each time they shuffle and pull the cards, they're building a psychic bond with the deck. They don't know it, but their spiritual energies are connecting with the cards. That makes the psychic forces of the universe guide them to pull the cards that has the answers they're looking for.'

'Are you right-handed or left-handed?'

'Uh … right-handed,' answered the woman. She raised her right hand. Every time I ask this question to someone, they raise their dominant hand.

'Okay, rub your hands so that you can activate the mini energy chakras of your palms and fingers, and then, with your left hand, pull a card to represent your present life situation.'

'Why the left hand?'

'It's the psychic hand. The dominant hand is that which does all the work of the material world. The non-dominant hand is that which does all the work in the spiritual realm.'

'Can I pull a card for my daughters?' the woman asked, enjoying the powerful thrill of a reading.

'How old are they?'

'The elder one is twenty-seven, and the younger one, twenty-three.'

'Ah, I'm sorry, we can't do that.'

'Why not?'

'Consent is important—not just in the material world, but also in the psychic world,' Aunt Meg had told me. 'Once people have satisfied their own curiosity, they'll always wish to know about those around them. "Does he love me?", "Will my mother-in-law sign the property over to us?", yada-yada-yada. Remember—when you do a reading, you're taking a peek into the psychic universe within a person. You're accessing their deepest, darkest secrets—the things that make them vulnerable and the things that haunt them, literally and metaphorically. So, if someone asks about someone else, even if is their child, you cannot allow it if they're above eighteen—unless they have themselves given you permission to read for them.

'But, beta, I just want to know when they will get married. Surely you can help put a mother's mind at peace?'

'However,' Aunt Meg added, 'There are loopholes around everything.'

I smile as I sip my tea. 'Shuffle the cards while thinking about becoming a mother-in-law within a couple of years.'

Aunt Claudine had taught me to always ensure that the customers leave with their spirits elevated. 'They come to you seeking hope during turbulent times. It's your duty to make sure they leave happy. And always take payment only in cash!'

'Oh, thank you so much, beta!' said the woman once everything was done. She bent to touch my feet.

I stepped back immediately and stopped her before she could. It was because Gran had told me to never let people touch my feet and to never touch the feet of others, even if done out of love and respect.

The reason is that Apana Vayu blows from the souls of the feet, expelling negative and wasteful energy. If we touch another's feet, we take on their toxicity as well as their negative karmas. Hugs are better because at least our heart chakras are uniting, spreading love. However, in case you don't feel like hugging, a simple namaste is enough.

After I bid adieu to the woman, I took the cash she gave me and placed it in a box before a small altar by my bedside.

The grand Golf Links mansion covered with ivy was gone. Life had taken me to live in this small studio on the roof of a four-storied town house in Defence Colony. It was cosy and let me live a minimalist life. After all, the practice of detachment is essential for a yogi. The landlady allowed me to use the entire roof area to grow all the herbs and vegetables I could in Delhi's climate conditions. I would often share my harvest with them and the other tenants.

Despite all the detachment, I still truly missed Gran and my aunts. I hope they're happy wherever they may be.

Chapter Nine

Apart from the virtue of taking roads less travelled by, Robert Frost taught us that good fences make good neighbours. However, I prefer Sylvia Plath and Emily Dickinson. Considering I was raised by a trio of witches, how could I not be drawn to literary 'madwomen'? However, little did I know that Frost's words would play such an important role in my life till Vir moved in next door. Though it would be at least three months before I would lay eyes on him.

A fortnight had passed since my sixteenth birthday when we were assaulted by the cacophony of a construction crew. Our mornings that once begun with a symphony of bird songs were now replaced by clanging, banging and drilling. The ivy that covered our walls were in turn covered with layers of soot and the road in front of the house was lined with trucks carrying bricks and sand. There was no room for the yoga students to park.

'Philistines!' Gran once groaned as she buttered a toast during breakfast. 'Not only are they ruining the beautiful façade of a classic Heinz architectural structure, but they are also so noisy going about it!'

'Tell me about it!' Aunt Meg moaned. 'I had three students walk out this morning before shavasana because they couldn't focus on nothingness.'

'Were they ever able focus on nothingness?' Aunt Claudine sighed, displeased with the dark circles under her eyes.

The collective sourness was alien to me.

'And they're painting it blue,' complained Gran. 'Blue! The house was perfectly beautiful with its ivory exterior, but they had to paint it blue! What ever happened to good taste?'

'Good taste and money rarely goes hand-in-hand,' Aunt Meg shook her head.

'Amen to that!' Aunt Claudine exclaimed as she mixed a shot of gin with her lemonade.

Not that we had anything against alcohol, but it was rather early for a drink. It wasn't even a Sunday brunch. I didn't dare add to the air of disgruntlement, instead choosing to keep my headphones on throughout the day. It was a pair of Beats by Dre that I got for my birthday, along with a new iPhone 6S in a delightful rose gold.

But it wasn't just to drown out the noise next door. I had become obsessed with Magdalena—a pop goddess who had just released her thirteenth album a few months ago. Yes, I was becoming *that* kind of gay guy!

I first heard her music three years ago, when she made a comeback after several years of inactivity, as she was building orphanages in Africa. Granted, her music was always there throughout my waking years, but that album blew me away. True, many did say that at fifty, she was playing catch-up with the crop of young starlets that were all vying for her musical throne. However, inspite of the ED synths, her brilliant lyrics along with her unique haunting voice shone through. Her latest album released a couple of months ago, where she was now experimenting with dubstep, triphop and trap—creating deceptively catchy tracks that dealt with heartbreak and abandonment. While everyone else was singing about partying and getting drunk or laid, she sang about the pain of divorce and the disillusionment with the material world.

'She was at her best in the 1980s,' Aunt Claudine would say whenever she caught me watching her videos on YouTube—which was constantly.

'Please, '90s Magdalena was her most experimental,' disagreed Aunt Meg.

'What has she done to her face?' Gran cried when she saw the edition of *Vogue Italia* that I had ordered because it featured her on the cover. 'I can hardly even recognize her!'

I didn't care what they thought. I guess all teenagers passionately defend their favourite artistes from haters. I totally 'stanned' Magdalena. My bedroom walls were covered with posters of her. I would save my allowance and bid on rare vintage vinyls and picture discs that I would have framed and put up on my walls. I once even contemplated getting a tattoo of her lyrics, but Gran forbid it.

'I'll give her this much,' Aunt Claudine said once when I was showing her a performance Magdalena did at the Grammy Awards, 'Her body is spectacular!'

'She is a level four Ashtangi,' I informed my aunts with a strange sense of pride. 'And her classical ballet training shows in her moves—smooth like butter!'

'Chill, fanboy!' Aunt Claudine ruffled my hair much to my annoyance.

After the construction crew left, we noticed a fleet of white Toyota vans with armed guards on the road outside. Never had I ever seen an AK-47 up close—almost fifty of them at that!

'Did you see how they've added those tacky stone lions outside their gate?' Gran muttered as we sat in our front lawn having afternoon tea in the gazebo while watching workers unloading furniture from four large moving vans.

'Tacky-tacky-tacky!' Aunt Claudine chimed. 'But at least the noise has stopped.'

'Small mercies!' Aunt Meg munched on a scone, 'Oh-my-god, will you just stop!' She snapped as she caught me taking a selfie while holding my blue periwinkle cup: #afternoontea #teaforlife.

'No phones at the table!' Gran declared, and snatched my phone from me. Thank God I had already pressed send.

'Madam ji!' A voice from behind startled us.

'Yes?' Gran arched a quizzical brow as all of us sized up the sweaty moustachioed man in a beige safari suit, wondering how he had the gall to just walk in without calling on the intercom first.

'Madam ji, myself Tejeshwar Rathi,' the man said. 'I am the PA of Mr B.L. Rajani.'

'And I'm supposed to be impressed by that?' Gran's sarcasm was delicious to my ears.

Not knowing how to react, the man continued, 'Madam ji, Rajani sahab and his family will be moving in next week, and would like to apologize for any inconvenience the renovations may have caused ...'

'So he sends you to do it for him? How charming!' Aunt Meg scoffed and took another bite of her scone.

'Now now, Margaret!' Gran only called Aunt Meg by her full name when it was time to reign it in. 'Let's not be so ungracious to our guest—albeit, an uninvited one!' She turned back to him and said, 'Please tell Mr Rajani that we accept his apology.'

'Thank you, Madam ji,' he smiled nervously. 'But the thing is—'

'Yes?' Gran's tone grew icy. I felt sorry for the poor guy as he tried his best not to tremble but failed.

'Madam ji, some of the trees on your property are branching over to ours.'

'Well, we can't exactly tell a tree how to grow and where!'

'T-True, but the thing is, their fruit falls into sahab's property, and he was wondering whether you would be okay to have them removed?'

'Absolutely not!'

'But Madam ji, Rajani sahab plans to build a pool with a patio there, and we wouldn't want the fruits and leaves falling into his pool and—'

'You can tell your Rajani sahab that our trees are older than I am, and if he wishes to cut them down because their fruit interferes with his gaudy renovations, then he might as well cut me down with them. Your property is big enough to build a pool a few feet away and I would graciously allow him to consume the fruits that fall. They're organic, after all!'

'But Madam ji ...'

'Mr Tejeshwar Rathi!' The temperature seemed to drop by a few degrees when Gran said that. 'May I remind you that you are trespassing on our property, and unless you wish to learn how we deal with trespassers, I suggest you leave immediately!'

'I'd leave if I were you.' Aunt Claudine smiled as she refilled her cup.

As soon as he had closed the gate behind him to scamper back next door, the four of us burst into a fit of giggles.

A few weeks later, we saw a car accompanied by armed escort vehicles drive up the road. The security guards at the property next door opened the gates and stood at attention, saluting as the fleet entered the property.

'There goes the neighbourhood!' Aunt Claudine sighed as we watched from the upstairs balcony that looked on to the newly renovated mansion. The entire household staff stood before the front door in black uniforms, while Mr Rathi ran over to open the door of the ominous car.

A stout man wearing a grey suit emerged. He barely acknowledged Mr Rathi's salute as he made a beeline straight for the house, followed obediently by a woman in a blue floral saree.

'You can smell the misogyny in the air!' Aunt Meg rolled her eyes.

'Oh, he's kinda cute!' Aunt Claudine's eyes sparkled when she noticed the boy who had emerged from the front passenger door. He was looking around at his surroundings.

'Oh, come on!' Aunt Meg playfully slapped Aunt Claudine's arm. 'He's young enough to be your son!'

'Well, if Magdalena can date men young enough to be her son, why can't I? Right, Jai?' Aunt Claudine winked at me and ruffled my hair.

I was too focussed on the boy to be annoyed by Aunt Claudine messing up my hair. He really was cute—at least from this distance—and was much taller than Mr Rathi. Just as he was about to go inside, he noticed us peering down at him.

'Hello, cutie pie!' Aunt Claudine called, waving playfully. Aunt Meg brushed her hand down almost immediately. There was something adorable about the way he blushed as he waved almost timidly back before entering the house.

Later that evening, Mr Rathi arrived with a package. This time he made it a point to ring the intercom at the gate before he entered.

'Compliments of Rajani sahab!' he announced, smiling. He handed me a big white box and scurried away before he got accosted by Gran.

'Oh, how charming!' Gran exclaimed when she opened the box later. Inside were mason jars filled with jams and pickles that seem to have been made with the fruits from our trees that had fallen into his property.

'There's a note!' Aunt Meg said, pulling out a white envelope.

'Well, don't just stand there—read it out!' Aunt Claudine said as she opened one of the jars. She looked delighted after taking a sniff.

'Dear Mrs Byrne,' read Aunt Meg. 'Apologies for any inconvenience caused by our moving in, as well as for my PA's intrusion into your private space. Please accept this as our olive branch. My wife made them just for you. With regards, B.L. Rajani.'

'At least he signed it himself,' Aunt Meg placed the note inside the envelope as she picked up a jar of lemon pickle.

'Well, it's the thought that counts,' said Gran, who did not seem to mind that she was addressed as *Mrs* Byrne despite being unmarried. I knew she'd probably find an apt moment to correct our new neighbour in the future.

The next morning, the gate intercom buzzed as Gran was lighting incense for the morning yoga class. It was about a half-hour earlier than the first students were due to arrive. Not wanting to step away from her rituals, she pressed the buzzer that automatically unlocked the gates.

I opened the front door and was surprised to see Mr Rathi, again in a beige safari suit.

'Hello, beta ji,' he said. It was so weird he called me that. 'I believe Madam ji teaches yoga?'

'Yes, we do.'

'Wonderful!' he beamed. 'Rajani sahab was wondering if he could join today along with his family.'

'Sure, they're more than welcome to! Do they have mats?'

'Yes, yes! We have mats. Can they start immediately?'

I wondered if he was paid extra to be so chirpy this early in the morning.

'Well, class doesn't begin till seven. However, students are advised to come at least ten minutes before so that class can start and end on time. It's seven thousand per head for a month.'

'No family discount?'

'No, sorry!'

'How about a free trial class?'

'We don't offer free trial classes!' It amazed me how the filthy rich could sometimes be so stingy with their money.

'No problem!' Rathi said, his smile still plastered on. 'Tell Madam ji to expect us!'

At precisely ten to seven, our neighbours entered—accompanied by an entourage of armed guards, much to the astonishment of the regular students. However, before they could enter, Gran came to the front door and said firmly, 'Sorry, this is a safe and sacred space! Please tell your guards to go home.'

Without hesitating, Rajani Sahab waved his hands. The guards saluted before exiting the premises with their rifles.

'Good!' Gran said, now smiling sweetly. 'You can remove your shoes there.' She pointed at the large wooden shoe rack by the door.

There was an eerie silence before class began. All the students tried their best not to gawk at Mr Rathi laying three cork mats in the front row. Rajani Sahab was dressed in a white kurta pyjama. His wife obediently followed and sat next to him in silence in a blue kurta and a pair of black sweat pants. The boy—who was definitely cute now that I saw him up close—was wearing a black Under Armour tank top and gym shorts. I couldn't help but check out his rather muscular legs.

'Will you be joining the class as well, Mr Rathi?' Gran asked.

'No, no, Madam ji,' he replied with an uncomfortable chuckle. 'I just—'

'Then you can go to the foyer and pay the fees to Jai—he'll create accounts for the new students.'

Before he could reply, Gran clapped her hands.

'All right everyone, let's sit in the child's pose to calm and centre ourselves …'

Mr Rathi handed me an envelope filled with cash and began filling out the details of the family on the iPad we used to keep the student roster. I quickly peeked at the information about the son: *Vir Rajani, 17, student …*

As Gran ended the opening prayer with three 'om shantis', I headed inside and took my place on her mat.

'We have a few newcomers,' Gran announced, walking around the class while the students sat in vajrasana. 'So Jai will be doing beginner variations of the sequence up front. Those who wish to take it easy this morning can follow what Jai is doing. The rest of you know the advanced variations, so please follow along. Okay, let's come up in our first downward dog, hold and breathe as we allow our body to slowly open …'

Vir's outfit blended in perfectly with the class, but his parents stood out like sore thumbs. I could tell both were uncomfortable seeing women wearing fitted tops and tight Lululemon yoga pants. All three of them were stiff as boards and got very self-conscious seeing the other students flow into the poses smoothly.

'Don't worry about what the others are doing,' Gran said when she sensed their discomfort. 'Focus on your own breath and your own practice. We can focus on others throughout the rest of the day. Now is the time to pay complete attention to yourself.'

'Um, excuse me?' It was Vir's mother, who was timidly raising her hand, almost trembling.

'Yes?' I ran over and squatted next to her as she sat in child's pose.

'C-can we turn on the AC, please?'

'Sorry, we don't turn on the AC during class. The purpose of the practice is to build the internal heat of the body. The AC would defeat the purpose. It could even trigger arthritis.'

Her face showed her dismay.

'However, if you wish, we can increase the speed of the fan.'

'T-thank you, beta!' she said, smiling sweetly.

'No worries!'

I turned up the fan and returned to the mat to continue showing the beginner variations of the day's sequence.

'Okay,' Gran announced towards the end of the class. 'We'll now start the finishing sequence. Those who can perform sirsasana, please get into a headstand. Those who can't can just lie down with their legs up against the wall.'

To our surprise, all three of the Rajanis performed headstands without a moment's hesitation. It was even more surprising that they could could hold the pose the longest of all the students.

After we ended the class with the closing prayer, all the students got up and rolled their mats while thanking Gran for the wonderful class. Mr Rathi promptly entered the room and rolled the mats for the Rajani family. Gran wasn't happy with that.

'Did you enjoy the class?' I asked Vir, who was sipping on the complimentary glass of iced tea that Aunt Meg always offered the students after class.

Before he could reply, his mother said, 'It was wonderful, beta!' Vir just cocked a grin. Someone had attitude!

'Have you done yoga before?' Aunt Meg asked as she handed Mrs Rajani a glass of tea.

'Oh yes!' She handed the glass to her husband before taking another for herself. 'We had a teacher who used to come to our home back in Jodhpur.'

'Oh, Jodhpur! How lovely!' Aunt Meg smiled.

'Yes, however, we heard that you were the best yoga teachers in Delhi, and since you lived next door, we thought why not do a group class.'

'It's a different feeling when we practice in a group!' said Aunt Claudine, entering the studio to prepare for the next class.

'Yes, it is!' Mrs Rajani smiled as she handed Meg her empty glass. 'Is this homemade?'

'Yes, our own special recipe!'

'Oh, you must share it with me! It's so delicious. How much sugar?'

'No sugar.'

'Really, but how do you—'

'Come on!' interrupted her husband, who had placed his glass on the table and was wiping the sweat off his forehead with a hand towel. 'We're getting late.'

The Rajani family headed out, followed diligently by Mr Rathi. Rajani Sahab shouted out orders on his phone all the way to the front gate. A part of me wished Vir would turn around to wave goodbye. *Oh well, he's not* that *cute*, I tried to tell myself.

Oh, who am I kidding?

Chapter Ten

'No honest man would need so much protection,' Gran sipped her tea as we watched Rajani Sahab return home one evening surrounded by his armed guards. 'If someone valued their privacy so much, I doubt they'd enjoy such a vulgar display of status and power.'

'Well, he is an arms dealer,' Aunt Meg smeared her scone with fresh strawberry preserve. 'He's also some sort of liquor baron.'

'That definitely explains all the gunmen surrounding him,' Aunt Claudine licked her rolling paper before she sealed her joint, 'Not to mention the fact that he's a member of the Rajya Sabha.'

'No honest men mix with politicians either,' declared Gran, turning to Aunt Claudine. 'Don't be greedy, my dear!' She smiled as Aunt Claudine passed her the joint she had just begun puffing. I guess I was old enough for them to smoke pot around. Oh well, at least it was home-grown.

'It's strange,' said Gran, passing the joint over to Aunt Meg. 'After their first month, they never returned to class.'

'It's a good thing,' Aunt Meg replied before taking a long drag. 'All the other students were so uncomfortable around them. Some even complained that they could feel Rajani Sahab checking them out during class.'

'I can attest to that!' said Aunt Claudine. 'Not that I mind gentlemanly attention, but he just came across as creepy! And who on earth practices yoga in a kurta pyjama?'

'Now now, girls!' Gran tut-tutted. 'In many ashrams, as well as in many conservative shalas, a white kurta pyjama is the standard uniform. He did mention he spent his youth at one of those state-funded yoga camps, where they were all made to wear something similar.'

'And yet, they're so stiff!' Aunt Claudine sighed. 'They claim they've been doing yoga regularly, but they can't even sit in sukhasana. And they refused to use a block, a bolster or a strap.'

'All bodies are different,' said Gran as she poured herself a cup of tea. 'Who knows what kind of teachers they've had in the past? We've had to heal so many students who came to us injured after being taught by inexperienced teachers. At least they can do headstands.'

'Yeah, that's actually rather strange!' Aunt Meg took a drag.

'Right? And what's the deal with the wife—what was her name again?'

'Damyanti.' Aunt Meg handed the joint over to Aunt Claudine.

'Thank you!' Aunt Claudine took a drag, 'Yeah, what's the deal with her? She almost had a panic attack when I was adjusting her in anandabalasana.'

'Probably one of those women who don't like to be touched by anyone but her husband.' Aunt Meg nitpicked at the crumbs of her scone.

'I doubt he even touches her!' Aunt Claudine giggled, 'Men like Rajani sahab stop touching their wives after a while. She's already given him an heir after all,'

'A male heir, nonetheless!' Aunt Meg rolled her eyes.

'Exactly!' Aunt Claudine said as she passed the joint over to Gran. 'Now her life revolves around standing beside her man when in the public eye.'

'More like behind her man,' Aunt Meg smirked. 'Probably had to drop every shred of her personality the minute he tied the mangalsutra around her neck.'

'Well, it *is* called a "mangal" sutra,' Gran said. 'I always found it interesting that "mangal" means both auspicious as well as Mars.'

'Patriarchy at its finest,' Aunt Meg commented as she plucked the joint from Gran's hand. 'Deciding that a planet that represents all things masculine must be auspicious. But it is said that wearing it helps strengthen one's immunity and regularizes blood pressure.'

'Mars does rule blood and vitality,' said Gran. 'Warfare too.'

'Of course, but why is it that a woman must wear one as a symbol of her marriage and not the man … are you on Instagram again?' Aunt Meg snatched my phone from me. I didn't dare protest.

'Oh, leave him be, Meg!' Aunt Claudine ruffled my hair. 'He's just in his swan phase.'

'He wasn't exactly an ugly duckling to begin with!'

Aunt Meg switched off my phone and placed it in her lap.

'True, he's always been a cutie!' Aunt Claudine said, pulling my cheeks. 'But he's over his awkward stage, now let him enjoy the fruits of his budding youth.'

'I'm sitting right here!' I protested.

'Oh, so you speak!' Gran smiled as she stubbed out the joint.

'Take away his phone and he comes alive!' Aunt Meg smirked.

'Well, it's not like you had anything worthy to talk about!' I retorted with a pout.

'Oooh …' Aunt Claudine chuckled. 'Someone's turning into a sassy queen!'

'And what would you rather we talk about?' asked Gran.

'The cute neighbour boy?' asked Aunt Claudine, reaching over to ruffle my hair as she liked to do.

Oh my god! Stop that!' I brushed her hand off.

'Someone's got a crush!' Aunt Claudine teased.

'Oh my god! I *do not!*'

'Well, he *is* a cutie. But not as cute as you!' said Aunt Claudine, pulling my cheeks again.

'Hopefully he doesn't age like his father!' Aunt Meg refreshed her tea.

'Oh my god! *Stop!*' I could feel my cheeks burn.

'Ha! Knew it!' Aunt Claudine's dilated eyes sparkled, 'Jai so totally has the hots for him.'

'Crushing on the boy next door? Ground breaking!' Aunt Meg smirked.

I ran upstairs to my bedroom as they giggled with delight at my obvious embarrassment.

Was 'crush' really an apt term to describe my feelings for Vir Rajani? I certainly was a little sad when he stopped attending class. Not that I cared. Okay, fine, I did. But maybe because it was so rare to see such a hot guy in class. The class was attended mostly by women; the handful of men who were regulars had begun as supportive husbands, but then couldn't get enough of the 'yoga high'. Anyway, none of them were cute.

It was such a delight to watch him practice. What he lacked in flexibility, he made up for in strength. True, he would do chaturangas as if they were regular push-ups, and he was definitely using his arm strength instead of his core to lift up into bakasana, which is why he could only hold the pose for a few seconds. True, I was more focused on his muscles and would wish he would wrap me in those arms of steel.

'Wipe that drool off your mouth!' Aunt Claudine whispered once during class when I was checking out his awkward prasarita padottanasana.

Then again, his stiff hamstrings could be blamed on the fact that he was a runner. I should have known he wouldn't return to class when one morning I saw him leave his home in a pair of Nike Lunarglides. Their fluorescent linings were faded and the edges were torn. I gazed from my bedroom window as he put on his earbuds and began running in the direction of Lodi Gardens, followed by a couple of uniformed armed guards.

He would barely speak to anyone in the yoga class. Not that one can talk during class, but afterwards people would usually exchange a few words over some iced tea. Not him. As soon as the class ended, the Rajanis would walk out leaving Mr Rathi to pick up their mats. Vir wouldn't even wish me a good norning before class. Well, none of the Rajanis did, but it hurt more to be ignored by Vir.

He didn't accept my follow request on Instagram either. Maybe I shouldn't have stalked him right after the first class … but still, it's just Instagram! Why even have an Instagram account if you wanna keep it private? I even sent him a request through my finsta, where I mainly share memes. No response. *What an asshole!*

I never noticed him leave his house except for his morning run. Those were the only times I got to see him, but he never looked up at my window. Then again, why would he? He sometimes had friends visit at odd hours of the night. Most were typical Delhi 'dude-bros' with cars that were obviously compensating for other shortcomings. There were a few girls who visited too. One of them was a leggy beanpole who always seemed to dress like Audrey Hepburn in *Breakfast at Tiffany's*. She'd always have her arms around him whenever Vir escorted her to the waiting chauffeur-driven black Mercedes. I never saw them kiss, but maybe they didn't engage in PDA in front of the staff. I still hated her though. Okay, hate is too strong a word, but I definitely didn't like her. One didn't need to be have clairalience to smell the stench of 'gold digger' reeking from her.

'Are you decent?' Gran knocked at my door.

'Come in,' I sighed as I sat up in my bed.

'I believe this belongs to you,' Gran said, handing me my phone before seating herself at the foot of my bed. 'You know we only tease because we love you, right?'

'I do,' I replied. 'Though sometimes, I wish you didn't treat me like I was still a child.'

'Oh, we can't help that, you'll always be our baby!' Gran said, laughing as she pulled at my cheeks. 'Besides, how can we resist when you're as cute as a button!'

'Oh my god, Gran!' I groaned as she chuckled playfully.

'Okay, how about we make a deal?'

'What sort of deal?'

'Well, if you stop burying your face in your phone when we have family time, we'll all start treating you like an adult. Responsible adults aren't glued to their phones.'

'Um, Gran … what century are you living in?'

'Uh-huh!' Gran tut-tutted. 'You're losing your focus. Don't think I haven't seen you playing with your phone during our meditations and rituals. Your magic, though awakened, is still being developed. The more you allow yourself to be distracted, the more you'll lose touch with it. Magic without mindfulness can lead to deadly consequences.'

'I guess,' I sighed.

'If you're good, maybe we'll share a joint with you.'

'Gran!' *What sort of grandmother promises* drugs *as a reward?*

'A really cool one!' Gran chuckled as she read my mind. 'Besides, there's a lot of magic to be explored with our friend Mary Jane.'

Before I could respond, we heard a loud crash. Gran and I rushed to the window, where she let out a cry of horror.

'Quickly, put on something decent, and meet us downstairs, I'll summon your aunts.'

Within a few minutes, the four of us were by the imposing wrought-iron gates of the Rajani residence. Gran waved her hands and the gates were swung open by her power of telekinesis.

The guards were in too much of a panic to notice us enter. All we could hear were the loud wails of Damyanti coming from an area on the long driveway that was encircled by the guards.

As we approached, we saw Damyanti in her night robe, howling away in horror. Vir's head was resting in her lap. The blood sharply contrasted against the white silk of the robe. She was cursing the heavens above, begging God to save her son.

'What happened?' Gran demanded as she broke through the circle of guards with the rest of us close behind.

'There was a fight, Madam ji,' it was Mr Rathi who answered. 'Vir baba stormed out. Before anyone could stop him, he got on his bike and roared away. But a stray cat crossed his path, and he swerved to avoid hitting it. He crashed into that tree.'

He pointed towards a large tree by the gate, before which lay a totalled Ducati. The four of us immediately went over to where Vir lay. Aunt Meg held Damyanti as Aunt Claudine told the guards to step back.

'What are you doing?' asked Rajani Sahab helplessly as he watched us kneel by Vir.

'Check his eyes!' Gran ordered me.

I gently opened his eyelids with my fingertips. I turned to Gran and nodded when I saw golden sparks of light. They were faint, but they were still there.

'Everyone, please back away!' Gran ordered. Mr Rathi immediately ordered the guards to step back when he saw the look on Gran's face.

'Go ahead,' she told me.

'But, Gran!'

'You've done it before, you can do it again!'

'B-B-But …'

'Now's not the time to panic! You want to be treated as an adult? Well, go ahead and show us what you can do!'

Before I could protest, Damyanti sobbed and cried, 'Please! Please save my son! Please save my Vir!'

I sighed and closed my eyes, focussing on my breath. Inhale five … exhale ten … inhale six …

'What the hell are you—' began Rajani sahab, but Aunt Meg silenced him with a look.

Inhale ten … hold the breath. I could feel a white light with golden flecks enter my crown chakra from above, while a golden light emerged from the earth below me through my root chakra. Both merged at my heart chakra, forming a ball of green vital energy. *Osculum Vitae.* I leaned in and kissed Vir on the mouth.

'What on earth—' Rajani sahab exclaimed, but was again hushed by Aunt Meg.

As our mouths touched, I exhaled slowly to the count of twenty, allowing the green vital energy to flow into Vir. As I finished the exhalation, I checked his eyes again. The sparks still were faint.

'Again!' Gran ordered.

I refocused on my breath and the green energy ball formed almost immediately in my heart chakra. I leaned in and exhaled into his mouth. But the sparks remained faint.

'Focus, Jai!' Gran said, placing her hand on my shoulder. 'Clear your mind and focus with love, not fear.'

I closed my eyes. It was hard. My mind was running around in circles. Every time I tried to focus, random things began to flash through it. Memes, Magdalena videos, weird memories from my past … Fuck! Now I understood what Gran had meant when she'd warned me that magic without mindfulness would lead to disastrous consequences.

However, just as Damyanti let out another wail—my mind went blank. *Finally!* I summoned the astral and earthly lights and allowed the green energy ball in my heart chakra to grow so large that I could feel it pour through my ribs. Without wasting a moment, I leaned over and kissed Vir on the mouth again. This time, the light filled his body within seconds.

'Look!' Mr Rathi cried in amazement. 'Vir baba's eyes have opened!'

Vir sat up with a coughing fit. Before anyone else could react, an ambulance entered the gates with sirens blaring. Vir was carried to the vehicle, and Damyanti climbed in with him. Rajani sahab's black BMW was summoned and he followed the ambulance with Mr Rathi.

'Wow, not even a thank you!' Aunt Meg snarked as we began walking home.

'We don't do it for the thanks, dear,' Gran wrapped her shawl around her shoulders.

'Still, basic manners and stuff!'

'Now, now, dear.' Gran tut-tutted. 'Pleasantries disappear in times of turmoil.'

'Well, on the bright side,' Aunt Claudine smirked, 'You had your first kiss with Vir!'

'Aunt Claudine!' I was horrified as the three of them chuckled away.

Though, I had to admit, I loved the sensation of his soft lips on mine. Pity he reeked of Scotch.

Chapter Eleven

How do you kill a god? Simple: you stop believing in him. That's easier said than done, however, because we humans can't help but believe in something. Even atheism is a belief system, for nothingness is also a divine force—perhaps the most misunderstood one. Believing in something helps us bring meaning to our lives. The human ego won't allow us to accept that our life is meant to be without purpose. Ancient Greeks glorified their heroes for they lived a life so noble that even the gods would make room for them in their pantheon. An unheroic life was considered a waste, for heroes live on in legends of their heroic pursuits that are passed on from generation to generation. Those tales would be embellished with each retelling.

Yogis, however, believe that even heroism is an illusion—for even an act of courage can build upon karma. To a yogi, the ultimate purpose of life is to detach from the illusionary material world of prakriti and connect to our true self. Doing so allows us to break free from the cycles of life and death, attaining samadhi or moksha or even nirvana. Of course, that is also way easier said than done.

Yes, we humans are believers, but we are also conquerors. Beyond just expanding political boundaries of kingdoms, conquest involves eradicating the beliefs held by the now-conquered territories and instilling the belief systems of the conquerers. We neglect to acknowledge that they we are all worshipping the very same deity, albeit in different forms. We are all one, after all.

An example of this is the sun. Vedic Indians referred to it as 'Surya', while Ancient Greeks named it 'Helios'. Egyptians had a Sun God—the mighty Ra—as did the Ancient Norse—who called him 'Freyr'. The Celts, too, had a similar diety named 'Lugh'. In cooler regions, the sun is seen as a benevolent deity who heals with his divine light—the source of spiritual illumination. But in regions with cruel summers, the sun becomes an egotistical god that makes man in his image. He is not worthy of being dubbed the 'king of gods'. Perhaps that's why Vedic myths considered Indra—the God of Rain and Thunder—to be the rightful one to sit on the throne of the heavens, for his rains were seen as a relief from Surya's intense heat. Yet, despite all these names and designations, it's the same sun that shines upon the earth.

'Do you know why Hitler chose the swastika as his symbol?' Gran asked as we prepared for my first-ever demon-banishing ritual.

I shook my head. I was too excited for the task ahead to really care.

'The swastika is a four-armed symbol that represents the motion of the sun, each arm representing the cardinal directions of north, south, east and west. Hitler was fascinated by Indian mysticism and would study ancient scriptures. The swastika appealed to him as a symbol of his ambition to spread his influence wherever the sun shone. Such is the power of symbolism.'

'But he lost.'

'Yet, even today, there are many around the world who still believe in his manifesto, and thus still use the swastika to spread their hate.'

'But the sun is light, Gran. How can light be used to represent hate?'

'Too much light isn't a good thing. Darkness is needed for the body to heal and for life to rest. Lord Rama is the scion of the Suryavanshi dynasty—the descendants of the sun. Though Rama was known to be an ideal man and king, his ideals eventually cost him the love of his life, Sita. Now, tell me: what is the path of the sun according to our human eyes?'

'East to west.'

'Can the sun ever rise from the west?'

'No, never!'

'Can it rise from the north or even the south?'

'Not at all.'

'Exactly, the sun must always rise from the east. It is its divine dharma to do so. Thus, Lord Rama was bound by his divine dharma to live up to his ideals. However, life is a force that's far too powerful and can cause even divine kings to fall due to their ideals. All suns must eventually set, and we all know how Rama's story ends.'

'So … what does this have to do with Hitler and the swastika?'

'Well, who won the war?'

'The Allied powers.'

'And you've seen how Allied powers would point two fingers up in the air in the form of a V?'

I nodded as I zipped up a backpack full of incense and candles. 'V for victory!' I recalled.

'Ah, but that sign was actually the symbol of a demon.'

'What?'

'There was a great occultist named Aleister Crowley, who infamously called himself "The Wicked Man on Earth" or "The Great Beast". Legend has it that he advised Sir Winston Churchill to use the "V" symbol against Hitler's swastika. For though the swastika represented the all-powerful sun, the V was the symbol of the demon Typhon—a Greek Titan that represented darkness and chaos. Thus, eventually, the Allies won because Hitler's sun had to set into darkness. That is the divine dharma of the sun.'

'But aren't demons evil?'

'Good and evil are just two sides of the same coin that's flipped to land in the favour of those who sit on the throne. All demons were once gods worshipped by now-forgotten civilizations. While the worshippers may be long gone, the energy created by their ceremonies for these demon gods still exists. Sometimes, foreign invaders had no choice but to include local ancient deities within their own pantheons, for the power of these gods was too powerful to wipe out. For example, the resurrected Christ was no different from the reborn Dionysus.'

'And where exactly have you been?' interrupted Aunt Meg, who had just noticed Aunt Claudine wander in, still tying her robe.

'A lady never tells,' replied Aunt Claudine playfully.

'You're no lady!' Aunt Meg shot back.

'Are any of us?'

'If you two are done with your bickering, let's move,' said Gran. She picked up a large leather-bound grimoire, which was a magical encyclopaedia. 'We have a long night ahead of us.'

'Thank you all so much for coming!'

Sana Hussain greeted us when we arrived at her plush home in Jor Bagh. She was one of the students at our morning yoga class. I noticed that her once rosy complexion was now pale and she looked exhausted.

'Where is he?' Gran asked as she entered, removing the hood of her robe.

'Locked in the bedroom. Come, let me take you to the living room.' We followed Sana inside. 'As you requested, I moved all the furniture away as well as the carpets and the paintings. And all the curtains have been drawn.'

Sana was usually a cheerful person who often brought homemade goodies to share with us and the rest of the students. However, for the past few months, Sana had been absent. At first, we thought that maybe she was on one of her family's lavish holidays. But after two months had passed, Gran took it upon herself to check on her.

'Is this okay?' Sana asked as she turned on the lights of her now-bare living room. The marble floors were polished clean as we had asked.

'Perfect!' Gran smiled before she turned to the three of us. 'Let's get to work!'

'Can I bring you all any ...'

'Brew these herbs in boiling water for five minutes,' said Aunt Claudine quickly, handing her a pouch of dried herbs. 'When done, let it sit for another five minutes, and then pour it in a teapot. Don't strain. By the time it's ready, we'll be done setting up. Don't bring it to us, we'll come to you ourselves.'

Sana nodded and hurried to the kitchen.

This was the first time I was casting a banishing circle, and so I had to follow the instructions exactly as prescribed in the grimoire. First, Aunt Claudine made a large circle with pink salt that stretched across the room. Iodized table salt could also have been used, but Gran insisted on pink salt this time, for this was no ordinary possession. Within the circle, Aunt Meg drew a black pentagram (a five-pointed star) using charcoal, ensuring each of the points touched the circle of salt.

Then we set up the crystals at the five points of the pentagram: green jasper for prithvi, amber for agni, aquamarine for apas, flourite for vayu and a large clear quartz for akasha. In the centre, Gran placed a large onyx crystal ball. Each elemental crystal had an accompanying white pillar candle—except for the large onyx in the centre.

Once all the preparations were done, Gran chanted briefly under her breath before placing a large grey stone dish on a small stand. The dish contained water blessed from the previous full moon ritual. She lit a white tealight candle underneath.

'I knew it wasn't just a regular fever,' said Sana, sighing as she sipped the brewed herbs that she had prepared as per Aunt

Claudine's instructions. We had joined her in the kitchen and each taken a cupful of the brew.

'It's a good thing you sought our help,' said Gran as she added a spoonful of honey to her cup. She knew she'd need the extra strength. 'Had you waited any longer, it would have been far too late for even us to help.'

'I was in two minds about calling you,' said Sana. 'But I suppose it was kismet that you called to check in on me.'

Sana Hussain was born as Savita Verma. She had fallen in love with Haider Hussain at university. Even though he belonged to an affluent and well-respected family, Sana's family was against the alliance because of his Islamic faith.

'It's not that we were religious at all at home,' Sana said. 'I mean, our idea of celebrating Diwali was going abroad for holidays to escape the post-festival smog.'

I still remember how she broke down in tears when Aunt Claudine's tarot cards revealed that her family had had a tantrik curse Haider and have him possessed by a demonic entity.

'You'll have to forgive them eventually, my dear,' Gran said comfortingly, clasping Sana's hand.

'How am I to forgive them? My children haven't even seen their nana and nani except through old photos. And now they do this! I converted to Islam of my own free will because I found so much peace and beauty in the words of the Holy Quran. Haider and his family didn't force me at all! He would have married me even if I didn't convert, but I wanted to. And they just ...' Sana began sobbing.

'They're only human, my darling,' Gran said, handing Sana a white handkerchief to wipe her tears. 'They're misguided by their own fear and ignorance. I promise you that in time they will accept you.'

'Highly doubtful!' Sana declared, handing Gran the handkerchief damp with her tears. Gran passed it to Aunt Meg.

'It's time!' Aunt Claudine said, tapping her watch.

My heart almost leapt out of my chest when two male orderlies carried Haider in as if they were bringing in a corpse. Gran had them place him in the centre of the pentagram, with his head facing the edge with the clear quartz. She then instructed them to retreat to the servant quarters and shower immediately. They nodded and left. The minute they left, Gran had Sana shut the door and then asked her to strip Haider of his robe. Haider was shrivelled and skeletal, his skin stretching against his ribs and his navel almost touching his spine. His eyes were bloodshot and drool dripped from his mouth.

Gran took out a jar filled with the blood of a goat that had been sacrificed earlier in the day. Dipping a sable brush into the blood, Gran began to paint alchemical symbols all over his body. I had never seen them before and only learnt about them later. Taking the handkerchief soaked with Sana's tears, Gran uttered a silent prayer as she wrung it tightly. We watched a few drops fall on Haider's navel, right where Gran had painted a large red circle. The tears sizzled the minute they came into contact with the blood, emitting a black smoke.

'Take your positions!' Gran commanded as she raised her arms. 'Hail to the powers of the North! Guardians of the watchtowers that rule the Earth! I call on you to oversee our work and bless this circle.'

'Hail to the powers of the East!' Aunt Meg raised her arms. 'Guardians of the watchtowers that rule the Air! I call on you to cleanse the air around us and allow the heavens to receive our work'

'Hail to the powers of the West!' Aunt Claudine called, making the same gestures as the others. 'Guardians of the watchtowers that rule the Water! I call on you to allow our powers to flow through us with the might of the sacred rivers.'

'Hail to the powers of the South!' I yelled, knowing it was my turn to raise my arms. 'Guardians of the watchtowers that rule Fire! I call on you to empower us with your strength to banish all evil!'

The flames of the pillar candles increased threefold and flickered wildly even as a rush of cold air raged around the room. Sana's eyes widened as the leather grimoire opened by itself. The pages flipped wildly and opened to a page that had an image of a beast with the head of an elephant with six tusks. It had a large belly, eyes that were wide open and a mouth that had half-swallowed a man, whose legs still stuck out. Its arms were long with fingers like talons of an eagle, and its feet were short and stumpy like a bear. It had a tail of a crocodile.

Sana knelt by the door, shaking with fear. Haider began screaming wildly as his body convulsed. With her eyes, Gran conveyed to Sana that she mustn't worry. Then she picked up the large onyx ball and whirled to face Haider.

'I summon thee, demon! Leave this body at once! You do not belong here. You belong to the pits of the underworld! Leave this body at once or face the powers of the light!'

My jaw dropped as Haider levitated above us and began spinning in circles.

'Quickly!' Gran ordered us to hold hands as she led us with a Latin chant. With each phrase that was uttered, Haider screamed louder and his body spun faster and faster. As we chanted, a white force field surrounded the circle. The minute it closed on top to seal us within a dome of brilliant white light, Haider's body dropped down, stopping a few inches above the ground.

Sana began crying when a cloud of black smoke emerged from Haider's navel, revealing the demon illustrated in the grimoire. As it stood upon Haider's chest, his body landed on the ground with a thud.

'You have two choices, demon!' said Gran, imperious as ever. 'Surrender to the light or return to the dark and fiery abyss from which you came!'

'Never!' The demon yelled and began to trumpet like an elephant, but to me it sounded like the roar of a lion. It tried to scratch us with its sharp talons, but Aunt Meg and Aunt Claudine fired beams of white light at it, causing it to wince in pain.

'Surrender now, demon!' Gran ordered as she held up the black onyx crystal ball. 'Or suffer the consequences!'

The demon tried to attack again, but Aunt Meg and Aunt Claudine shot two more beams of white light at it. It screamed, 'I will kill you all before I surrender!'

The demon's body began burning with a black flame. Soon, it began shooting balls of the dark flame at us. Gran pushed me behind her and joined my aunts in trying to neutralize the fireballs with their beams of light. It only laughed louder before making four more arms appear, which began shooting fireballs even faster.

Suddenly, my chest began to burn. It was mild at first, but the intensity grew with each passing second until I had to scream.

'What's wrong?' Gran asked, turning to me.

'Look out!' Aunt Meg yelled, blocking a black fireball. Gran quickly turned her attention back to the demon and was unable to tend to me as I cried in pain.

I could feel a fiery energy course through my veins. It felt as though my blood had turned to lava and that my skin would burn up any minute. Suddenly, with an even louder scream, I ripped open my robe and pushed past Gran and my aunts. My eyes were red like rubies, and the eye on my chest had turned a bright crimson. Before any of them could react, the eye emitted a large fiery beam that struck the demon straight in its heart, causing it to fall to its knees. I screamed like a banshee as the beam continued to destroy the demon. It howled in agony and disintegrated into a pile of ashes. At that moment, I collapsed and passed out.

When I opened my eyes, I was in the library back home, with my head resting on Gran's lap. It took me a while before I could sip the brew in the cup Gran held at my lips. As soon as I sat up, they all breathed a collective sigh of relief.

'I think we could all use a drink!'

Chapter Twelve

Our yoga classes were held seven days a week, except for national holidays. As it was Gandhi Jayanti, it was one of those rare days off and I could sleep in. It was a luxury that I always enjoyed thoroughly. But not this time, as I'd been awake all night.

How could I have slept after having one of the craziest experiences ever? My first official demon-banishing ritual took such a dramatic turn that it literally knocked me out. I pestered Gran all night long to explain how I managed to do what I did that with the 'eye' on my chest—and why was it there to begin with. Who was that hooded figure who had left that mark on me during the attack on my thirteenth birthday? However, as always, Gran promised to reveal all when it was the right time. It was an answer that obviously wasn't good enough for me, but there was no point in rushing Gran. She was a Taurian after all, and could not be made to do something before she wanted to do it.

So, this morning, instead of yoga I decided to dance! Lord knows I had all the energy for it. I was in the mood for some classic Magdalena from the '80s. Guilt-free pop exuberance was just what I needed then. Wearing just my shorts, I played one of my favourite tracks: 'Follow My Light'. The brilliant beats led to the infectious synth-heavy melody, and I grabbed a bottle of deodorant and began lip-synching along as Magdalena sang:

'Whenever I see you walkin' by, all I wanna do is make you mine. But you always leave me crying in the night. I can't keep these feelings locked inside.'

Even with a lack of sleep, my body was filled with so much energy that I couldn't help but begin to dance—

'I close my eyes and you're here next to me! Lost and abandoned, I want the sunlight—'

At that moment, Aunt Claudine entered my room in her nightie and joined my dance, singing along to the chorus:

'Follow my light to me, baby! I'll give my heart, please give yours to me! Follow my light to me, darlin' ... I'll give you love, won't you please set me free!'

Grabbing my hand, Aunt Claudine took me out of the room and led me down the stairs as we began singing the second verse:

'No matter what I do or what I say, time is always standing in our way! Caught under your spell, I can't escape! Everywhere I look I see your face ...'

Aunt Meg was entering the house carrying a basket of fresh produce from the kitchen garden. Before she could react, Aunt Claudine snatched her basket from her and began playfully grinding into her as she danced. Aunt Meg turned a shade that rivalled her tomatoes as we sung to her:

'Don't leave me here all alone in my dreams. Wake me up and make me believe all your magic ...'

Aunt Meg gave in, and to our surprise, she sang along to the chorus as the three of us began to dance like we were at one of Magdalena's concerts.

'Follow my light to me, baby! I'll give my heart, please give yours to me! Follow my light to me, darlin' … I'll give you love, won't you please set me free!'

Aunt Meg began letting loose, a sight that was so rare. She got on her knees and began waving her arms while singing the bridge:

'Follow my light to me … Darkness is such a lonely wonder …

Suddenly, we saw that Gran was at the top of the staircase, still in her nightie while singing along:

'Follow my light, I'll make you love me!'

She danced down the stairs, making us marvel at how agile her body was.

'It's not that hard, please just say yes to me!'

All of us began dancing about the living room to the final chorus, singing:

'Follow my light to me, baby! I'll give my heart, won't you give yours to me! Follow my light to me, darlin' … I'll give you love, won't you please set me free!'

As the music began to fade, we all burst into a fit of laughter and hugged each other.

'God, I just love '80s' Magdalena!' said Aunt Claudine, her eyes sparkling.

'I still say her '90s' stuff is far more superior!' retorted Aunt Meg as she tried to go back to her cool demeanour, but was too caught up in the infectious mood to succeed.

A sudden knock on the front door brought us back to reality.

The door was open as Aunt Meg had just walked in from the garden. I froze as I saw that it was Vir standing there. He was in his faded Nikes and a tank top that was covered in sweat. It looked like he had just come back from his morning run. How long was he standing there? *Oh crap!* I thought. *He's seeing me shirtless for the first time!*

'Um, hi,' he said cautiously. Gran and Aunt Claudine hastily fastened the robes of their nighties. Aunt Meg was in her gardening overalls, but my hands dropped to cover my crotch.

'Sorry, is this a bad time?' Vir asked, trying to hide a smile.

A few minutes later, Vir was with us at the breakfast table at Gran's invitation. She had pulled up an extra chair while Aunt Claudine had set a place for him. I had run upstairs to pull on a T-shirt, but was still embarrassed that Vir had seen me in that state of half-nakedness. Aunt Meg had fried some bacon, which Gran served Vir along with a helping of her famous scrambled eggs that had a hint of paprika to give it a little something special.

'So how did you get in through the gates?' Aunt Claudine asked as she poured him a glass of freshly squeezed pomegranate juice.

'Um, they were open.'

Vir had been a little taken aback when he had been asked to have breakfast with us. But slowly he was warming up to the idea. It was the most we had heard him speak ever since he arrived for his first yoga class.

'Open?' Gran arched a quizzical brow. 'Oh dear ...'

'That's my fault!' Aunt Meg walked over, holding the cast iron skillet that sizzled with the freshly fried bacon, 'I opened it to pay the newspaper boy for the month. I must have forgotten to close it after.' She walked around, serving Vir first the biggest helping before serving the rest of us. 'I still need to get used to the new electronic locks and stuff.'

'I hope I didn't intrude ...' Vir began, trying to maintain an air of formality, but seemed distracted by the delicious aroma of the bacon.

'Oh nonsense!' Gran said. 'An unexpected guest can sometimes be a delightful change. Now eat, my child, before your food gets cold.'

'H-H-How are you feeling now?'

I had mustered up the courage to speak, ignoring the playful kick Aunt Claudine gave me under the table.

'Oh!' Vir swallowed his bite. 'I'm good, thanks!' Our eyes met briefly, but before I could read into them, he turned to Aunt Meg and said, 'The bacon is delicious!'

'Why, thank you!' Aunt Meg seemed unusually delighted. 'The secret is in our homemade butter!'

'Jai churns it every week!' Gran sipped her pomegranate juice.

'Oh?' Vir turned to me. 'You churn butter?'

Before I could say anything, Aunt Claudine butted in: 'Of course he does!' She reached out to ruffle my hair, purposefully embarrassing me. 'When he isn't dancing about to Magdalena!'

'Oh my god! Aunt Claudine!' My cheeks turned red as Aunt Claudine chuckled. Vir smiled in a way that seemed so warm and so uncharacteristic of him. Well, at least from what little I knew of him.

'What brings you over, Vir?' Gran emptied the scrambled eggs onto Vir's plate as she walked over to place the serving bowl in the sink.

'Oh, um, er, I just wanted to, um …' He looked so cute struggling to find the words. 'I guess I just wanted to thank you for the other night.'

'Oh, there's no need to thank us!' Gran declared as she returned to her seat.

'We were just being good neighbours,' Aunt Meg smeared blueberry preserve on her croissant.

'And we absolutely love being good neighbours!' Aunt Claudine said with a playful wink at me. I wished I could bury my head in a pillow!

'What exactly did you do, though?' Vir asked as he gulped down on his pomegranate juice.

'What do you mean?' Gran was about to refresh his glass before Vir politely stopped her.

'Thanks, I'm good.' His smile was so dreamy when he dropped his attitude. 'I mean, I was told you guys came and did some weird ritual of sorts.'

'Weird ritual?' Aunt Meg bit into her croissant.

'I mean, from what I was told, I was injured really badly. I wasn't even wearing a helmet when I crashed my bike into the tree. But when we arrived at the hospital, the doctor said that the wounds were superficial. There were no signs of internal bleeding or bruises or anything …'

For the first time, I looked carefully at Vir. From the side, he resembled an emperor on an old Roman coin. His hair was shaved from the sides and the back, with long black locks on top. I think that hairstyle is called an 'undercut'. His strong jaw carried a full pair of lips that seemed as soft as pillows. Dimples would appear at the corners when he'd smile. His dark eyes were beautifully accompanied by well-defined brows that arched elegantly at the corners. I also took in how strong his shoulders looked … and had to stop myself from imagining my legs resting on his shoulders as he mounted me.

'… All I was told was that before the ambulance came, the two of you were giving me something that seemed like CPR or something.' Vir's gaze snapped me out of my thoughts.

'CPR?' Gran chuckled.

Vir smiled, flashing his dimples. 'Yeah, that's what I was told.' Suddenly, Vir's phone rang. His face dropped when he looked at the screen. He excused himself to the kitchen to answer.

Aunt Claudine turned to me and teased me by making kissy faces.

'Oh my god!' I threw my napkin at her. Aunt Meg joined in the teasing, making kissing noises. Oh my god! Not you too, Aunt Meg!'

I buried my face in my palms as Gran and my aunts burst into giggles.

'I'm really sorry,' Vir said as he re-entered the room. 'I've got to take care of something back home.'

'Oh, that's perfectly alright!' Gran said. She got up and headed over to one of the counters. 'We didn't get a chance to thank your parents for the lovely pickles and jams they sent before you officially moved in.' She called me over and gave me a basket that was covered with a white cloth. 'Please give these to your parents with compliments from us. These are Meg's special croissants. She's quite the baker.'

'Yeah! Master-baker!' Aunt Claudine said teasingly. Aunt Meg clearly wasn't amused.

'Um, they aren't my parents.'

The room suddenly went quiet.

'Oh?' Gran nudged me to hand over the basket to Vir. 'Is that so?'

'Um, it's a long story.'

Vir ran his fingers through his hair and thanked me as I handed him the basket. I found myself wondering if there had been an actual spark when our fingers brushed or if I had just imagined it.

'However, we would love to have you over for dinner tonight, if that's okay with you all.'

'Oh, we'd love to be over for dinner!' Aunt Claudine declared quickly. She got up and ushered us out of the kitchen. 'Jai would you be a dear and escort our handsome guest out?'

She truly knew how to embarrass me!

'Make sure you lock the gate!' Aunt Meg called after us.

The walk to the front door was uncomfortably silent, but as we stepped out and headed to the gate, Vir said, 'Your family is really something!'

'Yeah!' I mustered an awkward smile. 'I hope they didn't freak you out or anything …'

'Not at all!' His eyes sparkled. 'They seem really lovely.'

'They are.' I smiled too, oddly relieved that he liked them. 'So happy to have them in my life.' *Why did I say that? God, I'm such an idiot!*

'Wish I could say the same!' Vir's smile suddenly vanished. 'Anyway,' he said, turning to me as we reached the gate. 'I look forward to seeing you all later tonight.'

'Sure, can't wait!' *Ugh, why am I so cringeworthy?*

'Cool, later!' He held his fist out to me. In hindsight, I should have guessed he had meant to do a fist bump, but silly awkward me nearly leaned in for a hug. Thank God good sense prevailed and I extended my hand out … only it was for a handshake. He gave me a puzzled look, but shook my hand before turning and heading over to the two armed guards who were waiting for him outside.

I stood by the gate, watching him put on his earbuds as he led the guards back to his house. To my heart's delight, before he went through the gates of his mansion, he turned, smiled and waved. Waving back, I beamed as he disappeared into this house. I turned and shut the gate behind me. I was so overcome with joy that I couldn't help but twirl … only to spot Gran and my aunts standing by the front door giggling at me!

Ugh, such a blessing they are!

Chapter Thirteen

Chandni Chowk is one of those places that can either charm you or disgust you. A beautiful mix of the sacred—with the historic Jama Masjid, Sis Ganj Gurdwara, Fatehpuri Mosque and the Central Baptist Church—and the profane, with criminals such as pickpockets and scam artistes looking to fleece the avid tourists. Crowds queue up to bask in the historic splendour of the Red Fort and to savour the sinfully delicious treats from the street vendors in the Paranthewali Galli. One can sit down at the original Karim's or Moti Mahal for butter chicken that's still made with the same recipes that nawabs and kings feasted on. This is also the hub of wholesalers and retailers with shops kept in business by numerous generations of the same families. Yes, there is the smell of stale piss everywhere, but that can be said of even the posh south Delhi localities.

I knock on a door hidden down a poorly lit alleyway. 'What's the password?' asks a voice from behind the door. 'Humaira!' I respond. The door opens wide enough for me to sneak in.

I'm greeted by an almost seven foot tall man wearing a black salwar kameez, who frisked me for weapons before leading me down a dingy corridor. We walk through a second door and enter a small room where a bespectacled man sits at a small wooden desk.

'Javed bhai *hai*?' I ask the man, who nods and then gives a thumbs-up to the bouncer who had led me there. He opens a third door, and I hear Sufi music blaring from an ancient speaker system. I walk through the doorway and a waft of stale smoke makes my eyes water. I find myself in the middle of a crowded speakeasy illuminated by vintage red and blue disco lights. At the tables all around me are men of all ages smoking hookah—despite the recent Supreme Court ban.

Leading me to the far wall, the bouncer orders me to sit at a booth with plush leather seats that are torn at the seams. I smile as I hand him a hundred-rupee note. I always tip generously.

'PMC,' I say to the fresh-faced waiter as he walks over. He definitely doesn't look eighteen. PMC is my go-to hookah flavour. It's a delicious mix of paan—or betel leaf, known for its aphrodisiac properties—mint, which is sacred to Hecate, the goddess of witches and also an excellent herb for banishing stomach illnesses and exorcisms—and cigar.

'Tobacco, though dangerous,' Gran had told me once after catching me experimenting with cigarettes, 'has long been used by shamans across the Americas to converse with spirits. Sometimes it's even thrown into rivers to appease river gods. When burned as an incense, it purifies the air of all negativity, and its smoke has been known to cure earaches. However, mass-produced cigarettes use tobacco infused with thousands of carcinogens.'

Some say that hookahs are even more harmful than cigarettes. However, tonight, I need it for work. The waiter returns and whispers in my ear to follow him. He leads me through a kitchen, where in the whirlwind of chaos the staff seem thoroughly unconcerned by the rats scampering about. From the kitchen, we go out the back entrance and up a rusty spiral staircase to a balcony outside a small studio.

Unlike the speakeasy downstairs, the studio is illuminated by turquoise lamps hung from the ceiling. The room is carpeted and the walls covered in vintage dupattas sporting heritage embroidery. A large brass-coloured Khalil-style stand hookah with a fur-lined pipe is by a large cushion on the floor. I settle down on the cushion and the waiter hands me a small plastic nozzle and says that Javed bhai would be with me shortly. I take a long drag and blow out a large puff of fragrant smoke.

'Humans are created from clay and water, and the essence of angels is light,' says a voice from behind me.

I turn and see a figure wearing a green kaftan, with numerous crystal beads dangling around his neck. Before I can stand up to greet him, he signals for me to remain seated. 'Djinn were created on the day of creation from the smokeless fire that created our earth.'

'Javed bhai?'

The figure smiles. 'Javed bhai is only for those who need to fear me. You may call me Nafeesa behen.' With the lamps now clearly illuminating her face, I see that her eyes are lined thickly with kohl and the parts of her cheeks that aren't covered by her thick chest-length beard are rouged and contoured with pinkish highlights. The absence of a moustache reveals lips tinted in a rosy hue.

'Apologies, Nafeesa behen!' I say, smiling.

She claps her hands and a couple of servers appear carrying a tray laden with freshly cut fruit and a large crystal bottle of scarlet-coloured sherbet. The tray also holds three glasses.

'The third is for the djinn,' says Nafeesa behen as the servers place the trays before us and leave.

'The djinn drink sherbet?'

'Well, they also eat meat, bones and the dung of animals. The sherbet would be a welcome change.' She fills two glasses and offers me one. We clink our glasses together and take a sip at the same time, maintaining eye contact.

'Not bad!' I lick my lips as I place my glass down.

'It's my mother's recipe. Handed to her from her mother, who got it from hers, and … well, you don't need me to explain the powers of a maternal lineage,' says Nafeesa behen, smiling.

I nod and she continues, 'The djinn lived on earth long before humans, but it is unknown for how long. Some say it was a few centuries before Adam and Hawwa. The djinn were said to be equal in stature to angels. However, their ruler—Iblis, whom you probably know as Shaitan—refused to worship Adam. Thus, he was cast out of heaven along with his followers. After Adam and Hawwa left the Garden of Eden, the djinn mingled with their descendants to either haunt them or mate with them. Only a few humans were lucky enough to have a djinn as their loyal servant.'

A server enters carrying another hookah for Nafeesa behen. He hands her the fur-lined pipe after adjusting the coal. After he leaves, she continues, 'The great Sulayman ibn Dawud—whom you would know as King Solomon—used a magical golden ring to control the djinn and protect him from them.

The ring was set with numerous gems and in the centre was a large diamond that he would use to brand the djinn as his slaves. Some say Sulayman also forced the djinn to build the Temple of Jerusalem and even the city itself. The Quran tells us how the king had them make carpets, ponds, statues and gardens. And whenever Sulayman wanted to travel to faraway places, the djinn would carry him on their backs. Some say they would enchant carpets to fly him there.'

Nafeesa behen blows a majestic cloud of fragrant smoke as she continues, 'Like humans, the djinn have free will and are able to differentiate between good and evil. The Quran states that they were created for the same purpose as humans were: to worship Allah. They are responsible for their actions and will be judged at the end of their lives. Hell is filled with both djinn and humans.'

At this point, Nafeesa behen's tone changes. 'Why do you seek the djinn?'

'I don't seek the djinn,' I answer.

'What do you mean?' She appears to be caught off guard by my reply.

I take out a burgundy velvet drawstring bag from my pocket, from which I pull out a large gold ring that bore a large lapis lazuli.

'One of my clients was gifted this by someone who purchased it from one of your wholesalers. I'm not saying you are responsible for the trouble your ring has caused, but someone is clearly selling djinn-infested jewels to innocent people, for reasons only they know best.'

Nafeesa behen examines the ring carefully. Her face loses its rosy hue as she exclaims, 'Hai Allah!' She presses her earlobes with her fingertips and bites her tongue. 'You're right, this is definitely from one of my shops! But I assure you that I am not involved with this.'

'I know,' I say, taking another puff on the hookah. 'And I know you will take care of whoever is doing this.' I take out stacks of two-thousand-rupee notes and place them on the table. 'However, I need something from you.'

Nafeesa behen quickly puts the money in the pocket of her kaftan. 'What do you need from me?'

'You'll know when the time is right.' I blow out a cloud of smoke. 'I trust I have your word.'

'In'shallah!' Nafeesa behen says and kisses her fingers. She waves her hand in the air as if sending the kiss to the heavens.

'Excellent!' I smile. 'Now would you be kind enough to dispel the djinn from the ring? In spite of the terror it has caused, the ring holds deep sentimental value for my client.'

Nafeesa behen closes her eyes and begins to recite an Arabic chant with a hypnotically soothing melody before taking a lingering drag from her hookah. Placing the ring in her left palm, she blows out a cloud of smoke that covers the ring, which starts to vibrate wildly. The white vapours of smoke turn a deep shade of grey and begin swirling like a mini tornado. From the centre of the whirlwind appears a large being with a human torso and long limbs—but it has the head of a jackal and the tail of a scorpion.

The creature opens its mouth to reveal a forked tongue like a serpent. Nafeesa behen begins chanting in Arabic again, causing the djinn to howl wildly with the braying sound of a donkey. She removes one of her crystal necklaces, and I understand then that those are rosaries. Waving it in the air in three circles counter-clockwise, she throws it around the djinn's neck. It brays even more wildly before disintegrating into smoke that seeps into the crystals. Their colour changes from a pale pink to a dark onyx.

Nafeesa behen opens her eyes and regains her calm composure almost instantly. 'Another glass of sherbet?' she asks, smiling.

'Please!' I answer, blowing out another cloud of fragrant smoke.

Chapter Fourteen

It was a rare sight: Gran and my aunts dressed to the nines. Usually, they were either in their yoga clothes or ritual robes with minimal make-up. But tonight we were dining with the Rajani family, so they had put in an effort to dress up.

Gran looked quite regal in a black dress that flowed down to her Christian Louboutin suede pumps. Her hair was tied up in an elegant bun with a fuchsia lace wrap around her shoulders. Aunt Meg's Jimmy Choo ankle boots were well-matched to her tight black jeans and off-shoulder paisley peasant top. Aunt Claudine's virginal white knee-length number was decorated with art-nouveau red roses, and suited her daring personality. It made her long mermaid-like curls seem redder than usual.

'We're going to dinner, not walking the streets!' Aunt Meg remarked when Aunt Claudine met us downstairs.

'Honey, these heels were definitely not made for walking!' Aunt Claudine kicked her leg up playfully like a Rockette to show off her white Manolo Blahnik Paloma velvet sandals.

I had on a pair of indigo jeans with a white Henley-neck T-shirt. Gran refused to let me buy ripped jeans no matter how much I tried to convince her that they looked cool. She claimed that respectable people didn't wear clothes with holes in them. Oh well. Even though I looked pretty plain compared to them, mine was a classic look that could never go wrong. However, I did throw on a pair of ruby-red Converses to add an extra splash of colour.

We were escorted by a uniformed attendant to their grand living room, where Damyanti rose to greet us. She was dressed in an elegant turquoise Anita Dongre saree with white gold embroidery that perfectly complimented her platinum diamond necklace. We immediately felt severely underdressed.

'Forgive my husband's absence,' she said. 'Since last year's elections, he's been so caught up with work.'

I could tell Gran and my aunts weren't impressed by the gilded surroundings that resembled the lobby of an extravagant Dubai hotel, complete with a grand Swarovski chandelier.

'I didn't realize Mr Rajani was involved in the elections,' said Gran politely. A uniformed server arrived with glasses of champagne.

'Oh, you know how it is,' said Damyanti, smiling as she indicated for us to be seated at a big ivory and gold upholstered couch. 'Business and politics go hand in hand.'

Instead of sitting down, I walked over to the large wall-length oil canvas of a woman driving a green Bugatti. 'Is that an original Tamara de Lempicka?' I asked.

'Yes, it is!' Damyanti sounded impressed. 'We got it at Sotheby's last year, but had no space at our home in Jodhpur.' She turned towards Gran. 'So, when we moved here, I had our interior decorator find curtains to match the colours of that painting.'

'Indeed.' Gran smiled.

'I hope you don't mind my asking,' Damyanti began as an attendant arrived with a tray of assorted hors d'oeuvres, making sure to offer it to all of us before coming over to Damyanti, who shook her head gently to refuse. 'I was wondering where you are all from …'

'I'm sorry?' Aunt Meg raised a quizzical brow.

'Oh, it's just that, it's so rare to, you know, see a family of foreig—'

'Expats?' Aunt Claudine cut in, taking a swig of her champagne.

'Yes!' Damyanti giggled nervously as she toyed with her diamond bracelet. 'I mean, your accents sound pretty neutral, with barely any trace of …'

Before she could dig herself deeper into a politically incorrect hole, Gran quickly said, 'Well, I was born in India, as were my daughters.'

'Really?'

'Yes, my mother was Irish and my father was English. They came to India before Independence. Daddy was a research scholar who studied Sanskrit literature …'

'Sanskrit literature? That's fascinating!' Damyanti's eyes sparkled.

Another attendant came in and refilled everyone's glass, including mine. Aunt Claudine winked at me as my glass was refreshed, followed by Aunt Meg shooting me a look to not go overboard. Gran continued, 'Yes. So, Daddy was gifted our home by the Nehru government for his work, and while Mummy studied yoga with Babaji—'

'Oh, was this Shri Dhirendra Bhramachari Ji?' Damyanti interrupted.

'Oh no, our Babaji kept a low profile. He stayed away from all things political. Mummy said that he had renounced his own name by the time he was twenty, and thus, we just called him Babaji. He was the one who taught me yoga as well.'

'Oh?' Damyanti smiled. 'Is he still around?'

'Well, we don't know. When I was a teenager, he mysteriously vanished.'

'Vanished?'

'Well, we don't know exactly what happened to him …'

'Some say he took up hermitage somewhere in the Himalayas and lives a hermetic life,' Aunt Claudine recrossed her legs.

'Others say he has already attained Maha Samadhi and left this earthly realm,' Aunt Meg said as she dipped a small piece of bread into some herb mushroom pâté.

'And it's not like we could find him on Facebook,' Gran grinned as Damyanti giggled softly.

'Well, that is fascinating,' Damyanti said, smiling. 'Do you all speak Sanskrit too?'

'Of course!' said Gran.

'Hindi as well …' Aunt Claudine was bored but was delighted when more champagne was poured in her glass.

'It freaks out the auto drivers when we bargain with them.' Aunt Meg's blunt tone caused Damyanti to giggle again. It was clear that riding in an auto-rickshaw was an alien concept to her.

'So have you spent all your life in Delhi?' she asked my aunts.

'Well, we were born here, but I went to Woodstock for boarding school,' replied Aunt Meg.

'And I went to Welham's,' Aunt Claudine feigned a smile.

'Oh? Why not go to the same school?' Damyanti asked.

'Oh God, no!' Aunt Meg rolled her eyes.

'We'd have killed each other if we had!' Aunt Claudine definitely enjoyed her champagne.

'You know how teenage girls can be,' Gran said.

'Then how come you didn't send Jai to boarding school as well?' asked Damyanti, glancing at me as I was still admiring the Lempicka.

'Well, considering Jai's parents passed when he was just a baby, we felt it was best he stayed with us. He goes to St. Sebastian's—'

'Oh, St. Sebastian's is lovely, I believe!' Damyanti cut in, turning towards me now. 'Do you enjoy school?'

'Quit boring them with this ridiculous small talk!'

I turned in the direction of the voice to see Vir enter the living room. He was dressed in black from head to toe, with his fitted shirt unbuttoned generously to reveal his musclular chest in a way that didn't seem tacky. He looked even hotter all scrubbed up.

'Vir beta!' Damyanti got up to greet him, but he walked past her and headed straight to the ornate mahogany bar across the room. He pushed past the attendant standing there and poured himself a neat Glenfiddich before sprawling on a large chair across from Damyanti.

'I doubt anyone wants to talk about school at this time!' Vir said, taking a large swig. Clearly, his tolerance for alcohol had been developed from a young age.

Damyanti smiled nervously. 'Vir went to Mayo and—'

'Hated every single minute of it!' Vir rolled his eyes. 'Though it did give you enough time to get Tauji to leave his wife for you. Such a cliché: the secretary sucks cock to move up in society.'

Damyanti mustered all her composure. 'I was a senior executive at Rajani Enterprises—'

'Executive cocksucker!'

'Vir!' Damyanti was trying to hold back her tears.

An awkward silence followed.

'So, how come you stopped attending class?' Gran asked in an effort to ease the tension.

Damyanti snapped out of her moment of suppressed rage and returned to her smiling self. 'Oh, you see, it was a bit too much for us. I mean, you all seemed so advanced. We are used to doing the traditional hatha style of yoga. You know, simple classic poses that follow twelve rounds of Surya Namaskar ...'

'Oh, so you guys had a Sivananda teacher?' Aunt Meg asked.

'Oh yes!' Damyanti replied. 'He was from the Sivananda Ashram in Rishikesh. Even though he had his own studio, he would come over to our haveli every morning to give us private classes. Vir was interested in learning how to do a headstand, but otherwise preferred going to the gym instead.'

'That explains the headstands,' Aunt Claudine whispered to Aunt Meg.

'Yeah,' Vir said, overhearing her. 'It was cool to learn it, but nothing beats pumping iron.'

'Is that all you pump?' Aunt Claudine cheekily retorted, causing me to turn red. Thank God that Gran kept the conversation on track.

'Well, now I understand why you didn't continue with us,' she said. 'We teach Vinyasa-style yoga. It can be a bit intimidating for those who're used to a more structured class.'

Before Damyanti could say anything further, her husband walked in. We all stood up—well, except Vir.

'Pardon my tardiness!' said Rajani Sahab. He was dressed in a navy-coloured business suit.

'Long day at the office?' Damyanti asked as she walked over and gave him a gentle peck on his cheek. He seemed unmoved by her display of affection.

'If you give me a few minutes,' he said. 'I'll freshen up and join you all for dinner.'

He turned and headed upstairs, followed by Mr Rathi, who was carrying his boss's patent leather briefcase in one hand and a tan laptop bag in the other.

'I guess now we know why he has a male personal assistant,' Aunt Claudine whispered in my ear with a playful chuckle. Thank God no one heard her.

Dinner was set in a large dining room with a long rosewood table that could seat ten. Rajani Sahab sat at the head of the table. Behind him, a pair of grand antlers hung from the wall, almost framing his skull. He was in an elegant khadi kurta that seemed so simple compared to Damyanti's saree. Though if one looked closely, one could see the twenty-four carat gold threads that were seamlessly interwoven into the fabric.

Damyanti sat across the table with Gran by her side. She said, 'I hope you don't mind that I took the liberty of making our dinner vegan. Though our family is vegetarian, I assumed that you all must be vegan. After all, you are yogis—'

'Oh, that's thoughtful of you, my dear!' Gran cut in as the server served the first course of mulligatawny soup. 'However, we aren't vegan.'

'Oh, really?' Damyanti sounded curious. 'So then, you're vegetarian?'

'No, we eat everything.'

'Aren't yogis supposed to be vegetarian?' Rajani Sahab curled his moustache, which was thicker than the hair on his scalp.

'Some are,' Gran replied. 'However, nowhere is it written in the yoga sutras that one needs to be a vegetarian in order to be a yogi.'

'Nonsense!' Rajani's tone caught us by surprise. 'The Bhagwad Gita clearly states that eating meat is sinful.'

Damyanti chuckled nervously. Gran finished her first spoonful of soup before she replied. 'I suppose you're referring to chapter three, verse thirteen, which states *yajna-shistanshinah santo muchyante sarva-kilbishaih; bunjate the tvagham papa ye pachantyatma-karanat*.'

The Rajanis were clearly caught off guard by Gran's perfect Sanskrit. She continued, 'That basically translates to, "The spiritually minded, who eat food that is first offered in sacrifice, are released from all kinds of sin. Others, who cook food for their own enjoyment, verily eat only sin." That's not exactly advocating vegetarianism.'

'Yes, but isn't meat tamasic in nature?' asked Rajani sahab as he took a swig of his Scotch on the rocks.

'So is alcohol,' Aunt Claudine chimed in cheekily, causing him to sputter. 'But we all seem to enjoy it.'

'Alcohol doesn't involve killing life,' he retorted after regaining his composure.

'Tell that to the bacteria needed for fermentation,' said Aunt Meg, sipping her white wine. It went quite well with the mulligatawny.

Before Rajani Sahab could reply, Gran continued, 'Yes, meat is tamasic and so is alcohol. However, Lord Shiva is considered to represent the Guna of Tamas, while Vishnu represents Sattva and Brahma represents Rajas. And it is Shiva who is the Adi Yogi—the one who taught yoga to the world.'

'I believe he taught it first to Parvati?' Damyanti said, smiling as she sipped her wine.

'Indeed, he did,' Gran affirmed before having another spoonful of soup.

'And he teased her mercilessly when she couldn't sit in padmasana,' Aunt Meg continued the narrative to allow Gran to enjoy her soup. 'When the teasing crossed a line, Goddess Parvati pushed him into the river. There, they came across a fish who was spying on their lesson. That fish could recite all the shlokas he had heard, impressing Lord Shiva. He blessed the fish with a human form and thus was born Sage Mastyendra, who spread yoga to the world.'

'Oh, that's fascinating!' said Damyanti, her eyes sparkling.

'Whoop-di-freaking-doo!' Vir muttered under his breath. It was hard for me to even enjoy my soup considering its flavour was overwhelmed by Vir's musky cologne. But I was pleased to be seated next to him. Aunt Claudine and Aunt Meg sometimes shot me teasing looks from across the table but I did my best to ignore them.

'Yes, but imagine if Shiva ate the fish!' Rajani sahab snapped while signalling the server to clear his soup bowl.

'Well, there's this beautiful story in the Shiva Purana,' said Gran. 'One day, a farmer on his way to sell his produce in a nearby town came across a lone tribesman worshipping a Shiva Linga in the middle of the forest. The farmer was appalled that the tribesman was offering beef to the Shiva Linga as a form of worship. In a fit of anger, the farmer kicked him and shooed him away. He removed the offending meat from the Linga, replacing it with his fresh fruits and vegetables. The next day, he found the man by the Shiva Lingam again, offering his beef. The farmer lost his cool and began assaulting him mercilessly—'

'Naturally!' cut in Rajani sahab as a fresh plate was placed in front of him for the entrée. 'Only a total dolt would offer meat to the gods! Especially beef!'

'Well,' Gran continued, 'to the shock of both the farmer and the tribesman, the Linga magically transformed into Lord Shiva himself. Both fell to their knees and prostrated before the magnificent God. The farmer ran over to his cart and brought the finest of his produce over to Lord Shiva, seeking blessings for his family. To his shock, Lord Shiva kicked away his offering and proceeded to eat the beef.'

'Lord Shiva ate beef?' Damyanti asked in surprise.

'Indeed. When the farmer demanded—in the most respectful way, of course—to know why, Shiva told him that anything offered to him with love was as sacred as prasad, while something offered with anger and pride was akin to poison. Thus, the farmer's fruit was far less appealing to Shiva than the tribesman's beef,' concluded Gran. 'So, if meat is good enough for Lord Shiva—the father of yoga himself—surely it's good enough for us humble humans.'

'Nonsense!' Rajani sahab scoffed. 'This sounds like some convoluted liberal interpretation!'

'Here we go again!' Vir rolled his eyes. Rajani sahab shot him a look, which led to an incredibly awkward silence as two uniformed attendants appeared to serve our entrée—vegetable biryani and dal makhani. I did wonder how she managed to make the 'makhani' vegan. The silence lingered even when our drinks were refilled.

'I'm curious …' began Damyanti, finally breaking the silence. She turned to Gran. 'What exactly did you do the night of the accident?'

'Yes, what was that? I want to know too!' said Rajani sahab as he took a swig of his Scotch.

'Well, along with being yogis, we are healers,' Gran explained with a smile.

'Healers?' asked Damyanti, her interest piqued.

'Yes, we use the energy of the universe to heal those in need.'

'Oh, like Reiki?'

'Well, something similar …'

'Reiki doesn't make a boy kiss another boy on the mouth!' Rajani sahab shot at Gran.

'And what's wrong with a boy kissing another boy on the mouth?' Aunt Meg shot back as a nervous shiver ran down my spine.

'Oh, this is such bullshit!' Vir exclaimed.

'Behave yourself!' Rajani sahab snapped at him.

'Or what? You're gonna fetch your belt in front of company?'

'Vir, please!' Damyanti cried, trying to stop the situation from becoming worse.

'Oh shut up, whore!'

'Oh my!' Aunt Claudine was enjoying the drama.

'I'm done with this!' Vir stood, dropped his napkin on the table and stormed off in a huff.

Almost reading my mind, Gran said, 'Jai, why don't you go check if he's all right.'

Before Rajani sahab could say anything, I excused myself and got up to leave as Gran quickly began telling Damyanti how much she was enjoying the delicious biryani.

In the main foyer, I asked one of the guards where Vir had gone. He escorted me upstairs to a corner bedroom. The door was shut.

'Yes?' Vir responded through the door when the guard knocked.

'Vir baba …' the guard began hesitatingly before turning to ask my name. After I told him, he spoke again through the door, *'Jai bhaiya hain yahan pe!'*

Vir opened the door. But without even looking at me, he plopped back on his California king bed. Not knowing what to say, I instead quietly looked around the room. Unlike mine, which was filled with Magdalena posters as well as mementos collected over the years, Vir's bedroom seemed like a hotel suite. Devoid of any personality. I reasoned that he probably hadn't had the time to decorate yet, since they had moved in not so long ago. Or perhaps Damyanti wouldn't allow him to do any of his own decorating.

'My life is such a fucking mess!' Vir snarled as he turned over to lay on his side.

'Well …' I said hesitantly, before walking over towards the side he was facing to sit on a small loveseat next to the bed. 'We all come with our baggage.'

'Yeah right!' Vir turned to stare up at the ceiling. Another awkward silence followed. *The evening just gets better and better!*

'So,' I began again, deciding to test the waters by moving to sit at the edge of his bed. 'Mayo was …'

'Oh, let's not talk about that shit!' Vir kicked off his suede loafers and sat up. 'What's your deal?'

'My deal?'

'Yeah, you with your charmed little life next door!' Vir unbuttoned his cuffs and rolled up his sleeves, revealing a pair of strong forearms.

'I'd hardly call my life charmed.' I tried my best to make eye contact, though it was hard because all I wanted to do was dive deep into those dark pools that were the colour of coal.

'Bullshit! You live with a family that clearly loves you in a home filled with all the comforts imaginable. What baggage are you taking about?'

'I think we all have baggage—'

'Yeah, well, I bet you weren't snatched away from your own father when he was shipped off to an asylum by his snake of a brother who wanted complete control of the family assets. Had Dadaji not named me the sole beneficiary of the trust, I'd be there too, rotting away till my last breath. I was fucking ten when my mother took her own life because of the way Tauji and Dadimaa drove her up the wall with their fucking regressive ways!'

Vir got up and began pacing in front of me. 'Instead of letting me mourn her, they sent me off to Mayo, while Tauji conveniently replaced Taiji with that cunt because they deemed her barren. Of course, because Damyanti gave birth to a daughter—unfortunately, I might add—they let her stay on. Also probably because Damyanti gave great head. Pretty sure Dadaji was pleased too!'

I didn't know how to react, so I just remained silent as Vir continued his rage-filled pacing. 'I'm nothing more than a fucking asset to them, one that's meant to be groomed to take over the reins of their fucking empire! A fucking cult—that's what it is!'

Vir then stopped before me and looked me dead in the eye as I sat frozen. 'You know nothing of suffering! How would you? All you do is fucking dance merrily with your little haven of a family that loves you! What do you know about baggage?' He collapsed on the loveseat and sank his face in his palms.

'I was raped!' I said finally.

Vir looked up at me blank-faced at that. I continued, 'I was thirteen and a bunch of senior boys raped me in the boys' toilet at school.' I could feel my heart beating faster, but I couldn't stop myself. 'My mother died giving birth to me and my father died before I was even two. Ever since I can remember, I was bullied and beaten up in school. I was called everything from "orphan boy" to "hijra". I'm practically failing all my classes and have to give retests in at least two subjects every year before they can promote me. Sure, Gran and my aunts give me a warm home, but they're all I have. Who wants to be friends with the gay kid who's raised by a trio of "chudails"? I spend my days studying yoga and what not with my Gran and aunts because I don't have even a single friend to call my own. As much as they love me, I'm so fucking alone!' I couldn't stop the tears as my body was trembling, 'So don't you dare say that I know nothing about suffering. I come with my own baggage! We all do! The difference is, I learned a long time ago that instead of feeling sorry for myself, I had to be grateful for the blessings I do have! And I am grateful! I'm fucking grateful! But sometimes, i-i-it's j-j-just ...'

Wiping my tears, I got up to storm out. But before I could reach the door, Vir uttered softly, 'I'm sorry.'

Taking a deep breath to compose myself, I wiped my tears and turned around. 'It's okay!' I mustered a gentle smile.

Vir sat on the edge of the bed and patted the spot next to him. I sighed as I sat down. I could feel his heart lighten even as mine did. I didn't know what came over me, but I couldn't stop my hand from reaching out to hold his. He held on to it tightly looking me deep in my eyes, almost like he was inviting me to gaze deep into his soul. No words were needed. We just gazed into each other. I could see his aura turning a warm golden hue and tingles ran down my spine as we dove deep into each other's souls. Was it my imagination or was he about to lean in for a kiss? *Crap, what do I do?* I thought in a panic. *Do I close my eyes and lean in as well? Should I just let him take the lead? Should I man up and just—*

'I hope I'm not interrupting!'

I turned sharply to see the tall, leggy girl I had seen with Vir from my bedroom window. There she was, dressed in her Audrey Hepburn drag—she even wore a hat! Who wears a fucking hat?

'Aishwarya!' Vir exclaimed, smiling. He got up to greet her with a kiss on the cheek. I could tell that she didn't like me being there.

Kissing him back, she turned her attention to me. 'You're Jai, right?'

I stood up and held out my hand. 'Yes I am, pleased to—'

However, she cut me short: 'Your family is waiting for you downstairs.' The 'fuck off' in her smile was unmistakable.

I smiled and nodded at them before leaving the room.

'Well, that was fun!' Aunt Claudine held on to Aunt Meg as we walked back home.

'You certainly enjoyed the champagne,' muttered Aunt Meg.

'It was the best part of the evening!' giggled Aunt Claudine. She winked at the security guards by the gate as we left, much to Aunt Meg's annoyance.

Gran was silent. Clearly, she was not pleased with the way the evening had gone. Oh well, tomorrow morning she'd be in a better mood.

As we entered our gates, my phone chimed. I saw to my delight that it was a notification from Instagram: Vir had accepted my follow request and had followed me back! I wanted to leap with joy but controlled myself.

Gran and the aunts kissed me goodnight and we retired to our rooms. The minute I closed my door, I checked for further notifications. There was a message waiting for me in my DMs from the user 'theVirRajani': 'I need a friend too,' it said.

'I'd like to be that friend,' I quickly typed out and replied.

Almost instantly, Vir 'liked' my response.

I guess the night wasn't all bad after all!

Chapter Fifteen

I was in love with Vir Rajani. Okay, maybe 'love' was too heavy and serious a word. However, 'like' just seemed so superficial a term for the way I felt about him. It definitely was more than just a crush. Sure, my heart was crushed whenever Aishwarya appeared—always at the most inopportune moments, ruining any chance of something happening beyond lingering gazes.

Ugh! I couldn't stand her! It was such a strange feeling, considering I was raised to not only respect women, but to also always support and believe them. But, oh my god, I just wanted to smack her smug face in. Gran and my aunts would be so disappointed with me for having such feelings—especially Aunt Meg.

'Toxic patriarchy thrives when women are pitted against each other,' she would tell me often. 'Instead of creating a world of equality, it creates a world where men—well, straight cisgender men—are given all the privileges on a silver platter. Through centuries of trauma, women have been conditioned to compete and manipulate each other, diminish their light to appease men and live on the crumbs that the patriarchy deigns to offer them. Internalized misogyny runs through our veins like the Nile through Egypt. It's important for us all to fight against it. I'm not saying it will be easy, but we must carry on nonetheless.'

Aunt Meg obviously hadn't had to deal with Aishwaryas in her life. Then again, I didn't really know anything about her love life. Maybe I should actually take some time and discover things about my aunts and my family. After all, they are pretty much the coolest family ever but … Oh my god, Vir sent me a text!

theVirRajani: Up for a ride?

JaiGillYogi: Sure!

Okay, now I know it's super fuckboy-type behaviour to send a text in the middle of the night and expect someone to drop everything to meet. I reasoned that I was sixteen, and deserved to live a little. Even if I wasn't being fucked.

Vir looked so hot in his leather jacket as he waited for me on his new red Ducati 1299 Panigale S. No, I didn't particularly care about bikes or cars, but Vir did. He loved his bikes.

The first time he had taken me for a ride was a couple of nights after that dinner where shit hit the fan. I was very hesitant as I had never ridden on a motorcycle before—not even a bicycle, for that matter. I thought they were dangerous—and considering I saved his life after a motorcycle accident, it's not like I was entirely wrong.

'Don't worry, I'll be safe!' Vir had said, reading my thoughts. He grinned and handed me a spare helmet. It wasn't as fancy as his, which matched the bike—but it was a helmet nonetheless. I sat behind him as he revved the engine.

Before he could roar off, I tapped him on the shoulder and asked, 'Um, silly question, but what do I hold on to?'

He just took my hands and placed it on his waist and then zoomed off into the night. It took so much willpower to control my boner while my hands were pressed against his washboard abs.

A few rides later, I grew comfortable enough to rest my head on his back as he rode through the streets of Delhi. The route we took was always the same: we'd start with a round of the India Gate circle and then move on to Connaught Place, after which he'd take me across the DND Flyway, and we'd finish by zooming across the virtually deserted Greater Noida Expressway.

Delhi traffic rules were never enforced at night and Vir would speed through red lights. Even when the Delhi Police placed barricades for routine checks, they'd recognize Vir's motorbike and would allow us through. Sometimes, when the roads were chock-a-block full of trucks that could only pass through the city at night, Vir would take detours through service lanes and even colony roads. Every moment was thrilling!

We'd never really talk, at least not with words. I know it sounds strange, but every time my chest would press against his muscular back, I could feel our heart chakras merging. But for me, merging heart chakras seemed pretty normal when compared to some of the other things I've witnessed. No words were needed when our hearts would beat in unison.

'White tea has enough caffeine to energize you after a night out!' Aunt Claudine said one night when she caught me sneaking back in. 'How else do you think I manage to stay alert during morning yoga class after I return late from dates?' Her suggestion worked for the yoga classes on the mornings after those late-night rides, but I still felt sleepy throughout the day at school.

Vir would have me come over almost every afternoon after school. We'd always begin with the gym in the basement. I had pretty much figured out his workout routine. Mondays and Thursdays were chest and tricep days. Tuesdays and Fridays were for back and biceps. Saturdays were for shoulders and legs. Wednesdays and Sundays were rest days.

'Don't you ever stretch?' I asked one day when he groaned ferociously as he placed the squat bar on the rack.

'Should I?' Vir wiped the sweat off his forehead as a couple of attendants removed the weights off the bar and stacked them neatly.

'No wonder you were stiff as a board during yoga!' I teased.

A few minutes later, on a cork mat that hadn't been touched since he stopped attending the yoga classes, Vir was moaning in a mix of pain and release as I pressed on his back, helping him go deep into a paschimottanasana.

'Don't focus on grabbing your toes,' I whispered, 'Just place your palms on your shin and focus on leading with your back straight instead of hunched over. It's not about touching your forehead to your knees, it's about opening your spine and hamstrings.'

After fifteen minutes of a light stretching routine—well, light for me—Vir insisted that I do yoga with him on Wednesdays and lead him in a post-workout stretch routine on other days. Sundays were still be a rest day. Even God rested on a Sunday—at least the Judeo-Christian God.

'I don't really run,' I told him the one time he asked me if I wanted to use the treadmill.

'Why not?'

'Running stiffens your hips and hamstrings and constricts the space between the vertebrae of the spine,' I replied.

'Yeah?' he said, shrugging. 'Well, I need the runner's high—it keeps me sane!'

However, he agreed to stretch with me after every run.

After each workout, we'd spend time in the steam room. It was there that I could see him naked, so that was something I looked forward to. His body was like a chiselled Michelangelo sculpture. He told me that his way of escaping the pain of his reality was to lift weights—he'd been doing it since the ninth grade.

And yes, I saw his dick. Not that I was being a perv and staring! But I just couldn't help but quickly peek when he'd strip out of his sweaty clothes and wrap a towel around his waist before entering the steam room. It was never hard—why would it be? But, even flaccid, it was—for lack of a better word—meaty.

'Yoga gave you those muscles?' Vir commented the first time I took off my clothes in front of him.

I didn't know what to say, so I just shrugged.

'Is that a tattoo?' Vir pointed at the eye on my chest.

Not knowing what to say, I blurted out, 'It's a birthmark.'

'Interesting birthmark!'

'I'm an interesting guy!' I smiled, but the inner me cringed so hard at that response. I watch way too much porn.

We'd have quick showers after the steam room and then go to his bedroom, where we'd spend time talking about anything and everything.

'Why Magdalena?' Vir asked once after seeing probably the fiftieth Magdalena clip on YouTube on the large Smart TV screen in his room.

'OMG! Why *not* Magdalena?' The 'stan' in me had come alive. 'I mean, look at her move!'

'She's okay, I guess …'

'*Okay*?' My eyes widened. 'She's a creamy smooth pop-icon goddess! I mean, look at her here. She's fifty and doing a complex jump-rope choreography, while still singing live!'

'Oh, she couldn't possibly be singing live!'

'She def is! She always sings live! Except when she performs "Pose".'

'Why not that one?'

'Well, *Pose* is all about high performance intricate dance moves, paying tribute to the NYC Ballroom Scene. Magdalena always ups her choreography whenever she performs "Pose" on tour, and she needs to lip-sync it because it requires her to maintain her composure vocally with an air of being cool without trying hard …'

I doubt anything I said impressed him, but he looked so adorable as he smiled and listened along.

One day, I had him listen to the entire *Zephyrus* album. 'She was inspired to create this album after the birth of her daughter, Layla. Though all her lyrics are brilliant, in this album, she really bore her soul and it shows!'

Three tracks in, I could tell he was impressed with what he was hearing. By the sixth track, he couldn't help but drown in the album. By the time we reached the thirteenth and final track, we were laying in his bed staring silently up at the ceiling.

'Oh my god! You're crying!' I exclaimed when I rolled to my side to face him as the last song began to fade out—and saw that his eyes were wet.

'What?' He snapped out of his trance. 'No, I'm not!' He sat up and pressed his fingers on his eyes. 'It must just be the damn AC.'

'Oh my god! You so were crying!' I teased him as I sat up beside him.

'I'm not crying!'

'Ha ha! Someone's becoming a Magdalena fan!' I playfully hit him with a pillow.

'Am not!' He flung the pillow back at me.

'Are too!' I flung it right back at him.

Before we knew it, we were having a pillow fight, whacking each other as I teased him about finally opening his heart to Magdalena. All of a sudden, he leaped on top of me and we began rolling all over the bed in a strange sort of wrestling manner. He pinned me down and triumphantly grinned. 'I'm stronger than you, Yoga Boy!'

'Oh yeah?' I chuckled. 'We'll see about that!' I smoothly slid my leg over him from under his shoulder, catching him off-guard as I rolled on top of him. 'You were saying?' I stuck my tongue out cockily.

Letting out a moan, he pushed me off and after a few tumbles all over his mattress, he pinned me face down and locked my arms behind me as he sat on my back.

'Ha!' He leaned over, grabbed the back of my head and turned my face towards him. 'Now you're mine!'

'Oh really?' I laughed. 'I'm yours?'

'Yeah!' We both began to laugh. He turned me around so that I was flat on my back, then he laid on top of me. 'You're mine, bitch!'

'Oh, and now I'm your bitch?'

'Yeah? Problem?'

Before I could respond, our laughter faded and we just began to gaze into each other's eyes silently. I could feel chills run down my spine as he slowly traced my face with his fingertips with gentle feather-like strokes. Trusting the moment, I allowed my fingers to stroke his back as his body weighed heavier on top of me with every passing second.

It was as though we were trapped in this bubble where everything else began to blur. All I could see were his eyes. I could feel my heart grow warm as our heart chakras began to connect. It felt as though a golden light emerged from both our chests and fused, drawing us closer and closer. My eyes felt heavy as he slowly leaned in.

'Knock knock!'

Fucking Aishwarya! She broke our bubble as she announced her entrance with that grating, pretentious tone of hers. Vir sprung off the bed and ran over to her in a heartbeat. It was my cue to head home.

One afternoon, Vir and I were waiting in line at the Big Chill restaurant in the DLF Promenade after watching *The Intern* at the cinema. Vir was soon getting impatient. 'Why do you love this place so much?'

'Hey, I just cried buckets in the movie! I need me some Mississippi Mud Pie!'

'Yeah, but there's always a such a long wait to get in!'

'Because it's the Big Chill—it's epic! Besides, you don't complain when you're chowing down on your chicken pasta!'

As meat was forbidden in his home, the only time he could indulge his meat cravings was when he went out. However, sometimes I would sneak him some of Aunt Meg's bacon when I'd visit him.

'Vir!'

I didn't need to turn around to know fucking Aishwarya was standing behind us.

He immediately headed over to greet her with a customary kiss on the cheek.

'What are you two—?'

'Vir Rajani, table for two!' the host called out just then, and Aishwarya narrowed her eyes.

'I'm sure they'll make it a table for three!' she declared.

Using all her south Delhi girl wiles and charms, she got them to pull up a chair to our table and made sure she was seated next to Vir. She even placed her arm around his shoulders like a lioness marking her territory.

I barely got a word in as she kept eating Vir's ear off with gossip about her friend's circle. After a few minutes, I took out my phone and began scrolling on Instagram—hoping there were fun memes to drown out her voice. As soon as our orders arrived, she cooed when she saw my Mississippi Mud Pie: 'That looks too good to resist!'

Before I could say anything, she grabbed a spoon and scooped some into her mouth. To make matters worse, she began making annoying noises as she relished her mouthful. It made me wanna hurl. *Bitch!*

'So, Vir!' She had switched to an annoying baby voice as she fed him a spoonful of his pasta. 'I have relatives visiting this weekend so I can't host my annual Halloween party at my place. Would it be too much to ask to move it to yours?'

She began twirling her fingers through his hair and leaned in closer before continuing, 'You know how important my parties are! It would be such a shame if I couldn't host it this year! Pwease! Pwiddy pwiddy pwease!' She leaned in to kiss him. Such subtlety!

Gently pushing her off, Vir smiled. 'When you ask like that, how can I refuse?'

The squeal she let out caused a few tables to shoot us dirty looks. What on earth did Vir see in her?

'Is it okay if Jai comes?'

Aishwarya and I were both caught off guard by Vir's question.

'Um …' One couldn't miss the sheer disgust that Aishwarya tried her damndest to swallow. 'Sure, I suppose!' She turned to me, giving me a saccharine smile as she said, 'Do you even know what Halloween is?'

I'm a witch, bitch! What do you think?

Chapter Sixteen

As a child, I learned about Halloween mainly through American cartoons, movies and TV shows that would have special Halloween episodes. We in India did not celebrate this festival back then. However, over the past few years, people—mainly celebrities and socialites who just need another reason to dress up and celebrate—have begun throwing Halloween parties. Conservative pundits blamed it on globalization and the liberal agenda that was hell-bent on dividing the nation and making us abandon traditions to appear 'cool' to the West.

'What utter tosh!' Gran once said as my aunts and I were carving jack-o'-lanterns at our kitchen table a few days before Halloween. 'It's merely a harvest festival. All cultures have them along with festivals to honour the dead. How different is it from Pitru Paksha, which begins on the full moon of the month of Bhadrapada and goes on for all sixteen nights of the shradhs? Don't we pray for the souls of the deceased to attain liberation as they return to the earthly realm during that time? During that period, people who suffer from Pitru Dosha according to their janama kundlis must offer sacrifices to cleanse ancestral karma. In fact, even trick-or-treating has Indian roots!'

'Really, Gran?' I asked, curious. 'How does it have Indian roots?'

'People would practice Pind Daan, in which they offer food consisting of rice and black sesame seeds to feed the spirits of the dead while praying to bring peace to their souls.'

'Of course, nowadays, it's all about offering fun-sized Snickers and Mars bars to brats dressed up as superheroes and Disney princesses,' said Aunt Claudine as she lined a silver dish filled with sliced apples and pomegranate seeds with marigold flowers.

'Anyway, let's not be too bothered with faux-champions of tradition,' Gran sighed. 'We have Samhain to get ready for.'

Samhain, pronounced 'sah-win', was the end of the Witch's Year. It was a time when we bid farewell to the dying solar deity, who would be reborn during the winter equinox at Yule—also known as Christmas.

'Back in ancient times, winter snow wouldn't allow new crops to grow,' Gran said. 'Animals were slaughtered to ensure food was available throughout the winter, and their blood and bones were mixed into the earth to ensure the land would remain fertile even as it rested under the blanket of snow. Once spring arrived and the snow had melted, the land would be ripe and ready for planting to begin afresh.'

'Of course,' Aunt Meg added. 'Sometimes when the winter cold was particularly severe, they would plant fresh eggs in the field on the first day of spring. It would give it an extra boost of fertility.'

'Like Easter eggs?' I asked, loving the lore.

'Of course!' Gran exclaimed, sounding delighted by my inquisitiveness. 'Except it was traditionally called Ostara to represent the fertile earth goddess.'

'I still plant eggs in our garden every now and then,' Aunt Meg said while checking on the pie she had in the oven. 'They work better than any chemical fertilizer.'

'Animal blood and eggs, sometimes even the bones, are essential for the earth to rejuvenate itself,' added Aunt Claudine as she salted an offering dish with black salt.

'It's the circle of life,' concluded Aunt Meg as her pie started to fill the kitchen with its heavenly aroma.

This year, Halloween wouldn't be as lavish as our celebration back then. After all, I didn't have anyone to celebrate it with. But I had accepted that being a yogi meant leading a life of solitude.

I still needed to have a large bonfire around which to dance and bid farewell to the solar gods while embracing the dark aspect of the Goddess. However, there was not enough room in my tiny studio for that. But how could I not honour the dead?

The tenants in the flat downstairs were having a Halloween bash, but I remained on the terrace, naked except for the layer of ash covering my body. I was sitting in padmasana before a small coal fire. I didn't have any of my special magical tools to call upon the elements, so I used my fingers as substitutes. My thumb was my wand, representing the element of fire, while my pinkie was my chalice, representing the element of water. My ring finger was the pentacle of earth, while my middle finger was the atame, the sword of air. That left my index finger to represent the element of akasha, space or aether.

Focussing on my breath, I closed my eyes and joined my fingers into a sarva yoni mundra. This was done by bending the little and middle fingers of both hands while holding the ring and index fingers. Then the little and middle fingers were opened to touch the thumbs. If done properly, the hands form the shape of a vagina. It's beautiful, but only if one doesn't find shame and sin in the yoni.

Soon, I began to feel a sparkling silver shield of energy surround my body. A golden beam from the earth shot through the base of my spine, activating my root, sacral and solar-plexus chakras, while another golden beam of light from the heavens entered the top of my head, passing through my crown, third eye and throat chakras. Both divine beams met and fused in my heart chakra, allowing the golden light to flow through my veins and nadis all through my body. To the naked eye, nothing could be seen, but to those intuitively blessed, my body would appear like the long steadfast flame of a candle.

'Where is my offering?'

I didn't need to open my eyes to see that the Dark Goddess had appeared before me.

My spirit body exited my physical body, still bound to it by a silver thread through my navel. I prostrated before the fierce deity and offered a steel thali with a freshly slaughtered baby buffalo. It's amazing what the right butcher can sell you for the right price.

The Goddess licked her lips and began devouring the offering with the talon-like fingers of all four of her hands. After finishing, she let out a loud satisfied burp that made the trees tremble. Then she sat before me and raised her arm to offer blessings.

'Sit up, child!' she commanded.

My spirit sat up as I gazed at her. Skin dark as the midnight sky, her bare breasts were covered with a garland of human skulls, while her wild hair flowed about her like a thunder cloud. Her eyes were wide and bloodshot, while her third eye remained calm in the middle. I could see the blood at the corners of her mouth as she flashed a smile, showing serpent-like fangs that would terrify anyone who called themselves 'god-fearing'.

'Oh, great Goddess of darkness and chaos!' said my spirit with hands in namaste. 'I only seek your blessings for the task I am about to undertake.'

She thew her head backwards in a fit of fierce laughter that echoed in the polluted night sky. 'Oh, child,' she said finally, wiping the drool and blood off her mouth. 'Vengeance serves no one. For even the noblest of dharmic wars have never resulted in peace. Just more blood and corpses for me to feed upon. Your soul will never attain peace through it, and you'll spend numerous lifetimes bound to this earthly existence!'

'I understand, oh fierce one! But I'm afraid I have no choice but to avenge those who were taken from me.'

'That's not all you wish to seek.'

'No, oh queen of the night sky. I also wish to rescue the one I love from those who are hell-bent on damaging his body, mind and soul.'

'He can't escape his destiny. It's his ancestral curse! All you can do is delay the inevitable. You should know. Similar blood flows through your veins.'

'I understand, oh chaotic one, but I also know that destinies are meant to be changed. You, after all, are so fierce that the forces of karma bow before you. Had my heart's intent not been pure, you wouldn't have appeared before me this very night.'

'Flattery gets you nowhere, my child!' She burst into another fit of echoing fierce laughter, almost taunting me. 'But yes, I can never deny those with a pure heart. And now, to seal my protection for your mission of vengeance, I need your seed!'

'It is yours for the taking!' My soul body merged back with my physical body and I laid on my back with my eyes closed. I whispered a forbidden mantra under my breath as the Goddess began grinding into me, screaming wildly as thunder roared and lightning flashed across the sky.

I lay still while she had her way with me, riding faster and faster. The skin around my groin burned and blood from her womb flowed all over my body. As I uttered the final 'om', she dug her talons into my chest near the heart. Then she leaned over and licked my face with her bloody tongue before leaping off me and flying off into the night sky, leaving me trembling on my rooftop.

I'm coming for you, Vir!

Chapter Seventeen

'Aww Gran, please let me go!' I begged the morning of Aishwarya's Halloween party.

'I wouldn't have said no had it been any other night!' Gran said as she closed the doors of the yoga studio. The final morning class had just ended. 'But not only is tonight Samhain, but it is also a Saturday …'

'Yes, I know Saturday nights are perfect for magic … night of Saturn, the ruler of karma, magic, witches, yada yada. But Gran, it's just this once!'

'I said no!' Gran walked past me and headed to the kitchen where Aunt Claudine was brewing a fresh pot of tea and Aunt Meg was frying the morning bacon.

'Please, Gran? Pretty, pretty please …' I whined as I followed her.

'Oh heavens, child! Stop begging like a greedy pup!' Gran exclaimed as she sat down at the table. 'You've been spending far too much time with that boy anyway. Now you want to abandon your family on perhaps the most important night of the year to cavort with—'

'Isn't his girlfriend the one throwing the party?' Aunt Meg cut in as she transferred the sizzling bacon to our plates.

'Oh, sweetie,' Aunt Claudine said, shaking her head. 'Falling for a straight boy with a girlfriend ... that's not going to end well.'

'You seem to know from experience!' Aunt Meg joined us at the table.

'At least I'm smart enough to know not to fall head over heels for them.' Aunt Claudine bit into a slice of brioche as she teased Aunt Meg, 'Unlike this one who has fallen for the boy next door.'

'Oh my god! I haven't "fallen" for Vir!'

All three of them shot me a look as if to say, 'Really bitch?'

'I *haven't!*' Obviously, I was lying.

'Denial ain't just a river ...' Aunt Meg said drily.

'It's just one night, Gran!'

'One very important night!'

'Please! It's not like I ask for much!'

'Till the next Magdalena album comes out,' said Aunt Meg, sipping her tea.

'Oh my god! Whose side are you on?'

'Oh, we're picking sides now?'

'Oh, leave the boy be!' Aunt Claudine said. Finally someone came to my defence! 'They'll be plenty of Samhains that fall on Saturdays.'

'That's not the point,' Gran said, glaring at Aunt Claudine. 'Our magic depends on us observing our rituals, especially on the holy days.'

'Oh, we have seven other ones and Yule is just a couple of months away. Besides, we couldn't exactly celebrate them when we were in boarding schools for most of the year, and our magic is just fine!'

'That's not the point! And he isn't in boarding school, so he can't excuse himself from—'

'Oh my god!' I yelled, standing up in a rage. 'I have finally found a friend in this world, who not only accepts me for what I am, but also wants to share a special day with me. I've spent all my life by your side, learning all about magic and obediently following all your lessons. Can't I have *one* night for myself?'

'Are you done?' Gran said curtly.

I sighed and sat down in a huff. We finished breakfast in ominous silence. When she finished eating, Gran got up and retired to her room without another word. After she left, Aunt Claudine leaned over and kissed me on my cheek.

'Don't worry,' she said, ruffling my hair. 'Leave Gran to me. You just figure out what to wear tonight!'

'Oh, thank you, Aunt Claudine!' I hugged her tightly.

'Anything for you, baby boy!' She kissed me on my cheek.

'I really wish you wouldn't encourage him like that!' Aunt Meg complained as she got up to do the dishes.

'Oh, lighten up! Let the boy have some fun!' Aunt Claudine shooed me away as she joined Aunt Meg at the sink to help her.

'Are you sure this is what you wanna go as?' Aunt Meg arched a quizzical brow when she saw me in my costume that evening.

'Oh, come on, he looks adorable as Dr Frank-N-Furter from *The Rocky Horror Picture Show!*' Aunt Claudine said. She made me twirl in my black leather corset and booty shorts, complete with fishnet stockings. She had even cut up a spare set of stockings to make fingerless gloves for me. 'By the way, I've borrowed your boots to spare him the agony of heels.'

'The eyeliner is a bit much, don't you think?' Aunt Meg shook her head.

'Be thankful I didn't put on lipstick!' Aunt Claudine said as she kissed me on my cheek. 'Besides, even if no one gets the reference, he can just say he's a punk rocker from the '70s.'

'Do you like it, Gran?' I asked her nervously as she looked closely at me.

'Hmm …' she began, scratching her chin. 'Something is missing!' She got up, took off the string of pearls from around her neck and put it around mine. 'There you go, now it's perfect!'

My heart skipped a beat as I gave her a big bear hug. 'Thank you, Gran!' I lifted her up and spun her around.

'Oh child, put me down!' she said, chuckling. The minute I put her down, I began attacking her cheeks with kisses. 'Okay! Okay!' She laughed as she playfully pushed me off. 'Just make sure you enjoy yourself fully!'

'Make good choices!' Aunt Meg rolled her eyes.

'Aw, I love you too, Aunt Meg!' I ran over to give her a hug and kissed her cheeks too.

'Ew! Get off me!' Aunt Meg yelled. I giggled because I knew that she hated being hugged and kissed.

'And remember,' Aunt Claudine said as she led me to the front door, 'You're not Cinderella, so don't worry about the clock striking twelve!'

Aishwarya had spared no detail for the party. The guards surrounding Vir's mansion were dressed as Stormtroopers from

Star Wars. Even though the masks were covering their faces, I could tell they were weirded out by my costume. When I showed them the invite that Vir had DM'd me on Instagram, they opened the gate and had me escorted to the front door.

There, a female attendant dressed in a French maid costume offered me a welcome drink—a speciality cocktail in a margarita glass that had vapours steaming out of it. I noted the mini skull resting on the rim where the slice of lemon would be. As she led me to the living room, I noticed all the male attendants were dressed up as butlers, while the women were all French maids. *Way to humiliate the help, Aishwarya!*

However, the decorations were great: the hallway was decorated with fake cobwebs and plastic skeletons, and the jack-o'-lanterns filled with LED candles looked really cool. I seemed to be the only guest who had put some thought into their costume. All the men seemed to have come dressed as superheroes, and their costumes were clearly complete sets bought online. The women were in their regular club outfits and had merely added hair bands with cat ears or devil horns with flickering LEDs.

I stood by the wall, looking for Vir in the crowd. I noticed there was was a DJ who was dressed as a vampire and spinning tracks I had never heard. Not that I didn't listen to anything besides Magdalena, but this just seemed like random club bangers I assumed one would play at raves in Ibiza. The strobe lights added to the effect.

Almost twenty minutes passed, but there was no sign of Vir. There was no else I really knew there, and the few who did notice me just looked me up and down before laughing cruelly as they walked away. It's not like I'm not used to being teased, but it hurt more because that place had kind of become a second home for me. Well, at least the gym and his bedroom. The DJ continued jumping as he hyped the dancing crowd, who were gyrating to his beats.

Were all parties this boring? Maybe I should have stayed home and been a part of the Samhain ritual. Maybe I could still make it back in time.

'And what are you supposed to be?' A guy dressed up as the Green Arrow leaned over and yelled in my ear so that he could be audible over the music.

'Have you seen *Rocky Horror*?' I yelled back.

He shook his head. Of course he hadn't.

'I'm a punk rocker from the '70s!'

'Awesome!' He raised his hand to high-five me.

I smiled and high-fived him back. 'Have you seen Vir?'

'Nah, man!' He sipped his bottle of Corona. 'But let's get you a drink!' He took my empty glass and handed it to a passing butler before grabbing my arm and leading me through a sea of sweaty dancers over to the bar. The mixologists were shirtless and were performing juggling tricks with liquor bottles as they prepared drinks.

'What ya having?' Green Arrow yelled in my ear.

I wanted to say a merlot, but this didn't really seem like a wine party. 'Gin and tonic!' At least the juniper berries would keep help keep things magical this Halloween.

'One G&T coming up!' said a mixologist, opening a bottle of Tanqueray immediately. My drink came with the signature mini skull on the rim.

'To Halloween!' Green Arrow clinked his fresh Corona bottle with my glass and we both took a sip.

'Hey, Pranav,' said a familiar voice. 'Who's your friend?'

I turned to see Aishwarya in a 'bandage' dress that left very little to the imagination. Her hair was pulled back into a high ponytail on top of her head. No doubt thanks to expensive extensions, the hair then flowed down to the small of her back. Her face dropped when she recognized me. 'Oh, you made it!'

I shrugged and sipped my drink as the Green Arrow went over to Aishwarya and asked, 'You two know each other?'

'He's Vir's neighbour, the one I was telling you about!'

'Ah, the gay kid next door?' He laughed and extended his hand towards me. 'Sup bro, I'm Pranav!'

Before I could introduce myself, Aishwarya butted in, 'And what exactly are you dressed up as?'

Not wishing to explain my costume, I replied, 'I'm a '70s' punk rocker!

'You don't say!' The daggers were pointed.

'What about you? Who are you meant to be?'

'I'm Ariana Grande, duh!' She flipped her ponytail for effect. I had to give her props for not dressing up like Audrey Hepburn. Then again, that would just have been any other day for her.

'Oh, I love her new song, "Focus"!' I said. It is her party after all, might as well try to be pleasant. 'It's such a total bop!'

'Thanks!' she said, but her eyes said *Fuck off.* She turned to Pranav. 'Have you seen Vir?'

'Nope! But why bother, let's have some fun, babe!' Pranav tried to get Aishwarya to dance, but she just pushed past him and stormed over to a bunch of girls on the other side of the bar.

'Women, am I right?' Pranav tried to fist-bump me, but I just smiled back. Aunt Meg wouldn't have liked it if I encouraged any negative talk about women—even if it was about my arch-nemesis, Aishwarya. *Fucking Aishwarya!*

'Wanna meet Charlie?' Pranav yelled in my ear.

'Huh?' I had no idea what he was talking about.

Chuckling, Pranav grabbed me by my hand and took me over to a row of booths on the other end of the grand ballroom that were set up just for the party.

'Hey, fellas!' He said to boys sitting there. They were dressed as different members of the Avengers. He fist-bumped them all in turn before introducing me with, 'Our friend Jai wants to meet Charlie!'

Before I could say anything, one of the guys took out a packet of white powder and poured it on to the table. He began making lines of it with a credit card, as another guy began rolling a two thousand rupee note. Pranav grabbed it and used it to inhale a line of powder into one nostril. He howled like a wolf as it hit his system.

'Um, I think I'm just going to …' I began, turning to leave. But Pranav yanked me closer.

'Dude, don't be such a pussy!' He grabbed the back of my head and turned me around the face the group of boys, whose chuckling reminded me of Sahil Hada and his hyenas from school. It couldn't be them under those costumes, could it?

'I really am not into …' I tried again, but Pranav's grip tightened and he forced me to lean over the table as another boy began making a line next to my face with the credit card.

'Come on buddy, this is how to party!' Pranav yelled, as the rest of them joined in his deviant chuckle. One of them began to press the rolled-up note to my nostril. My heart began to beat rapidly. I didn't know what PTSD was like, but it must feel like what I felt in that moment.

However, just as another boy pressed my other nostril, Pranav let go of my head. I quickly got away from the table and saw him being choked by a tall man dressed as Robin Hood a la Errol Flynn.

'Back the fuck off, Pranav!' said Robin Hood, whom I then recognized as Vir. He shoved Pranav against the wall, causing him to fall with a thud.

Before Pranav could get up, Vir caught my hand and dragged me outside to the pool area. Some of the guests were splashing about in the pool with their costumes sprawled on the patio. Walking past them, Vir led me over to a wrought-iron gazebo decorated with fairy lights. It was in a quiet part of the garden, where even the blaring Ibiza beats seemed distant.

'You okay?' Vir asked as he sat me down on a bench.

I nodded, still breathless but able to admire how sexy he looked in his green outfit that was generously unbuttoned.

'Sorry about that,' he said as he sat down beside me.

'Some friends you have!' I scoffed.

'They're Aishwarya's!' he retorted, removing his costume hat and running his fingers through his hair. 'I don't really know any of them beyond the few times she's brought them over for house parties.'

'Oh!' A part of me felt very happy to know that I still was his only friend. Maybe he really did need me as a friend in his life.

'Did they make you ...'

'No, no,' I assured him. 'You came just in time to sweep me off my feet.' I playfully punched him on the shoulder.

'I shouldn't have said yes to having the party here. But you know how Aishwarya is!'

I didn't really, but I just nodded along.

'I hate that she's such a party girl! Always the same people, the same music, the same drugs ...'

'So why do you put up with it?'

'It's complicated ...' he began before sighing. 'You wouldn't get it.'

'I could try,' I said, hesitating before I placed my hand on his. He turned to look me in the eyes. 'It always helps to talk about it.'

'I don't want you to,' he said, gazing deeply into my eyes. 'I want what we have to be separate from all of this!'

'What we have?' Inner me cringed, but I couldn't help drown into his coal pools.

'You know what I mean.' He began to lean in closer.

'I do?' My eyes began to get heavy as I leaned in.

'Yeah ...' he said, and I could feel his warm breath. '... You do ...'

'There you are!'

Fucking Aishwarya. Such perfect fucking timing!

I sighed as Vir got up to greet her with his usual 'Hey, babe!'

Ignoring my presence, she pulled Vir away. 'Come on! Everyone is dying to meet you! What are you even wearing? Ugh … I wanted you to come as—'

I sighed as she dragged Vir inside. Eventually I followed them back into the house and headed over the bar to get another gin and tonic. Finding a quiet wall to lean against, I let my thoughts wander. *Why, Vir?* I thought. *Why are you with her when you clearly can't stand anything about her?*

But I had to admit that they did look good together. I could see them eventually having their wedding pictures in *Vanity Fair* or something. Knowing Aishwarya, she would make sure they were on the cover. I looked over where Aishwarya was cackling away with her friends as she held on to Vir. Though he was good at masking his agony, Vir did not fool me with his fake grin as he stood by her side patiently.

This G&T was definitely strong! Maybe it was a double shot. Or maybe it didn't mix well with that weird welcome drink. What was in that? Yeah, I should get outta here. Maybe I could still make it in time for the ritual.

I placed my glass on a table and began walking towards the door of the grand ballroom. However, just as I pushed the door open, the music stopped.

'This one is a special request for a special friend!' yelled the DJ into the mic.

My heart skipped a beat as a very familiar '80s' baseline began to play, followed by an addictive synth melody. The crowd moved aside as Vir stood in the centre of the dance floor, extending his hand out to me. My jaw dropped in amazement as he began to lip-sync to Magdalena's 'Follow My Light'.

Whenever I see you walkin' by, all I wanna do is make you mine ...

I walked over, shaking my head in disbelief as Vir began dancing with me.

But you always leave me crying in the night, I can't keep these feelings locked inside.

'How do you ... ?' I whispered wonderingly, amazed that he knew the steps.

'All those Magdalena videos you keep showing me, how could I not?'

He smiled as he began singing along:

I close my eyes and you're here next to me! Lost and abandoned, I want the sunlight

We sang together as we broke out into Magdalena's dance moves.

Follow my light to me, baby! I'll give my heart, won't you give yours to me? Follow my light to me, darlin', I'll give you love, won't you please set me free?

Soon, others had joined us on the floor, trying to copy the steps. However, all I could see was Vir. His eyes were locked with mine as we joyfully danced away. *Am I dreaming?* I thought. *This is so surreal! Oh, I don't care!* I just didn't want it to end.

Follow my light to me, baby! I'll give my heart, won't you give yours to me? Follow my light to me, darlin', I'll give you love, won't you please set me—

'You fucking bastard!'

Aishwarya yanked me away and threw her drink in my face. Immediately the music stopped as everyone looked on in shock!

Before, I could even wipe my face clean, Aishwarya slapped me. 'You fucking fag! Who the fuck do you think you are! Coming to my fucking party and blatantly hitting on my boyfriend! Why, I oughta—'

She raised her hand again, but Vir caught it and pulled her away. 'Stop it!' he yelled. 'You're making a scene!'

'I'm making a scene?' Aishwarya shouted back in disbelief. '*I'm* making a scene?' Her eyes were livid.

'Just calm down.'

'*Don't you fucking tell me to calm down!*'

I just ran out as fast I could in Aunt Meg's boots. My heart was almost about to pop out of my chest, but I didn't stop as I ran past the attendants and pushed open the front doors. I ran past all the Stormtroopers outside, ignoring their snickers as they opened the gate. As I reached our front gate, I collapsed on the pathway and began wailing in agony. Tears burned my cheeks as I curled into a foetal position. *This was such a mistake!* I berated myself. *Such a big fucking mistake! Oh, I should have just stayed home! Maybe I've offended the gods for skipping the Samhain ritual for the sake of a party! Ugh! I should have just listened to Gran …*

'Hey!' I felt a hand touch my shoulder. I turned around to see Vir, kneeling besides me. Fuck, I forgot to lock the gate!

'I'm sorry for what happened,' he began. 'I just—'

'We can't do this!' I yelled, pushing his hand off. 'You can't keep doing this to me!'

'What do you mean?'

'Oh, cut the crap! You know what I'm talking about! You know this is more than just friendship! Aishwarya certainly does!' I could feel my blood boil the minute I said her name. 'You can't say that this isn't something more. Something deeper!'

'I told you, it's really complica—'

'If it is so complicated, then why are you here?' I was shivering, but I mustered up all the strength I had. 'Why are you here, Vir? You can't just keep dangling our friendship knowing well that it's way more than that. Don't even try lying to me and denying the way you feel about me! If you think it's fun to play with my feelings this way, then please leave me alone! I was happy before you came, and I don't really need you to—'

He kissed me! Not on the cheek, but on the mouth! My eyes widened in shock before I gave in within seconds as his arms wrapped around me. His lips were so soft and tender. With every passing moment, the intensity of the kiss grew until I could feel chills up and down my spine as my heart began to glow in a golden light along with his. I melted in his arms as he rolled on top of me, pressing my body beneath his as he pinned me against the earth.

Suddenly, he pushed me away and we breathlessly stared into each other's eyes. Snapping out of his trance, he just got up and just ran out the gate. *What just happened?* I thought as I picked myself up.

No longer could I feel the burn of Aishwarya's slap against my cheek. The world around me was spinning as I fumbled my way back home. Just as I opened our door, my phone began to vibrate. Unzipping the pocket of my leather booty shorts, I pulled it out to see that Vir had sent me a message with a red heart emoji.

He loved me! He really loved me!

Chapter Eighteen

Shakespeare once said that the course of true love never did run smooth. I guess he would know, considering he was said to be a gay man in love with Henry Wriothesley, the third Earl of Southampton, as well as, William Herbert, the third Earl of Pembroke. True, he was married to Anne Hathaway (not the Academy Award winner), but I suppose that was due to the circumstances of the time.

I remained in my love bubble with Vir, but after that Halloween party, he wasn't allowed to invite me over. He never did explain why, but I assumed it was because of his uncle. Considering how that family dinner went down, it wouldn't take a genius to figure that his uncle was a raging homophobe. I wouldn't dare have him over at ours. Not that Gran and my aunts would have an issue with it, but as open as their hearts were, the secrets held within our home couldn't be revealed to anyone outside of the family.

However, that didn't stop us from sneaking out for our nightly bike rides. But now we would hardly ride. We'd just head straight over to the Greater Noida Expressway and find a quiet spot in some abandoned wooded area to make out.

'Oh my god, it felt so good to kiss Vir! His mouth was so hungry for mine, devouring me with every breathless moment.

I'd cry out loud each time he sank his teeth into my neck. I'd quiver in delight as he'd feast upon my nipples. I found it so hot when he'd cover my mouth to stop me from breathing, dangling me on that borderline of life and death. My eyes would roll over to the back of my head, but he instinctively knew when to pull away, as if he could feel my heartbeat slow down. It just drove me wild. However, I could never do the same to him. It was this strange power dynamic between us where he had to dominate. I was happy to submit.

As the crisp November night chill nipped through the air, his strong muscular chest felt so warm against mine. His skin tasted musky and manly, but there was this sweet note of vanilla that made it delicious. I always wanted to know what cologne he used, but I'd be so caught up in the moment that I'd forget to ask.

'No!' he would whisper when I ran my hands down his pants, which seemed to desperately want to release the monster entrapped within. 'I don't want our first time to be like this!' But one night, I didn't take no for an answer. With a quick thrust, I rolled on top of him and began kissing down his neck and all over his chest, taking a deliciously scenic route all over his abs with my tongue as I made my way down to his belt.

'No,' he said feebly, but before he could stop me, I unbuckled his belt and unzipped his fly. I couldn't help but gasp as he stood before me, rock hard, begging to be worshipped.

It was saltier and warmer than the rest of him, and it throbbed against the flicker of my tongue. I let instinct take over as I worshiped him deeper and deeper. I didn't know if it was all the porn or Magdalena' album *Desire*, but I felt this weird surge of power as I took control of him. I was grateful that all the years of yoga had taught me to breath solely through my nose without the aid of my mouth.

Letting out a powerful growl, he pushed me off and pinned me down on my chest, as he stripped off my pants. He lifted my bare hips in the air and buried his face between my cheeks. Our kisses never prepared me for the pleasure I felt as his tongue invaded me. I could feel tears roll down my cheeks as I screamed in sheer delight.

He skilfully manoeuvred my body on top of his as he laid down. Together, we formed a sensual yin-yang. We worshipped each other. He was my god, I was his goddess. We had no doubt that our union would move mountains.

Pushing me off, he pulled my face over as we kissed each other, while our hands began stroking each other. Our collective moans probably scared the chirping cicadas into silence as I dug my fingers into his Herculean back as his teeth sunk deep into my neck.

'Oh fuck!' he screamed as I felt warm streams of ecstasy shoot between my legs. He lost all self-control before collapsing on top of me. We laid there for what seemed like an eternal silence, only broken by the sound of our echoing heartbeats.

Only when he rolled off me did I see that his torso was covered with my essence. I was so wrapped up in the moment that I didn't realize that we had both come simultaneously. We stayed lost in each other's eyes for a few more moments.

'Fuck! What time is it?' Vir exclaimed when we heard the birds begin their morning song.

'Clearly way too late!' I said, snapping out of my trance and starting to gather our clothes, which were spread all over the grassy earth.

'Or too early,' he said. He smiled as he gave me a soft tender kiss.

As much as we wanted this to go on, we knew we had to slip back into reality and return home. *Oh well, there is always tomorrow night,* I told myself. Thank God there was plenty of white tea at home.

On our way home, I couldn't help but admire the sun peering out from the grey Yamuna river as I started to imagine the life we would have together. We'd probably get married and move somewhere we could live our lives without any fear or judgement. Maybe London? Or New York? Or maybe even Paris? Oh, it had to be Paris! It was the city of love. We'd live in a cute little apartment in Montmartre like Amelie, where'd we'd begin each day with coffee and croissants. Okay, maybe tea instead of coffee, but the croissants were a must. He'd go off to work while I'd teach yoga classes in a studio I'd lease. How would one say 'Downward Dog' in French? *Chien tête en bas?* Fuck it, I'll just use the Sanskrit names. It'll make my classes appear more exotic.

We'd spend our evenings out at various charming cafes where accordion players would serenade us with Edith Piaf numbers. Vir would slip them a Euro or five to play a Magdalena song just for me. Over long weekends, we'd travel to smaller towns, and lap up all the culture and the fine wines. And during longer breaks, we'd explore other parts of Europe. Maybe Gran and my aunts could visit us during the summer when Delhi became a sweltering mess. Of course, we'd winter here because the European snow would be too much to bear. Oh, such bliss! I could almost see it all hap … whoa! What the—

A car swerved dangerously close to us, almost causing Vir to skid. Luckily, he managed to stay upright. *Fuck!* I thought. *Delhi traffic always knows how to wreck an idyllic—*

Another car swerved dangerously close, making me snap out of my dreamlike state. My eyes widened with horror as I realized that four cars had surrounded us. Suddenly, one of them overtook us and made a sharp turn to the side, skidding to a stop right in front of us. Vir hit the brakes hard, stopping merely inches away from a collision.

Before Vir could remove his helmet to hurl insults at the offending driver, I felt a couple of hands pull me off the bike. I was punched in the stomach and collapsed on the road. I felt my soul leap out of my body, and, hovering above, I could see three men kick me mercilessly all over my body. I wanted to fight them off, but I couldn't return to my body. My soul just dangled in mid-air, attached to my body by a silver energy cord through my navel.

I saw Vir in a brawl with four other men. It took me a moment to realize that one of them was Pranav—the guy from the Halloween party who had dressed as Green Arrow and tried to force me to snort cocaine. The rest of them must be his friends. *Oh fuck! What is going on?* Vir shook off his assailants and ran towards me. He grabbed one of the guys who was kicking my almost lifeless body and punched him in the face. But soon the others had grabbed Vir and one of them kicked him in the shin, causing him to fall over. Soon, they had overpowered him. Pranav began punching him repeatedly in the stomach.

I hurled myself at them, but my hands went through their bodies because I was still my soul self. I just had to return to my body, but every time I tried to do so, my body would keep rejecting me! *No! Fuck!* I thought in a panic. *I have to save Vir! They'll kill him! They're gonna kill him!*

'Enough!' said a familiar voice.

I turned to see Aishwarya exit the car behind us. *Fucking bitch!* My soul flew over to slap her, but, of course, she couldn't feel it. She just walked past me and headed over to Vir. Pranav grabbed Vir by his hair and turned his bloodied face towards Aishwarya.

'This time you're lucky it's just me,' she said, and slapped him. She snapped her fingers, and the others let go of Vir. He fell on the ground and lay there as they all returned to their cars. As she passed my prone body, Aishwarya kicked me in the stomach and spat on my face. The look on her face was a sort of evil I had never seen before.

Aunt Meg opened the front door to see Vir carrying me in his arms, shouting, 'Please! You have to save him!'

Without wasting a moment, Gran had Vir lay my body upon an old blanket. I was still in my soul body, hovering above them all. I watched Gran wave her hands above my lifeless body, as Aunt Meg started to tend to Vir's wounds. Aunt Claudine began sending messages to our students that today's yoga classes were cancelled.

'How is he doing?' Aunt Claudine asked Gran when she was done.

'Not good!' Gran sighed. I could tell how hard it was for her to be calm at this moment, but calm she remained.

'It's my fault!' Vir cried in a state of despair. Aunt Meg was bandaging his torso after applying a herbal medicinal paste on his wounds. 'I should have never dragged him into my mess. I'm so sorry, I—'

'Oh hush, child!' Gran snapped at Vir, trying her hardest to keep cool. 'There's time for that later!' She turned to Aunt Meg. 'Are you done?'

'I am!' replied Aunt Meg as she tied the final knot of the bandage. She handed Vir an ice pack to place on his head before heading over to Gran and Aunt Claudine.

Gran closed her eyes to centre herself while my aunts began chanting the Maha Mrityunjay mantra while waving their arms in the air to remove all blockages in my energy shield. I could feel my soul-self tingle warmly. But suddenly, I heard a sinister laugh.

I turned and saw the black hooded figure who attacked me on my thirteenth birthday. Its face was covered with an onyx shield as dark flames surrounded its body.

'I told you, you'd be mine!' it said and laughed maniacally. Then it shot a fiery lasso towards me. However, before the lasso could reach me, a beam of white light appeared and disintegrated it. I turned to see Gran's soul-self hovering behind me.

'Adele Byrne!' laughed the hooded figure as it hurled a beam of black light towards Gran. She expertly shot another beam of white light, stopping his attack.

'Leave now, Daddy!' Gran's soul-self screamed.

Daddy?

'You'll never lay claim to Jai's soul!' Gran screamed, firing another beam of white light that knocked the hooded figure back. Before it could get up, Gran leaped high and kicked it straight in its face. Then she launched a blindingly brilliant surge of white light that disintegrated the evil figure.

Moments later, the eyes on my physical body flickered open. I sat up with a surge of energy in a breathless coughing fit, my soul-self having been reunited with my body. Gran and my aunts hugged me and showered me with tear-filled kisses. My body felt no pain, just the collective warmth of their love. It was almost as if nothing had happened.

I turned to look at Vir, but before I could say anything, Gran yelled, 'You!' She shot Vir a look that made him sit up in a cold rush of fear. 'You have a lot of explaining to do!'

As do you, Gran, I thought to myself. *As do you!*

Chapter Nineteen

'Okay, so let me get this straight,' Aunt Claudine ran her fingers through her hair, 'After your crazy ex-girlfriend—'

'That's a sexist term!' Aunt Meg countered.

'Honey, she chased them down and had a bunch of goons beat the living daylights out of him …'

'The situation's a whole lot more nuanced than that—'

'Hush!' Gran shouted, raising her hands. 'Both of you!'

As the room descended into silence, Gran sighed and turned to Vir. 'So, what was her name again?'

'Aishwarya,' I answered before Vir could reply. I wanted to say 'Fucking Aishwarya', but I didn't think Gran was in the mood for it.

'Yes, thank you,' she said to me before turning back to Vir. 'So, after Aishwarya left the two of you to rot, you don't remember how you both arrived at our doorstep?'

'I know it sounds crazy,' said Vir. He was sipping a tea with ginger, peppermint, lemongrass and honey, but what he didn't know was that it was no ordinary tea. It was Aunt Meg's special 'truth serum'. 'But a strange white light hit us and … I don't know… teleported us here?'

'White light?' Gran arched a quizzical brow.

'Yeah! I don't know how to explain it. It was just so surreal.'

'That explains how they got in despite the gate being locked,' Aunt Meg refreshed everyone else's cups with lavender tea.

'It's true,' I said. I don't know why I wanted to rush to Vir's defence, as everything he said would be believed anyway because of the truth serum. 'I saw it all through my soul-self. We were just surrounded by white light, and next thing we knew, we were by our doorstep.'

Gran remained silent as Vir continued, 'I'm sorry, I shouldn't have gotten you all mixed up in my mess.'

'Well, too late for that!' Aunt Claudine tied up her auburn hair in a loose top knot.

'But why would she go so far as to try and kill you?' asked Aunt Meg. 'I get "hell hath no fury as a woman scorned" and all other sexist literary tropes, but I severely doubt most would go to such extremes to avenge a broken heart.'

'It's not to avenge a broken heart,' Vir replied. His cup was almost empty. 'It was to remind me of my duty.'

'Your duty?' Gran asked even as she gestured to Aunt Meg to give him more enchanted tea.

Vir sighed, 'It's a long and really complicated story.' He thanked Aunt Meg with a gentle smile as she refilled his cup. 'I don't even know where to begin.'

'Well, the beginning is always a good place to start,' Gran said after Vir took a sip. 'Go on, tell us!'

'Do you know of the Cabal?'

Upon being greeted with a collective silence, Vir continued, 'My family belongs to a clandestine fellowship that traces its origins to before history even began being recorded. It is called the Cabal. Aishwarya's family is also a part of it. Some say that the Cabal existed even when Atlantis floated upon the ocean, and that it led to its eventual sinking. Families that are a part of it are born to lead and control the world. It's not that we seek global domination. We already have it. Our duty is to merely maintain that control through any means possible.

'The best way to keep the power alive is through marriage among Cabal families. When a male heir is born, the elders arrange his match with a suitable girl from another Cabal family. In my case, that girl is Aishwarya.'

I looked towards Aunt Meg, wondering if her truth serum was working. She nodded, reading my mind.

'So … your family controls the world?' Aunt Claudine asked.

'Only a small part of it. It's a complex hierarchy. Imagine if the world is a human body. The heart is core of the Cabal that consists of the thirteen original bloodlines of power. They're the board of directors who take care of the larger narrative of history. From war to global economies, and even colonizing and de-colonizing nations.

'Think of them like primary colours that are at their purest state. Aishwarya's and my family are a result of those colours mixing together over millennia. We're heavily diluted to form our own individual shades, and in the scheme of things, our family are like the fingertips of the human body that represents the world. Our power and reach is nothing compared to those who sit at the heart. However, it's far greater than what most people believe. And thus, through our marriage, we're supposed to start a whole new off-shoot to the bloodline.'

'And thus,' Gran sipped her tea, 'You and Aishwarya are said to take over control after your marriage?'

'In a matter of speaking, yes.' Vir sighed, 'Like all children of the Cabal, we have been extensively trained in the five core disciplines of control—government, religion, finance, science and mass media. Eventually, we assume high positions in all these areas of power. Never in front of the camera, of course. We leave that to outsiders who are willing to sell their souls.'

'Sell their souls?' Gran asked. As much as she tried to hide it, I could see her spine stiffen.

'Yes. The only way many rise in the world is through the act of selling their soul. A Faustian pact, so to speak. But instead of making a deal with the Devil, they make one with the Cabal. All those you see in the spotlight—world leaders, members of royal families, captains of industry, CEOs, even mass entertainers with huge fan followings—are mere puppets who've sold their soul to the Cabal. They hold no real power. They're merely following orders, allowing the grand plan of the Cabal to succeed.'

'And what exactly is this grand plan?' Gran asked.

'Chaos!' Vir declared. He sipped the truth serum before continuing. 'It is what I've been taught since childhood. You see, all creation comes from the "Source". Some call it God, others call it Brahman, some even call it the Intelligent Infinity. When the Source becomes "aware" of itself, it seeks to experience itself, and thus we have a Creator that is born or manifested. Each universe is assigned its own individual creator—a subdivision of the original Creator. And thus, with each universe form many galaxies. Within each galaxy are solar systems, where planets revolve around the Sun—the Logos–or "God Form" that divides itself energetically to create various planets. Each planet has it's own Logos, and within that planet, there are various other Logos in the form of elements and nature. Thus we have various pantheons of ancient civilizations. It's why all planets, including the sun and moon, as well as, all forms of nature are always seen as divine. They are all but fragments of the Source.'

'But what does the Cabal have to do with all this?' Gran asked as Aunt Meg refreshed all our teas, including Vir's truth serum. 'Again, I only speak of what I've been taught.' Vir sipped on his enchanted brew, 'You, of course, know the story of Adam and Eve and the Serpent in the Garden of Eden?'

'Yes,' Gran said. 'According to Judeo-Christian beliefs, God—or Yahweh—created Adam and Eve and bestowed upon them all the divine beauty of the Garden of Eden.'

'Until, of course, Eve took a bite of the forbidden fruit of knowledge and fed it to Adam,' Aunt Claudine added.

'Which led to millennia of men blaming women for all miseries of the world,' said Aunt Meg.

'Very true!' Vir replied. 'However, it wasn't knowledge that they gained from the forbidden fruit—it was free will.'

Vir paused to let this sink in before continuing, 'The Cabal believes that Yahweh wanted his creation—mankind—to live in an absolute perfect harmony, to follow his divine will. However, he ignored a very important part of the Source—Darkness—for with infinite light comes infinite darkness. So, to balance Yahweh's enforcement of light, Lucifer "fell" from heaven to enforce free will, because free will is the divine right of the third density.'

'The third density?' I asked, confused.

Vir sipped his tea before answering. 'It is in service of the planet's evolution. You know of the seven chakras, don't you?'

We all nodded.

'Well, think of the evolution of our planet in the terms of the chakras. Each chakra represents a density. The first density, represented by the root chakra or muladhara, was when the world was a spinning ball of fire and chaos. Over millennia, it cooled into a lifeless mass. The second density, or the svadishtana chakra, is when water emerged, and life was created from its depths. Life made its way out if the water and populated the earth with flora and fauna. That's why water is seen as a divine mother in ancient cultures. Water is the womb that nourished life, which began as rocks from solidified lava, and then evolved into plants, trees and then animals. Some of which, through the process of evolution even exist till this date.

'Now tell me,' Vir asked, 'What separates Man from animals?'

'The ego,' said Gran, her eyes sparkling.

'Precisely, the ego is what led to Earth's evolution to the third density. Man sees himself as separate and above all of nature because of his ego. And thus, he seeks to dominate and control nature to his will. Plants blindly follow the divine rhythms that nature by automatically taking in their energy from the Sun to grow and prosper. Animals blindly follow nature's divine rhythms as well. Even the most carnivorous predators only hunt when hungry, because that's how nature created them.

They harmoniously flow seamlessly like the divine waters of the earth. As earth shifted to the third density, Man came into being. Any guesses which chakra this corresponds to?'

'Fire!' I answered. 'The manipura chakra.'

'Bingo! When Ancient Man struck two rocks, he discovered fire, and thus sought to control nature. Through this, he learned farming, which is nothing but manipulation of Earth through the elements. Thus allowing civilizations to be created from small farming communities to the political nations we see today.'

'Okay, but what does this have to do with free will and Lucifer?' Aunt Meg emerged from the kitchen table with a charcuterie board laden with various cheeses and cold cuts. There had been no time to cook up a proper breakfast.

'Well, please understand that this is all just a metaphor.' Vir continued, 'Imagine in the Garden of Eden, Adam and Eve had no control of the elements. They just existed in their bubble and were in a way, slaves to their surroundings, depending only on what was created. When Lucifer descended upon earth, he gifted them the Forbidden Fruit, which basically awakened their free will. True, in the Bible, they say that Adam and Eve discovered their nakedness and covered themselves out of shame. However, man needs clothing to protect himself from the elements. That free will not only helped man create fire, but also to grow crops and build homes. The earth was full of potential, and only man had the free will to go beyond the surface of what appears before. God created the grapes, but man, through his free will learned to ferment those grapes into wine. Thus, had they just remained faithful to Yahweh, mankind would have remained naked in paradise, ignorant of their potential. However, because free will is the divine right of mankind, who are the reflection of the Source in the third density of existence, Lucifer had to feed Adam and Eve the forbidden fruit.'

'So you're saying,' Aunt Meg started as she smeared a cracker with cream cheese before placing a slice of salami on top, 'Lucifer feeding Adam and Eve the Forbidden fruit led mankind developing an ego, which eventually led to the evolution of modern civilization?'

'Even social media is basically a consequence of Lucifer feeding them the forbidden fruit. Free will allowed man to basically invent. Thus we have the world we're in.'

'So, you're all essentially Devil Worshipers?' I asked.

This was beginning to get really twisted.

'Well, the Devil is just a Christian concept,' Vir replied. 'A bogeyman to control the masses in blindly following dogma—a dogma created by man himself. Remember, Yahweh is just one of the many diluted forms of the Source, as are the various other divine beings of all the world's religions. We humans are an even more diluted form of the Source. As is Lucifer. Lucifer is known as the fallen angel, but he is much more than that. Lucifer is the morning and the evening star. He who rises before the sun and shines brightly even after it has set. Lucifer is a divine being who is responsible not only for mankind gaining free will, but also for the planet to evolve from the second density to the third. Eventually, it will be Lucifer who will make the planet evolve into the fourth density.'

'And how exactly does Lucifer plan on doing that?' Aunt Claudine dipped a cracker into hummus before biting into it.

'As he's always done—allowing mankind to choose.' Vir replied.

'Choose what?' Gran sipped her tea.

'Well, now that we're in the third density, all life has to evolve further. Evolution is the natural path of energy. However, since free will is the gift of the third density, man has to choose between the path of service to others, as well as, service to self. Service to others is in the form of helping others in life—be it through charity, or goodwill, or even something like teaching yoga or anything that helps increase love and peace in our lives. Service to self is basically when we want to only selfishly hoard wealth and power at the expense of others. In service to others, we uplift mankind. But in service to self, we only uplift ourself at the expense of mankind.'

'So then isn't your family and the Cabal basically choosing the path of service to self?' Gran desperately needed more tea.

'Not exactly,' Vir continued, 'the Cabal is essentially the divine offshoot of the Lucifer Soul Group.'

'Come again?' Aunt Meg refreshed our teas, and gave Vir an even more potent dose of her truth serum.

'The Cabal—at least the thirteen original bloodlines—believe that they contain Lucifer's blood within them. As you know, before Eve, Adam was born with Lilith.'

'Yes, the first woman,' said Gran. 'She was attached to Adam by the tailbone.'

'But she was banished from the Garden when she refused to submit to Adam,' Aunt Meg added.

'Yes, however, Lilith was not just human. Adam contained Yahweh's essence that wanted everything to be controlled by his will. Lilith contained the polarity of the feminine divine force—the Goddess principle,' said Vir. 'Thus, when Adam tried to dominate the Goddess, Lilith's refusal to submit led her to reject Yahweh's desire for full control. After she was banished, she mated with Lucifer, and it was their offspring that eventually led to the creation of the thirteen original bloodlines.'

'So … you're basically a descendant of Lucifer and Lilith?' Gran asked, her eyes wide.

'A very distant descendant of Lucifer and Lilith,' nodded Vir. 'As is Aishwarya.'

'And how exactly does the Cabal fit into the evolution of the planet?' Aunt Meg asked. 'Simple, we create chaos in the world, testing the will of man. Every single decision man makes impacts his soul. From lying, cheating and even murder. From giving birth, helping the elderly and the less fortunate, and even choosing between chocolate or vanilla—all of it accumulates karma. The more karma man accumulates, the more he remains trapped within the earth. Being yogis, you know that the only way to overcome the trap of constant karmic cycles, is to detach and attain moksha—the ultimate liberation.'

We all nodded collectively.

'Well,' Vir cracker in hummus and placed a green olive on top before eating it. 'This is delicious by the way!'

Aunt Meg smiled as Vir continued, 'The ultimate liberation just means mankind evolves into a fourth density being. If they choose the path of service to others, they evolve into angels or devas. If they choose the path of service to self, they evolve into demons or asuras. The Cabal and their descendants already know their future is to evolve into demons in the fourth density. While we remain in this earthly third density, our duty is to create so much chaos that man has to exercise his free will in order to evolve.'

'You're destined to eventually become a demon?' I asked, horrified. I didn't want any of this to be true.

'Unfortunately, yes!' Vir answered. He grimaced as he sensed my heart break into a million pieces. 'This is all part of the divine play, and the Cabal and its descendants are playing the role of the divine antagonist. The fact that I'm born into this family is because it's my karmic destiny to help prepare the world for "the Harvest".'

'*The Harvest?*' All of us exclaimed in a unison of shock.

'Haven't you wondered why the world has become far more chaotic in the last couple of centuries than ever before? We're on the cusp of evolving into the fourth density. As more and more plants and animals are becoming extinct, the human population is growing at alarming rates. Souls are being trapped in the human plane because of accumulating karmas that are so heavy that attaining moksha is all the more difficult on the path of service to others. Thus, the Cabal is bent on bringing more chaos into the world, luring mankind to choose the path of service to self. The cusp officially begun on the twenty-first of December in the year 2012.'

'When people were worried that the world would come to an end due to the Mayan Calendar ending?' exclaimed Aunt Claudine.

Vir nodded. 'The souls of the humans that have been dying after that date are either ascending to the angelic realms or descending to the demonic realms, depending on their karmas. They will respectively evolve into fourth-density angels or fourth-density demons. However, it's not that easy.'

'How so?' Gran asked.

'Imagine your soul upon dying is being measured on a divine scale.'

'Like how in Egyptian mythology, Anubis measures our heart against a feather,' Aunt Meg added 'If the heart weighs heavier than the feather, the soul is sent to the realm of the underworld. If the heart weighs lighter than the feather, the soul is sent to the realm of the Gods.'

'Exactly!' Vir sipped on his truth serum, 'Thus, in a way, we're enabling man to choose whether to keep his heart heavier than the proverbial feather or not. After December 2012, all humans souls are being measured on this divine scale. However, the rule is, the soul must be at least 51 per cent in service to others to evolve into a fourth density angel, while 95 per cent in service to self to evolve into a fourth density demon. The fourth density is, after all, represented by the heart chakra. The heart is, after all, the source of all our divine power. That's why lovers pledge to give each other their hearts instead of their brains, or kidneys, or livers. Just by being born into this family, my heart is already heavier than that feather.'

'Vir … ' I said softly. The shards of my heart disintegrated further.

'And this is why Aishwarya attacked us. To remind me of my duty to not only my family, but the Cabal. And, of course, my eventual destiny.'

The room descended into an ominous silence when he finished speaking.

'What's after the fourth density?' I couldn't help but ask.

'Well, there is the fifth density, which is represented by the throat chakra. That's the centre of communication. That's the realm of all the spiritual messengers—the archangels, the prime demons in Judeo-Christian beliefs, but also the various deities of other religions across the world—Thor, Zeus, Indra, Osiris, Isis, etcetra. This is the realm where major battles are fought between divine beings of light and their nemeses—deities of chaos and darkness. After that is the sixth density, where the paths merge.'

'Merge?' asked Gran.

'Yes, merge!' Vir ate a slice of apple and continued, 'Like how in the third density, the path divided into the paths of service to self and service to others, they merge back into a singular path in the sixth density. Remember, we are all part of the divine ultimate Source. The sixth density is represented by the third eye chakra. The chakra that banishes all illusions and shows us the truth. And the truth is that all dualities—good and bad, light and darkness, joy and sorrow, service to others and service to self—they're all part of the Source. When the soul ascends to this state, it's commonly known as achieving Christ or Krishna Consciousness. After the soul has attained that, it has the choice to either return to earth and participate in the divine play of the third density, or merge with the Source in the seventh density—the crown chakra. We all will eventually get there. It's what we're destined to do. However, the path we choose is what makes this divine play, all the more interesting.'

Vir's words caused us all to descend into an ominous silence.

Finally, I spoke up. 'Where does that leave us?' I asked. My eyes couldn't hide the pain of knowing Vir was born to be a demon.

Before he could reply, the intercom of the gate buzzed. Aunt Meg went to answer, before rushing back in moments later yelling, 'It's Mr Rathi and he's demanding that Vir come out at once, or else they'll storm in with a bunch of armed guards!'

'Fuck!' Vir shouted, standing up. 'I must—'

'Come with me!' Aunt Claudine said, grabbing his hand. 'There's a secret passage that leads from the house to the main road.'

'*Secret passage?*' I asked, stunned to learn yet another secret.

'Never mind that!' Aunt Claudine then turned to Gran and Aunt Meg and said, 'Stall them for about five minutes!'

After Aunt Claudine and Vir had left through the kitchen door and disappeared into the back garden, Gran and Aunt Meg walked over to the front door. Taking a deep breath, they pressed the button that unlocked the front gate. Within a few moments, they opened the front door before Mr Rathi could knock.

'Mr Rathi!' Gran said, smiling sweetly at the waiting man. 'So nice of you to visit!'

Chapter Twenty

'Madam ji, I don't have time for tea!' Mr Rathi protested as Gran and Aunt Meg whisked him inside after making sure he removed his shoes.

'Oh nonsense!' said Gran, sitting down beside him on the large floral couch in the living room.

'There's always time for tea!' declared Aunt Meg, handing him a cup of lavender tea that she re-heated from earlier. True, she hated doing that, but time wasn't exactly on her side.

'B-B-But Madam ji—'

'I hope you understand that we don't allow guns inside the house,' said Gran, feigning grave concern. 'Guns aren't very "yogic", after all. You wouldn't want to be responsible for tampering with the spiritual energies of a yogic environment, now would you, Mr Rathi?'

'Drink up!' said Aunt Meg. She was being uncharacteristically cheerful. 'Wouldn't want your tea to get cold.'

I couldn't help but smile as I saw Mr Rathi sip his tea hesitantly so that he wouldn't offend Gran and Aunt Meg, who could be quite intimidating when they laid out their 'charm'.

'Oh, this is really nice tea!' Mr Rathi exclaimed.

'Why, thank you!' said Aunt Meg, grinning. 'I grow the lavender myself.'

'Wonderful!' After another sip, Mr Rathi regained his resolve. 'Madam ji, we're looking for Vir baba.'

'And you thought he'd be here?' asked Gran.

'Well, we—'

'Honestly, considering all the guards you keep around your home, I would have thought they would be aware of Vir's whereabouts twenty-four-seven.'

'Yes, but—'

'Of course, boys will be boys,' said Aunt Meg, trying her best not to roll her eyes at her own statement. 'One can't always keep them caged.'

'Of course, but—'

'Now, honestly, Mr Rathi!' Gran said. 'Do you really expect us to know where he would be?'

'We haven't exactly seen him since the Rajanis stopped coming for yoga classes,' Aunt Meg added.

'Of course, there was that rather delightful dinner next door,' Gran reminded Aunt Meg.

'Ah yes!' Aunt Meg exclaimed. 'How could I possibly forget that very *delightful* dinner?'

'It *was* delightful. Wasn't it, Jai?' Gran turned to me, prompting me to nod cheerfully.

'Yes, but—' Mr Rathi tried again, but was interrupted this time by a knock on the door.

'Now who on earth could that be?' Gran waved her hand at Aunt Meg to go answer it. As she left to do so, Gran turned to Mr Rathi and asked, 'Are you enjoying the tea?'

'Oh!' Mr Rathi said, hurriedly taking another sip, 'Very much so!'

'I'm glad!' Gran declared.

'Look who decided to join us for tea!' Aunt Meg said as she came in with Damyanti, who was looking as elegant as ever in a rather lovely azure sari. I supposed it was too early for heavy jewels, but she, of course, had her mangalsutra on.

'I'm sorry for the intrusion,' Damyanti said even as Mr Rathi stood promptly to attention, bowing ever so slightly. 'But I don't know if you've heard the news?'

'The news?' Gran asked even as Aunt Meg gestured Damyanti to the couch. Mr Rathi wouldn't dare sit in her presence and so he remained standing.

'Well, our good friends at the police department informed us that Vir's bike was found abandoned in the middle of the road ...'

'Oh dear!' Gran was so good at feigning surprise! 'That doesn't sound good! But what brings you all here?'

'Well, we know Vir and Jai would often go off on bike rides in the middle of the night,' said Damyanti, looking at me. 'And so we thought Jai might know where he was.'

'Bike rides in the middle of the night?' Gran exclaimed, shooting me a look.

Before I could say anything, Aunt Claudine sauntered into the living room. 'My my my!' she exclaimed. 'What do we have here!'

'Ah, there you are, my dear!' Gran said. 'Did you hear that Vir's motorcycle was found abandoned in the middle of the road?'

'Oh dear!' Aunt Claudine said in a show of surprise that was as good as Gran's. 'Shouldn't you all be searching for him?'

'We are, but—' Damyanti began, before being interrupted by her phone ringtone. 'Excuse me !' She smiled as she fished it out of her blue Birkin, 'Hare Krishna! Oh, that's wonderful … I'll just send Tejeshwar over … Thank you! Jai Shri Krishna!'

Damayanti smiled and she breathed a sigh of relief. 'Vir's back home!'

'Oh, how wonderful!' Gran cheered. Damyanti ordered Mr Rathi to return home immediately, and he scurried off.

'I'm truly sorry for the inconvenience—' began Damyanti as she turned towards us.

'Nonsense!' Gran declared. 'We're just glad he's all right. Now, my dear, we can't let you leave without having some tea first.'

'Oh, that's really kind, but I really don't want to be a—'

'Oh, it's no bother at all!' Aunt Meg said. 'I've just brewed a fresh pot!'

Before Damyanti could protest further, Aunt Meg headed over to the kitchen with Aunt Claudine following.

After a moment of awkward silence, Damyanti said, 'I'm truly sorry for disturbing all of you this morning.'

'Oh, don't be silly!' Gran said with a smile. 'We can imagine how disturbing this must be for all of you.'

'It's not just that,' Damyanti sighed. 'Vir hasn't been the same since he stopped taking his medication …'

'Medication?' Gran asked.

'Well, it's a long story, I wouldn't want to bore—'

'We have the time,' said Gran, placing a comfortingly hand on her shoulder.

Damyanti sighed and nodded. 'The thing is,' she said hesitatingly. 'Vir was diagnosed as bipolar and schizophrenic a few years ago.'

'Oh my!' Gran placed her hand on her heart.

'It was around the time his father passed away,' Damyanti continued. 'Vir suddenly began accusing Rajani sahab and me of some grand conspiracy, something about plotting against him and his parents. Many times he would have violent outbursts, mostly directed towards me ...'

Gran comforted Damyanti as she shed a few tears, but my mind was racing at a million miles an hour. *Is Vir sick?* I wondered. *Did he make all that up about the Cabal and demons and stuff?*

Damyanti dabbed away her tears with the tissue Gran handed her before continuing, 'When he was in a stable condition with the medication, Rajani sahab thought it would be best if he went to Mayo to complete his schooling. He did rather well there, even skipping the eleventh grade because of his exemplary performance. However, around the time we moved here—right after he finished school—he began acting up again. My husband and I would try our best to help him get better, but he would continue to rebel with one violent outburst after another. You saw how he almost killed himself that night when you saved him. We hoped that he would start his medication again, but he refused to.'

'Clearly,' Gran smiled thoughtfully.

'When we woke up this morning to the news of his abandoned bike, we were all so worried—'

'Who's up for some tea?' called Aunt Meg as she returned to the living room carrying a sterling silver tea tray. Aunt Claudine followed carrying a platter of sliced tea cake.

'Oh, you didn't have to go through all this trouble!' said Damyanti as I promptly got up to pull the wooden coffee table closer to the couch.

'Oh, no trouble!' declared Aunt Meg as she poured a steaming cup of tea for Damyanti. 'We're always happy to have people over for tea.'

'And do try the cake!' Aunt Claudine said, handing her a slice that had been smeared with preserve. 'This is the preserve you sent us!'

'Oh, that's lovely!' Damyanti sounded delighted as she took the cake. 'I do again apologize for the trouble we caused when we sent Tejeshwar over to ask you to cut the trees.'

'Water under the bridge,' said Gran. 'And I must say, your preserves and pickles are absolutely delightful.'

'Thank you!' Damyanti blushed as she bit into her cake. 'I've always loved to cook, ever since I was a child. Of course, now I hardly get the time, but when Tejeshwar told us that you wouldn't cut the trees, I felt it would be best to make a peace offering. I must say, those are the sweetest oranges I have ever tasted. Even today, we make our morning juices with them.'

'That's nice, my dear!' Gran said, smiling as Aunt Meg and Aunt Claudine took their seats.

'So, what did we miss?' Aunt Claudine asked as she bit into her cake.

'Well, Damyanti was telling us about Vir being bipolar and schizophrenic; he's gone off his meds.'

'Oh dear!' Aunt Claudine's eyes widened.

'That's scary!' Aunt Meg chimed in.

'Indeed!' Gran said, and then turned to Damyanti. 'Please have your tea before it gets cold.'

'Ah yes!' Damyanti sniffed the aroma as she lifted the silver cup. 'Oh my, this is heavenly! What's in it?'

'Oh, just some peppermint, ginger and lemongrass,' replied Aunt Meg.

'Sweetened with some organic honey we have shipped from Kashmir,' Aunt Claudine added.

'It's got a hint of saffron too,' said Gran. 'Drink up, my dear!'

Damyanti smiled and took a long sip. 'Oh this is delicious! Have you used fresh herbs?'

'Straight from our garden!' Aunt Meg flashed a diabetic smile.

After Damyanti took another long sip, Gran said, 'So, my dear, you were telling us about Vir's condition.'

'Ah yes!' Damyanti took a third sip before placing the cup, now half-empty, on the coffee table. 'Well, you see, Vir has been off his meds, which is causing him to have these violent outbursts. Of course, the medication is just to keep him numb so that he curbs his rebellion and just follows through with the protocol as dictated by the Cabal.' Damyanti's eyes widened as she clasped both hands over her mouth. We all exchanged knowing looks. The truth serum had kicked in!

'You were saying, my dear?' Gran eyes twinkled as she smiled.

Damyanti shook her head as her eyes remained widened with horror with her hands firmly clasped on her mouth. Then she suddenly got up and made a dash for the door. Before she could even leave the room, however, Gran waved her fingers and the living room doors automatically closed. Aunt Meg swiftly conjured the silver cord from her navel and attached it to Damyanti, forcing her to walk back to the couch and sit down.

'W-W-What's going on?' Damyanti cried, visibly shaking.

'There, there, my dear!' Gran said, smiling sweetly as Aunt Claudine walked over to Damyanti and started to glamour her with her eyes. 'You wouldn't want to be so rude as to leave without finishing your tea.'

'I wouldn't dream of it!' said Damyanti as she fell under Aunt Claudine's spell.

'Of course!' said Gran. 'Now, please, have some more tea and tell us about this Cabal.'

Damyanti slowly sipped her tea and began, 'The Cabal is all powerful and all-knowing. They're far greater than you can ever imagine.'

'So, all that about Vir being bipolar was ...?'

'Sheer nonsense to throw you all off the track. We are sworn to keep the secrecy of the Cabal. Vir's father refused, so Rajani sahab and Bade Papa had to dispose of him and Vir's mother. The Cabal doesn't tolerate those who refuse Lucifer's will.'

'And how did you get involved with them?' Gran pressed.

'I was working as Rajani sahab's executive assistant, but he saw how ambitious I was, and initiated me by making me sell my soul.'

'And how did you sell your soul?'

'Like how all outsiders do. He took me to the grand lodge in Jodhpur for my initiation.'

'Grand lodge?'

'Every major city around the world has a grand lodge for the Cabal. All members meet there regularly where they not only initiate those who wish to sell their souls, but also follow through with the orders given by the those who are at the heart of the Cabal.'

'And where exactly is the heart of the Cabal?'

'That I'm unaware of. I am not a bloodline member.'

'But the Rajanis are?'

'Yes, as are many families throughout the nation. Vir is being groomed to take over on his twenty-third birthday after he marries Aishwarya.'

'He won't!' I burst out, unable to control myself. 'You can't do that to him!'

'There's nothing you can do about it!' retorted Damyanti. 'It is his destiny. He will follow through unless he wishes to meet the same fate as his parents!'

Before I could say another word, Gran shot me a stern look that silenced me. She turned back to Damyanti and asked, 'What does the Cabal seek to do with Vir?'

'I do not know as I am not a bloodline member. However, I do know that the future of the nation depends on Vir marrying Aishwarya on his twenty-third birthday.'

'Why his twenty-third birthday?'

'Again, I do not know. I am not a bloodline member. I am merely there for ceremonial purposes and to be the matriarch of the Rajani family till Aishwarya joins our family through marriage!'

'How empowering!' Aunt Meg couldn't help but remark.

'What will happen to Vir now?' Gran asked after ensuring Damyanti drank more tea.

'He will be placed under house arrest, and Rajani sahab will break his rebellious resolve.'

'How will he do that?'

'Usually a good belting works. If not, we will have him shipped off to a secret location, where senior members of the Cabal will do it for us.'

'And how will *they* do that?'

'Again, I do not know. I am not a bloodline member.'

'That's all we're going to get out of her,' said Gran with a grimace. 'Let her go.' She turned to Damyanti and said, 'My dear, you'll be kind enough to forget everything you've revealed to us, won't you?'

'Of course!' said Damyanti with a smile, still lost in Aunt Claudine's glamour spell.

Gran waved her hands, making Aunt Meg and Aunt Claudine break their respective spells. As Damyanti snapped out of her trance, Gran continued as if nothing happened. 'My my, look at the time! I'm sure you must be on your way!'

Damyanti checked her phone. 'Oh dear! It's almost noon! I should be heading back!' She got up and politely said goodbye. Aunt Meg escorted her out.

When Aunt Meg returned, Gran turned to me. 'Okay, I guess now it's time we tell you all about that mark on your chest!'

Even after all the crazy things I'd heard and experienced that morning, I was still not prepared for what I was about to learn.

Chapter Twenty-One

'Why did you not tell me this before?'

My head was spinning after listening to what Gran had to say.

'Now now, there's no need to panic!' said Gran, offering me some more tea to calm my raging nerves.

'Panic doesn't even begin to describe what I'm feeling,' I retorted in a cluster-fuck of emotional rage.

'Well, to be honest, we didn't really expect it to happen so soon and—'

'Clearly!' I shouted, pacing up and down the kitchen. 'I mean, it's one thing to find out that the love of my life is basically destined to lead a Cabal and evolve into a demon—'

'The love of your life? Really?' Aunt Meg said sarcastically.

'Meg! Be a little sensitive!' Aunt Claudine snapped.

'They've barely known each other for a month, and at sixteen, what does he know about—'

'Margaret!' Gran said impatiently. 'This isn't the time!' She turned to me and began, 'Jai, please be seated and calm down so that we can explain further.'

'What else is there to explain? I've already heard that your father—my great-grandfather—was an occultist who not only sold his soul to the Cabal, but also evolved into a demon and then marked me to follow in his infernal footsteps? Wonderful! Fabulous! Oh, this is just fucking awesome! What's next? Are you going to tell me that I'm the spawn of Lucifer?'

'Are you finished?' Gran was in no mood to indulge me.

'No, I'm not finished!' I yelled, continuing to pace. 'I'm so not fucking finished!'

'Fine, go on, get it out of your system. When you're done with your temper-tantrum, we'll discuss this further.' Gran folded her arms and sat steadfastly on her chair.

Letting out a sigh of sheer frustration, I plopped back down and took a deep breath. When I stopped shaking, I took a sip of the freshly brewed lavender tea and said to Gran, 'Okay, I'm calm.'

'Are you absolutely sure?' Gran asked, locking eyes with me.

I took another deep, cleansing breath and another sip of tea before nodding.

'Okay,' said Gran. 'Yes, Daddy was an occultist who sold his soul to the Cabal, but there's a reason why he did so. You see, Jai, the magic we practice—which is passed down by the women of our clan—it's the natural magical life-force that makes the world go around. It's pure! It's divine! It's what makes us witches—'

'You were the first boy born in our family, and it took us all by surprise,' Aunt Claudine chimed in. 'It's because we were always taught that men had no access to this natural magical force.'

'But since you're gay,' Aunt Meg added. 'It meant that you had access to our magical lineage.'

'I know that,' I said, picking up my teacup. 'Aunt Claudine explained it to me.'

'You're male,' Gran continued. 'And Daddy wanted a male heir to pass on his demonic lineage.'

'So, only men can evolve into demons?'

'Well …' Aunt Meg was about to go on a feminist tirade, but Gran shut her up with a stern look.

'Not exactly. However, masculinity and patriarchy doesn't have access to our kind of magic,' said Gran. 'But there is magic that's accessible to them. It's a kind of magic that was developed by ancient occultists such as Plato, Ptolemy and Solomon, and passed down through the Middle Ages by Heinrich Cornelius Agrippa, Nostradamus and John Dee. It was further developed by the likes of Grigori Rasputin, Eliphas Levi, Papus, Arthur Edward Waite and Aleister Crowley. It is demonic magic.'

'Demonic magic?'

'As you've seen, our magic flows through our veins like a wild river. It's the goddess energy that is a birth right of women. Men, however, have been jealous of that since the beginning of time. The only way they could tap into the magical energy is through making pacts with demons through complex ceremonial rituals—usually performed in large gatherings with precise astronomical and astrological calculations.'

'Okay, but how does your father fit into all this?'

'Unbeknown to us, Daddy was a power-hungry despot. Yes, he sold his soul to the Cabal, but that's only because he couldn't access the magic that Mummy had in her naturally.'

'All this for power?'

'Never underestimate a man's thirst for power. History has taught us well about the amount of blood that's shed in the name of seizing power.'

'How come your mother didn't know about this? Why didn't she stop him?'

'Unfortunately, she was in love.' Gran sighed.

'It wasn't the first time that love has led to the downfall of a witch,' Aunt Claudine remarked.

'Or a woman, for that matter,' Aunt Meg added.

'What about the mark in the shape of an eye on my chest?'

'The eye is the symbol of the Cabal,' Gran replied. 'Inspired by the all-seeing-eye of Providence, it serves as a reminder that the Cabal is watching our every move. It symbolizes the eye of Lucifer, who is always watching man's actions in order to judge souls in the afterlife.'

'I'm being spied on?'

'Not exactly, it just means that you've been given access to both our kind of natural magic as well as demonic magic. We ourselves have no idea of what your magical potential is. It's far greater than ours! However, it all depends on the path your soul has chosen.'

'And what path has my soul chosen?'

A collective silence fell upon us.

'Well?'

Gran sighed, 'We don't know!' She pushed her cup aside. 'All we know is that it was best we teach you the values we had. The rest is your own journey.'

'What if I don't want to take this journey?'

'You have no choice!' Gran said with a grimace. 'Your soul had already chosen its path before you were born to us. Before Daddy passed from the physical realm into the demonic realm, he performed a mighty ritual in which he wished for a male heir. We thought his ritual didn't work because I never gave birth to a son.'

'However, Jemima did!' Aunt Claudine said.

'How does my mother fit into all this?'

'We don't know,' Aunt Meg said. 'However, she's the only one of us who got married and had a child in wedlock.'

'That was unlike most women of our lineage,' said Gran. 'It took us all by surprise when she did, but of course, she was young …'

'And in love!' Aunt Claudine sighed.

'This is so messed up!' I buried my head in my arms on the table.

'Magic is messy! Our magic and demonic magic too. That is why not everyone can walk a magical path. The scars are too deadly for most to bear.'

'So now what?'

'We don't know!' Gran said with a sigh.

'This is unchartered territory for all of us,' said Aunt Claudine, running her fingers through her hair.

'All we can hope is that we've taught you well, and that you make the best choices possible,' Aunt Meg said.

'It's the best we could do,' said Gran softly, placing her palm upon mine.

'What about Vir?'

'What about Vir?' Aunt Meg shot me a look.

'How do we save him?'

'He's not ours to save!' Aunt Meg replied bluntly.

Before I could say anything, Gran said, 'His destiny is mapped out for him. There's nothing we can really do about it.'

'But Gran!'

'Dear boy, we're powerless compared to the Cabal! We're just three witches who live their own life. He's part of a sinister legacy that's been in control of our realm since the beginning of time. It's a miracle that they don't know our true identity!'

'What do you mean?'

'Who do you think was responsible for burning witches?' Aunt Meg cut in. 'By disempowering women—especially witches—the Cabal has spread its toxic patriarchy down the millennia. Patriarchy has always feared the true power of womenkind, and thus actively sought to suppress us! That's why we keep our powers a secret from the world, making them believe we're just yoga teachers or tarot readers or even reiki healers. Through our silence, we've been able to survive!'

'But surely there must be a way!'

'If there is, we don't know it,' Gran grimaced.

'Gran, I know Vir, he's not like the rest of—'

'Oh, shut up!' Aunt Meg snapped.

'Margaret!' Gran exclaimed.

'No, this is ridiculous!' Aunt Meg roared. She looked me dead in the eye. 'Just because you've spent a month with him, you think that you know him so well? It's only today that we discovered that not only does he belong to the Cabal, but is also set to take charge after his marriage to Aishwarya! You know nothing about him!'

'That's not fair!' I shouted back.

'Life isn't fair!' Aunt Meg yelled louder, standing up. 'I've already lost one sister because she fell in love! I won't let you endanger any of us because you think you've fallen in love! Love isn't the path for us witches! Love is what curses us! It's best you just forget him!'

'Margaret, that is enough!' Gran said, standing too.

'He deserves to know the truth!' Aunt Meg shot back.

Before Gran could say anything, I ran up back to my room. It's only after I locked the door did I allow myself to howl. I could feel my eyes burn as tears rolled down and the veins on my throat almost popped with each painful wail. I couldn't believe all that I had heard today! I refused to believe it! This can't be the way I'm supposed to live my life—a life lived in secrecy without knowing the joys of love. *Fuck magic!* I thought furiously. *Fuck the Cabal! Fuck this fucking eye on my chest!*

I ripped my shirt off and stared at the eye on my chest with rage, and then began beating my chest with my fists. *Fuck you! Fuck all of you! Fuck this cursed life!* If this is what it meant to live a magical life, I wanted nothing to do with it! Fuck it! FUCK IT ALL.

I collapsed on my knees, with my chest now covered in indigo bruises. But the pain was nothing compared to what was in my heart! I couldn't give up on Vir. My heart wouldn't let me. There had to be a way! There just had to be! If only I knew how.

For the first time in my life, I wished I had a mother.

Chapter Twenty-Two

'Waheguru ji!'

I bowed my head as the attendant handed me my token after taking my shoes before I entered the sacred space of the Bangla Sahib Gurudwara. After washing my hands in the communal sink, I dipped my feet into a trough of flowing water, and then touched my forehead to the first of many white marble steps that led up to the grand courtyard.

I had always marvelled at the large gilded dome that crowned the holy structure. It was a prime example of eighteenth-century architecture, though over the years many modern additions had been added. These new constructions mimicked the old style but couldn't compare to the original structure. When I was a child, it would shimmer under the glow of the full moon. Now floodlights illuminate it under the smoggy night sky. Nevertheless, it remained a work of beauty.

Even so close to the witching hour, people flooded to offer prayers at the gurudwara. The doors to the heavens truly have no closing time. At least it wasn't as crowded as it usually is during the day. As I arrived at the topmost step, I picked out a saffron scarf to wrap around my head. I joined my hands in namaste as

I chanted a holy verse that Gran had taught me. It was from the Rehras Sahib—the evening prayers of my father's family.

I entered the grand gilded doors and kept my head bowed as I walked the heavily carpeted path over to where the head priest sat before the sacred text—the Guru Granth Sahib. He was fanned by two attendants with silvery fluffy fans that represented the sacred hair of Guru Nanak, the first of the ten gurus.

Placing a hundred-rupee note in the donation pit, I prostrated before the holy text and offered a personal prayer, seeking help for my mission ahead. Of course, a short prayer would have to do, as there was a queue behind me. I then proceeded to donate another hundred to the holy minstrels, who were led by a melodious man whose eyes sparkling with spiritual fervour through his heavily bearded face. I made sure to add a donations for the accompanying harmonium and tabla player as I made my clockwise round of the holy square. Usually, I would sit for a bit and marvel at the large crystal chandelier that hung in the centre, but there were more pressing matters at hand.

Next, I stood in line for a serving of the holy Karah Prashad, which was served all day to all devotees. During the day, there would be two lines to accommodate the rush. However, at this hour, there was just one. I bowed and offered both hands out, right palm on top of the left. The sewadar smiled and served me a large handful of the delicious halwa made with sweetened wheat flour and desi ghee. I couldn't help but smile when I discovered that it was scrumptious as it used to be when I was a child. Devotion can even turn deathly venom into sacred ambrosia.

After taking a sip of the holy water offered by a turbaned volunteer, I whispered prayers as I damped my scalp with the few remaining drops still in my hands. I then headed to the Nishan Sahib, the tall flagpole that bore a triangular orange flag with the Khanda—the holy symbol of the Sikh faith. The Khanda depicted a double-edged sword surrounded by a chakkar in the middle, flanked by a pair of single-edged swords called kirpans that represented the dual characteristics of Miri-Piri. The symbol represented the integration of both the spiritual and temporal realms, treating both with equal sovereignty.

After touching my forehead to the base of the flagpole, I made a clockwise circle around it while chanting a verse of the Rehras Sahib. Then I headed over to the Sarovar, which is the holy pond of the gurudwara. Usually, devotees would immerse themselves in this pond as doing so was supposed to cleanse their body, mind and souls of all sins and their karmic repercussions. I, however, had different intentions.

With barely a minute left for the witching hour to begin, I looked around for a quiet spot to disrobe. I left my underwear on as Kachera, or underwear, is one of the divine five Ks of Sikhism, along with the Kesh—uncut hair covered in a turban; the Kanga—a comb to maintain the hair; the Kara—the iron bracelet of faith; and the Kirpan, which is the holy dagger.

As the witching hour began, I discretely stepped into the Sarovar. The large koi fish scattered hurriedly as I walked deeper into the pond. Once I was waist deep, I took a deep breath and chanted, '*Wahe Guruji ka Khalsa, Wahe Guruji ki Fateh*!' Then I immersed myself fully into the icy cold water that was warmed by divinity.

'I was wondering when you'd appear,' said the small boy—no more than eight years old—sitting at the bottom of the Sarovar in a perfect padmasana. Surrounding him was a halo of divine light that prevented the water from wetting his gold silken robes and matching turban.

I prostrated before the sacred being but he commanded me to arise. Touching my third eye with his ring finger, he blessed me with the ability to not only breathe underwater, but also speak.

'Praise to you, oh holy one!' I said as I sat in padmasana too, holding my hands in namaste. 'I come seeking your blessings for a task that perhaps is beyond my own individual capabilities.'

The boy smiled. 'The glories are in the Lord's own hand,' he said. 'He blesses those with whom he is pleased. You live your life making earnest efforts and make your life happy through rightful earnings. Meet the Lord through contemplation and your anxieties will be dispelled.'

'I am but one,' I said. 'And those I seek to fight are many and far more powerful and have many sinister forces at their command.'

'The evildoer is a demon, who knows not the Master,' said the boy. 'He is a madcap, who understands not his own self. The sinner, like the deer hunter, bows twice as much. What can be achieved by bowing the head when a man goes with a filthy mind? The blind fools are without wisdom and blind is their understanding. They who are bereft of the Lord's grace, obtain not honour ever. Foolish and unwise are they, who seek to rule over others. For the only one who is True is the Lord.'

'I'm fearful, oh holy one! Though my cause is noble, I fear that my actions could perhaps result in altering the fate of the world as a whole—'

The divine child interrupted me with a chuckle. 'There are millions of worlds below and above ours,' he said. 'Man's mind is tired of this great search. It cannot reach the end of His vastness. How can the infinite be reduced to the finite? You are the embodiment of light, O yogi! Recognize your essence. Make wisdom thy mother, contentment thy father and truthfulness thy brother. One whose heart is filled with his Infinite Light meets with Him and shall never again be separated from Him.'

'I am hardly one who could be called noble,' I said, bowing my head. 'Though I have trained well for this, my mind is filled with doubts and—'

'If we serve humanity in this world, then we would be welcomed in the court of God.'

I couldn't help but smile at the boy. 'How did you do it?' I asked. 'And at such a young age?'

He giggled and said, 'I just followed the fate laid before me. Like you, I was called to it at a young age. Without doubt, I followed through, and till my very last breath, I served as a divine medium of the Lord's work. My mission, however, ended before I could even turn nine. You have lived far longer. Surely, the Lord sees great virtue in your spirit, and thus grants you this long life. As long as you serve others and desire the good of mankind, you must perform your deeds with humility and follow through with your mission.' He smiled and extended his arms. 'Give me your right hand.'

I obeyed, turning my right palm upwards as I extended it to him. He gently placed both his cherubic palms around my wrist and closed his eyes. As he chanted under his breath, I could feel a surge of energy work its way up my veins and fill my heart, eventually spreading all over my body. Though we were underwater, I felt as though I was floating through the heavens above.

'Open your eyes, O yogi!'

Upon my doing so, I found a golden kara around my right wrist. Filled with a joy that I couldn't express, I prostrated before the divine child and thanked him profusely.

'Falseness shall come to an end,' the boy said as he raised his hand to bless me. 'Truth shall ultimately prevail.'

I bowed before him before swimming back up to the surface. As the first rays of the morning sun pierced through the darkness of the night sky, I took my first breath over water.

I'm coming for you, Vir.

Chapter Twenty-Three

I spent the entire day locked up in my bedroom trapped within the silence of my sorrow. My brain was numb from trying to process everything that had happened. Barely escaping death only to discover that the man I loved was destined for damnation—and if that wasn't enough, my own soul was marked to be sacrificed to the demonic cause by none other than my own great-grandfather, whose soul had descended to a demonic existence. The one thing that I truly sought—a love that could fill my soul—was considered to be a curse for me and my kind.

A knock on my bedroom door interrupted my wallowing.

'Hey!' It was Aunt Meg. 'You okay?'

I turned to lay on my side so that my back faced her. I was in no mood to talk to her after everything she had said to me.

'Still mad at me?' She walked in and closed the door behind her. I ignored her even when she lay down next to me. 'You know I love you, right?'

'Isn't love a curse for our kind?' I brushed her off as she tried to hug me.

'Only the romantic kind.' She wrapped her arms around me. 'The love we have for you is far deeper than that.'

'You could have fooled me!' I pushed her off again and sat up.

'I know I was harsh with you earlier,' said Aunt Meg. 'But understand that everything I said was for your own good. You're not the only one who's suffered a broken heart.'

I remained silent. Aunt Meg lifted my chin with her fingertip, making me look her in the eye. 'Jai, there's obviously more in your heart than the pain of losing Vir,' she said. 'This kind of silent anger can't just be over a boy, of all things …'

'Do you hate me, Aunt Meg?' I could tell that my question caught her by surprise.

'Heavens, no!' Aunt Meg gasped. 'What would make you think that?'

I shrugged. 'I don't know. Maybe because I'm a boy?'

She looked puzzled, so I continued, 'I mean, sometimes you keep going on and on about the evils of patriarchy and about how men have suppressed women and stuff. Sometimes I feel as though you're personally attacking me.'

'Oh sweetie, no!' cried Aunt Meg. She hugged me and kissed me on my cheeks. 'That's not true at all!'

'It sure feels that way sometimes,' I said, turning to stare at the floor.

Aunt Meg sighed. 'Jai, I don't hate you,' she said. 'I don't hate men either. Sure, I hate the toxic effects of patriarchy, and how it's so ingrained in the very part of the world we live in. However, maybe I sometimes do go overboard. Sometimes I forget you're a boy …'

I gave her a look, and she smiled in response. 'You know what I mean! But I can see how my behaviour is pretty toxic too.'

I sighed. 'Sometimes you can really be harsh, Aunt Meg. I know it's the way you love, but you know, it can really sting.'

'Jai, I'm truly sorry!' Aunt Meg's voice quivered a little. 'I can't even begin to imagine what you're going through. But know I'll always be by your side!'

'We all will!' chorused Aunt Claudine and Gran, who had decided that it was the right time to enter the room. They came and sat around me on my bed.

'Even if Daddy has marked you with the Eye of Lucifer, we'll never leave you!' Gran declared, embracing me. My aunts joined in the group hug.

'As for your Aunt Meg's harshness,' said Gran began. 'Think of her as the holy neem. Bitter in taste, but oh so good for you. Plus, I'm here to balance it out with my sweetness!'

'While I'm here to add that spice that makes life all the more fun!' Aunt Claudine added with a giggle as she ruffled my hair.

I couldn't help but crack a smile, though my heart still ached.

'Don't worry, my child,' Gran said as she sensed my pain. 'We may not be able to take on the Cabal, but when one door closes …'

'… a secret passage opens!' Aunt Claudine finished.

'What do you mean?'

We went down to the garden where the branches of the fruit trees hung over the boundary wall of the Rajani mansion.

'One of the many reasons we refused to let them chop off the trees was because they hid a little secret escape hatch!' Gran said with smile as she pulled at a stray branch that lay on the ground. My eyes widened when I realized the grass at that spot was just a small strip of Astroturf, which was lifted away when the branch was pulled. Underneath was a hatch with two wooden doors sealed by a big iron bolt.

'This is a secret underground passage that we had built into the house,' Gran explained. 'There's an array of tunnels and secret passageways underneath. Witches need to have a means of escape when times get drastic.'

'Is this how you got Vir home without anyone seeing him?' I asked Aunt Claudine.

She nodded. 'It leads straight to the gazebo by their pool. Thank God they let that be during their renovations.' Reading my mind, she added, 'Don't worry, I told Vir to come here after midnight, when the others in his household are fast asleep. You may not get to go on your nightly bike rides, but you're more than welcome to bring him home. Just be sure you let him go before the morning sun, so that they're none the wiser!'

'Speaking of which!' Aunt Meg said suddenly, checking the time on her phone. She kicked the iron bolt open. The doors opened and my heart skipped a beat as I saw Vir climbing a wooden ladder to the surface.

The minute he had pulled himself out into our garden, I jumped into his arms, kissing him so wildly that he almost fell back into the hatch.

'I think we should let them have their moment!' Gran said quickly. Aunt Meg closed the doors of the escape hatch and the three of them headed back inside.

'Have fun, you two!' Aunt Claudine called playfully.

'Use protection!' Aunt Meg warned.

I ignored them both and continued to kiss him wildly, running my fingers through his hair, pulling him close to me. It felt so good to feel his warmth against me …

'Ow!' he yelled out in pain as I squeezed a part of his back.

'What's wrong?' I asked, jumping off him.

Vir sighed and turned around to lift his T-shirt, revealing fresh bruises. He didn't have to explain that it was from his uncle belting him. I wanted to cry, but before I could shed a tear, he placed a finger on my lips to silence me, followed it with a tender kiss. 'Let's not waste whatever time we have on tears.'

'I promise I'll be gentle!' I kissed him back softly.

'Yeah right!' He teasingly grinned as he spanked me on my bottom.

Time flew by as we collapsed on my bed, naked and breathlessly gasping as we spent a couple of hours ravaging each other.

'How many Magdalena posters do you have?' He chuckled as I threw a pillow at him.

For the next few weeks, we fell into a routine that involved me waiting for him to climb out of the escape hatch at midnight, and at around four in the morning, helping him go back home before their night guards did their final patrol of the premises. Most of our hours together were spent in passion, but sometimes we did manage to talk.

'What're you thinking?' I asked him once as I rested my head upon his chest, allowing my mind to be soothed by the sound of his beating heart.

'I'm thinking about how I wish we could just escape from all this,' Vir replied, tracing the nape of my neck with his fingertip.

Kissing him on his chest, I said, 'Well, in a way, this is our escape.'

Vir sighed, 'You know what I mean …'

Before he could finish, I leaned in closer and kissed him softly. 'I do, but I don't want to spend the little time we have with each other worrying about vague what-ifs. I just want to use this time to enjoy what we have at present.'

He kissed me tenderly. 'Why are you so good to me?'

'Because you deserve every bit of it!' I kissed him back before I surprised him with a rather hard tweak to his nipples.

'OW!' Vir screamed before his eyes sparkled. 'Come here you!' I yelped as he pulled me over for another round.

One night, he surprised me with a startling revelation.

'Seriously?' I sat up in disbelief. 'You've never had sex with Aishwarya?'

Vir shrugged and said, 'Cabal brides are supposed to be virgins on their wedding night.'

'That's just twisted!' I shook my head. 'What about the men?'

'Um …' Vir thought for a second before saying, 'You know, there's no rule about that.'

'How freaking convenient!' I smiled as I kissed him.

'Isn't it though?' He winked as he rolled me over as I screamed in delight.

Another night, he truly surprised me!

'OMG! Where did you get this?' My hands were trembling as I held an imported bootleg DVD of Magdalena's seminal

Haute Aspiration World Tour, which hadn't ever been released in its entirety. There were just a few clips featured on the documentary *Daringly Truthful,* which was shot during that tour.

'It's amazing what one can find on eBay these days,' Vir said, smiling seeing my sheer delight.

'OMG! This must have cost a fortune!'

'You're worth every penny!' He kissed me tenderly.

'Oh we're so totally watching this!'

We made popcorn before popping the DVD into my laptop and began basking in Magdalena's glory. There she was, dominating the stage with a troupe of gorgeous dancers.

'So all of them are gay?' Vir asked with arm around me.

'Yup!' I replied, not taking my eyes off the screen. 'Except Orville. He's the one with the frosted tips. Though we fans all feel he's just deeply closeted and repressed!'

Just as she began singing 'Follow My Light', Vir smiled, 'Oh I remember that song far too well!'

As he leaned in to kiss me, I pushed him back. 'After the concert!' I said impatiently.

Vir sighed and rolled his eyes, but I could tell he was happy to see me so ecstatic.

A few nights later, we were feasting on brownies that Aunt Meg had baked for us.

'OMG! These are so freaking good!' Vir said, muncing on his third brownie.

'Aunt Meg's an amazing cook!' I declared as I bit into another one.

'That's really surprising.'

'Why so?'

'I dunno! I guess considering she's such a feminist and stuff, I would have figured she would hate spending time in the kitchen and stuff.'

'Um! Stereotyping much?' I playfully hit him with a pillow.

'Hey!' Vir grabbed me and kissed me with chocolate stains all over his mouth.

'Ew! Gross!' I giggled as I pushed him back.

One night, I caught him by surprise.

'You sure about this?' Vir asked as he looked me in the eye. In his hand was a condom that I had just brought out.

'More than ever!' I replied, kissing him softly.

'You know that there's no going back after this, right?' he said. I could tell that he was concerned about what had happened to me back when I was thirteen.

'Why would I want to go back?' I said. 'Besides, in my heart, you'll still remain my first. That's how I want to remember it.'

Vir kissed me gently as he climbed on top of me. With each passing moment, our kisses grew deeper and deeper. Pulling at my hair, Vir sank his teeth into my neck, marking me as his territory as I dug my nails into his strong muscular back. 'Tonight,' he whispered, 'it's all about you!'

Kissing me gently, he made his way down and took me in his mouth. My body quivered as he devoured every inch of me. He pinned my wrists against the bed, making sure I couldn't move a his warm lips surrounded me as his tongue flickered wildly, making me scream out oh so loud. I wanted to please him more, but he made sure I just laid there as he feasted upon me. Letting out a loud tearful cry of bliss, I collapsed as he swallowed me whole, making sure not a single drop escaped his ravenous tongue.

As I laid breathless, Vir rose up and kissed me tenderly. Without wasting time, Vir flipped me over and began nibbling on my ear as he shoved a couple of fingers in my mouth, making me warm them up before he entered me with one of them, ever so gently. Pushing my face into the pillow to muffle my cries, he made a trail down my spine with his tongue before he reached my cheeks. Spreading them wide, he devoured me again with his mouth as he widened me simultaneously with his fingers. It was the kind of pain that only someone that loves you could inflict. I was loving every minute of it.

'You ready?' he whispered in my ear.

I just sighed breathlessly in reply.

Ripping the wrapper with his mouth, he skilfully covered his rock hard throbbing self with the condom. Before he entered, a trail of drool spilled from his mouth, making sure I was warmed up for him. Thank God he pushed my face harder into the pillow because I began screaming wildly as he nearly tore me apart with the first thrust. Pleasure set in as our bodies synchronized into a lustful rhythm. With each thrust, I could feel the world around me blur into a rose-tinted haze. He flipped me over and made me sit on his lap. His lips locked with mine as he continued to thrust deeper and deeper into me. I could feel the earth tremble as the bed creaked.

Finally, he lay back and let me take control. With his body between my thighs, I rode him as if he was a wild stallion that I had to tame. He moaned louder and louder, matching my cries of passion as I got wilder and wilder. I could feel him throbbing with each thrust. No more was there any pain. No more were there any haunting remains of any trauma. No more was there a Cabal. No more was there anything that kept us apart. It was just us! Just the two of us! *I love you, Vir! I fucking love you, Vir!*

With a final thrust, I collapsed on top of him, breathlessly gasping for air. We drifted off to a slumber with our hearts beating as one.

'Oh fuck!' Vir shouted, waking me up with a shake.

'Oh crap!' I gasped as we saw the rays of the morning sun burst through my windows.

Pulling on our clothes, we ran over to the fruit trees by the boundary wall. I couldn't believe we were so late. So fucking late!

'Hey hey hey!' he said suddenly as I pulled off the Astroturf that hid the doors of the escape hatch.

'What?' I asked, my mind racing.

'I love you,' he said as he kissed me softly.

'I love you too!' I said and kissed him back. 'Now go, already!' I kicked the iron bolt open with my foot.

Before we could open the doors, they burst open. My eyes widened in horror as I saw several AK-47s pointed at us.

Chapter Twenty-Four

'No tea for me today?'

Damyanti's scarlet lips curled into a deviant grin as she imperiously sat on the couch in our living room. I was by her feet, on my knees with my hands bound behind my back with duct-tape. I couldn't bear to look Gran and my aunts in the eye as I was crippled with an overwhelming cloud of guilt. It didn't help that right next to me was an armed guard with an AK-47 pointed at my temple. He had been given orders to shoot if I dared to move a muscle. It was hard to stay still as the sight of Vir being dragged kicking and screaming by a bunch of guards back to his home kept flashing before me.

'It doesn't have to be this way, Damyanti,' said Gran, speaking with a vulnerability I had never heard before. 'He's just a child—'

'A child who would single-handedly bring down an entire empire!' Damyanti snapped. 'Did you think I would allow the fate of our family to be brought down by a bunch of witches?'

Before Gran could speak, Damyanti continued, 'Yes, I know exactly what you all are! Of course, I had my doubts, but that morning when you thought you could put me under a spell and have me reveal all my secrets, you all ended up revealing yourselves! Then I knew for sure.' She smiled as she opened the locket of her mangalsutra, revealing a small camera that was in the shape of an eye. 'The Cabal truly does see all.'

'Damyanti please, just let Jai go!' Gran's voice trembled.'He's just a boy in love, he can't be held responsible for—'

'Oh, the responsibility is not all his, I know that!' Damyanti snapped her fingers as she placed a cigarette in her mouth, and Mr Rathi rushed to light it. After blowing a cloud of smoke that smelled of cloves, she continued, 'After all, his deeds were encouraged by the three of you. Then again, what would witches know about instilling good values in a child!'

'That's rich, coming from you!' Aunt Meg snapped back.

Damyanti let out a sinister chuckle, dropping ashes on the couch before saying, 'My my my! Such moxie! Especially when inevitable doom is upon you all.'

'Whatever you wish to do,' Gran said, grabbing Aunt Meg's arm to remind her to keep calm. 'All we ask is for you to let Jai go!'

'Oh, but you see, I can't let him go!' said Damyanti, flicking her cigarette and causing ash to singe the couch. 'This isn't just about his little perverse love for Vir!' She stood up and walked over to Gran and my aunts, who were seated on chairs pulled close together. There was a gunman behind each of them ready to pull the trigger when the order was given. 'We couldn't care less about that. After all, infidelity of all kinds is encouraged by the Cabal. I should know, I benefitted from it.'

'Then what is it that you really want?' asked Aunt Claudine, trembling in her seat as Damyanti stood before them.

'Your elimination!' Damyanti's declared, her lips curling as she walked over to me. One of the guards yanked at my hair, causing me to yelp as my spine arched backwards. Taking a gilded dagger from Mr Rathi, she sliced open my T-shirt, revealing the mark on my chest. 'His soul has clearly been marked for us!' She turned to Gran. 'Your father made a pact with Lucifer, offering to sacrifice the first male heir of his line. After all, Lucifer doesn't allow someone who doesn't belong to the sacred bloodline access to his power without something in return. However, we had to make sure he was defiled by one of us. After all, there's no power in chastity!'

'Of course, usually it's done by the elders of the families, as it has been done since the beginning of time.' Damyanti snapped her fingers and the guard let go of my hair, causing me to collapse to the floor. The guard then kicked me on my thigh to make me sit up straight again. 'However, since Vir is said to take over command after his marriage to Aishwarya, I suppose it would have to do.'

Before anyone could say anything, Damyanti continued, 'Now, you must be wondering why Jai was chosen. What's so special about him? Well, allow me to tell you. After all, one must always know the truth before they pass.' She laughed and stubbed out her cigarette on the couch, leaving a black ashy hole in the fine upholstery.

'I'm sure you all know that the Cabal relies on demonic magic for their power,' continued Damyanti. 'However, for such power to work, one needs the blood of a witch that's been stained by Lucifer's curse. Why else do you think witches were burned in all cultures around the world? Not for some feeble sense of morality. Then again, all morals of the faiths have been instilled by the Cabal.

'Before a witch was burned, she would be defiled by elders of the Cabal posing as high-ranking men of the clergy and royal courts. Never kings and popes, though! That would just be far too obvious. Besides, we needed them to turn a blind eye towards us and distract the world with wars, famine and what not so that the Cabal could operate secretly in the background. And when that defiled witch would be burned, her powers would feed Lucifer's spirit, and through him, the Cabal would be empowered to rule for an entire century.

'Of course, they went a little overboard during the Dark Ages, leading to most witches hiding their powers. Men are so rarely known to curb their lust. However, despite that, we'd always found witches. But none ever had a male heir. Especially one that had Lucifer's blood flowing through his veins. Yes, Jai's lineage has been diluted by generations, but the fact that he bears the eye on his heart goes to show not only that Lucifer's darkness is potent within him, but also that he has harnessed its energy before!'

Suddenly, the memory of me vanquishing the demon at Sana's home during the exorcism ritual flashed before my eyes.

'Of course, the minute Vir revealed that he defiled your precious little self the night before,' said Damyanti to me, digging her nails into my skin as she pulled my cheeks. 'We knew we had to act fast. Time is of the essence!'

How could Vir betray me like that? Almost instantly, as though she had read my mind, Damyanti said, 'We have our ways of finding these things out.' Patting my cheek, she turned to Gran and said, 'You don't think it was just sheer coincidence that we moved next door to you? Everything had been meticulously planned by the Cabal! We've been watching you ever since we learned of the birth of a male heir that carried the blood of one who had sold his soul to Lucifer. True, we were taken aback by the fact that he was gay. However, that's when the Cabal chose our family to carry out their mission.

'The Rajani family was wrought with shame when they found a preteen Vir in the arms of one of his schoolmates back in Jodhpur. They had begun conversion therapy, hoping it would work to turn him straight. However, Jai being gay played in our favour. And thus we groomed Vir to be the—what's that phrase again? Ah yes! The honey trap! And like the hungry little bee, Jai fell straight into the Cabal's trap.'

As Damyanti let out a deviant cackle, my heart broke into a million little pieces and a deep rage filled my being.

'Of course,' Damyanti continued, still facing Gran and my aunts. 'There's also the role you three must play before we sacrifice Jai's soul!' Damyanti nodded at the guards, who kicked the chairs they were sitting on, causing them to fall on the Persian rug below. As Damyanti walked towards them, she continued, 'There's this delightful little chemical that's formed in our blood whenever a young one witnesses great trauma. I forget what its scientific name is, but to explain it in magical terms: when it's secreted and mixes with the blood, it turns the soul more appetizing for Lucifer. And what would be more traumatic for a child to see than his family destroyed before his very eyes!'

'NO!' I cried out in sheer anguish, and the guard behind me kicked me before yanking me back upright by pulling my hair.

'Oh, don't worry, child!' Damyanti said, turning to me. 'It'll be over before you know it. After all, witches burn faster than regular humans.'

As Damyanti let out another deviant cackle, I could feel my body burn with a rage I had never experienced before. However, before I could burst, Gran caught my eye and silently told me not to lose control.

'Oh dear!' Damyanti composed herself. 'I've been monologuing all this time and forgot to ask you all if you had any last words.' She walked over to Gran and the aunts, bending over to look them in the eye. 'Well, do you have anything to—'

Aunt Meg suddenly spat in Damyanti's face. She screamed as the phlegm burned into the skin of her cheeks. The guards stared in horror as Damyanti's face burned.

'Now!' Gran commanded as all three of them stood up and clapped their hands together, causing a sonic boom to ripple through the room. The guards fell over as the all the glass cabinets and windowpanes shattered into fine fragments.

Before the guards could get up, Gran raised her arms, causing all the guns to levitate in the air. As she flung her arms outwards, the guns flew out of the window, exploding in mid-air once they were a safe distance away from the house.

As the guards charged towards them, Gran and my aunts held hands and began levitating themselves. Then they began spinning like a vortex, causing a bright scarlet light to flow from their bodies. They circled throughout the room, flinging all the guards out of the windows.

'Quickly!' Gran yelled, grabbing my hands. We ran up the stairs, but just as we reached the top, below us another horde of guards stormed through the front door. This time they were firing their guns. Aunt Meg and Aunt Claudine turned and waved their hands. An emerald light emerged from their hands, causing the guards to fall like dominoes. Then they turned to follow Gran and I to the rooftop, sealing the door shut behind us.

'This should buy us some time!' said Gran, before she and my aunts began chanting a sacred mantra I had never heard before. Within minutes, a shield of sky-blue light surrounded us. When we were cocooned within the forcefield, Gran turned to me and said, 'Whatever happens, do not move!'

We saw grappling hooks shoot up from below, clinging onto the parapet. The guards were trying to access the roof by climbing the walls. As they neared the top, Gran and my aunts began shooting balls of fire at the nylon cords they were using to climb, causing them to burn up. The guards screamed as they fell back down. But almost immediately, we heard loud thuds at the door to the roof. It was being forced open.

'They shouldn't be able to break it down easily,' said Aunt Meg. But she spoke too soon, as the doors flew open just then. A horde of demonic beings rushed out, with a seething Damyanti behind them. Before any of us could react, they charged towards us, flinging Gran and my aunts in opposite directions.

I froze in fear—never before had demons been able to break through our forcefield. Then again, never were we attacked by so many simultaneously. I helplessly watched Gran and my aunts levitate mid-air, shooting beams of white light at the demons.

'Get the boy!' Damyanti screamed, and a couple of demons charged right at me.

'No!' cried Gran. She tried to fly towards me, but the demons grabbed her legs and flung her far away.

I cried in horror as the demons began beating Gran mercilessly. I wanted to run over to her, but Damyanti had me in a deathly grip. She swung me around and slapped me so hard that I fell to the ground. I screamed as Damyanti pressed her steel-edged stiletto heel deep into my palm. She laughed as the demons continued to attack my family mercilessly, rendering them powerless.

'You're weak, my boy!' said a familiar voice. I looked up to see the dark hooded being before me. My great-grandfather! 'My daughter and her daughters never did teach you how to defend yourself, did they!'

He cackled and I realized that he was only visible to me. 'You can make it all go away,' he said. 'You can make it stop!'

'How?' I asked weakly, barely able to speak. My body trembled with a deep rage unlike anything I had ever experienced before as Damyanti dug her stiletto deeper into my palm.

'Yes! That's it!' said the hooded being. 'Let that anger build up. It's what's going to set you all free! Don't stop it! It's a part of you that's been suppressed for so long. Build it up, Jai! Build it up!'

I could feel lava burn through my veins as my heart boiled with hellish fury. I could see my skin turn a reddish hue as the fires of Tartarus enflamed within me.

'Burn, Jai! Burn!' screamed the dark creature. 'Don't allow your weakness to suppress it! Don't you love your family? Don't you want them to be safe? Burn away, Jai! Burn more and more and more! Don't be the pathetic little coward that's been raised to suppress his rage! Let it explode! Let it escape! That magic has been trapped within you far too long! Let it out! It demands to be free!'

I began to scream as steam started to spout out from my pores. My tears had turned into fiery flames.

'Let it out, Jai! Do not suppress it!' the being screamed into my face. 'Do not let your cowardice suppress your true self! Burn, Jai! Burn! BURN!'

The fire surged through my being like a hundred raging suns as I flung Damyanti away with a loud yell. As I stood up, the eye on my chest opened wide and began shooting a deep scarlet light from it. The pain was too much to bear, but I couldn't stop it. I wailed louder and louder as the deep scarlet light blinded me. Before I knew it, I was levitating in the air. My voice climbed to octaves it had never explored as my body began spinning like a vortex, shooting the scarlet light in every direction with an uncontrolled intensity. But moments later, my body came crashing down.

As I got a hold of my senses, I let out a scream of horror. The bodies of my family lay on the ground before me. They were in flames. The hooded being levitated above, cackling with evil joy.

'I told you that I'll get you!' he crowed. 'I told you that you'd kill them all, just like you killed your mother! And you did kill them! Praise Lucifer!'

Then he charged at me.

All of a sudden I was surrounded by a blinding white light. Everything before me began to disappear. The white light covered every inch of my skin, causing my body to disappear before my very eyes. Soon, everything turned dark.

'Wake up, Jai,' I heard a voice call out gently. 'Wake up!'

It took me every ounce of strength I had left to slowly open my eyes. The blinding white light slowly faded away to reveal a white-bearded face. Green eyes sparkled warmly as they gazed at me.

'Welcome, Jai!' said the white-bearded man with a smile. 'I've been expecting you.'

Chapter Twenty-Five

'Why does the Tower come between the Devil and the Star?'

I remember asking Aunt Claudine this as a child when she first began to teach me how to read the tarot. It was an afternoon in the library, and on the large apothecary coffee table we had laid out the major arcana of the Tarot in three rows of seven. The Fool card was on top by itself.

'Well, remember what I told you about the Majors being symbolic of a journey?' Aunt Claudine sipped her lavender tea.

I nodded and she continued, 'Think of the Fool as the hero of the journey.'

'Why would the Fool be a hero?'

'That's because a hero is often seen as a fool by the world,' answered Aunt Claudine with a smile. 'The world doesn't like heroes until they prove themselves. Thus, in the first row, we have the Fool discover the magic of the world around him through the Magician. The High Priestess reminds him that there are mysteries far greater, which are still hidden. The Empress distracts him from the mysteries with the luxuries of the material world, while the Emperor reminds him of the obligations one has if one has to live in the material world. The Hierophant acts as his teacher, revealing all the laws of both the material and the spirit world. The Lovers is where the Fool has to choose whether he wants to revel in the material world, or discover the mysteries of the spirit world …'

'And the Chariot is where the Fool sets off on his quest?'

'Very good, Jai!' Aunt Claudine exclaimed. She ruffled my hair and planted a kiss on my forehead before turning her attention back to the cards. 'Now, the second row is an interesting one. Some decks place the Strength card after the Chariot; while others place Justice. I personally prefer placing Justice, because once the Fool is off on his heroic quest, he has to seek the karmas of his actions. Remember that he is a fool after all. His excited state leads to mistakes, and he faces the consequences of those mistakes through the card of Justice. After that, the Hermit reminds him of the importance of quiet reflection. This is important because until then the Fool has learned from external sources. Now he has to learn from the greatest teacher of all: his inner self, his soul. Only when he learns how to listen to his soul can he discover the laws of the divine spirit world with the Wheel of Fortune. Armed with what he's learned, the Fool learns to build his Strength.'

Aunt Claudine held out a card and said, 'See how this woman is taming a lion?' I nodded as I looked at the card, which had a smiling woman petting a wild lion. 'Notice,' she continued. 'She's not using a whip like a lion tamer, nor is she wearing armour of any kind. Yet, she has the lion like a little kitten, purring with her touch. That's true strength because she's without fear. Ignorance has been wiped out through contemplative reflection that the Fool learns with the Hermit. Once his strength has built up, he learns to let go of all that doesn't serve him with the Hanged Man. The Hanged Man smiles despite being hung upside down because there's no greater joy than realizing that all you need to face the world is a strong heart filled with love. This is why Death follows, symbolizing the Fool's transformation from a wanderer to a hero with purpose. Temperance follows Death to remind him to use his newfound skills and strengths to defeat the adversary. Do you remember who that is?'

'The Devil!' I replied, pretty proud of myself.

'Indeed! The Devil is the sum of all our fears and ignorance. When the Fool faces the Devil and fights him, the Tower is destroyed. The Tower is either the Devil's castle of false beliefs, or the Fool's palace of shaky foundations—because in his excitement to be a hero, he forgets his lessons. Then we have the Star, who comes as a ray of hope. Creation is only possible with destruction. Nothing new can come while the old still exists. Everything that's created must be destroyed, and everything that's destroyed must give way for something new to emerge. If that didn't happen, the world would just come to a standstill and life has no meaning. The Star reminds the Fool to keep hope alive. If the Devil defeats the Fool, then the Fool must maintain hope. He can always restart his journey and face the same Devil again.'

Aunt Claudine stopped when she saw me looking blank. 'You remember how when you play Mario,' she said. 'Mario has to keep defeating Bowser at various stages. Right?'

I nodded.

'Well, when Mario defeats a lesser beast in the early stages, he meets Toad, who tells him that the Princess is in another castle. This leads Mario to the next stage, where he fights and keeps defeating the monsters till eventually he makes his way to the final stage. There, he meets Bowser. Right?'

I happily nodded again as she was now speaking a language I understood.

'Well, think of all those various stages as the Moon. Mario doesn't know where he's headed, but believes in the path that lays ahead. Each stage has greater monsters, and the obstacles on each new path get trickier and tricker. Mario reaches the final stage, where he fights Bowser, destroys him and eventually rescues Princess Peach. It can be compared to the Fool returning to the Devil and eventually defeating him, shattering the Tower. The Star gives him hope that even though the war isn't over, he's won a battle. This prepares him to fight again. When he finally finds Princess Peach, he celebrates that victory with the Sun.'

'And what about Judgement?' I asked, picking up the card showing an angel blowing a trumpet to lure the souls of the dead from their graves.

'Ah, that's where we count all the points Mario scored by killing the various monsters, as well as all the coins he collected along the way.'

'So, good karma is kinda like the coins?'

Aunt Claudine's eyes widened in delight. 'Why child, you are positively uncanny!' she exclaimed. Kissing me on the cheek, she continued, 'So yeah, that's basically a tally of all the good karma that the Fool—in our example, Mario—has accumulated over the various stages he conquered.'

'And the World is his "happily ever after"?'

'Yes, indeed it is, but it's only temporary,' replied Aunt Claudine.

'Why is it temporary?'

'Well, that's because life is an unending journey. Unlike Mario, we have many more stages and worlds to conquer. In this lifetime, as well as other lifetimes in the future. Life moves on and thus we need to move along with it. There are many Devils to defeat and many Towers to shatter. But only when we succeed in doing so can we evolve further.'

Before I could ask her any further, a loud clanging sound echoed throughout my mind. The memory had been a dream, and now I was awake. As my eyes adjusted to the morning light, my soul started to ache again as visions of Gran and my aunts as burning corpses flashed before my eyes.

Six months had passed since I had arrived at Babaji's secret ashram, which was hidden above a momo cafe in the chaotic ghetto of Majnu Ka Tila. It was officially known as New Aruna Nagar Colony, but those who lived there would refer to it as 'Chungtown' or 'Samyeling'.

Legend has it that during the reign of Sikandar Lodhi, an Iranian mystic named Majnu met Guru Nanak—the first sacred teacher of the Sikhs—when he ferried the guru across the Yamuna river. Majnu became devoted to the guru, who was touched by his devotion and decided to stay and preach in that area. Majnu would ferry without charge those seeking the guru's blessings. When the time came for him to leave, Guru Nanak blessed the space with his divine boons. Majnu remained faithful to him till his very last breath.

Later, Baghel Singh Dhaliwal built the famous Majnu Ka Tila gurudwara to commemorate the sacred spot. Towards the end of the eighteenth century, Guru Har Gobind—the sixth Sikh guru—stayed there as well, and it remains one of the oldest Sikh shrines in Delhi.

'Hurry up!' called Tempa, peeping into my dingy dormitory as the hallway light formed a halo around his shaved skull. 'Babaji is about to begin the morning class!'

I sighed as I dragged myself out of bed and into the tiny bathroom. I turned on the tap, filling a blue plastic bucket with water that was never warmed. The shock of a cold bath in the Delhi winter was nothing compared to the pain I felt within.

After we stood in tadasana reciting the opening mantra, Babaji spoke.

'Ekam …'

We raised our hands in urdvahastasna.

'Dwei …'

We bent forwards to touch our foreheads to our knees in uttanasana.

'Treni …'

We lifted our heads to flatten our backs so that it remained parallel to the floor.

'Chatvardi …'

Pressing our hands on the floor, we kicked our legs up before floating into a stable chaturanga-dandasana.

'Pancha …'

We uncurled our toes and raised our heads as we balanced our torsos on our palms and the nails of our toes in urdhva-mukha-svanasana.

'Sho-dasha…'

We curled our spines and moved into our first adho-mukha-svanasasna, holding our downward dogs for five breaths.

Babaji was beloved amongst the Tibetan refugees that called Majnu Ka Tila a home. The Indian government had made our country a safe haven for those escaping from China's occupation of their homeland. But I still hadn't spoken much to him because I was filled with guilt and shame for what had transpired. In fact, guilt and shame did not begin to describe what I felt. After all, I killed the only family I had.

I stayed silent for my first week at the ashram. Finally, Babaji told me that he'd only speak to me once I snap out of my funk. As I hadn't yet managed to do so despite six months passing, he still kept a silent distance from me, speaking to me only when he led the class.

The intense yoga classes were the only thing keeping me sane. Though this style of yoga was quite spartan, unlike Gran's classes. With her, there would be new sequences daily, depending on the ability of the students as well as the mood and energy of the class. But Babaji's classes would only have one set sequence: five rounds each of the two styles of surya namaskar, followed by a series of standing poses to build strength.

When Babaji noticed that my body was flexible and strong from all the years of practice, he placed me with the advanced students. We would perform an additional set of arm balances and complicated binds and splits. Beginners performed mostly forward bends to cleanse the system of toxins, while the intermediate level would focus on backbends and core-strengthening work.

There were many other differences between Gran's classes and here. Gran and my aunts would often joke around in class, making the students laugh. This was to remind them not to take yoga too seriously and remember that the most important thing was to enjoy the journey. Babaji, however, was almost militant. No one could progress to a higher level until they had mastered all the poses of their respective series.

Gran would insist on people using props such as yoga blocks, straps and sometimes even chairs and balancing wheels. Here, the only prop allowed was the mat beneath our feet. The mats were thick jute mats that were locally produced—very different to the luxuriant Manduka mat I was used to practicing on. Instead of the colourful yoga gear worn by Gran's students, the men in the ashram wore just a plain white dhoti, while the women wore a matching white kurta on top. Babaji, however, wore a colourful tunic as he walked around the class. The shala would be silent during class.

After the morning class, we'd have a simple breakfast of seasonal fruits, followed by whatever the staff at the momo café would prepare for us. After a quick bath, I'd report downstairs at the café, where I would work as a server. The customers were mostly locals from the neighbourhood, but during the lunch rush, there would be students from the north campus of Delhi University. They would stuff themselves with the various varieties of momos and thukpas, but the bill for a table of five rarely crossed a thousand rupees. No wonder the students loved coming here so much.

As Gran and my aunts had trained me to clean up after myself and do my own laundry, adjusting to ashram life didn't really take time. I did miss my king-sized bed with its body-contouring mattress after a few weeks of sleeping on the small hard cot in my tiny room. But I still slept well after two intense yoga classes and a day of waiting tables at the café.

I'd constantly dream about my life with Gran and my aunts. Oh, how I longed to be hugged by Gran! I missed Aunt Meg rolling her eyes, and I would give anything to have Aunt Claudine ruffle my hair! The café's milky masala chai could not compare to Aunt Meg's freshly brewed herbal teas. The momos, though delicious, only made me miss home, which always smelled of fresh baking.

Every time I remembered Vir's betrayal or Damyanti's taunts, my blood would boil. Despite the yoga, I'd wake up sore and stiff from the guilt and shame. Maybe I needed this spartan existence. Perhaps this was part of my punishment for falling so blindly in love. Was it even love? I didn't have the strength to examine what Vir and I had had.

Some nights, I'd wake the entire street with my howling. Those were the nights I was plagued by the visions of the burning corpses. I'd be put straight back to bed by other ashram residents after being made to sip turmeric milk. However, I would be too scared to sleep again. I'd just stare up at the dark ceiling, which was stained by years of seepage that gave my room a mouldy stench. I guess I deserved sleepless nights. I deserved far worse!

'Babaji!' Tempa wailed as he refused to do a headstand, disrupting the silence of the shala.

'Hush!' Babaji fluffed his cloudy beard as he stood before Tempa, who trembled fearfully in child's pose. 'You've been with me for almost five years, boy! Today you're going to do a headstand whether you like it or not!'

'B-B-But Babaji …'

'No buts! Get up now!' Babaji clapped his hands, signalling to us to stop and watch. 'No one will progress further till Tempa can do a headstand!'

As I watched Tempa quiver in fear, I was reminded of what Gran would say in class: 'The only thing that prevents us from attaining a headstand is fear. Once we let go of that fear and open our hearts, we will see the world from a completely different point of view. Getting into a headstand will become a breeze.'

'Are you going to get up, or do you need one of Babaji's kicks?' Babaji said with a wide smile as the class burst into gentle giggles.

'B-B-Babaji please!' Tempa begged. 'Tomorrow, I promise you that I'll get up—'

'I've heard your "tomorrows" for five years now!' Babaji chuckled. 'Now get up, or else you'll get—'

'No Babaji, please!' Tempa said, prostrating at Babaji's feet. 'I-I've eaten too much today. I'm afraid I'll—'

Thwack! Babaji kicked him on the bottom, and almost magically, Tempa assumed a headstand. The class burst into applause. Barely a second later, however, Tempa was on the verge of losing balance. But Babaji held his legs and said, 'Now come on! Focus on your breath, and engage your core and pelvic floor …'

'N-No, Babaji!' Tempa said, trembling. 'P-P-Please let me—'

'Hush!' Babaji said firmly. 'Don't make me kick you again!'

'B-B-But ...'

'No buts! Just engage and—'

Before Babaji could complete his sentence, Tempa screamed and farted louder than the engine of a Bullet motorcycle. We immediately noticed a brown stain growing on his dhoti. Babaji let go of Tempa's legs and he fell to the floor. Within a second, he had picked himself up and went scampering out of the shala holding his bum.

A deafening silence fell upon the room as we watched in shock. Before Babaji could process what had happened, I let out a quiet giggle. When Babaji turned in my direction, I don't know what came over me, but I burst out laughing. It was soft at first, but I could feel my belly rumble as I laughed louder and louder. Soon, everyone began laughing along with me.

I couldn't stop, laughing louder and louder. Soon, I was rolling all over the floor laughing. It was like a deathly burden was being lifted off as my body released every bit of pain trapped within with each fresh bout of laughter. I couldn't remember the last time I had laughed so hard. I kept rolling about, grabbing my now aching belly until Babaji grabbed me and engulfed me in a big bear hug. That was when my laughter turned into a tears of release.

After what seemed like an eternity, I finally sighed into the warmth of Babaji's cuddly body. He lifted my face and looked me in the eye. 'Good boy, Jai!' Babaji said, smiling softly as he kissed me on my forehead. 'Now I can finally talk to you!'

Chapter Twenty-Six

Babaji was unlike any one I had ever met before. Then again, how many people had I really met? Though, I can imagine he'd be a culture shock to anyone who'd meet him for the first time. His cloudy white beard that fell below his chest almost blended with the shockingly white curls upon his head, yet his skin radiated with a youthful glow that made him seem as though he was barely in his thirties. When I asked him how old he was, he just replied, 'Oh, I stopped counting after eighty!'

'And when exactly was that?'

Babaji took a sip of his masala chai with his pinkie extended before saying, 'I think that was probably a couple of years before Aurangzeb was coronated at Shalimar Bagh.'

When I asked what his name was, he replied with a nonchalant shrug, 'Oh I forgot it ages ago!'

'You forgot your name?'

He chuckled playfully and said, 'Well, no one's really called me by my name for so long. They just call me "Babaji", and I let them. Besides, what's in a name? That which we call a rose, by any other name would smell as sweet!'

'Shakespeare?'

'I'm a yogi, my boy, not a philistine!'

As his protégée, I was given the task of waking an hour before class began and sweeping the floor of the shala. Once class ended, I had the additional task of mopping the floors. I was told that I should be able to see my reflection in the faded mosaic tiles. Tempa was given the same task, but he did the evening shift. It allowed him a few extra winks in the morning.

During class, Babaji was firm with his instructions and would keenly observe each of us as we did the poses. If one met him for the first time, one wouldn't believe he was a great yogi. He towered over us all with a heavyset frame that made him look like Santa Claus. Yet, he moved with the grace and elegance of a swan. Even when he'd walk, it would seem as though he was floating. I couldn't help but be awestruck whenever he'd demonstrate a complicated yoga pose with movements smooth as butter.

'Yoga is for any body and every body!' He would smile as we would applaud him as he smoothly existed the posture.

Wednesday was the official 'holiday' of Majnu Ka Tila, a day most shops would be shut and cafes would not serve meat. Every week on Wednesday, Babaji would have me follow him as he walked around the narrow alleyways. He'd be dressed in colourful kaftans and sing-song his way as he'd greet all the locals, waving as though he was a royal princess with one hand, as he fanned himself with an elegant floral lace hand fan. Children would run up to him to hug him and gift him flowers. He would delightfully place them in his hair and sometimes even in his beard. The children would laugh as he made funny faces to tease them.

Every week, he'd be invited over to a different café or restaurant for lunch, which was the only meal he'd eat all day. His green eyes would sparkle whenever food arrived at the table. They'd make an exception for him and serve meat even on Wednesday, and boy did Babaji enjoy his meat: pork, buffalo-beef, turkey, fish and, of course, chicken. He'd devour his food with a pair of wooden chopsticks. He'd squeal like a child when he was served his customary two scoops of ice cream after every meal. The flavour would be the only thing vanilla about him.

The minute he'd wipe the last bit of the ice-cream dish with his finger tip, there'd be a long queue of people waiting to see him. They'd come with common colds, fevers, scars, open wounds, broken bones, as well as broken hearts and quarrelling in-laws. He'd listen patiently while they talked before placing his hands on wherever the affliction. He would exhale slowly and that would be enough to cure them. They'd smile and bow gratefully as they left. They knew well not to touch his feet.

'Vishnu has four arms that carry the sacred weapons used to defeat his enemies,' Babaji once said during class when Tempa was struggling with a pincha mayurasana. 'The first carries a lotus, so that he can communicate sweetly with his enemies in the hope of reaching a fair compromise. If the enemy resisted, he would blow his conch shell, because sometimes sweetness falls short and we must use raise our voice to put a point across. If the enemy is still stubborn—in this case, Tempa's laziness,' Babaji smiled at Tempa who was sweating buckets as his forearms balanced his body in a dolphin pose, 'Vishnu would use his mace, because when words—both sweet and harsh—fail, a good spanking is needed!' *Thwack!* Babaji swatted Tempa on his bottom, making him lift his legs high. He held his pincha mayurasana for a few seconds before collapsing.

After we all applauded his feat, Babaji continued, 'Laziness is the biggest enemy of a yogi, for laziness leads to ignorance, which leads to fear. Fear leads to guilt, which leads to shame, and then the heart stops learning how to love. When the heart stops loving, the body loses the will to live, and then the soul is trapped and tortured within a loveless life, desperately waiting for life to end so that it can be reborn again.'

'What's the fourth weapon?' Tempa asked, wiping his sweat with a towel.

'The chakra, or discus,' Babaji answered as he walked over to the front of the class. 'The mightiest of weapons. When the enemy doesn't understand with even a beating, Vishnu must deploy his chakra so that the enemy is finally …' Babaji looked Tempa in the eye as he drew his thumb across his neck, mimicking the sound of a decapitation. Tempa gulped in horror, causing Babaji to laugh. 'Oh don't worry, Tempa!' he said. 'With enough beatings, you'll be spared the fourth weapon!'

Tempa had been with Babaji for five years. His parents ran the momo café that hosted the shala above. They were fed up with him for having failed his way through college and were almost on the verge of disowning him. Babaji assured them that he'd sort out Tempa's laziness. Tempa and his family were grateful for everything Babaji had done for them.

'You should have seen him when I first took him under my wing!' Babaji said as he puffed on his hand-rolled joint. 'Stiff as a board and would need a bucket of water to be splashed on him just to get him out of bed.'

'I've gotten better!' Tempa huffed.

'There's always room for improvement!' said Babaji as he fanned himself. Tempa shook his head and retired for the night, leaving just Babaji and me on the rooftop under the night sky.

'Why did you disappear on Gran?' I asked as Babaji finished his masala chai.

'Oh, I taught everything I could to Adele,' answered Babaji, running his fingers through his beard. 'Just as a teacher appears when a student is ready, he must leave when the student must progress on their own. Too much dependence is bad for the soul, no matter how good the teacher or student is. An insecure teacher holds on to a student, crippling their growth. An ignorant student clings on to a teacher, giving him too much power and leading to the teacher's soul being corrupted.' He took a long drag before continuing, 'Besides, I had places to go, things to see, people to do!'

I almost choked at his last statement, causing Babaji to break into a jolly belly laugh. 'I'm a yogi, not a saint! Besides, the body has its needs. And like twinks, "daddies" never go out of style!'

I guffawed at that. Babaji had a way of surprising me with his colourful remarks. I knew that he enjoyed having nightly companions, and would be amazed by how many young men would throw themselves at him. He'd just be minding his own business as he fanned himself during his strolls through the alleyways, and out of nowhere, a young stud would give him the eye. Moments later, he'd have them over in his chambers for a delightful romp. He had four rules—no students, no one under twenty-one, no one more than once, and the last but most important one—no virgins.

'Virginity has nothing to offer!' Babaji once confided in me. 'Celibacy blocks the sacral chakra, causing the kundalini life force to remain perpetually blocked. If one isn't comfortable with his sexual nature, one can never grow spiritually.'

'What about priests?' I asked as I reluctantly sipped my masala chai.

'There's a reason sexual scandals plague the clergy of all faiths!' he replied with a puff on his joint.

I couldn't disagree with him.

'That's why you couldn't defeat those demons that were attacking your family,' he said suddenly. I froze as he stared me dead in the eye. Before I could say anything, he continued, 'Adele and her daughters taught you plenty, and taught you very well. But there was only so much they could teach you until you popped your cherry. The sexual trauma doesn't really count. That just allows magic to emerge. It's only when you finally give consent to it can you really take your powers to the next level. The more actively comfortable you are with your sexual being, the powerful your magic becomes.'

'Why is sexual trauma so necessary for magic to emerge? I mean, that's glorifying rape!'

'It wasn't always that way!' Babaji sighed as he stubbed the joint into the parapet of the roof before flicking it over. 'Before patriarchy took over the world, sexuality was revered and magic flowed freely. Man became power-hungry and would seek it through any means necessary. Thus, it became hard for man to access inner magic. As shame crept into the sexual narrative of the world, magic got suppressed. What was once a birthright for everyone became scarce, flowing down lines of only a select few who dared to live a life that threatened the status quo.'

'But still, why rape?'

'Ah my boy, it's a question of the chicken and the egg. What came first? Was it the sexual trauma that triggered the magic, or was the magic so powerful that it attracted the sexual trauma so that it could be released? In all my years roaming across this earth, I still haven't found the answer to that. However, with time, not even sexual trauma was powerful enough to release the magic within our soul. Except, of course, for witches.'

A silence fell upon us as the nightly spring breeze blew. I couldn't help but wonder if Vir intentionally took my virginity the very night before Damyanti cornered us. Was it all part of an elaborate ruse, to attack and destroy us when I wasn't powerful enough? Then again, they could have easily attacked us even before that. After all, if my being a virgin did indeed keep my powers limited, Vir didn't have to lead me on the way he did. Maybe he was trying to help me access my powers to defeat the attack? I could feel my head throb as my mind drowned in an endless ocean of what-ifs.

'How old are you again?' Babaji asked as he lit another joint and took a leisurely drag.

'I'll be seventeen in a few months.'

'Hmmm …' Babaji said thoughtfully. 'Remind me to revisit this conversation when you're eighteen.'

'Why?'

'You'll see!'

His eyes sparkled with a childlike twinkle and I didn't know whether to be excited or fearful of what was in store for me.

Chapter Twenty-Seven

'Happy birthday to you!' sang Babaji and Tempa's family, clapping merrily. Tempa emerged from the kitchen, carrying a small round chocolate cake lit with nineteen candles—an extra one for good luck.

'... Happy birthday, dear Jai!' They sang and cheered loudly as Tempa placed the cake in front of me. 'Happy birthday to you!'

'You were born in a—Ow! What was that for?' Tempa cried as Babaji swatted him in the back of his head.

'Hush!' Babaji shot him a look before turning to me. 'Now close your eyes and make a wish.'

As I closed my eyes, I couldn't think of anything I wanted more than for Gran and my aunts to be at peace wherever they were.

It was unbelievable how quickly time flew by. It almost felt like I had just teleported over to Babaji's shala at Majnu Ka Tila after that tragic morning. I remember when I asked him how I ended up there and he just responded, 'There are forces greater than you and I, who watch over us. When needed, they perform such miracles, protecting us when we need it most.'

Though Babaji did his best to make me feel at home—and I was so grateful to him for that—I still desperately missed my family. Yes, I could finally laugh again and my sleep was now sound. Yet, there remained that hole in my heart. I did my best to hide it, but Babaji knew that underneath it all, I had a deep sorrow that never seemed to go away.

'Hurry up now!' Tempa's mother scolded. 'All the candles will melt and there'll be more wax than cake!'

'And I'm hung—Ow!' Tempa whined as Babaji swatted him again.

'Hush!'

I smiled and blew out all nineteen candles with a single rushed exhale as everyone cheered.

Tempa's mother spoiled us with a feast. We began with large bowls of chicken thukpa that Tempa slurped greedily. An assortment of steamed momos and a mouthwatering shapale followed by a massive serving of buff sha datchi filled with yak cheese. Babaji was delighted when he was presented with two scoops of vanilla ice cream at the end. It was perhaps the only time I saw him eat after sundown.

'What are we doing here?' I asked as I followed Babaji into a nearby crematorium.

Babaji kept walking without answering. Though the lights of the gurudwara were lit, the temple was unusually dark. Babaji had insisted that I walk barefoot all the way from the shala wearing just my dhoti and nothing else. Due to the heavy monsoons, avoiding puddles became trickier than usual. They smelled of many things other than rainwater.

Moments later, we came upon a small mud hut that had a large thatched door. After Babaji knocked, a couple of men came out. They were completely naked, with ash smeared all over their bodies and over their thick dreadlocks.

'Is everything ready?' Babaji asked in a whisper. The ash-covered men nodded and stepped away from the door. Babaji suddenly grabbed me by my hand and pulled me inside the hut. The thatched door was shut behind us by the two men who stood guard outside. The room was lit by a lone diya, and when my eyes adjusted to the light, I froze in fear as I saw a fresh corpse of a woman before me.

I let out a cry of disgust, only to have Babaji cover my mouth with his palm. I looked again at the corpse. Her eyes had been gouged out and the cavities were filled to the brim with ghee, as were her nostrils, mouth and other orifices. All over her body were sacred symbols that were precisely drawn with what I thought at first was henna. It took me a few moments to realize that they had been drawn with dried blood.

Babaji ordered me to strip naked. When I looked at him in horror, Babaji said, 'Either you do it yourself, or I'll do it for you!'

'B-b-but ...' I stammered in sheer panic.

'Trust me!' Babaji whispered sternly.

I didn't know what scared me more—what lay ahead or what Babaji would do to me if I refused to obey. Shivering, I untucked my dhoti and let it drop to the floor. He immediately began pouring an oil with a pungent aroma on the crown of my head. I could feel by body tremble as Babaji began rubbing it roughly into my scalp. As he began anointing my torso with the oil, I was shaking wildly.

'Hold still!' Babaji spanked me lightly on my bottom as he continued to massage the oil deep into my skin, making sure it was absorbed by each pore, including my fingertips. After what seemed like an embarrassing eternity, he took my palm and poured the rest of the oil in it. 'You know what to do.'

I shook my head nervously, but after Babaji shot me a stern look that sent chills down my spine, I slowly began massaging the tip of my shaft.

'All of it!' Babaji commanded in a stern whisper as my hands barely feathered the tip. Not wanting to anger him, I took myself completely in my hands and massaged well. It sickened me that I became hard inspite of being filled with fear and disgust. I was hoping it was enough, but Babaji coughed, reminding me that I had skipped my balls. When done, Babaji nodded.

'Now fuck the corpse!'

'WHAT?' My eyes widened with horror.

'You heard me loud and clear!'

'B-B-But—'

'Don't make me ...' Babaji raised his hand at me, causing me to flinch. Never had he even raised a finger at me. Tonight, his green eyes burned with a severe darkness.

'The path of magic isn't all sunshine and rainbows!' Babaji whispered, 'To access powers greater than ever, you must perform the first ritual—overcoming your fear. Within this corpse lays divine sacred power that is desperate to be transferred to you. If you do not harness it, not only will your powers never grow, but that magic will fall in the hands of far more sinister forces. If you let fear paralyse you, you'll never be able to grow strong enough to walk the path that's been destined for you, causing your soul to wander endlessly, tortured in the realm of purgatory. If you overcome your fear, you'll open doors and access forces so great that nothing will stop you from ascending on your path. Now go! Your destiny awaits!'

Babaji gently pushed me closer to the corpse. I hesitantly looked back at him, desperately hoping that this was just some sort of sick joke. The stern look he shot me made that hope disappear. The stench of the pungent oil blended with the foul odour of the corpse. I sighed and slowly laid upon the corpse.

Never did I think I would have sex with a living woman—let alone a dead one! *Fuck, this is so fucking creepy!* I thought with a shudder. But I knew I had no choice but to do as Babaji directed. I steeled myself and prepared myself for the deed, hoping against hope that I survive it.

Oh fucking hell! I wanted to hurl so badly, but I was more fearful of what Babaji would do to me if I didn't obey him. As I slowly slipped my embarrassingly hard self into her, suddenly, the corpse began to come to life.

'What the ...' *Thwack!*

Before I could finish my cry of disgust, Babaji kicked me on my bare bottom, causing me to enter her fully. As every oily inch entered her ghee-filled self, the corpse suddenly animated. Laughing wildly, she yanked me and rolled me over so that she was squatting on top of me. I froze in horror with my eyes wide open as my heart thumped wildly as though it wanted to escape my ribs. The re-animated corpse laughed wilder and wilder as her ghee-filled eyes and mouth began glowing like red lumps of coal. How the fuck was I remaining hard throughout?

From the corner of my eyes, I saw Babaji was sitting in padmasana. His eyes were rolled over to the back of his head, revealing just the whites as his lids flickered and as his lips mouthed a silent mantra. The corpse slapped me tightly across my face, almost daring me to look deep into her eyes as she rode me wildly. I screamed out loud in pain when she dug her fingernails into my torso as her body gyrated intensely against mine.

Babaji made a fist with his hand and kissed it gently before blowing harshly towards me, causing golden sparks to flow from his fingertips. The minute they landed on my chest, I felt a rush of energy coarse through my veins, filling me with a strength I knew nothing of. I began thrusting more and more inspite of my disgust. I could feel the eye on my chest beginning to burn as I screamed out loud as I could feel myself near climax.

As my screams grew louder, the corpse wailed even louder as if to outdo me. I could see flashes of brilliant white light appear throughout the room as the eye on my chest continued to burn through my skin. The sheer force within me was growing with each passing second, making it harder to control myself. Oh fuck! Oh fuck! Oooooooohhh fuuuuuuuuuuuccccckkkkk!

The corpse let out a bloodcurdling, banshee-like wail. What took just a few seconds seemed to last an eon as I released every bit of myself inside of the corpse as her supersonic pitch almost shattered my ear drums. Before I could even catch a breath to recover, the corpse fell upon me, lifelessly stiff and cold. I screamed wildly as I pushed it off me, panting breathlessly.

Perhaps time passed. Perhaps it stood still. But before I could process what I had done, Babaji let out a joyfully robust roar of laughter. I couldn't tell if he was happy with what had happened or was just perversely thrilled at my state.

I quickly rolled over and began to throw up violently. Babaji, still laughing, came over and held me comfortingly as streams of black bile flew out of my mouth in long viscous streams. I coughed roughly as the last remnants left my body, feeling completely drained. Babaji enveloped me with a big bear hug from behind.

All of a sudden, I felt extremely light, as if I could float into the heavens above. As the chill of disgust left my body, Babaji turned me around and kissed me on my forehead, comforting my shaken spirit.

'Welcome to the world of magic!' he said.

Chapter Twenty-Eight

'Okay, I still don't understand how me doing it with a corpse is meant to help me release fear?'

I broke the silence as Babaji and I sat in the backseat of a rickety white Maruti Swift that was stuck in a massive jam along ISBT. It was my first time in a taxi, and also the first time I had left Majnu Ka Tila since I had arrived in a flash of white light on that fateful morning.

After my ordeal at the crematorium, I spent all of the next day in bed—except the times I had to run to the bathroom to throw up more black bile. I don't know what was more exhausting: the frequent vomiting or cleaning up afterwards. It was only after the evening class that Babaji visited me and ordered me to dress pretty. When I told him I didn't exactly have anything pretty to wear, he went and ordered Tempa to find me something. Tempa lent me a pair of jeans and a white crewneck T-shirt. I also had to borrow a pair of sneakers that pinched the sides of my feet.

'It's an ancient tradition that predates even me,' Babaji replied as he fluffed his beard. He was looking rather charming in his fuchsia Hawaiian shirt with a black T-shirt underneath. It was so strange to see him out of his kaftan—and in a pair of cargo shorts! 'We see a corpse as something vile, but what we don't understand that it too is a thing of beauty, as it once contained a soul. When a soul departs, the corpse becomes a shell, yes. However, there is still magic within it that's inaccessible to most because of their fear of tampering with the dead. Many sages would access this hidden magic by either eating the corpse or partaking in intercourse with it. Some would even trap demons and wandering spirits within the corpses to create zombie slaves to do their bidding.'

'So now zombies exist!'

'Of course!' Babaji chuckled. 'So do vampires, ghouls, djinns, werewolves … along with angels, faeries, elves, goblins, mermaids and the lot. Man has yet to even discover all the species of flora and fauna that live on the surface of our earth and in the depths of our oceans. The spirit realm has far more beings than even the most creative soul can dare imagine.'

He paused for a moment before he asked, 'What planet rules love?'

'Venus!' I answered.

'What else does Venus rule?'

'Well, sex, sexuality, the ova, the sperm and thereby our ancestral lineages.'

'What else?'

I thought for a bit. 'Well, it rules femininity, it's the fertile aspect of the goddess energy. It also rules beauty, glamour, luxury, jewels, cars and even art and artists.'

As our taxi began to move at the pace of a snail, Babaji said, 'Venus also rules the dead.'

My eyes widened with surprise as Babaji continued, 'Venus possesses a power that no other cosmic being possesses. The ancients called it "Sanjeevini Vidya"—the knowledge of immortality. You know how devas are constantly waging a war with the asuras?'

I nodded.

'Well, the asuras would never die. Venus would simply use her Sanjeevini Vidya to resurrect them. Lord Yama, the god of death, was merely an agent of Venus.'

'But aren't asuras evil?'

'Dear boy, asuras and devas are merely two spectrums of the Infinite Source energy that tread different paths. Good and evil are just moralistic divisions that block us from accessing the Source's energy. Nothing is purely good, and nothing is purely evil. The same sun that warms us and allows life to prosper can torture and even kill those who are exposed to it for too long. We can't really say it is good or it is evil. It is what it is. Thus, Venus teaches us to find beauty in the world, even in the darkest and most fearful spaces that man is too scared to go.'

'And that includes corpses?'

'Especially corpses.'

'Why do devas fight with asuras?'

'Asuras guard all the treasures of the world. The devas fight them to access those treasures, as those treasures can allow the devas to wield the power of the heavenly realms.'

When he saw that I looked blank, Babaji smiled and asked, 'What is a diamond made of?'

'Coal,' I answered. 'A form of carbon.'

'Think of the asuras as being guardians of a mighty coal mine that's deep under the ground,' explained Babaji. 'The devas battle the asuras, and through that battle coal is extracted. Some of that is used as fuel. But upon some pieces of coal, this divine battle is fought even more fiercely—those are the ones that become diamonds. It's symbolic of the incredible amounts of heat and pressure a piece of coal endures in order to become a diamond. Of course, a diamond needs to be cut and polished so that it can become brilliant. That cut and polish happens when the asuras fight with the devas to retrieve what's been stolen from them. Now if we look at it from a moralistic view of good and evil, the devas were evil for stealing the coal from the asuras. However, had they not done so, there would be no fuel and there would be no diamonds.'

'I never thought of it that way,' I said, my mind blown by that explanation. 'But why does Venus resurrect the asuras and not the devas?'

Babaji turned to the driver and asked, '*Bhaiya, thoda maal phoonk sakta hoon?*' He smiled as he took out a hand-rolled joint.

'*Aapse kya behes kar sakta hoon?*' replied the driver, grinning as he succumbed to Babaji's infectious charm. '*Bas mere liye kuch rakh dena.*'

Babaji guffawed as he handed the driver a second joint from the breast pocket of his shirt. Lighting his joint, Babaji took a leisurely drag and blew out of the window before turning to me. 'Do you know the story of the Samudra Manthana?'

'When the devas and asuras churned the celestial ocean?'

'Indeed! You see, the devas and the asuras wanted to access the greatest treasure of all, which was buried deep in the depths of the celestial ocean. According to the Bhagvata Purana, Vishnu took on his Kurma avatar—the divine tortoise. In this avatar, Vishnu swam to the depths of the celestial ocean, where the devas and asuras placed the holy Mount Meru on his shell. Vasuki, the king of the Nagas, offered the use of his body to twist Mount Meru so that they could begin churning the ocean like how milk is churned into butter. Wrapping himself around the middle of Mount Meru, Vasuki let the devas grab his tail and the asuras grab his neck. He didn't trust the devas with his neck, because he feared that Garuda, Lord Vishnu's eagle, would eat him. They began to churn, and churned for eons until they finally cracked the base of the celestial ocean. Out came the infernal Halahal—a poison so deadly that even Vasuki feared its deadly venom.'

'Shiva drank it, right?' I asked. 'Because all poisons are neutralized by his divine grace?'

'Ah, but even though Shiva was mighty enough to handle it, the sheer volume was far too much—even for him,' answered Babaji. 'So, Shakti took Vasuki and wrapped him around Shiva's neck, letting the poison remain there. That's why the throat chakra is so important, for its where poisons can be neutralized. That's why, as a yogi, I can smoke this ganja without getting any of its negative aspects. Shiva is, after all, the Adi Yogi. Ganja is perhaps the mildest of the poisons he enjoyed now and then.' Babaji smiled as he took another leisurely drag. 'Do you know what happened after?'

'Amrita flowed out, and the devas took it for themselves …'

'Double-crossing the asuras. Not a very good thing to do, is it? Faltering on your word of honour. Of course, along with Amrita—the nectar of immortality—Lakshmi also emerged from there. Kind of like Aphrodite rising from the foam of the ocean on the banks of Cyprus.'

'Wait a minute! Do you mean that—'

'Indeed, Lakshmi is the daughter of the asuras! At least according to some versions of the tale. And the minute she emerged, Indra swept her off her feet and took her to his heavenly abode, where he made her his queen!'

'Without her consent?'

'Breaking consent has been part of magical legacy since the very beginning of time, and this is perhaps the earliest recorded history of it. Well, if we can call it history,' Babaji said, pausing to take another drag before continuing. 'However, Lakshmi is far more powerful than Indra. She is the Venusian aspect of the goddess. You see, Indra was an insecure king, and was perpetually paranoid of his possessions being taken away. Therefore, he tried to suppress Lakshmi—not unlike how patriarchy tries to suppress magic and women in general even today. However, Lakshmi has a mind of her own. She leaves anyone who tries to hold on to her like a miser. Magic has left so many souls who've suppressed others and is never accessible to those who dare suppress her.'

'And thus, patriarchy never has access to pure magic!'

Babaji nodded and giggled. 'And so, Lakshmi went to Vishnu, who never really sought her,' he continued. 'He was too busy trying to preserve the world. That is why Lakshmi joined him, for her powers only come to those who wish to help mankind. Thus, magic remained with witches and yogis and those walking the spiritual path, who wish to use their powers to help mankind.'

'But you still haven't told me why the asuras were resurrected!'

Babaji chuckled and said, 'My, such impatience! Lakshmi was the daughter of the asuras, correct?'

I nodded.

'Well, because the devas double-crossed the asuras and greedily swallowed every drop of the Amrita, Lakshmi promised to resurrect the asuras if they died in their eternal battle with the asuras. The devas were already immortal. If they didn't have the asuras to fight with, all the magical potential of the world would end. So, in a way, the asuras are essential in preserving magic.'

Babaji smiled when he saw that I was stunned by this new perspective. He asked, 'What's another name for Venus?'

'Um … Aphrodite? Astarte? Ishtar?'

'No. Think about the sky—what else is Venus is known as?'

I thought for a bit. 'Um … the morning star?'

'And what is another name for the morning star?'

My eyes widened with a shocking realization. 'Lucifer!' I cried.

'Bingo!' Babaji smiled. 'The deity revered by the Cabal!'

'B-B-But how …'

'Dear boy, remember how the sun is both benevolent and cruel. Similarly, Venus has different sides to her. All spiritual deities are essentially neutral. Their power is only corrupted by those who believe in it. No "god" really asks others to kill in their name. Anyway, we've arrived! Time for your next test.'

We stepped out of the taxi. I realized we were standing at the entrance of the Lalit hotel.

'What are we doing here?' I asked.

'Well, you passed the test of fear,' replied Babaji. 'Now you must pass the test of guilt.' He led me through the lobby and down the steps to Kitty Su, the hotel's nightclub.

'I don't get it,' I whispered as I followed him.

'Well, Venus rules sexuality, right?'

'Yeah?'

'And Lakshmi, the Venusian aspect of the goddess, is the consort of whom?'

'Vishnu ...'

'And Vishnu is the deity of which chakra?'

'The sacral and svadishthana chakra ... but what does that have to do with—'

Before I could finish, Babaji waved like a princess to the bouncer standing by the door. He allowed us to skip the queue and enter. Once our wrists were stamped by the door hostess, we were inside the crowded nightlub. The DJ was playing a remix of a vintage Bollywood track.

Babaji led me over to the bar. I watched with amazement as he twirled his fingers, causing the patrons to move aside and make way for us. He turned to me and asked, 'What's your poison?'

'Gin and tonic!' I answered immediately.

As we sipped our drinks, Babaji twirled his fingers again, and the music seemed to fade out. When no one else reacted, I realized that the effect only applied for the two of us. We could speak without shouting. 'You've only had sexual intercourse twice,' said Babaji. 'The first time was without your consent, and the second under the spell of love.'

'Vir put a spell on me?' I asked in shock.

'I'm being metaphorical! Jeez!' exclaimed Babaji as he sipped on his Cosmopolitan. 'The point is, apart from those two times, you haven't really had sex on your own terms. The corpse from last night doesn't count because of reasons that are pretty obvious. Guilt is the demon of the svadhisthana chakra. Queer individuals and women have been burdened with centuries of guilt regarding our sexuality thanks to patriarchy. The first step towards overcoming it is to start not only enjoying sex on our own terms, but also accessing it whenever and wherever we want to. Besides, you haven't really had sex since you arrived at my shala, which was almost two years ago! Aren't you craving it?'

I couldn't really disagree.

'So, to access that aspect of your magic, you need to come to peace with your sexual desire and its pleasure without any trace of guilt. Hence, what better place to find it than a gay bar!'

'This is a gay bar?' I was surprised that I hadn't even noticed.

'Oh for heaven's sake, boy! Get out of your self-absorbed inner monologue and have a look around!'

I did look around and was surprised to see so many gay men dancing about. It was my first time at a gay bar. I didn't even know they existed in Delhi. It was so exciting to see so many men feel free to be themselves. They were tall, short, skinny, muscular and everything in-between. It almost made me feel safe being amongst so many of my tribe. *Can I call them my tribe?* I wondered.

'Pick one!' Babaji sipped his cosmopolitan.

'Huh?' I shot him a confused look.

'You heard me!'

'I did, but I can't just—'

'Oh hush!' Babaji said before swallowing the last drop of his pink drink. 'Just pick a guy you find hot and point him out to me.'

I looked around through the sea of people dancing. They were all attractive in their own ways, but no one particular who caught my … oh hello there! My eyes sparkled with delight as I saw a tall man standing by the bar ordering a Barcardi and Coke. Though I couldn't make out his features in the dim light, I liked how his muscles protruded from the tight black Armani shirt he was wearing. He had the sleeves rolled up, revealing strong forearms. His pants did nothing to hide his bum. I informed Babaji that I had made my choice.

'Wow, a Muscle Mary!' said Babaji, rolling his eyes. 'Typical!'

'So now what do I do?'

Fishing out two condoms from his pocket, Babaji discreetly slipped them into the pocket of my jeans. 'Well, your test is to seduce him and enjoy him in the loo,' he declared.

'What?' My eyes widened in shock.

'Venus, sex, sexuality, svadhisthana chakra, guilt … go!' Babaji nudged me closer to the hottie.

'But why two …'

'One for you and one for him … versatility is part of the joy of being a yogi!'

'B-b-but why the loo?'

'Venus rules bathrooms!'

Before I could protest, Babaji twirled his fingers, causing the music to return to its regular volume. At the same time, a young twink came over to Babaji and said, 'Come to me, Daddy!' Before the twink pulled him over to the dance floor, Babaji gave me a final nudge, causing me to bump into the hottie.

'Oh sorry!' I exclaimed, thankful I didn't cause him to spill his drink.

'What?' the hottie asked, leaning in. I had forgotten that now that the music was loud, I had to scream over it in order to be heard.

'I'm sorry for bumping into you!' I yelled in his ear, getting a whiff of his deliciously musky cologne.

'No worries, cutie!' He smiled as he clinked his glass with mine. It had been so long since I had looked someone so handsome in the eye.

'You got a name?' he asked.

'J-J-Jai!' Fuck, how could I stutter!

'Huh?' He leaned in closer. Fuck, his cologne was so hot!

'Jai!' I yelled louder.

'Nice name!' he said. 'I'm Suraj!'

I smiled, but then there was an awkward silence between us as I was not sure how to take it forward. We just stood by the bar, sipping our drinks and watching the crowded dance floor. I couldn't help but smile as I saw Babaji being twirled by not one or two but *three* twinks, who took turns grinding against him.

'This one's for Jai!' announced the DJ suddenly. I saw Babaji wink at me. My heart skipped a beat when the opening bars of Magdalena's 'Wild Wild Woman' began to play.

'OMG!' I yelled in the hottie's ear, whose name had already escaped my mind. 'I freaking love this song!'

'Really?'

'OMG! It's like my jam!' As the eight-o-eight drums began to echo, a strange surge of confidence filled my being. I grabbed on to the guy's hand and said, 'Let's dance!'

Suddenly, I didn't have a care in the world as the music took over my soul. I began lip-syncing along to the infectious chorus: 'Hey-yeah-yeah-yeah-hey-hey-hey-hey I'm a wild wo-man a wild-wild-wo-man!' As the second verse began, the hottie began grinding against me. I wrapped my arms around him as our bodies pressed against each other. His arousal was very apparent through his tight pants.

Beyond the hypnotic effect of Magdalena's voice, I felt a surge of desires coursing through my veins that I thought I had lost a long time ago. I was so overcome with guilt over all that transpired that I hadn't even touched myself throughout my stay at Majnu Ka Tila. As my body grinded against the hottie, I could feel that guilt melt away.

'Wanna get outta here?' the hottie yelled in my ear as the song segued into another one. I led him straight to the loo as per Babaji's directions.

As we entered the men's room, we guffawed as there were already two couples making out in different corners. Giggling, we found a stall just for ourselves. The minute he locked the door, I jumped upon him, kissing him with a ferocity that

I had never felt before. With a swift stroke of my fingers, I unbuttoned his shirt in an instant, revealing his muscular torso. He had popping pecs and abs one could grate cheese over.

'Whoa!' he exclaimed, his eyes widening with amazement. 'How did you do that?'

Magic, I grinned to myself before starting to kiss him again.

Chapter Twenty-Nine

Over the next few months, I gained a whole new sense of confidence and comfort within myself. I would fearlessly walk up to anyone I fancied and within moments, I'd have them eating out of the palm of my hands ... and elsewhere too. My appetite was insatiable, and Babaji would always encourage me.

I'd never bring them over to my tiny room at the ashram, as the bed wasn't big enough for the two of us. I'd always go to theirs. Many times, they couldn't host, so we'd find a quiet alleyway or a shady spot behind the bushes in a park. Sometimes they would offer to rent a room at a nearby hotel. Babaji also arranged a room for me at the Lalit whenever I'd go out for a night of dancing at the nightclub there.

'Sex is a powerful exchange of magical energy,' Babaji would tell me. 'Make sure you shield your aura beforehand so that you don't unconsciously give off your power. Once done, cleanse your chakras with light green and electric violet light so that you don't pick up on their energy as well. Apart from that, feel free to go crazy!'

Magic coursed through my veins unlike ever before. I didn't need to focus so hard on visualizing light and colours anymore.

Seeing auras and energy fields became almost second nature. I also began appreciating my looks more. I told myself that I was now a bonafide hottie with a yoga-chiselled body that could drive men wild with its flexibility. It felt so good to be in control.

Vir never let me be in control, so I never experienced how addictive it could be. Whether I topped or bottomed, I was always in charge. My pleasure took priority! Of course, I made sure that they enjoyed themselves too. After all, greater pleasure comes from giving than just receiving. However, it was more fun being on the receiving end of things.

Babaji would train me in the empty shala between classes. He convinced Tempa's parents to excuse me from working at the café as I needed time to train. Only Tempa complained as he'd have to take over my shifts.

'You need the work to overcome your laziness!' Babaji chuckled as he playfully swatted the back of Tempa's head, 'Maybe then you'll be able to hold your handstands longer and firmer!'

I learned how to snap my fingers and light candles. By twirling my fingers I could then make the candles levitate and fly around the room without the flame extinguishing. I'd also learned how to hold a stranger's palms and access visions of not only their past in this life, but also past lives. I would only do this with their consent, of course.

However, all that was only the tip of the iceberg. There was so much more to learn. Babaji promised to teach me as much as he could. 'Do not abandon all you've learned from your family,' Babaji said one morning as he sipped his masala chai after an intense training session. 'It's your foundation. Keep it strong and keep nourishing it. It'll ground you. Magic without grounding is as deadly as the venom of a cobra.'

Placing his empty glass by the windowsill, Babaji twirled his hands and a demon appeared.

'Do not be afraid!' Babaji instructed. 'This is just a low-level entity. It's under my control, so it can't harm you. Focus on your breath and shoot it with white light.'

Closing my eyes, I took a few deep breaths. Then I extended my arms, and as I exhaled sharply, a beam of white light surged from my hands, vanquishing the demon instantly.

'Excellent!' Babaji said with a grin.

The next day, he summoned another low-level demon. This time he didn't control it, allowing it to attack me. Before I could strike, the demon pushed me, making me fall back and crash into the wall. As I screamed in pain, Babaji twirled his fingers and created a lasso of white light that he tossed around the demon's neck. The demon fell to its knees like an obedient dog.

'Demons won't wait for you!' Babaji scolded me. 'You have to attack them before they can get to you!' Releasing the demon, Babaji ordered me to attack. Before the demon could leap towards me, I shot him with a beam of white light, causing it to disintegrate in mid-air.

'Better!'

The next day, the demon Babaji conjured was mightier. Even when I attacked it with a shot of white light, he just swatted the beam away and kept charging towards me. I leaped about, avoiding the demon. I didn't know if it was because of my intense yogic training or the magic coursing through me that I was almost levitating at times. I somersaulted and cartwheeled to avoid the demon's attacks.

'You're wasting too much time!' Babaji yelled as I kept up the chase. 'Vanquish it now!'

As the demon took a mighty leap towards me, I swirled and kicked it right in the face. As I did so, I could feel a shield of white light cover my body. A surge of white light was emitted from my leg, blowing the demon to smithereens.

'Finally!' Babaji said. He took out his pink lace fan and left to have his lunch.

Weeks passed as I trained against stronger demons. Each fight was now gruelling in its intensity. Though I would be exhausted afterwards, I was amazed by how my body's physical and magical strength grew after each encounter. The fights began to resemble old kung-fu movies, with me doing gravity-defying acrobatic stunts. It was as though I was one with the wind as I glided through the air with by body flowing like a river.

One day, Babaji summoned the most powerful demon I had come across. The others were mostly smoky, formless entities, but this one towered over me and looked very real. I shivered as I looked upon its grotesque form. Its lower body was like a gigantic furry tarantula with eight limbs that oozed pus. It had the torso of a human and two muscular arms with sharp talons like those of an eagle. It had the head of a lizard with a forked tongue and shark-like fangs.

'Attack!' Babaji ordered.

But before I could even blink, the demon swatted me across the room. Restraining it with a white-light lasso, Babaji ordered me to get up at once and fight again. But as soon as I got on my feet, the demon swatted me to the other side of the room. A layer of paint cracked as I smashed into the wall. Before I could get up, the demon grabbed me again and flung me into the opposite wall as I screamed in pain.

'Pathetic!' Babaji shouted. He snapped his fingers and the demon vanished. He left the room, fanning himself.

The next day, I fought the same demon again, and it was a repeat of the previous performance. The demon flung me around like a child would do to a toy. It repeated the next day, and the day after, for almost a month. I made no progress.

As Babaji shook his head in disgust and left the room after another defeat, I yelled after him, 'Why the fuck can I not vanquish it?'

'Because you're weak!' Babaji turned and said sternly.

'I am trying! I really am!' I yelled back. 'But it's no use—that demon is far too powerful for me.'

Babaji shook his head again before leaving.

The next day, the demon continued to have its way with me. After three rounds, before he could send it away, I shouted in anger and frustration, 'How the fuck am I supposed to defeat it?'

'Well, clearly Adele didn't teach you well!' retorted Babaji as he coolly sipped his masala chai.

'What do you mean?' I couldn't believe what he had just said.

'Clearly, she failed you not only as a teacher, but also as a parent—well, a grandparent.'

Before I could say anything, he continued, 'She spoiled you. As did your aunts. Coddling you with cakes and whatnot, not even teaching you how to protect yourself from demons.'

'But—'

'I mean, she knew what would happen to you after seven years of magical training, but never did she warn you. She was always a secretive one. And when you were traumatized, what did she do? Teach you a few parlour tricks to give you a false sense of confidence? Pathetic!'

I could feel my blood boil with every word, but I let him continue. 'All that big talk about empowerment, for what?' Babaji scoffed. 'You grew up to be a whiny little sissy boy that spends all his time monologuing internally, too afraid to speak up or speak your heart's desire. And then letting her insidious father—a despicable man who evolved into a fourth-density being of darkness—mark you with Lucifer's eye. Did she ever tell you about it or why he did so? Not until it was too late, in any case. I knew there was a reason she was no longer worthy of being my student!'

Too far, Babaji! I said to myself. *Too fucking far!* I could feel a fiery anger coursing through my veins as he continued, 'And then you fell in love with a boy who was set to take over the reins of his bloodline in service to the Cabal. A Cabal she knew all about, but never once thought to warn you about. And you, like a pathetic little twerp, fell head over heels for the first boy who showed you a morsel of kindness. Thinking you could love someone so quickly! What do you even know about love? Not that pathetic mollycoddling Adele and her daughters raised you with. Those hugs and kisses made you soft. A soft little pansy boy!'

'STOP IT!' I shouted, standing up. My eyes burned with rage. I could feel the eye on my chest burn as a fiery surge flowed through me like an volcano about to erupt.

'Oh, now you stand up!' Babaji scoffed. 'Had you learned how to do so a long time ago, you would have been able to save your family. But no, pathetic little weakling that you are, you allowed Adele's father to manipulate you, and thus you burned them alive. That's what your weakness did. It made you kill them. You burned the only family you knew!'

'ENOUGH!' I bellowed. Suddenly the eye on my chest shot a powerful red beam of light towards the demon, causing it to catch fire. As it let out a supersonic squeal of horror, Babaji commanded, 'Now!' He released the demon from the white-light lasso.

I began fighting it with a ferocity unlike ever before, knocking it back with punches and kicks as white light shot out through my limbs with an intensity I could barely control. The demon wailed with every mighty blow. Finally, it fell on its back and was unable to stand up. I let out a mighty scream as a blinding white light emerged from the eye on my chest, blowing it to smithereens. I collapsed on my knees as it all grew dark.

When I opened my eyes, I saw Babaji laughing like a child. As I slowly sat up, he walked over and sat beside me. 'You've now passed the test of shame,' he said.

'Huh?'

His green eyes twinkled as he said, 'Oh my boy, there was so much anger trapped inside of you. Anger is the poison of your solar plexus, or the manipura chakra. Its enemy is shame. That shame was eating away at your soul. Only when you were able to let go of your shame could you discover that bit of magic that was dormant within you.' He pointed at the eye on my chest. 'The eye of Lucifer is a powerful symbol,' he continued. 'Shame prevents you from accessing it. Hence, I had to trigger you to enable you to do so. No hard feelings, okay?' He extended his hand.

I hesitantly accepted it. 'You didn't mean all that, did you?'

He quickly enveloped me in his embrace, soothing my body with his cuddly self as he whispered, 'Not a single word.'

Chapter Thirty

'Prana is the essence of magic,' said Babaji as he sat before me in padmasana. 'Prana is the life force that flows through everything that breathes, and through everything that doesn't. The Chinese call it Qi, the Sufis call it Ruh, while the ancient Greeks call it Pneuma. The great Kabbalist mystics call it Ruah, while in Latin it's referred to as Anima, the animating principle of life. Everyone has access to it, but only witches and yogis have the ability to channel it to create magic.'

'Is that why pranayama has to be practiced by all yogis?'

'Precisely!' Babaji replied. 'But pranayama is useless without physical practice. After all, the body is the temple of the soul. The soul needs Prana to thrive, but if the body isn't strong enough to handle it, the soul is trapped in a lifetime without experiencing its full potential. Adele did well to begin your physical training at such a young age. Most people only start yoga later in life, often after their body is injured due to afflictions of the physical, emotional or mental realm. Once they get on the mat and maintain a regular practice, they do experience many benefits. However, for most it remains just a physical practice. It would take them lifetimes to learn how to harness the true power of their prana. That's why you were perhaps born into a family of witches—your soul must have experienced yoga through many lifetimes, but it's only in this one that it was ready to experience not only the power of prana, but magic as a whole. That's why you took to it without any resistance. Your soul removed all traces of doubts about your mission—'

'My mission?'

'To walk the path of service to others. Magic is of no use if it's just used for personal gain. That is why even great psychics can never predict their own lives. They can try, but they'd never be as accurate about themselves as they would be for complete strangers. If they were, they'd all be billionaires by playing the stock market. Magic when used to benefit oneself backfires severely.'

'But Gran and my aunts would charge people for their services. I mean, I've seen people pay them with briefcases full of cash. Isn't that basically serving the self?'

Babaji let out a jolly chuckle. 'Dear boy, even witches and yogis must eat! And what's money compared to helping people in their hour of need? Magic is energy, and energy needs to flow. That's why money is taken in exchange. After all, money is Lakshmi! I'm sure you know that everything Adele and her daughters did for those who came to them was worth what they paid.'

I couldn't help but agree.

'Many people with gifts feel guilt and shame when it comes to charging for their gifts,' continued Babaji. 'People, however, never value anything done for free—which is why plantation owners in the United States never considered their slaves as human beings who deserved a life of dignity. Those that do offer something for free, beware of them. They lure you in with the promise of something free, but they will come to collect eventually, and that cost will be deadly. Just like Rumpelstiltskin in the old faerie tale offered to weave straw into gold for free to help the miller's daughter, but once she married the king and gave birth to her first child, Rumpelstiltskin demanded the baby be given to him. Most nefarious cults offer something free—a personality evaluation, perhaps, or an invite to join a weekly meditation circle. Once you've taken the bait, they start luring you with promises to elevate your soul, provided you spend thousands on their courses. And let's not forget how they shame you into giving them regular donations.'

'Is this your way of asking me to pay you?'

'Oh God, no!' Babaji exclaimed. 'I teach you because of a promise I made to Adele. You see, in a past life, she was my teacher.'

'She was?' My eyes widened.

'Indeed!' Babaji smiled and continued, 'I recognized it while she was still in her mother's womb. When her father chose to sell his soul to the Cabal, Adele made me promise to teach you everything I possibly could so that you wouldn't fall prey to the Cabal. Thus, I took you on as my protégé.'

'So, what am I supposed to defeat? The Cabal?'

Babaji guffawed. 'Oh no, you can't really defeat them. They were on a sacred mission before history could even be recorded. They exist to serve a greater purpose. To bring upon chaos in the world.'

'But why? Why chaos?'

'If it wasn't for chaos, we human beings wouldn't have the ability to access our free will,' he explained. 'Without free will, we'd be no better than zombies. It's only through free will that we can make choices. Each choice—be it as small as deciding what outfit to wear in the morning or as big as deciding whether to end life support for an ailing relative—is one between the path of service to the self and the path of service to others. Through these choices our soul evolves through the payment of karmic debts.'

'But then how does a soul break this karmic cycle? I mean, as long as we live human lives, we're stuck in this seemingly endless karmic cycle because every day we're faced with numerous choices. Even getting out of bed in the morning is a choice.'

'That's where the paths come in handy. Through service to the self, we entrap ourselves so much in the karmic cycles that our soul shifts its polarity. Then, once it's ready to shift to the fourth density beyond the human body, it becomes demonic in nature. However, through the path of service to others, the soul learns the true divine joy of giving. Thus, it eventually evolves to the angelic realm in the fourth density.'

'Do you think Gran and my aunts have evolved into fourth-density angels?'

Babaji sighed. 'I don't have the answer to that. Their karma is theirs, just as your karma is yours and my karma is mine. I took a vow to never leave my body till my soul was ready to evolve into the fourth-density angelic realm. I've been roaming the earth for centuries, doing my bit to serve those in need. Perhaps in previous lifetimes, I accumulated so much karma that I'm still paying it off. Not that I'm complaining—I've led an incredibly fun life and had so many adventures along the way. I saw the world evolve through the ages. However, I never got attached to it. Attachment corrupts the heart, making us insecure within ourselves, robbing us of the ability to enjoy the present moment. Perhaps that's why I even let go of my name. After all, our name is the first identity given to us, allowing our ego to be formed right from birth. The ego thrives on attachment.'

'Why are you telling me this?' I asked, making Babaji give me an odd look. I quickly explained, 'I mean, not that all this hasn't been enlightening. But we've spent so many months intensely training to fight demons and developing my powers. Surely there's a reason for it beyond expanding my worldview?'

Babaji shook his head. 'Ah, the youth of today!' he complained. 'So impatient!'

Before I could protest, Tempa entered carrying an earthen teapot that had vapours swaying from its spout as if they were dancing.

'Did you follow the instructions to the letter?' Babaji asked as Tempa placed the pot before us.

'I'm lazy, but not stupid!' Tempa retorted. 'Now will that be all? The lunch rush is about to begin, I need to get ready and—'

'And what are we supposed to drink out of?' Babaji asked, making Tempa look puzzled at first. He bit his tongue in shock when he realized that he forgot to bring cups or glasses.

'Oops! Sorry!' Tempa said, grinning haplessly.

As Babaji raised his arm to swat him, Tempa squealed and ran away.

'Not stupid, indeed!' Babaji shook his head before turning to me. 'Lord knows what sin I must have done to deal with that dolt!'

Tempa rushed back in, panting as he placed two earthen cups between us. Before Babaji could scold him further, Tempa ran back out. I couldn't help but giggle.

'So, do you want to know why I was telling you all that?'

I nodded as Babaji began pouring steaming green liquid from the pot into the cups. 'You've overcome the tests of fear, guilt and shame,' he said. 'And you've done well so far …' He handed me a cup.'Today is the test of grief!'

'Grief?' I asked as I took my cup, surprised that it was cold even though steaming vapours danced by the rim.

'Prana is circulated through our heart chakra, also known as the anahata chakra. Just like the heart pumps blood through our veins, the anahata allows Prana to circulate throughout our body. Grief is the demon of the heart. And your heart is full of it.'

Before I could question further, Babaji commanded, 'Drink up!'

As I brought my cup close to my lips, my nose crinkled at the incredibly foul odour. 'What the hell is this?'

'Never you mind that!' Babaji said. 'Just close your nose and down it like a shot of tequila!'

Knowing there was no point arguing, I drank it all in one big gulp, surprised by the fact that it tasted like nothing. Even water had more taste than this!

'Good boy!' Babaji said and then drank a cupful himself. He then extended his arms with his right palm facing down while his left faced up. 'Now, put your hands in mine.'

Once I did so, Babaji commanded, 'Now, close your eyes and focus on your breath. Do not do anything; just let whatever happens, happen.'

The moment our palms joined, I felt an electric rush flow through my spine.

'Now open your eyes!'

When I did, I found myself standing waist-deep in a lake under a starless night sky that was streaked in various shades of green, illuminated solely by a full moon that glowed with hues of blue and violet. As I swayed gently in the lake, I noticed the ripples in the water were tinted in yellow, orange and red. Before I could ask where I was, Babaji's voice echoed:

'This is your heart, Jai!'

'Why is it so dark in here?' I shivered and realized I was naked in the icy water.

'That's because it's plagued with grief, Jai!' Babaji's voice echoed.

'Why is it—' before I could finish my question, I yelped in panic as I felt something icy cold brush against me. It was Vir's lifeless, naked body floating in the water!

'You know why it's grieving,' Babaji's voice echoed again as I stared at Vir. Even though he was stiff as a board and icicles were forming around his nostrils and mouth and his skin glowing in a frightful shade of indigo, I still couldn't help but fall in love with him all over again. *No!* I thought. I couldn't let myself! Not after what …

'Why am I here?' I yelled at the sky above as my mind began racing like a wild gazelle.

No answer.

'Babaji!' I yelled again. 'Why have you brought me here?'

The silence was frightening. As Vir's icy body brushed against my waist, I let out a yelp of disgust and pushed it away. It floated away a little, but immediately floated back and knocked me in the stomach with its head. I pushed it away more forcefully, but it returned again, hitting me harder. Argh! With a mighty exhale, I channelled all my strength to push Vir's body away, causing it to float a few feet away. However, it once again torpedoed towards me. This time, it threw me off balance and made me fall into the water.

Before I could stand up, I felt something grab on to my ankle. I began screaming as I splashed about the water, desperately trying to kick myself free while keeping my head afloat. But it was of no use. The more I struggled, the more I was pulled down. Then I realized that Vir's body stood before me. As I tried to grab on to his arm in the hope of saving myself, Vir dunked my head in with both his hands, plummeting me to my watery fate.

Suddenly, I found myself in a lavish bedroom. Before I could take in the luxurious surroundings, I let out a cry of horror as I saw a child lying on its back as a much younger Rajani sahab belted him. With each strike of the sharp and heavy buckle, the child cried tears of sheer agony. I couldn't bear to see any further. Vir's young face was red with tears as he wailed. *Oh God!* I thought. *Make it stop! Make it stop!*

I then opened my eyes to find myself in a hospital room. I saw a slightly older Vir strapped to a bed with his mouth gagged with a cotton gauze. Rajani sahab stood before him along with Damyanti. There was also a doctor in full surgical garb who was holding two rods in his hands with wires tied to a big machine.

As Rajani sahab nodded, the doctor prodded Vir with the rods. My eyes widened with horror as Vir's screams of pain were muffled by the gauze. He was being electrocuted.

'Don't worry, Rajani sahab!' said the doctor, removing his mask and smiling. 'We'll shock the gay out of him in no time!'

Fuck! No! This can't be real! No! Make it stop! Please make it stop!

I was transported to a large hall. Torches hung on marble columns illuminated a gilded ceiling. The floor was tiled like a chess board. Surrounding me were a horde of people wearing scarlet robes with black hoods covering their heads. Around their neck was a purple scarf with golden edges and embroidered on the chest of their robes in thick golden threads was the symbol of an eye similar to the one I had on my chest.

I saw Vir, who was now around the same age as I last saw him, kneeling naked before three men who sat on gilded thrones. Their robes had more elaborate golden embroidery. Above each throne, grand antlers hung on the wall. The ones in the centre were attached to what seemed to be a skull of a mighty stag.

'Praise Lucifer!' yelled the three men as they stood and raised their arms in the air.

'Praise Lucifer!' echoed the horde, raising their arms as well.

The man in the centre walked towards Vir, stopping barely a step away from him. Three hooded attendants walked up from the crowd and grabbed a rope that descended from the ceiling, knotting it around Vir's ankle.

'Stand before us!' The main leader commanded Vir, who stood up slowly and turned towards the crowd, his head bowing in shame. The main leader nodded to the attendants, who tugged at the rope, causing Vir to be dangled upside-down.

'You see, oh brothers!' The main leader's voice echoed in a deep baritone. 'We have a traitor amongst our midst!'

The horde began to boo wildly, stopping only when the main leader raised his hand to silence them. 'Lucifer trusted us to follow his divine will,' he said. 'Since the dawn of time, we have served him loyally in his quest for domination through chaos.'

'Praise Lucifer!' The two sub-leaders yelled as they raised their arms, causing the horde to do the same. The main leader raised his hand to silence them again before continuing, 'However, for the first time in our history, we have someone who refuses to follow through.'

The crowd again booed wildly, only to be silenced by the main leader. 'Do we take kindly to traitors?' he asked.

'NO!' The crowd yelled.

The main leader said, 'Perhaps it's time we taught the traitor a lesson!'

The crowd cheered in agreement as the attendants presented the three leaders with large brass staffs. Taking them in their hands, the three circled Vir who, despite dangling in mid-air, remained as still as he possibly could.

'Let us begin!' the main leader yelled.

The three leaders raised their staffs and the horde fell to their knees, chanting ominously in Latin. The main leader struck the first blow on to Vir's back. 'Praise Lucifer!' he shouted.

As the chants grew louder and louder, each of the leaders took turns beating Vir, making his body oscillate like a pendulum.

They yelled praises to Lucifer with each strike. Vir took each blow silently, almost as if he felt he deserved it.

Fuck! This can't be happening! No! Make it stop! Please make it stop!

'Stop it!' I shouted as I ran up to the leaders, but every time I tried to grab them, I just fell through them. They couldn't see me nor feel me. It was as if I were a ghost.

'NO!' I screamed, trying to stand before Vir's dangling body in order to protect him from the blows. But it was no use. The brass staffs passed through my body as if it was just air as they continued to beat Vir.

Oh no! This can't be happening! Please! Stop! Stop it! Stop it! STOOOOOOPP!!

All of a sudden, I was back in the lake. This time I could see Vir's body curled in a fetal position by the grassy bank. Splashing my way through the lake, I ran up the shore and threw myself upon him.

'Vir!' I cried as I frantically kissed him all over his face. 'Oh Vir! What have they done to you?'

'He truly did love you, Jai!' Babaji's voice echoed. 'So much so that he wanted to give up his birth right so that you could be saved. They wanted to offer your soul as a sacrifice.'

'Why?' I looked up at the dark sky, holding on to Vir desperately.

'Within you flows not only the blood of Lucifer, but generations of magic. Witches, when sacrificed through the Cabal's nefarious rituals, have their magic transferred to the Lucifer Soul Group, allowing them to continue their reign for centuries. However, your sacrifice would empower them till eternity. You are, after all, the first male child of a witch.'

'That can't be true! I'm just a—'

'It doesn't matter if it's true or not. It is what they believe. Belief is a force so powerful that it can even make the sun rise from the west. Their belief has been empowered for eons.'

'Oh God, this is so fucking twisted ...'

'It is what it is. However, Vir stood up for you. He wanted to spare you and leave behind the Cabal. You've now seen the consequences of his actions.'

I sobbed as I held Vir's body in my arms. Babaji's echoing voice asked, 'Do you still love him, Jai?'

'Yes!' I shouted immediately without a shred of doubt. 'Yes! I love him!' I kissed Vir softly as I whispered, 'I love you! I truly love you!'

'Then you must forgive him. He was not responsible for what happened to your family, just as you weren't. You were both pawns in a greater nefarious scheme. Forgiveness is the only way you can alleviate yourself from the demon of grief. Forgive him, Jai! And with that, forgive yourself!'

I sobbed as I held onto Vir's body, kissing him softly on the lips. I wrapped his lifeless arms around me and cried salty tears upon his chest. 'I forgive you,' I whispered, trembling. 'I forgive you, Vir!'

I closed my eyes, and when I opened them again I found myself back in the shala, sobbing with my head resting on Babaji's thigh.

Gently, Babaji kissed me on the forehead and said, 'I can teach you no more.'

Chapter Thirty-One

I never thought I would return to the chapel of St. Sebastian's, but here I am after so many years, back to perhaps the place where it all began. I had never been here at night before. There was a weird sort of comfort in seeing that nothing had really changed. The same gilded dome, the same stained-glass windows that still possessed that hauntingly beautiful quality, the same bench where Nikhil Sahni kissed me before he took me to the … oh, let's not go there.

Despite it being night, the frankincense and myrrh still remained potent in the air. It was surreal that despite hating school so much—and all the shit that went down during those days—I still found a sense of peace here. Maybe it's because Babaji helped me defeat all traces of fear, guilt, shame and grief from my physical and energetic bodies. Or maybe it was because I was so focussed on my mission that I didn't dwell on the past.

'You've changed so much since the last time you were here,' said a voice beside me.

I turned and smiled at the divine being sitting beside me on the bench. His brilliant halo caused the dark chapel to glow. 'What, no arrows?' I asked.

The divine being laughed and said, 'We never carry our wounds with us when we ascend to higher realms.'

'I suppose you already know why I'm here,' I said. I removed my black overcoat as the divine being's aura made me feel quite toasty despite the city being in the midst of a cold wave.

'I do,' the divine being answered. 'But I still feel you're acting recklessly. There are other ways to go about it.'

'Time, unfortunately, isn't on my side,' I said. 'Besides, sometimes one needs to be a little reckless for the sake of the greater good.'

'Is it really for the greater good?'

'Aren't all great battles fought in the name of love? After all, you are the patron saint of warriors and even athletes.'

'I'm also the patron saint of the holy death!'

'Death hasn't really been a fear of mine.'

'Death isn't only about the physical. Pain is after all just an expression. Death is the doorway of transformation. What you're about to do could very well transform the fate of the world. Are you sure you can handle that?'

'Well, I've spent almost all my life preparing for it.'

'And you've prepared well,' said the divine being. 'But you know how it is. I must deliver the warning before I give you the boon you seek. All blessings come with a curse.'

'Just as all curses bring along a blessing.'

The divine being gently laughed and said, 'I do admire your chutzpah! It's indeed admirable.'

'Well, I had some really good teachers that enabled me to build that kind of faith in myself.'

'As did I,' the divine being sighed. 'It was hard to conceal my faith in his holiness back in those times. Despite my best efforts to do so, I was reproached by Diocletian. He had me bound to the stake and then ordered the archers from Mauritiana to shoot me down with the arrows. Though I didn't die, had it not been for Irene, the widow of Castulus, I would have remained there for all of eternity. I suppose that's God's way of reaffirming my faith.'

'I don't think I have the luxury of being rescued by anyone,' I said.

'The path you walk is a lonely one,' the divine being said. He placed his hand on my shoulder, causing tingles to run down my spine. 'You have to be your own source of inspiration as well as your own rescuer.'

'Do you think I'll be able to save myself after what I'm about to do?'

'In your heart, do you believe you're doing it for noble reasons or selfish ones?'

'I don't know,' I sighed. 'I know I have to rescue Vir from the Cabal, but what if it triggers a series of events that drown the world in doom? Would my act of rescuing one put the lives of countless others in jeopardy?'

'I'm not a fortune-teller,' replied the divine being with a smile. 'But I do know that everything that happens is for the greater good. After all, what happened to you here started you on your journey.'

'I doubt many would consider my journey as "the greater good",' I sighed. 'I've lost so much in the process …'

'But what you've gained has been more.'

'Debatable,' I scoffed. 'But you know, life moves on, and we need to make the best of what's given to us.'

The divine being smiled and said, 'Well, for that you need to keep your faith alive. Your heart knows what's in store even before your intuitive mind does. As long as your intentions are pure, the divine takes care of the rest.'

'Are mine pure?' I asked as I looked him straight in the eye.

'If they weren't,' he replied. 'I wouldn't have appeared before you tonight. Neither would have the others when you sought them out.'

The divine being slowly opened his robe, revealing his shimmering torso covered with holes where arrows had once pierced his skin. Taking my hand in his, he made me dip my index finger in one of the punctured wounds on his chest, right above his heart. As he dug my finger in deeper, I could feel beams of white light flow through my veins as if an icy breeze blowed through me. Upon pulling my finger out, I was surprised to see my fingertip was red with fresh blood that smelled incredibly real.

As I looked up at him, the divine being led my finger to my lips. Almost instinctively, I put it in my mouth, sucking upon it gently. I was pleasantly surprised to find that it tasted like honey. With each stroke of my tongue, I felt a surge of divine energy envelop my being. It was like I was standing under a waterfall where light slowly covered the crown of my head, working its way down my face to my neck and shoulders. As it flowed down my arm and chest, I felt so mighty and powerful. When the light flowed down my knees and calves, I felt weightless. And by the time it bathed the soles of my feet, I was levitating, floating about as if I were in space without the weight of reality bringing me down.

The divine being laughed as I gently landed on the bench after I removed my finger from my mouth. 'I don't think you need any confirmation of your faith, do you?' he asked.

'I guess not,' I replied with a smile.

'When is your quest?'

'Tomorrow night.'

'Ah, well, then you must leave now. You need all the rest you can get. Even the greatest warriors can't fight a battle without a good night's rest.'

'I doubt I'll manage to sleep with all this adrenaline coursing through me.'

'Ah, but you'll find a way,' he said. 'You've been taught the meditations to do so. If they fail, I'm sure your aunts taught you how to brew the right kind of tea to help.'

I couldn't help but laugh at that. 'Thank you for coming to me!' I said.

'Thank me once you return successfully!' With that, the divine being slowly faded into the night.

Immediately, the warmth disappeared and I felt the chill of the Delhi winter. Quickly putting on my coat, I walked over to the altar and lit a fresh white candle. I placed it on the prayer stand that was littered with the melted wax of candles that burned throughout the day. Genuflecting before the giant statue of the Holy Madonna holding the Baby Jesus in her arms, I marked myself with the sign of the cross before staring up at the large mural of St. Sebastian bound to a tree with arrows piercing his body. I couldn't resist winking at him.

Don't worry, Vir, I thought. *Tomorrow, I will rescue you. Even if it means my death!*

Chapter Thirty-Two

I was a month shy of turning nineteen when Babaji took me to Daryaganj to meet Gran's accountant, Mr Gupta. I was sad that my time with Babaji was drawing to an end. However, it was time for me to spread my wings and fly solo. It was essential for my progress. Babaji assured me that he would still be around to guide me, if needed.

Mr Gupta's beige cabin's décor seemed stuck in the 1970s. White fluorescent lights illuminated a calendar featuring Goddess Lakshmi in her Gaja avatar. She was seated on her bright pink lotus being showered with gold coins by two white elephants as she smiled, blessing those upon whom her gaze fell. 'Do you want the good news or the bad news first?' asked Gupta as he peered at us through his bifocals.

'The bad news, I guess!' I said, shrugging. I didn't even know that Gran had an accountant. I guess she needed someone to manage her estate, considering she lived lavishly. Money was never something we discussed growing up. She considered it incredibly tacky to do so.

'Well, as you were under the care of Babaji,' said Gupta, bowing his head towards Babaji and holding his hands in namaste before continuing, 'There was no one to tend to the property in Golf Links. Due to the new political reforms, all houses granted by the government had to be given back to the state. As you know, that house was a gift to your family from Prime Minister Nehru, and thus Mr Rajani could take it over. He demolished it so that he could build a base there for his political operations.'

I was incredibly saddened to hear that the last trace of my childhood had been destroyed.

'However,' Mr Gupta continued. 'Adele ma'am had named you as her sole beneficiary, as did your aunts. So, you do have a comfortable nest egg in your trust. But most of that is invested in various bonds that are still to mature—so liquidation isn't possible. I wouldn't recommend it anyway. Living on the interest alone will allow you to live a rather comfortable life. Not as comfortable as Golf Links, but maybe we can find you something grand in Sohna Road ...'

Before the shock of potentially living in Gurgaon could sink in, Babaji spoke up, 'Gupta Ji, surely you know people who can help him find something nice in South Delhi?'

'As you can see,' the real estate broker smiled as he showed Babaji and me a small unfurnished 'barsaati' on the roof of a newly renovated builder flat in Defence Colony, 'the space is cozy, but the terrace is massive with such a gorgeous view of Sukun Park! One won't find a better place than this in your rental budget. Plus, the hardwood floors are state of the art ...'

'And the bathroom?' Babaji turned to him.

'Freshly done up, Sir ji!' The broker smiled as he opened the bathroom door, 'Italian marble, with a beautiful granite slab.

All the fittings are American Standard, and look at these large full length St. Gobain mirrors!' He smiled as he pressed the buttons that lit up the bathroom, bathing it in a golden glow. I quite liked the fact that large mirrors were lined with bulbs, making it look like a vanity of a star's dressing room.

Seeing how pleased I was, Babaji turned to the broker, 'We'll take it!'

Along with a faithful accountant, Gran also had an incredibly loyal lawyer—a rarity in these times—who procured an Aadhar card and a PAN card along with a host of other legal certificates for me to ensure that I didn't run into any trouble with the law. I was truly thankful that I didn't have to deal with the bane of endless red tape.

Tempa hugged me tearfully when it was time to leave the ashram. 'I'm going to miss you!' he said.

'I'm going to miss you too, Tempa!' I too couldn't help but tear up a little.

'Come on now!' Babaji said as he yanked Tempa off me and enveloped me in a warm embrace. 'Don't worry, you'll find me when you need to!'

'Come see us when you're craving delicious momos!' Tempa said, grinning.

Babaji kissed me on my forehead before he left the room. He never looked back.

The landlady was an old widow who lived on the ground floor. She rented out the first and second floor too.

'Thank you, Mrs Ahuja!' I said as she handed me a cup of green tea. I was grateful it wasn't milky.

'Oh, please don't be so formal with me, beta!' she said with a smile. 'Call me Sheila Maasi!'

Sheila Maasi was of great help. She spent the next week scouting the furniture market of Amar Colony. 'Some of the things are new, but a lot of it is vintage furniture that's refurbished,' she said. With her brilliant bargaining skills, she managed to get me a single wooden bed with a matching armoire and a chest of drawers for an unbelievable price. I was also amazed that she got the vendors to send their staff to help set it all up for free. I needed to learn those skills from her.

'Beta, don't fall for the big grocery stores in the main market!' she told me as we walked through the sabzi mandi of Kotla Mubarakpur. Vendors arranged their produce in their stalls and yelled while bargaining with their customers. 'Those are more for the expats and the lazy nouveau riche who are driving out most of the older residents. All the big restaurants in Delhi get their vegetables from here! I've been coming here ever since I got married. They all know me well.'

'How come you never moved abroad with your children, Sheila Maasi?' I asked, carrying three bagsof vegetables.

'Oh, my children keep telling me to move with them. But, beta, they have their own lives to lead, and I'm far too old to adjust to a new country and a culture that's alien to me!' She wiped her brow with her dupatta. 'Besides, I have my friends here, and belong to five different kitties! I've got enough to keep me occupied!'

My new kitchen was tiny, but I was happy that there was a state-of-the-art stove and an oven big enough to roast an entire turkey. I had enough money to buy a new iPhone XS Max with a Magdalena case and a Manduka Pro yoga mat in a beautiful shade called 'black magic'.

Shiela Maasi watched wide-eyed as I sprinkled sea salt on the mat before scrubbing it with a damp wash cloth.

'All this effort for a yoga mat that costs over a hundred dollars?' she asked.

'Maasi, it's a Manduka!' I exclaimed, in response to which she shook her head and said, 'You young people have your own crazy fundas, I tell you!'

At the crack of dawn the next day, I took my mat over to Sukun Park, where local residents did their morning walks. The grass was lush due to the monsoons, and the flowers were blossoming with pride. As most children were at school, the sand pit, the swings and slides were empty. Equally deserted were the small basketball and badminton courts.

I waved at Sheila Maasi as she walked around the track with her morning walk group before spreading my mat on the badminton court where a few younger people were performing aerobics and calisthenics exercises. There was also a yoga teacher who was teaching a bunch of seniors some basic yoga moves. I felt it would be rude to intrude.

Sitting in padmasana, I closed my eyes and folded my hands in namaste. I chanted the Gayatri Mantra softly, and after saying my final 'Om shanti', I stood up in tadasana. I began my first round of surya namaskar. As I held my final downward dog for five breaths, I couldn't help but notice that many people were checking me out. Perhaps it was because I had removed my shirt and was just clad in my tiny yoga shorts. *Hope they're enjoying the view*, I thought.

I balanced on one leg and wrapped the other over my shoulder in durvasana. That was when the watching people burst into a round of applause. By the time I got out of shavasana, there were over a dozen residents surrounding me, asking, 'Beta, do you take classes?'

Over the next few weeks, I had to arrive at the park at 4 a.m. so that I could do my practice for two hours. At six, I would teach my first class, which was mainly for senior citizens and beginners. At seven-thirty, I'd do a higher-intensity class geared towards younger people. The evenings were for those who couldn't make it in the morning. Starting with just a handful of students, I had over fifteen in each class by the end of the first month.

'Never refuse a student,' I remembered Gran telling me once with a twinkle in her eye. 'You never know the blessings they'll allow into their lives the minute they step on to their mat.'

I was shy about asking money, but Sheila Maasi said, 'You're providing a great service by teaching yoga. You must charge for it!'

'When are you joining my class, Sheila Maasi?' I asked with a smile.

'Uffo!' she said, waving her hand dismissively. 'I'm too old and too stiff to do yoga!'

I wanted to tell her that no one is too old for yoga, and stiffness goes away the more we practice. But I recalled Gran's sage advice: 'Never force someone on to the mat! They'll come when their soul is ready for it. Perhaps when they injure themselves at the gym or are cursed with the banes of old age.'

'What have you ordered?' Sheila Maasi handed me a large brown packet that she had accepted from the Amazon delivery agent on my behalf. When I opened it to reveal five brand new tarot and oracle decks, her eyes widened, 'Oh, you read tarot cards?'

Soon, my afternoons were flooded with numerous tarot reading appointments. At first, people were hesitant as they thought my rates were far too expensive when compared to other astrologers and psychics they had visited. However, I soon had a customer so ecstatic with the results that she began to spread word about how good I was.

It was embarrassing to have my drawers stuffed with cash. Mr Gupta offered to help me invest my money. 'Jai beta, don't worry,' he said. 'Just as my father and I helped Adele ma'am to manage her finances, I will help you too! Just make sure you always accept payments in cash. Spend as much as you like at the end of the month, bring over whatever is left. I'll help you invest it.'

After a few months, Gupta helped me buy a car. I chose a black Hyundai Creta with all the fancy extras and a high-end stereo system after Gupta's advice: 'Don't go for a Mercedes or something flashy. It'll arouse too much suspicion from the tax authorities.' I couldn't resist spending on clothes though. I had to find a second armoire just to accommodate my new clothes.

The biggest money-maker for me was demonic exorcisms. Though most of my clients were women who were either searching for a man to marry or were suffering at the hands of cruel in-laws, I was amazed how many of my clients were victims of demonic activity.

'Delhi is full of tantriks and corrupt priests that are more than happy to perform demonic attacks for a suitable fee,' Babaji once told me.

'Why would anyone attack people with demons?'

'Never underestimate human greed and their lust for power,' he replied. 'Blood has often been shed over property and inheritance. Some are even willing to torture their daughters-in-law for the sake of dowry.'

I would be asked to exorcise demons from personal possessions, houses and even offices. I no longer had access to Gran's grimoire nor the various magical tools my aunts would use. Therefore, I had to use the only tool I had—my body.

'Your palm contains all the elements of magic!' Babaji told me once during training. 'The thumb is fire, the little finger is water, the ring finger is earth, the middle finger is air and the index finger is spirit. These are your new magical tools. Make sure that you douse them in pure vodka before and after all magical work, to wipe away all demonic entity. Vodka is made from potatoes, which is the perfect vegetable to neutralize all negative magic.'

Of course, I grew my own potatoes! I also grew carrots, tomatoes and peas. Soon, I didn't have to go to Kotla Mubarakpur to buy vegetables. I always gave Sheila Maasi a weekly supply of fresh produce along with the freshest herbs—especially lavender, with which I taught her to make tea.

'Oh, this is delicious!' Sheila Maasi had said after her first sip of lavender tea.

She asked me to make my own herbal infusion mixes so that she could sell them to the members of her kitty. I'd bake cakes and other goodies for her using Aunt Meg's old recipes, and Sheila Maasi wanted me to sell even those! But I refused as I didn't have the time. I also insisted that she keep a percentage of the sales revenue generated by the herb mixtures she sold. After all, she was going out of her way to promote me as a yoga teacher and a tarot-reading psychic too.

I didn't even need to promote myself on Instagram, but I still had an account to post thirst traps. It helped to have one to connect with my Grindr and Tinder profiles. Of course, I was on those apps! Sure, I could always go once a week to Kitty Su to dance and go home with a handsome stranger, but sometimes I just wanted to get straight down to it.

I never hosted any of my dates. My barsaati was where I did all my psychic work, my meditations and other magical activity. Not that there was anything wrong with fucking where you pray. Babaji had taught me well about the divine aspect of sexuality and how it enables one to attain divine bliss. It was just that I wanted to keep my love life separate.

Thus, it would usually be at their homes. If they couldn't host, my trusty car had enough room to have some fun in a quiet corner of a dark alley. It kept me away from the nosy neighbours too. I didn't want to embarrass Sheila Maasi with the questions she would get about all the men I would potentially bring home almost every night.

My life was going great until I saw Vir one fateful afternoon.

It was during one of my many shopping trips to the newly opened mall called the Chanakya, which was a petite version of the DLF Emporio Mall. I was walking out of the Hermès store, delighted with my purchase of a gorgeous button-down shirt that had just come in stock, when my heart almost stopped as I saw Vir emerge from another store with Aishwarya. She was dolled up in her usual faux-Audrey-Hepburn look, while he just looked miserable. Incredibly handsome, of course, but it didn't take a gifted psychic witch to see that behind that smile was a soul aching in misery.

Placing my thumbs in the space between my middle and ring finger, I blocked my energy field. It was a trick that Babaji taught me that helped to not be noticed. Not that it made me invisible, but people would not recognize me.

I followed them through the mall as Aishwarya took him from store to store. She shopped away while he just sat around, lost in his phone. She would be fawned over by all the sales reps whenever she'd emerge from the dressing room, strutting around the store as if it were her own personal fashion runway. She basked in the oohs and aahs of the sales reps, who were gleeful at the thought of the big commission that awaited them after her platinum card would be swiped.

I don't know why I felt a little spurt of joy that Vir seemed to ignore her, keeping his head buried in his phone. It was as though this was the universe's way of showing me that he didn't love her. *How could he love her though*, I wondered, *if he loved me?*

My heart skipped a beat when our eyes met. Almost immediately I turned and hurried to the elevator. I knew that he was now following me. I pushed the elevator button repeatedly as my pulse raced. *God! What's taking it so long?* I thought as I felt him approach closer. Thankfully, it was a Sunday and there was a huge sale on, so the mall was more crowded than usual.

The minute the elevator doors opened, I rushed in before people could get off it. Bad etiquette on my part, but can you blame me? I just wanted to get out of there. I harangued the elevator attendant to press the button for the ground floor and breathed a sigh of relief when the doors closed just as Vir was a few steps away. As much as I wanted to turn around and look at him, I didn't. Lord knows what trouble would arise if I did.

That night, I decided to astrally project into Vir's home. Casting a circle of sea salt, I lit four white pillar candles in each direction and placed a clear quartz next to each of them for the sake of clarity. I added an onyx to ground and protect me. Laying inside naked, I closed my eyes and chanted a sacred mantra that allowed my soul-self to exit my physical self with a silvery cord attached to my navel.

Soon, I was in Vir's bedroom and caught him coming out of the shower. Fuck, he looked so hot with that towel wrapped around his waist. I don't know why I was happy to see that he was still working out. However, my heart sunk when I saw his body was bruised. Rajani sahab must still be beating him. There was also that strange ceremony I saw him being tortured by the Cabal in when Babaji was teaching me the lesson of grief.

Suddenly, Vir just collapsed on the bed, crying. As much as I wanted to hold him and comfort him in my arms, I knew that I couldn't. I was already violating many unwritten magical rules by astrally projecting into his personal space without his consent. *After all we've been through, I don't need it,* I told myself. But I knew that Aunt Meg would never accept that logic. I justified it as an extremely exceptional circumstance.

Before I could go on with my own internal moral debate, Rajani sahab entered. Vir immediately sat up, wiping away his tears.

'After all this time, you're still a weepy little faggot!' Rajani sahab said in disgust.

Vir just remained silent as his uncle continued, 'Don't worry, once you're married next year, the Cabal will fix you for good!'

With that, Rajani sahab stormed out of the room. As soon as the door slammed shut, Vir began to weep silently. I couldn't stand to see him like this. After all this time, I knew I still loved him. Even if he didn't love me back, I loved him far too much to see him like this.

The minute my soul-self returned to my physical body, I arose with sheer determination. I was going to rescue Vir! I didn't know how, but I had to save him.

I'm coming for you, Vir!

Chapter Thirty-Three

'Thank you for having us here, Jai bhaijaan!' Nafeesa behen said as she elegantly sat on the large turquoise floor pillow upon the throw rug that I used to define the 'living room' of my barsaati. She had instructed her three towering bodyguards to wait outside on the terrace.

'It's my pleasure to have you here!' I said, smiling as I offered her a glass of special rose sherbet. She wasn't much of a tea drinker, she had told me, claiming that it gave her a migraine.

'Ever since the Supreme Court banned sheesha, the police has become more vigilant with their raids,' she said, taking a sip of her sherbet and revealing her perfectly manicured nails. 'Gone are the days when a simple bribe would solve the problem!'

'I understand,' I said, sitting down on a slightly larger pillow and spreading a black silk cloth between us.

'It's a cute little place you have here! You've filled it with good energies.'

'Thank you, I try my best! Forgive me for not having a hookah at home.'

'Oh, it's all right!' Nafeesa behen said. She fished out a velvet pouch from the pocket of her green kaftan. Her clothes contrasted beautifully with the shades of pink, lilac and mauve she used on her lips, eyes and cheeks. 'Besides, one would never find better sheesha than my little establishment anywhere in the city.'

'I don't doubt that for a second,' I said as she began taking out an array of rings with colourful stones and placing them on the black silk.

'Just like there are people of different races, creeds and sizes, there are numerous kinds of djinn. Those trapped in the golden rings are powerful during the day, while those in the silver rings are at the most powerful at night.'

'What if the night turns to day?' I asked, admiring the beauty of the rings.

'Ah, then we'll need white gold!' she answered. Swiftly packing away the golden and silver rings, she left only three rings on the cloth between us. 'I apologize for the lack of vareity. White gold isn't in so much demand these days.'

'Do the stones have any significance?'

'Of course!' Nafeesa behen replied. 'The amethyst one will put a person to sleep for a thousand nights, while the pink tourmaline works best for matters of the heart.'

'What about for breaking and entering?'

'Ah, then you best go with the black diamond!' Nafeesa behen said, picking up the third ring. 'This is a powerful one. It'll seep within all the crevices of the bricks and stones of even the mightiest of towers and disarm all guards on watch. However, it's a temperamental one. If it's not fed well after, it'll turn on whomsoever is wearing the ring. Do you have the carcass of a donkey?'

I nodded. 'I've kept it sealed in the trunk of my car.'

'Excellent! When you're done with your task, feed it immediately!'

'What if my task takes longer than usual?'

'Have you not planned well?'

'I have, but you know how even with the best-laid plans, things can go awry.'

'Hmm …' said Nafeesa behen, scratching her long, curly beard. 'Well, just be sure you aren't wearing the ring when it begins to attack. Unless you want to be the djinn's dinner. Once fed, the djinn shall return to the ring and remain there for twenty-four hours. I'll have one of my men return to collect it from you.'

'That's really nice of you.'

'You're taking on the Cabal, so I doubt you'll have the energy to navigate Chandni Chowk afterwards,' said Nafeesa behen with a smile. She picked up the ring and gently kissed the large black solitaire before slipping it on my right index finger.

'I just hope it's all worth it!' I said as I admired the beautiful white-gold ring with the princess-cut black diamond that brilliantly reflected the lights of my barsaati.

'No matter how great the task, if your heart is noble and your intentions are pure, Allah shall always protect you!'

As I escorted Nafeesa behen down the stairs, we were greeted by a rather surprised Sheila Maasi, whose eyes widened in shock at the sight of the three bodyguards all dressed in black. I only remembered that it was Lohri when I noticed her carrying bags full of peanuts, popcorn and black sesame seeds to the bonfire party being held in the neighbourhood.

As they opened the main gate, Nafeesa behen turned to Sheila Maasi. She bowed gently and said, 'As-salamu alaykum, aaka jaan!' Not sure how to react, Sheila Maasi just smiled, though the lines on her forehead showed her fear. Nafeesa behen turned to me and winked before she climbed into the black vintage Ambassador that awaited her. I couldn't help but admire the floral pink curtains in the car's windows that matched the thick, fluffy seats. After waving goodbye as the car zoomed off, I turned to head back upstairs, but was stopped by Sheila Maasi.

'Jai beta!'

'Yes, Sheila Maasi?' I answered, not sure how to react to her fearful expression.

'Who was that?' Her shivering hand gripped mine.

'A friend. Why?'

'Beta, please don't bring such friends over,' she said, slowly letting go of my hand. 'We don't like their kind around here.'

I wasn't sure whether it was her transphobia or her Islamophobia talking—perhaps both. I shook my head and headed back upstairs. *I'll have to have a word with her about her bigotry later,* I thought.

'You're a fool!' Babaji declared as he stubbed his joint into the parapet of the tiny balcony at the shala the day after I had astrally projected into Vir's bedroom.

'Maybe I am, but I know I have to save Vir from the Cabal!'

'You do realize that it won't just end there? Messing with the Cabal could probably set off a greater chain of events that would alter the course of the world!'

'I have no choice! Vir's life is at stake. Tonight's the night before his twenty-third birthday. Tomorrow he'll be married to Aishwarya and be forced into a life where his soul would be damned forever!'

'His soul was damned the minute he was conceived within his mother's womb!' Babaji said, fluffing his beard before starting to fan himself with his pink lace hand fan. 'Besides, I can't protect you in this endeavour. I'm a teacher, not a fighter!'

'I'm not asking for your protection!' I went before him and genuflected, catching him by surprise as I took his hand and placed it on the crown of my head. 'All I'm asking for is your blessing!'

'What is this? A bad Bollywood movie?' Babaji pulled his hand away. Before he could continue, Tempa entered the shala.

'Mumma was asking if Jai would like some ...'

'Not now, you cretin!' Babaji shot him a deadly look, causing Tempa to squeal as he ran away. 'You're tying to be the big hero in a fool's quest! Don't you know that revenge is never fulfilling? An eye for an eye leaves the whole world blind!' He took out another joint and began frantically searching for his lighter.

'It's not about revenge, Babaji!' I said, offering him my black onyx lighter.

Babaji lit the joint and took a long drag. It seemed to calm his nerves before he asked, 'Then what is this about?'

'It's about justice!' Despite Babaji scoffing at me, I continued, 'It's not about what his family and the Cabal did to mine. I've healed from those wounds. You helped me do so—'

'And you still want to mess with them? Clearly my lessons weren't enough!'

'Babaji, Vir may be born to lead this chapter of the Cabal, but he is clearly miserable about it. He's being tortured by the life that's been decided for him. I won't be able to live with myself if I didn't at least try to save him from it. I love him ...'

'Oh good lord!' Babaji scoffed and rolled his eyes. 'This isn't some grand romantic tale of olden times, and you're no knight in shining armour! Besides, does he even love you?'

'I don't care if he loves me!' I said. 'I'm not doing this so that we can live happily ever after. I know love is a curse for me. Believe me, I've experienced it! But I can't deny that, even after all this time, I truly love him. I'll only be able to live in peace knowing that I've saved his soul.'

'What makes you think his soul is yours to save?' Babaji said before taking another long drag. 'You can't really go about saving the soul of every tortured individual crying for help. Everyone is responsible for the hand life deals them. It's the path their soul chooses even before birth! No, I won't be involved in this!'

'I'm not even asking you to do so!' I said as I looked him straight in his eyes. 'I'm just asking you to bless me so that I'm able to succeed in my mission.'

'How do you expect me to bless you when you're walking to your death?'

'Pain is just an expression,' I reminded him. 'Death is just a doorway!'

'I knew one day you'd use my own teachings against me!' Babaji sighed as he fanned himself.

'Babaji, you taught me that yoga is nothing but preparation for death—'

'That's different!'

'Be that as it may, this is the path that I've chosen. Your approval or disapproval won't stop me from treading it, no matter how reckless it may be.'

'Then why have you come here?'

'As I said, I've come to seek your blessings,' I replied. 'You're the only family I have left. If something happens to me, at least you'll know about it. If nothing else, at least you can pray for my soul to find peace after I leave this body.'

Babaji sighed. 'There's no stopping you, is there?'

I quietly shook my head. Babaji nodded in resignation.

As I drove through the streets of Delhi, Babaji's instructions rang through my mind.

'Like Aleister Crowley advised Winston Churchill to use the 'V' symbol to defeat Hitler's regime, you too will need certain magical tools to take on the Cabal. The eye of Lucifer is a powerful symbol, one that can't be defeated by just one. We live in a country where almost all major faiths live in harmony—well, at least until politics get involved. But the Cabal has worked that to their advantage over the centuries. You can't do it all in one night. You'll need to space out the rituals throughout the year before you carry out your task.'

'Why so much time?'

'Well, apart from giving you enough time to think before you act, such blessings need time to marinate within your body. When is his birthday?'

15 January.

'Ah, how quaint! Born on a harvest so that his soul can be harvested!' Babaji sighed.

I parked my car near Janpath and checked the time on my phone before I locked it in the glove compartment. I had precisely five minutes before the witching hour. I checked my reflection in the rearview mirror of my car. What could one wear to a battle that would require the use of agility? Yoga pants, of course! On top, I had on a black full-sleeved active jacket that's usually worn by runners. It was perfect to move around in.

Best magic happened only when barefooted, but my thick ankle-length socks would have to do if I wanted to keep from freezing. Putting my keys in the inner pocket of my jacket, I zipped up and covered my head with the hood. Then I quietly ran to the gate of the Cabal's lair.

'Seriously?' I had asked Babaji that afternoon. 'The lair is in Janpath?'

'What better place to hide than in plain sight in the midst of chaos?' Babaji had answered. 'In the Tibetan market, a tiny lane that leads to the gates of the Cabal's grand lodge. It's where Vir would be undergoing his ceremony. You'll recognize the gate by its two pillars—one black, one white—on which the eye of Lucifer is engraved.'

When I approached the gate, I noted that there were two guards. Taking a deep breath, I waved my fingers and made their guns fall. As they bent over to pick them up, I exhaled as I parted my fingers wide, causing the guns to slide a few feet apart in opposing directions. They ran after their guns, bewildered, as I channelled the Udana Vayu housed in my throat chakra and began to run towards the gate. Before they could pick up their guns, I had taken a mighty leap and jumped over the gate.

After landing inside the compound, I quickly hid behind a tree before quietly creeping towards the grand hall. There, I noticed four armed guards at the front and a few others at each corner. They were all alert and I thought they couldn't be as easily fooled as the two by the gate.

I whispered an Arabic incantation that Nafeesa behen had taught me as I rubbed the black diamond ring on my index finger. Almost instantly, a large black smoky being towered before me. I stood in awe as the djinn took its form. It had three horns protruding from its tiger's head and silvery stripes that ran across its black body. It had the torso of a human, but with camel legs a hump that protruded from its back. It crossed its arms and bowed to me, closing its deep blue eyes as it said, 'I am here to serve you, my liege!'

I pointed to the giant red-bricked edifice before me, and the djinn nodded. It disintegrated into a puff of dark smoke and flowed over to the building, surrounding it with an ominous smoky cloud. Within seconds, all the guards began coughing before they fell to the floor. The moment they stopped spasming and lay still, the two heavy wooden doors opened wide.

After I entered, I was pleased to find that all the guards inside were lying unconscious too. *I must send Nafeesa behen a token of my appreciation*, I thought.

'As you enter the foyer, you'll find three doors before you,' Babaji had told me. 'Ignore them. They're illusions! The actual door to the ceremonial hall is hidden behind a large statue of Lucifer in his Baphomet form.' I noticed the large stone statue of Lucifer in the western corner of the foyer. It was almost eight feet tall.

I couldn't help but feel intimidated when I saw that it had the face of a goat and two horns protruded from its skull. In the centre of its forehead was the eye of Lucifer and the expression on its face was mocking—almost like Mona Lisa's grin. One hand pointed up at the heavens, while the other pointed to the earth—to symbolize the Cabal's control of all that is above and below.

'Between its crossed legs will be a protruding caduceus,' Babaji had said. 'At the point where the two snakes meet will be an orb. That orb is a secret button. Push it and the statue will move to reveal a dark corridor. It will lead to the ceremonial hall.'

I found the button and pressed it. The statue duly moved to the side with a dull shriek as wheels rubbed against small metallic tracks. As soon as I could squeeze past it, I ran through into a dark tunnel. I saw a reddish light glow at the other end. As I neared it, I slowed down to a walk until I reached a staircase. It led to the grand ceremonial hall that was just like in the vision I saw during Babaji's test of grief.

Flaming torches illuminated the room and the gilded ceiling reflected in the checkerboard floor. I crept behind a pillar near the top of the staircase to see what was happening. In the centre was the horde, dressed in their scarlet robes with black hoods covering their heads. They were chanting in Latin as the three leaders sat on their thrones, urging them on. When they finished the chant, the leaders stood, raised their hands and yelled, 'Praise Lucifer!'

'Praise Lucifer!' echoed the horde.

'The time has come, brothers!' the main leader spoke. 'Tonight, we shall harvest the soul of our next leader!'

The horde cheered wildly until the main leader raised his hand to silence them. 'Bring them out for the harvest!' he commanded.

Suddenly, a door opened right next to the pillar I was hiding behind. Placing my thumbs between my middle and ring fingers, I tightened my fist and ducked behind the door. I saw Damyanti walking past me. She was naked with her long hair undone, covering her bare breasts. She seemed to have undergone plastic surgery on her face, but I could still see the scar around the spot where Aunt Meg had spat on her and made her skin burn.

Damyant was holding a large silver tray laden with a crystal decanter filled with wine, a brass ceremonial dagger and a small bottle of oil. She had a smug look on her face as she descended the stairs imperiously to the crowd's cheers. When she reached the elevated platform upon which the three thrones were, she turned to face the crowd and raised the tray above her head. The cheers grew wilder.

Walking up the steps, she bowed to the three leaders before placing the tray on a large stone altar. Then she raised the dagger in the air with both hands and roared, 'Praise Lucifer!' Her voice echoed through the hall. 'Praise Lucifer!' the horde yelled back. Two doors behind the thrones opened. Out of the one flanked by black pillars emerged Aishwarya, naked in all her glory.

She beamed as she walked towards Damyanti. After bowing before the three leaders, she laid down on the stone altar. The cheers grew louder and wilder as Damyanti began oiling

Aishwarya's naked body. There was something perverse in the way the horde shouted in ecstasy.

When she was done, Damyanti bowed and stepped aside. The three leaders approached Aishwarya, who lay motionless, her body glistening in the candlelight. As the two sub-leaders began massaging her breasts, the main leader slid his hand inside Aishwarya, causing her to moan out loud. There was no pleasure in her cries as her eyes widened with each thrust of his hand.

Aishwarya let out a final gasp of agony before the main leader removed his hand from inside her. 'She is ready!' he declared. 'Bring out our future leader!' There were more cheers as Vir emerged from the other door behind the throne—the one flanked by two white pillars. Unlike Aishwarya, Vir kept his head bowed down. I could tell he was hating every minute of it.

Vir approached the three leaders and genuflected before sitting on the altar, facing the horde. They cheered wildly as Damyanti began massaging the oil into Vir's skin. She then, stepped back as Aishwarya sat up and took some oil in her hands. She too began anointing Vir's flaccid self. My blood began to boil seeing Vir this way.

When Aishwarya was done, the main leader shouted, 'Praise Lucifer!'

The horde echoed his cry as he took the ceremonial dagger in his hand. The main leader said, 'Brothers! Now our future leader shall deflower his virgin bride! When he succeeds in doing so, we'll cut her gently with this dagger and mix her blood with his seed. Then we will add the mixture to the ceremonial wine and we shall all drink the blood of Lucifer!'

The horde dropped to their knees as the leaders returned to their thrones. They began a chant as Vir laid on top of Aishwarya.

'*Ruo Rehtaf ohw ni nevaeh*,' the horde chanted along with the leaders. Vir hesitantly began kissing Aishwarya's body as she laid still with her legs spread, ready for him. '*Dewollah eb yth eman! Yht modgnik emoc, yht lliw eb enod, ni htrae sa ti ni nevaeh. Evig su siht yad rou yliad baerd, dna evigrof su sessapsert, su ew evigrof esoht tath sessapsert tsniaga su …*' The main leader grabbed the dagger and raised it in the air as he continued leading the horde in the chant. '*Dna dael su ton otni noitatpmet, tub reviled su morf live. Nema!*'

I quickly rolled up my sleeve, revealing the golden kara that was presented to me bu the divine child in the pond. '*Sat Naam Waheguru!*' I whispered, causing the kara to grow threefold in size and begin to resemble the chakra of Vishnu.

'Praise Lucifer!' the three leaders cheered.

'Praise Lucif—' the horde began before collectively gasping as something swirled passed them and knocked the dagger out of the leader's hand. Vir and Aishwarya stopped and looked up upon hearing the commotion.

'Who dare intrude here!' bellowed the main leader even as everyone stood and began looking around.

'I do!' I roared as I grabbed the golden kara when it circled back to me.

'Jai!' Vir exclaimed. His eyes widened in joy.

'Seize the intruder!' Damyanti shouted, and the horde began running towards me.

Okay Jai, I told myself. *Time to kick ass!*

Chapter Thirty-Four

Tapping into my Udana Vayu, I leaped off the top of the staircase, somersaulting in the air a few times before landing in the centre of the hall. As I landed, the horde pounced on me. But my body was surrounded by a halo of red light as I tapped into the Prana Vayu of my heart chakra to fight them off. Rising high on my toes like a ballerina, I extended my leg as I pirouetted. It created a chaotic vortex that made the horde go crashing into the walls and pillars.

I landed in skandasana and crouched deep with my hands in namaste, facing the three leaders standing high on their platform. Vir and Aishwarya sat up, shocked.

'Ah, the son of the witch has arrived!' the main leader laughed. 'And he's learned a few tricks of his own.'

'I mean to cause no harm!' I said as I stood. 'Just let Vir go and I shall be on my way!'

The three leaders began to laugh and Damyanti joined in. The main leader turned to Damyanti and commanded, 'Finish him!' Damyanti smiled at me, her naked body glowing in a sinister shade of red. Suddenly, she screamed and she charged towards me. Tapping into my Udana Vayu again, I leapt in the air, and she just ran past me.

I landed and mocked the leader. 'Is that the best you got?' But then I turned around to see Damyanti holding swords in each of her hands. *Where the fuck did she get them from?* I wondered as she began whirling the swords about, her eyes glowing with a reddish glint. As she took a mighty swipe at me, I did a back flip and barely avoided the sharp blade. It did trim a few strands of my hair, though.

I removed my karra and enlarged it into a chakra again. Then I sent it flying at Damyanti and knocking the swords out of her hands. They fell to the floor with a metallic clang. My kara returned to me as I smirked at Damyanti. She leapt to pick her swords up but I twirled my fingers, making the swords leap towards Damyanti and slice her hair off. Then they pierced a pillar and were stuck there. She ran to pull them out, but when she was unable to, screamed in frustration.

I turned to face the leaders, 'Seriously? That's all?'

The leader softly chuckled.

Upon turning, I saw Damyanti spread her arms wide and began chanting softly. Dark smoke emerged from the pores of her skin and began circling me, taking the shape of demons. I counted thirteen of them as they surrounded me. I flung my kara at the demons and decapitating them all. However, not only did the decapitated demons grow new heads, but also the fallen heads grew new bodies. Now there were twenty-six demons. Fuck!

I began fighting them off with all my might, but with each blow, they would disappear into smoke only to re-emerge behind me. I kept fighting until one of them caught my ankle and swung me around in circles. Then it threw me against the wall. I got up immediately and took a deep breath. Using the eye on my chest, I emitted a large beam of white light towards the demons, making them disappear.

But before I could breathe a sigh of relief, not only did the demons reappear larger and mightier than ever, but also they had now doubled to fifty-two. *What the fuck?*

'Using the eye of Lucifer on his own demons?' asked the main leader as he and the others laughed. As their laughter echoed through the ceremonial chamber, the demons began having their way with me. Flinging me around as though I were a toy, they knocked the wind out of me with every blow. I fought as hard as I could, but it was of no use. The demons were far too powerful. With a mighty blow, I was flung to the ceiling. I screamed as the gilded edges pierced through my skin before I fell hard on the floor.

'Stupid little witch boy!' mocked the main leader. They all guffawed as I panted slowly, barely able to look up. The main leader turned to Vir and said, 'See what happens when you try to fight the Cabal?'

Damyanti headed over to the platform, handing the main leader the ceremonial dagger that had fallen on the floor. Accepting it, he turned to Vir again and said, 'Now finish the deflowering ritual!' Then he turned to the demons and commanded them to hold me down. 'Let him watch every moment!' he shouted.

I tried to scream, but only a shallow gasp escaped my lips. Vir gazed at me with a painful expression as he laid back on top of Aishwarya. No, I couldn't let them succeed. I had come way too far to fail! *No, Vir!* I shouted in my mind. *Don't do it! I love you! I love you!* As the sinister laughter of the leaders echoed louder and louder, I saw Vir thrusting away into Aishwarya. I felt so helpless, but I knew I had to do something!

Come on, Jai! Get up! Get up! Get UUUUUAAAAAAAHHHHHHH . . .

Suddenly, I felt a fiery surge of energy shoot through my spine. I shot up and levitated, causing the laughter to abruptly halt. I screamed wildly as electricity coursed through my veins, causing each cell of my body to burn with rage. My jacket ripped apart and my yoga pants became like shorts as my body grew almost three feet taller. I let out screams of agony as four pairs of arms emerged from my shoulders. I could feel my head burn as long strands of hair grew from my scalp.

The Goddess had entered my body!

Immediately, the demons began attacking me, but the Goddess was far too mighty for them. She ripped their limbs off, savagely tearing them apart with her talons even as she laughed with a bloodcurdling cackle. Before their fallen limbs could reanimate, she opened her mouth wide, unleashing her blood soaked tongue, swallowing them whole in one swift swoop. After she had finished off all the demons, she stood before the three leaders.

Allowing my face to emerge from her, I spoke as the leaders stared at me. 'Release Vir now!' I commanded. 'Before you live to regret it!'

The main leader began clapping slowly. 'Well, well, well!' he said with a sinister chuckle. 'You've certainly changed from that snivelling little faggot you once were. However, you didn't think it would be so easy to defeat the Cabal in the abode of Lucifer, did you?'

Before I could reply, a loud roar came out from the top of the staircase. I turned to see that the giant Baphomet statue had come to life. It was taller than its statue form, its body covered in fur and it's eyes glimmered as if they were soaked in blood. As Lucifer leaped at me, the Goddess took over and kicked him into a pillar. Swiftly recovering, Lucifer leapt up and dug its talons into the Goddess's midriff. However, instead of blood, white light emerged, glowing like St. Sebastian's halo. It made Lucifer's skin burn.

The Goddess lifted Lucifer's body with all ten arms and tossed it into another set of columns, causing them to crash. However, Lucifer quickly recovered and charged at the Goddess, piercing her belly with one of his horns. She let out a bloodcurdling yell even as St. Sebastian's brilliant white blood burned Lucifer's horn, causing it to fall off his head. The Goddess yanked the severed horn out of her belly, which sealed up almost instantly.

Lucifer and the Goddess charged at each other again from opposite sides of the chamber. However, just as Lucifer came within reach, the Goddess grabbed his horn and pierced it deep into his third eye. He let out an earth-shattering yell and crashed on the ground with a loud thud, causing the entire building to tremble. Then he disintegrated into a fiery pile of ashes.

The Goddess left my body immediately, and I fell to the floor as my normal self. I quickly got up to see that the three leaders had escaped with Aishwarya, leaving Vir and Damyanti behind.

As I ran towards them, Damyanti grabbed the ceremonial dagger and held it against Vir's neck.

'You miserable little brat!' Damyanti spat in disgust. 'Do you think just by saving Vir, you can stop the Cabal? Ha!'

As the rays of the sun began creeping through the windows, I noticed black smoke slowly seeping in from the crevices in the walls. Damyanti continued, 'The Cabal is mightier than you think. Vir is just a small puppet. Even if you help him escape, they'll just replace him. Their agenda is never compromised. So give up while you—'

Vir stomped on Damyanti's foot, causing her to scream. Elbowing her in her stomach, he pushed her away and ran over to me, wrapping me in his arms. Before I could enjoy his warm embrace, I eyes widened in horror as I flung him over, causing Damyanti to stab me in the stomach with the dagger!

'No!' Vir shouted as I grabbed on to Damyanti, pulling her down with me. I rolled her under me and sat astride her, holding the dagger in my hands. Even as I stared down at her with rage, she began to laugh.

'Fool!' she said. 'Killing me won't do you any good! I know you witches can't take a mortal life! It will only cause you to lose your powers! I know all about that delicious little loophole! The whole Cabal does! So kill me if you must, but enjoy a powerless life as the Cabal hunts you down to finish you off once and for good! Just like we finished your family! Oh wait, you did that for us!'

Before she could finish her laugh, I slapped her hard with the back of my hand. It was the first time I hit a woman, I noted despite the circumstances. 'I'm not going to waste my time killing you, you bitch!' I yelled. 'But he will!'

When Damyanti turned her head towards where my finger pointed, she let out a loud scream. The djinn stood before us, licking its lips. As Damyanti turned back to look at me, I lifted her hand to reveal that I had slipped the black diamond ring on her finger. I rolled swiftly off her just as the djinn pounced and began feasting upon her flesh.

My vision blurred as my wounds took their toll. I began to slowly pass out even as Vir held me in his arms. He looked so beautiful, but everything was growing black around me as my eyes began to close.

'No!' Vir held me close as my body went limp. 'No, you can't die on me! Wake up, Jai! Please wake up!'

Epilogue

'Okay, I understand that L is for Lesbian, G is for Gay and B is for Bisexual,' Sheila Maasi said. 'And yes, Bisexuality is not just something people claim to be when they can't decide ...'

'And that's because?'

'Because one can't choose what they are, just like a rose can't choose to be a tulip. And a garden is only beautiful when all flowers blossom with joy.'

'Very good, Sheila Maasi!' I said. I was proud of her, as she proved that one is never too old to learn and expand their worldview.

'But beta,' said Sheila Maasi. 'I still get confused with T. I know it means Trans, but is it transgender or transsexual? And what's the difference between the two?'

'Sheila Maasi, it's simple. A transgender person is someone who may have been assigned a sex at birth but identifies with another gender. Basically, their internal sense of who they are does not match the sex they are assigned at birth. The term "transsexual" is used to convey that an individual's experience with gender involves undergoing hormone treatment or gender-reassignment surgery. They are both valid terms, but we must not call someone transsexual unless they ask to be referred to in that way.'

'Hey bhagwan!' Sheila Maasi cried as she shook her head. 'So complicated!'

I smiled to myself. It would take many more afternoon teas to help her understand terms like non-binary, genderqueer, intersex and the many other colours of the rainbow. But hey—at least she was willing to learn. Slowly, but surely, she'll get there.

Of course, I survived that night, as I am here to tell my story. I guess swallowing St. Sebastian's blood that night at the chapel gifted me with the ability to regenerate. Just like Lucifer too regenerated himself after that mighty battle. Venus, after all, does have the power to bring the dead back to life.

And like Lucifer, the Cabal still exists. The battle between the devas and the asuras is indeed an eternal one. I didn't care though, because Vir was safe with me.

We had tickets to see *Birds of Prey* at PVR Director's Cut, but he was late. They always played thirty minutes of commercials before the movie started, but I wanted to see all the trailers—especially the one for the upcoming *Wonder Woman* sequel. I kept calling his phone, but it was not reachable.

Not in the mood to hear the Airtel lady telling me to call again later, I decided to walk around the food court. Not that I was hungry or anything, but crowded spaces were the best to read auras.

Oh yeah, remember when I began my story, I told you that I'd teach you how to read a person's aura? If you can't, that's okay, no better time like the present. Okay, pick someone. Anyone around you. Doesn't have to be a friend or family member, but I suppose they wouldn't mind giving you their consent. Remember, consent is important for all magical activities. Picked? Cool! Now just stare at them. No, not like a creep! Just take a deep relaxing breath and stare at them. If your heart and mind are open to even the possibility of magic, you'll slowly see a silvery halo around their body. That's the etheric body, the layer that connects the physical body with the aura. Its brightness depends on how much you practice, and how much faith you have in yourself. Once you see the etheric body, seeing the aura is a breeze.

'Jai!' A voice called out from one of the stalls at the food court. I turned and saw a vaguely familiar face waving frantically. As I approached closer, my eyes widened with delight.

'Tempa?' I shouted as I rushed over to him. He looked so different now that he had grown his hair. His eyes still had that lovely sparkle as he flashed his pearly whites.

'Oh my god! What are you doing here?' I asked as I reached over the counter and gave him a big hug.

'Oh, I've expanded our little café into a chain!' Tempa beamed with pride. 'I guess Babaji did kick the laziness outta me!'

I couldn't but laugh at that. 'How's Babaji?'

'He's good! Being a badass as usual!'

'I bet!'

'Tempa sir,' the chef called out from the little kitchen window. 'We need you in here!'

'Coming!' Tempa called. 'Listen, you gotta try these new stuffed cheese momos that are our new speciality—'

'Maybe later? My movie is about to start!'

'Tempa sir!' called the chef again.

'Ugh!' Tempa shook his head. 'Okay, after the movie then. My treat!'

'For sure!'

'And don't stuff yourself with popcorn!' Tempa shouted as he rushed into the kitchen. I couldn't help but wonder if he was treating his staff the way Babaji would treat him. *I hope not!* I thought.

Anyway, where was I? Oh yeah! Are you able to see the silvery etheric body? No? Don't worry, it just takes practice. Once you're able to see the etheric body, just keep patiently staring. Soon, you'll see a cloudy mass surrounding the etheric body. That's the aura.

The colours may not be apparent at first, but with practice you'll be able to see them, and they'll reveal everything you need to know about the person. A red aura surrounds one who is strong-willed, while adventurous souls tend to have orange auras. Creative ones have bright yellow auras, while nurturers have a green aura. If it's a light blue aura, the person is a free-thinker, while more darker blues tend to be gentle and thoughtful. Violet ones are rare and they are spiritually inclined, while pink auras surround people who love to love …

'Jai?' It was a different voice. I turned to see someone vaguely familiar.

'I guess you don't remember me, huh?' asked the man with a grin. He was cute, for sure, but for the life of me, I couldn't place him.

'Sorry …' I said with an apologetic smile.

'Well, it's been a long time, and man, you've totally grown!' he said as he extended his hand. 'It's Nikhil!'

My jaw dropped in surprise. 'Nikhil Sahni?' 'Oh my god! Fuck! Quickly snapping out of my daze, I took his hand and he pulled me into a weird bro-hug-handshake thingy that was rather clumsily awkward.

'Wow!' I said, feeling weird. 'This is a surprise!'

'Yeah! Tell me about it!'

'What are you doing here?' I asked. I wondered where Vir was.

'Oh, I'm here with my boyfriend, Kunal!' He turned to wave at a guy standing in queue at the KFC. He waved back at us.

'Wow, when did that happen?'

Nikhil smiled sheepishly and said, 'Well, it's a long story. It took me a while to come to terms with what I was, but Kunal really helped me through it.'

'Wow … that's amazing!' Nikhil Sahni had come out of the closet and found himself a boyfriend!

'Yeah, my parents freaked out when I came out to them. We're all in family therapy now. Kunal recommended a good shrink.'

'That's really nice,' I said. 'I'm happy for you.' I truly was.

'Listen,' Nikhil began. 'I know it's probably not the best place or time to say this, but … I truly am sorry for what happened that day—'

'Hey, it's okay, I—'

'No, it's not okay. I still feel so incredibly guilty about everything. I guess there was so much anger in me because I hated myself so much. Every day I was filled with so much shame and guilt because …' Nikhil sighed as he trailed off, before continuing, 'I know nothing I say can justify what I did, but all I ask is that you find it in your heart to—'

'Sorry! Sorry!' I heard Vir's voice call. 'I know I'm late!' He arrived and gave me a tender kiss on the cheek. Before I could introduce the two of them, Vir extended his hand to Nikhil and said, 'Hey, I'm Vir!'

'Nikhil,' he said and they shook hands. Vir's look asked me silently if this was the same Nikhil. I nodded in confirmation.

I grabbed Nikhil's hand, gently looked into his eyes and said, 'I forgive you.' Just by saying those words, I could feel a gentle wave of energy flow through us and make our bodies lighter as though a mighty burden had been lifted off us. I understood then that to forgive truly is divine.

'Well, we had better hurry,' said Vir impatiently. 'They've probably begun playing the national anthem. It was nice meeting you,' he added tersely to Nikhil.

I was proud of how Vir had bounced back after his ordeal at the hands of the Cabal. He was eager to get back to normalcy and Mr Gupta had helped him get an internship with his son at a branch of his firm. Vir had also begun studying for MBA, but had chosen an online course despite me encouraging him to go and study full-time. He told me that he didn't want to be far away from me, but I could tell that he was afraid that the Cabal would get their hands on him again.

He would sometimes wake up in the middle of the night screaming and covered in a cold sweat. He didn't have the luxury of a magical recovery from trauma so I wanted him to visit a good therapist.

'I don't know why you always have to wait till the credits end?' Vir rolled his eyes as we left the theatre. It was almost one in the morning, and the cleaning crew had already begun mopping the lobby. *I guess we'll have to visit Tempa's stall another time,* I thought to myself before answering, 'Because there's always a special scene that tells us what to expect in the sequel!'

'You can just look it up online!'

'I could, but you know much fun it is to play "spot the Indian" whenever the end credits roll. Especially in the VFX section!'

Vir rolled his eyes as he shook his head. But I knew he found my quirks adorable.

'Shall we?'

'Wait, I gotta go pee!' I announced.

'Oh, come on!' cried Vir, exasperated.

'I'll be back in a jiff!' Before Vir could protest, I gave him a quick peck as I ran towards the men's room that was now empty. I guess even the attendant had gone home. Who could blame him?

As I splashed water on my face after washing my hand, I grabbed the heated face towel and began dabbing my face with it. Before I could even finish, my phone began to chime. Vir definitely was getting impatient. Turning it off, I tossed the towel into the bin and headed out. However, just as I grabbed on to the handle, a sinister laugh echoed throughout the gilded men's room.

My eyes widened with horror when I saw my great-grandfather in the mirror, his black hood covering his face. I stood frozen with fear as his laugh continued to echo thunderously.

'You thought you could get away from me, did you?' he roared as his hands emerged through the glass, rushing towards me. 'I'll have you! Your soul shall be mine! Even if it's the last thing that I do!' His deafening cackle caused my heart to almost burst as he began to choke me. I could feel his dark presence squeeze the life force out of me.

'What's taking you so … hey, you okay?'

I snapped out of my daze and turned around to see Vir standing at the door. I quickly turned to look at the mirror, but only my reflection looked back at me.

'Jai, is everything okay?' Vir asked, sounding concerned.

'I'm okay!' I said, forcing a smile. I wasn't sure what to make of what happened.

'You sure?'

I wasn't, but it wasn't the time to worry Vir. 'Yeah, let's go!'

I doubt that would be the last time I'd be haunted like that. But I guess that's the path I was born to walk on. I'll just have to focus on the joy of the present moment. It's better than dwelling on the past that once was or worry about a future that's yet to come.

Despite this little bubble of joy I live in now, a part of me knows that the curse of love will hit me eventually. Till that happens, I'm determined to live every moment to the fullest. Happiness, after all, is in our own hands. Right?

Welcome to my world.

Gratitude

I first thank the divine muses, who inspired me to create this work during perhaps what were the darkest times in our world's history, as well as, my own personal turmoil. A big thank you to Anuja Chauhan who out of the kindness of her magnanimous heart, opened doors that even in my wildest dreams I would have never thought were possible for me to walk through. I'm so grateful that Ananth Padmanabhan took a chance on a new author with a story that had never been told before. Words can't begin to describe how much Swati Daftuar not only believed in me and Jai's story, but also how she went above and beyond to nurture me throughout the editorial process. Thank you Shalini Agarwal and Tanima Saha, for helping to turn my manuscript into this finished book we have with us today. They say a we should never judge a book by it's cover, but I'm so thankful to Ramnika Sehrawat and the extremely talented design team for gifting me the fruits of their incredibly creative labour. I still have to pinch myself because it's such an honour to be part of the Harper Collins family.

Thank you Shibani Bedi, for encouraging me night after night to deliver her a chapter for her reading pleasure. Thank you Sumiran Annamaria Kashyap, for being a magical source of inspiration. Thank you Rayman Gill, for being part of the journey from the minute it was a vague idea that I pondered upon during a cocktail-fueled lunch after a yoga class. The three of you have been so instrumental in my journey, as well as, keeping me sane before, during, and (hopefully) after the pandemic.

My skills as a story-teller have their roots in the theatre, as my very first play was written and performed at the Akshara Theatre, to rave reviews and thunderous applause. To the divine Jalabala Vaidya, for being such an iconic force and encouraging me to push my artistic boundaries to new heights. To Anasuya Vaidya, for her immense patience and sheer force of will, and ever supportive spirit. To Nisa Shetty for being my 'Belle' and for your love, trust, and friendship, Dhruv Shetty for your compassionate spirit, and Yashna Shetty whom I can't wait to see how she dazzles the world. Thank you to the entire Akshara family for accepting me and making a special place for me within your hearts.

Words cannot express the deep gratitude in my heart to my fabulous yoga teacher, Seema Sondhi, who not only inspired me to first step foot on a yoga mat, but lovingly nurtured my journey along the way. Thank you for giving my feet roots, my arms wings, and opening my heart to the wonders of the yogic path. The incredible Anuška Iliji for teaching me how to be kind to my body and be mindful as a whole. The lovely Bindiya Sabharwal for being such a force of strength without compromising on kindness. There would be no Yogi Witch without the three of you helping me rediscovering my body, mind, and soul – on and off the mat!

A special thank you to Bharath Shetty and the entire team at Indea Yoga, Mysore – for not only helping me take my practice to a whole different level, but for also helping me fight my own personal demons during those spartan, but lovely, five hundred hours.

Rodger Shawn Christopher, thank you for being a yogic inspiration, and sharing a deep love for our Queen!

Thank you Roma Singh, for helping me discover magic within this and many other universes across numerous lifetimes.

Thank you Nishant Singh for his invaluable 'straight man' take on the story. Special shoutout to Akshat Sharma, Isha Vajpeyi, Dhruv Gupta, Chiragg Khatri, and Mark McCaul.

This novel wouldn't be possible if it wasn't for the amazing team at Café Bokan, for providing me with a comfortable haven that enabled me to write into the wee hours of the morning. Thank you for treating me like a princess!

A special thanks to my sister, for being the first person who accepted me when I came out, and for forever being a protective force that's constantly watching out for me every step along the way. I probably wouldn't be the person I am today if it wasn't for you. Thank you!

About the Author

Zorian Cross is a multi-award-winning theatre professional based in New Delhi. Since 2009, he's acted in over thirty-five productions, written over fifteen scripts, and directed ten productions – including a jukebox musical, a cabaret, and an original ballet that he conceived. His plays have been performed in over thirteen cities across the world, including Sydney, Brisbane, Chicago, and Dubai. His short play, 'The Coming Out' is still regularly performed in Bangalore. Along with that, Zorian's also been a guest writer with numerous publications, including ScoopWhoop, iDiva, NDTV, and is currently writing a weekly column withLifestyle Asia India. Along with this, Zorian is also a certified Ashtanga, Vinyasa, and Yin Yoga teacher, as well as, an Occultist – specialising in Tarot, Astrology (Vedic and Western), Kabbalah, Eastern and Western Schools of Mythology and Mysticism. As an ardent activist for the LGBTQIA+ community, and feminism on the whole, Zorian has appeared frequently on various news channels to share his point of view, as well as, doing his bit in the quest for equality, equity, and liberation. Don't be surprised to find him performing stand up at one of the various comedy clubs across the city – tickling your funny bone with love, and a naughty twinkle in his eye.

30 Years *of*

HarperCollins *Publishers* India

At HarperCollins, we believe in telling the best stories and finding the widest possible readership for our books in every format possible. We started publishing 30 years ago; a great deal has changed since then, but what has remained constant is the passion with which our authors write their books, the love with which readers receive them, and the sheer joy and excitement that we as publishers feel in being a part of the publishing process.

Over the years, we've had the pleasure of publishing some of the finest writing from the subcontinent and around the world, and some of the biggest bestsellers in India's publishing history. Our books and authors have won a phenomenal range of awards, and we ourselves have been named Publisher of the Year the greatest number of times. But nothing has meant more to us than the fact that millions of people have read the books we published, and somewhere, a book of ours might have made a difference.

As we step into our fourth decade, we go back to that one word – a word which has been a driving force for us all these years.

Read.